Darlin' Bill

A Love Story
of the
Wild West

Darlin' Bill

*A Love Story
of the
Wild West*

by Jerome Charyn

ARBOR HOUSE / NEW YORK

For Michelle Lapautre and Marvin Charyn

This book was completed with the help of a grant from the National Endowment for the Arts. I would like to thank the Endowment for its kind support.

Library of Congress Catalog Card Number: 80-6673

ISBN: 0-87795-283-3

Manufactured in the United States of America

10 9 8 7 6 5 4 3 2 1

Salome

One

Drat that camel! He was chewing the walls again, and I figured the veranda would break. I sent out Archie to scare him off, but you know how colored boys can be with a camel. He was next to useless for camel scaring. I yelled at him from the veranda.

"Archibald, you chase that camel, or pa will give you a licking you won't forget."

So he went up to the camel and made a face at it.

"Silly," I said, with the veranda knocking like it was in a storm. "That's not how to scare a dromedary. You have to beat it on its hindquarters with a stick. Smash it good, and he'll behave."

But Arch only stared at me and he began this lecture. "Drome-

3

daries don't have more than a single hump on them. This is a Persian camel."

Archie's from Boston, where they educate the colored boys. He was a sailor until they "stole" him from the wharves. But it wasn't pa's fault. If pa didn't buy him, Archie would have gone to some plantation and died of malaria.

"Archibald, don't give me any of that Boston sass. You chase this Persian camel before the veranda drops into mama's garden, with me in it."

I wasn't going to move off the veranda to please any camel. I would have sailed down and cracked all my bones if the schoolmaster hadn't come along. Henry Ovenshine knew how to treat a camel that likes to swallow the paint off people's houses. He walloped the camel on the rump with mama's garden hoe. That devil with the two hills on his back blinked and then looked into my eyes and let out a noise that was worse than the whinny of a sick horse.

I could feel the camel's breath on me. It was a wind of sugar, salt, and sour paint. His nostrils closed. He scraped his head against the side of the house, whinnied some more, and ran near the ocean, like a dunce who wobbled all the time and had a beard that went down to his knees.

"Doctor Ovenshine, that was mighty thoughtful of you."

He had thick black eyebrows that jumped on his face. Pa imported him out of Connecticut to run the girls' school. I don't believe he was a doctor at all. He'd give you a couple of *parlayvoos*, but he didn't have a camel's acquaintance of French, Latin, or Greek. All he knew was Marco Polo and a few mad kings. He lived with us, in pa's house, ate our food, slept upstairs, in the back.

"Somebody ought to shoot those dromedaries," he said, "or put them in quarantine."

"Archie says dromedaries don't have but one hump. These are Persian camels."

Doctor Ovenshine hooked up his eyebrows. He could get real angry if you disputed his word. "What does Archibald know! You tell Archibald there's a two-humped version of the dromedary, and we have a pack of them wandering around this island, doing no good."

"Tell him yourself. Archie's standin' right here."

Ovenshine ignored him. You think he would discuss the camel situation with pa's colored boy? He went into the house, tucking his coattails behind him and slamming doors to show people that the schoolmaster was about. That faker. He'd put on his studying cap and expect black Hannah to rush over with something to eat, because you couldn't have a scholar peruse his books without bread and butter in his face.

Archie was sulking near the camel's footsteps. "I don't like that man, Miss Sally. He's got the longest nose and the littlest hands in creation."

"It's no crime to have small hands."

Arch went around to the stables to lather pa's horse, and I whispered dromedary, dromedary, dromedary. Black Hannah saw me through the window and shook her head. "Is you insane, girl? Whispering to a house."

I didn't answer her. Things are running strange. Ships coming into the harbor and letting camels loose. Some genius in a silk hat, probably a sea trader, got the idea that Persian camels would become the horse and donkey of the West. The camels arrived, but nobody bought a single one, and that trader man dumped them on us. Now the camels have their pick of the island. The gray old men of the city don't know what to do. Should they pass an ordinance making it illegal for camels to exist? Who's going to arrest the critters? I never heard of a calaboose that can keep a dromedary from breaking through the door. Maybe Justice Morrissey will sign a piece of paper that will move the dromedaries across the channel and into the state prison. But they'd only chew down the prison walls. We can't get rid of them. It's best to leave the camels in Galveston, where they have oleander bushes to hide in and windows to chew.

Pa came home with Justice Morrissey and the mayor's people. They were waiting for the tiny general with the golden sword. Dust was flying at the house. You'd think it was the dark before a hurricane. It was only General Smith. You could hear him clomping on his stallion. It was a big, beautiful roan with white legs, and when he sat on him he could command the whole island and half of Texas. This was the general who conquered Nicaragua, and would have had Panama to himself, if traitors and pirates hadn't forced him out of there. But the general was going back in. Pa helped him raise an expedition to capture Nicaragua again, and they were meaning to plan the expedition tonight.

The general had once owned a country, but he couldn't get down from his horse. I had to fetch Archie from the stables for General Smith.

"Archie, quick, the general's here, and he can't get down from his horse."

"Then let him sit until the wind blows him off his saddle," Archie said. He was an ornery boy, but pa had a liking for him, and it wasn't in his heart to sell Archibald.

"Damn you, Nicaragua Smith."

"Don't cuss," I said. "And get movin', Arch."

He went out to the general, who was still up there on his chestnut horse, Victory Fire. It wasn't only pride that said a general couldn't dismount by himself. The general was stuck. His legs were too short to climb down the side of a stallion.

Archie locked his fingers together and made a stirrup out of his two hands, and the general stepped down, his weight falling onto

Arch. The muscles popped on Archie's neck, but his knees didn't buckle. You never saw Archie dip while holding a general in his hands. You could have followed the moon waiting for the general to touch ground. That's how long he clung to Arch.

Pa winced, because he knew how it felt to be another man's stirrup, and the general walked into the house, carrying the scabbard to his golden sword.

"Archibald, are you hurt?"

"No, miss Sally."

"I'm glad. I thought the general lamed you."

"Smith couldn't lame me," Arch said, but something wasn't right. He moved with a stutter and dragged his feet around.

"Should I ask black Hannah to banditch your foot?"

"Hannah couldn't banditch a crow's ear," he said, and he was back inside the stable. I wouldn't go into the house. All those men jabbering about this country and that. You'd think they owned the world. The planters and the merchants and the mayor's people were behind the general's expedition. They were supporting him with money and guns. It wasn't their blood they were meaning to deliver. They had to drum around for recruits. The general ran this "card" in the Galveston *News:*

March 1, 1859
Patriots
Fall in! Fall in!
A Company of Brave Men to fight the heathens in Nicaragua, will
be raised at Galveston, on a plan that will offer the
Greatest Inducements
to those anxious to free Nicaragua, and at the same time secure
FAT SNAPS!
It's been decided to have this Company composed
Entirely of OFFICERS
As follows, 1 General, 2 Colonels, 3 Lieutenant Colonels, 6½
Majors, 12 Quartermasters, 11 Captains, 18 First Lieutenants, and

the balance to be filled up with Second Lt's which will be the lowest position in the Company. In order to secure at once the services of so many brave men, the Nicaraguan Expedition will pay each volunteer on arrival in Nicaragua, a Bounty of $75.13, and furnish clothing, all covered with buttons and gold trim, also Rations, Tobacco, and WHISKEY, and at the close of the Expedition all volunteers who decide to remain in the Nicaraguan Free State will receive land warrants for 29 farms apiece, to comprise not less than 6000 acres, with the privilege of locating them in any part of the Free State

Apply at once, to Head Quarters, 19 Water Street

You couldn't find the general's name on the "card." It was illegal to raise a private army and go galavanting in foreign jungles, where you had to wrestle with imbeciles and snakes. So the general kept quiet about himself. But who could forget Nicaragua Smith? He wasn't a bit taller than Sally Blackburn. And I'm twelve, a schoolgirl at Doctor Overshine's, with Latin that's nothing but camel talk out of the doctor's head.

The general had scars and burns on his eyebrows. And he had a golden sword that he took from the infidels before they threw him out of the country. He could nick off a bull's nose without leaving a scratch. But I've never seen the bull or the bull's nose. The general talked a whole lot about his Christian state in the jungle. He's going to cut Nicaragua off the map and start the country of Ishmael. What's so Christian about that? I've read the Book. Ishmael was an Arab.

There was the knock of bare feet over my head. The schoolmaster, Henry Ovenshine, was making traffic on the veranda with a clay pipe in his mouth. He wore his britches, thank God, or he would have been as naked as a prairie chicken. This Doctor of Philosophy couldn't tolerate a shirt on his back when he was dreaming in the open air.

He must have come out of his dream, because he smiled down

from the veranda. I didn't like it. It was the devil's smile, with a crease on his lips. I moved closer to the house, so I wouldn't have to look at that schoolmaster. But then I had to listen to this jabber about the glorious free state of Ishmael. The planters were angry that they couldn't get enough colored boys for the "cotton mines." It was the old talk about slav'ry and how the Yankee government was interfering with their lives. Ishmael would solve the problem. It could become the "safe harbor" that the cotton men needed. Traders would ship colored boys from Africa into Ishmael and hide them until they could be smuggled over to Galveston.

Drat all their Ishmaels!

I could see the general through the window. He took the planters' gold and nodded his burnt eyebrows. Justice Morrissey said Galveston ought to break away from Texas and the Union and become its own Ishmael. "What's Texas got to do with us?" Everybody hoorayed, but the mayor's people told him it wasn't a practical idea.

Pa sat in the corner, like it wasn't his house. Why was he going along with General Smith? Pa owned twenty-seven darkies, and he leased a number of them out to merchants and planters. Did he want another twenty-seven from the Nicaraguan Free State? If you asked him, he'd say it wasn't commerce at all. He'd have a funny look in his eye and talk of Galveston as the Queen Bee of the South. *Seize Nicaragua and we control the Isthmus. That's our future.*

I went upstairs saying to myself, what's so special about the Isthmus? Here they were palaverin' about the high cost of colored boys and preparing an expedition with eighteen first lieutenants and not one corporal in the bunch, to fight for Ishmael, a country that didn't exist, when they had camels in their yards, dromedaries that were eating everything in sight. And the chief justice of the island, Morrissey himself, couldn't raise a platoon to rope the

camels somewhere. That's island justice. Gold for Ishmael, and
not a penny for the camel situation.

I undressed and got into my night shimmy. I stayed off the
veranda, because Ovenshine was nosing about. I could smell his
pipe tobacco through the window. That man. He'd give us lessons
to do on the Peloponnesian Wars, but he didn't have a notion
where Peloponnesia was. He liked to talk about kings. He told us
how the great king Xerxes acquired two hundred wives and fought
with every one of them until his strength fell away and he was
strangled in his chariot by a common soldier. The girls in Ovenshine's school wept over this sad king, pretending to ourselves that
we were part of the king's harem. *Oh, Xerxes, slain in your
chariot.* We all hankered to be wicked, wicked wives. But Ovenshine was a fool, outside of harems and kings. And he was on the
veranda minus his shirt.

The skunk came through my window without a knock or a how
do.

"I'll scream," I said. He wouldn't have dared come in if mama
had been around. But she was with the Women's Auxiliary,
knitting socks for captains and lieutenants of the Ishmael army.
And the mayor's people were jabbering so loud, pa couldn't have
heard a thing if Ovenshine ravished me and all and I died of
shame and whatever filthy disease the schoolmaster was carrying.

I shut my eyes and said, "Don't you touch me, Doctor Ovenshine."

He started to laugh. "You're too skinny for a man to touch
. . . and too damn proud."

"I'm not skinny," I said. "And don't you laugh at me."

"Why not?"

"I'll tell pa you walked into my room."

"You wouldn't. I know you, Sal. It's not in your constitution
to snitch."

Who learned him so much about my constitution?

"Why'd you come in here if it wasn't to touch?"

"Sally Blackburn, you've got a mind full of soot."

"What do you expect from a girl, when her own teacher tells her stories about harems and slobbering kings?"

He was laughing again. "How can I teach you history without some entertainment?"

"I didn't know entertainment was in the curriculum, Professor Henry."

"I'm not so sure I want to visit with such a rambunctious girl. Good-night," he said, but he didn't walk out on the veranda. He stuck to my room.

He put his chin down into my hair, and that skunk squeezed my chest. I wasn't going to swoon to satisfy him.

"Why are you shaking, Sal?"

"I'm not shaking, Doctor Ovenshine. Only you . . ." Before I had the chance to finish, he was on the veranda with his clay pipe. I figured, poor Doctor Ovenshine, he thinks he's Xerxes and I'm one of his wives. I got into bed. I had a dampness on me. Ovenshine put me into a sweat.

A critter was brushing the wall outside. It was the camel chewing paint. It felt like he was lifting the house and dragging it into the dunes. But the expedition planners down in pa's library didn't complain. I'd swear they never heard the camel breathe. That's how hot they were to get the general into Nicaragua. Let the camel eat. I'll kiss him if his face comes through the wall.

Two

Ishmael.

You could almost see that country if you looked out onto the Gulf. Ishmael was going to bubble up slaves for us, and cure the ills of cotton men.

The man behind the cure was Nicaragua Smith. The general had pearl buttons on his uniform for embarkation day.

Archibald drove us to the harbor for a last look. The wharves were crowded with quality folk. The general's steamship, the *Lorelei*, was waiting for him and the Nicaraguan volunteers, all the majors and captains and lieutenants the island could hold. You had to pretend they were "emigrants," and not an army, because the federals were about, guarding the port. But nothing could keep the general from wearing his uniform. He was in silver, gold, green, and red, the colors of Ishmael. He rode up the gangboard on his stallion, Victory Fire, and was the first man on the *Lorelei*. We shouted and clapped, and the Women's Auxiliary stretched out a silken banner with the words, GOD BLESS OUR GENERAL AND HIS BRAVE VOLUNTEERS.

The *Lorelei* had two sails, since she was entering rough waters, and steam wasn't so reliable. You could never tell where the engines might blow up. The *Lorelei* could be stranded in the middle of the ocean, with a stallion on board, and the "emigrants" would never see those packets of land the general had promised them. Most likely they'd die of starvation and some horrible ocean fever. All the hours the Women's Auxiliary spent knitting socks would have been for naught. So the general insisted on sails.

The whistle blew, we waved good-bye, and the *Lorelei* chugged up the channel to Bolivar Point, with the general saluting us from his horse. Then they were out to sea, and the expedition was launched with that army of "emigrants."

We drove home, with Archibald in pa's straw hat and butternut pants. These were his carriage clothes.

You could tell how pleased pa was, with Archie up front, holding the reins. A carriage boy who had a broader vocabulary than most quality people. Pa gave him our name to wear. He was Archibald Aloysius Blackburn now. And it didn't matter that the general, in order to raise some cash, had gone into pirating colored sailors, in cahoots with Justice Morrissey. The general grabbed colored boys off any ship that called at Galveston, and the chief justice signed them into slav'ry, right under the noses of the federal troops. But Archibald was a special case. Pa took him in, and it was more like adopting than buying a boy.

Every other colored boy on the island was jealous of Archibald. They didn't play checkers or shoot darts with their Misters. They couldn't talk white men's politics. They'd never heard of Bishop

Berkeley and John Locke. Arch had two years at the Boston Freeman's Academy, with Harvard professors, until he went off to sea. Pa'd rather converse with Archibald Aloysius than with that Doctor of Philosophy upstairs, or sit with mama and me.

But it didn't seem to matter to Arch. He ran away and sold his carriage clothes to some peddler on Mechanic Street and hid out in the dunes, living like a dog.

Justice Morrissey heard about the Negro in the dunes. He was fat and lazy, and he had lots of gold lying around from the colored sailors he'd helped to steal, but he was also chief justice of the island. He captured Arch and brought him home to pa on a leash.

"Whip him, Benjamin, whip him good."

Pa didn't have the heart for it, whipping a boy who could discuss John Locke.

"Archibald Aloysius, confound it, will you not sell your clothes?"

"The devil was in me, Master Ben, and he's gone out of this poor nigger."

"Balderdash," pa said. "You know how it disturbs me, Archibald, when you lie so boldly to my face. Couldn't you think up a better excuse?"

I'd listened to them arguing over demons many, many times. Archibald, pa, and John Locke didn't believe in the devil. Doctor Ovenshine was different. He claimed the devil was in every pocket. So you couldn't shake him out of your pants.

Pa was finished questioning Arch. It was almost like Justice Morrissey had led *him* back from the dunes, and not Arch. That's how ashamed he was. He walked into the house.

I wasn't going to let Archibald off so easy. There's lots of ways to whip a man. "You ungrateful boy," I said. "You had better clothes than anybody. Why'd you run?"

"I figured I'd ride me a camel over to the mainland and become a cattle boy."

"We have plenty of cattle on the island, Arch. And when did you acquire a love for cows?"

"I didn't," Arch said. "I'm a seafaring man. But never mind. I'd take that camel up to Boston and visit my two brothers."

"Heck, pa would give you passage money, if it was just for a visit."

He tossed me a look with his gray eyes that made me feel lower than an imbecile, a camel, and a mule.

"I wasn't meaning to come back," he said, and he went off to the stables.

I had to side with pa. Visiting is one thing, but running away from your Mister is a crime. I know it was wrong what the justice did, stealing Arch, but pa had his bill of sale, and Archie belonged to him. We're not an unholy island. Justice Morrissey may be a swindler and all, but what can he do, when planters and merchants are dying for colored boys?

He had to dig Arch out of the dunes again. But pa wouldn't whip him to satisfy the chief justice. He began giving Arch out to hire. Pa leased him to merchants in town. No one would take him steady. Arch fell in with a bad crowd. He committed robberies. Pa had to pay the justice to keep Archibald out of jail. It gave him a sore heart, watching the boy deteriorate. So he took Arch into the house and tore up the bill of sale. "Go on, Archibald Aloysius, you're a free man."

"Free, Master Ben? How? Free niggers don't have much of a chance in Texas. The bounty hunters would grab me quick, once I stepped off this island, and sell me to a planter along the Brazos."

"I wouldn't allow that," pa said.

"What's the use? The bounty hunters would take me to another river bottom, far away."

"Then I'll get you on a ship to Boston and find a captain who isn't a thief."

"Beg your pardon, Master Ben. They're all thieves . . . I'd rather stay here."

He put on a fresh straw hat and he drove pa's carriage, but Archie just couldn't behave. He broke into mama's pie safe and had himself a bellyful of pies. It was black Hannah who took the broom to him. "Varmint, no-account skunk, stealing from the Missis."

It was worse than any whipping. Arch rolled on the floor, with his hands over his head. The rage was in black Hannah, and mama had to stand in front of Hannah, or she would have broomed Arch into the next world. Arch was blubbering, not from the welts he had, but from the shame of it. A boy with his education sneaking after pies!

Arch recovered from his shame and went right on stealing. It was terrible to watch. He graduated from pies to silver and gold. The bad city crowd had learned him to pick locks like a fiend. He opened pa's money chest with a strip of wire. But he wasn't a complete rascal. He only took the smaller pieces of gold.

You just couldn't have Archibald in the house!

Pa had to deal him to the state prison, hire him out to the prison masters, because no one else would tolerate such a thief. But the penitentiary couldn't hold Arch for very long. He got himself a rope and climbed right out of prison. They caught him in the swamps, and they put chains on Archie, like a regular convict. Pa grieved over it, because Archibald was still his favorite boy, but he had to stop protecting somebody who grubbed pies and gold.

Pa had his mind on the country of Ishmael. June, July, and August passed, and it got to January and no news from the general. Ships that went near Nicaraguan waters came to Galveston with conflicting reports. The general was alive. The general was dead. It sounded like bunk to pa and me. Then rumors started to drift in, talk of fierce fighting, infidels slain with the golden sword, the general persisting against unbelievable odds, the lieutenants gaining a jungle stronghold, with the flag of Ishmael going up.

It didn't help the planters, this jungle flag. They couldn't get their cotton to market without the African boys that Ishmael was supposed to provide. People forgot about General Smith. It was an election year. They had that Black Republican to consider, Abraham Lincoln of Illinois.

The whole island shuddered at the idea of Lincoln. A big-jawed man with lumps on his face. Pa said he'd stepped out of a coffin to run for president. He'd drink our blood and make the darkies lord and master over us. We'd have a darkie mayor and a darkie chief justice, and Galveston would disappear into the Gulf, a wandering island of camels and ghosts. We put up tar scarecrows in long frock coats, a hundred Mr. Lincolns, so the island would have a picture of Black Republican rule.

The girls threw all their strength into the production of scarecrows. We hung a tar critter by the neck in Doctor Ovenshine's academy. It was a warning to him. We suspected Ovenshine of being a Lincoln-lover, since he came from Connecticut and all. But you couldn't snare Ovenshine with any monster doll.

Professor Henry got to school in his sombrero. He sat down and ignored the critter hanging over his desk. Well, we were the daughters of quality people and we weren't going to let him make light of our work. He couldn't hide in Xerxes' harem every morning. We asked him what his opinions were on Father Abraham and the Black Republican party.

Professor Henry had to peek out from behind the doll's legs.

"That muddleheaded Abe! Vote for him? He'd make a good camel keeper. He could ride up and down their humps all night."

Fools that we were, we had a laughing fit. But he could only get a few titters out of me. I wasn't taken in by his camel talk. He wouldn't reveal his politics to schoolgirls. He was intending to marry one of us. Ovenshine was poor as a mouse. He didn't come to Galveston to start a school. There's no profit in schooling girls unless you can steal their hearts and take yourself a bride.

Emilia Salmon was the most likely candidate. She was seventeen and the dummy of the class. Her pa is the richest merchant in town. If Ovenshine can cozy up to the Salmons and "catch" Emilia, he might inherit her pa's store. It's a pagoda right on Market Street, the Salmon Emporium, with iron pillars and gaslights that blaze up over the roofs until you'd swear the town was burning. We call it the "Salmon fire."

That fortune will go to Ovenshine, wait and see. Emilia drools over his speeches and the sentences he writes on the chalkboard. She wouldn't care if the schoolmaster was the blackest Black Republican. She'd marry him anyway. That's how dumb Emilia is. Ovenshine has to give her extra lessons after class. There's little arithmetic and lots of crawlin' going on with Ovenshine's hands. Emilia's big for seventeen. She has the teats of a milking cow. She'll sit with that skunk in the schoolhouse practicing long division.

Before you can say *parlay-voo,* he's got his elbows inside her shirtwaist. It's the funniest sight, Emilia squirming with her eyes shut, and Ovenshine busy as a gravedigger in Emilia's "front yard." We spy on them from the window. We giggle sometimes, and then you get this feeling in your throat, because you imagine that varmint with his wrists climbing up your belly, the hair on his arms grazing your skin, and the more disgustin' it gets, the more you'd love to scream.

Her pa would murder Emilia if we ever snitched, and they'd throw Ovenshine in the penitentiary, with Archibald Aloysius. That wouldn't bother me, but you can never tell what schoolmaster they'd give us in Ovenshine's place. We'll stick with Professor Henry.

A BLACK Republican couldn't get a vote on the island. Galveston went for Breckinridge of Kentucky. But the Democrats were split. The fools put up *two* men, Douglas and Breckinridge, and Father Abraham crawled between them and took the country by surprise. Justice Morrissey said the white man was finished in the United States. We'd have to join the camels in the dunes, before Abraham and the colored boys marched into our homes and "married" the best Galveston wives and young girls, including mama and me.

"Nooooooo," the justice snorted. "Nooooooo." The Union was a sick old bull, he said, and it was time to break away from her, or become sick bulls ourselves.

"Yes," spit Justice Morrissey, "a bull with a shrunken pizzle and horrendous gray balls."

Pa frowned at him. "Aaron, don't talk like that in front of the child."

"Sally a child?" the justice said, pinching my ear with stubby fingers, like I was that old she-bull, the United States. "Sally's more a woman than some ladies I know."

"Aaron," pa said, *"enough."*

Were they talking about the bad ladies that lived on Postoffice Street? Some took care of sailors and the general riffraff, and some were reserved for the gentry of the island. It depended on which door you went in. Is that where pa goes when he tells mama he's visiting the phrenologist in town to get his skull examined?

"Benjamin, what's the matter? Did you ever see a bull wear long johns? And what in tarnation do they learn her at school? Doesn't that idiot, Ovenshine, give her anatomy lessons? Bulls have pizzles. It's a fact of life."

Pa turned away from him. He wasn't going to continue the subject of bulls without long johns. But I didn't have to listen. I had things to do. The girls in Ovenshine's college formed a patrol. We took the Lincoln dolls and set them on fire. They burned all over the island, their tar faces melting off, to show our true feelings on the Black Republican menace.

Galveston was in a fury over Lincoln. South Carolina had dropped out of the Union, and Texas was figuring to do the same thing. Governor Sam came to the island to warn us about the evils of secession. He had white hair and a stringy neck, Sam Houston, and he wasn't so popular in 1861. People remembered how he'd chased the Mexican Army across the San Jacinto and into hell, captured Santa Anna in his military underwear, and set up the Lone Star Republic. But he got us into the Union, and people wanted out. The rabble hissed at Sam as he went to the courthouse to give his speech. Justice Morrissey was quiet, but his crowd of followers said, "Let's hang the old buzzard!"

Mr. Sam reached the courthouse alive. The door was locked. Morrissey had a grin on his face. Pa cursed this island that wouldn't let Sam speak, and he led the governor to the Tremont Hotel. Not even Justice Morrissey or the mayor could shut a hotel on the governor of Texas! Mr. Sam stepped out on the wooden balcony at the front of the hotel and hushed the rascals with one throw of his white eyebrows. He was ten feet above us all. It was like having Moses in Galveston.

Breaking with the Union would land us "in fire and rivers of blood." The rascals heckled him for that. They couldn't halt his tongue.

> "Some of you scorn the idea of bloodshed as a result of secession, and jocularly propose to drink all the blood that will ever flow in consequence of it! But let me tell you what is coming on the heels of secession. The time will come when your fathers and husbands, your sons and brothers, will be herded together like sheep and cattle at the point of the bayonet; and your mothers and wives, and sisters, and daughters, will ask, Where are they? And echo will answer, where?"

He never did finish his speech. Too many folks were out on the balcony with Mr. Sam. It started to rock. Pieces split off, and you had an avalanche of wood. Mr. Sam had to step indoors.

"It's an act of God," Justice Morrissey screamed. "The angels fixed it so Mr. Sam would have to give his tongue a rest."

The rascals haw-hawed and they marched with the chief justice to the whiskey houses on Mechanic Street. Mr. Sam was left with a crippled balcony and empty spaces underneath.

Our Moses didn't do much good; they wrote up a bill of secession in the statehouse, and the people ratified it. Mr. Sam was thrown out of the governor's palace, because he wouldn't swear allegiance to the new Confederate nation.

A Committee of Public Safety was formed on the island. It tried not to bump too much with the federals that were still around. But it took control of the port. You had two countries in Galveston until the federals packed up and left the island.

Who do you think sat at the head of the Committee? Morrissey himself. He had the keys to the customshouse in his pocket. The lighthouses belonged to him. He was the dictator of Galveston. Pa wouldn't talk to Morrissey. But the justice came around to make peace. He was awful fond of pa.

"I won't have any person in my house who was rude to Mr. Sam."

"Lordy, Benjamin, was I supposed to feed him sugar? We've gone through a revolution, and he was on the other side."

Pa relented, and they got to talking about Ishmael. Casualty lists had been posted, but it was almost two years since General Smith rode his stallion onto the *Lorelei*. We could read off the wounded and the dead, and the names of deserters and all, but no one could say if the general took Nicaragua or not.

"Ishmael's a stupid dream," Justice Morrissey told pa.

Morrissey was more than a dictator. He was the prophet of Galveston. Soon as he said *Ishmael*, Ishmael appeared. It was as much of a country as you could fit on a boat. The *Lorelei* drifted into Galveston, through the morning fog. Its side wheel was gone, and it only had one sail. Some fish with big teeth must have chewed up the *Lorelei*'s deck, because it was the flattest steamship you ever did see. Where was the army of officers, the colonels and majors with buttons and gold trim? Monkeys crept away from the boat, men with long fingernails and beards down to their bellies, and not a boot among them.

You couldn't find a stallion on that ship. The general had to go on foot. He crept along with his monkey men, an empty scabbard knocking between his legs, like a bull's pizzle.

He sat in the nearest whiskey house, and whimpered into his sleeve. It wasn't Ishmael he was grieving for. He mourned the death of his beautiful roan. The infidels had shot poisoned arrows into the rump of Victory Fire. That sick, dying horse carried the general through the jungle on a journey of eighteen miles, spitting a thick foam of blood, and never lay down on him until they got to the general's camp.

He had Ishmael in his palm, he said. He'd have beat the dickens out of those infidels if Costa Rica, Guatemala, El Salvador, and land speculators from the States hadn't overpowered him at the last minute. People nodded yes, yes, and they pitied the general and his expedition and the two years he lost in Nicaragua, but they weren't so interested now. He should have come back a year ago, when there was still some fever over Ishmael.

Galveston was at war.

Confederate guns had opened fire on the Yankees hiding in Charleston harbor, and we were waiting for Mr. Lincoln to strike back. We didn't have time for jungle stories. We had rifle pits to dig and breastworks to put up. Uncharitable folks said the general should have died with his horse. Then he could have been a little bit of a hero, instead of the failed conquerer of a country that nobody cared about. It wasn't much of a homecoming for Nicaragua Smith.

Three

O<small>UR MILITIA</small> took to the rifle pits, but the invasion never did
come. Why should the Yankees overrun an island of camels, little
girls, and tiny forts, when their gunboats could sit at the entrance
of our harbor and bottle up the whole darn place? It was dis-
couraging. We had to live with Yankees in our rear yard. They'd
lob a few shells into the dunes, and that was the war.

"Merciless times," the justice said, "merciless times," and he
knocked on our door at three o'clock in the morning. Pa was in
his nightshirt. He called down from the bedroom window. Morrissey had five riflemen with him.

"Aaron, what the devil is going on?"

"Sorry, Benjamin. We've come to arrest the schoolmaster. I

25

charge him with being a Yankee spy."

"That's ridiculous," pa said from the window.

Morrissey set his jowls to shivering. "Benjamin, you're challenging me in front of my men."

"Well, sir, do you have a writ in your possession that compels you to take him out of this house?"

"Of course I have a writ," Morrissey said. "What's the matter with you? I'll still chief justice of the island."

Pa came downstairs to look at the writ. It was legal. He had to hand Ovenshine over to the chief justice. Morrissey was running special tribunals all over the island, arresting this man and that, and holding them in the courthouse jail.

It was Ovenshine's misery to be a Connecticut man. He was no more of a spy than the girls in his class. But that didn't bother the chief justice. Morrissey had to keep awake on an island that the Yankees had put to bed. So he went around arresting people. Soon he'd arrest the camels and the dogs.

Pa said it was an outrage and *he* was going to defend the professor against Morrissey's tribunal. But meantime we didn't have a soul to write on the chalkboard and hug Emilia Salmon after hours. We missed Marco Polo and Xerxes' chariot. So we plotted to get Xerxes back.

We declared ourselves a secret society. Xerxes' Harem. Galveston's eleven finest daughters curtsied to the Confederate guards and broke into the courthouse.

"What's this?" Justice Morrissey said, hobnobbing with one of his tribunals.

"We brought our college to Doctor Ovenshine," I said, sweetly as I could, because you can't holler at a justice and win.

"That's impossible," the justice said. "He's a spy. He has to go before the tribunal . . . Sal, you take your friends and run on home, you hear me?"

But I played deaf to him. "Justice Morrissey, you'll have to arrest us too. We're not leaving until Professor Henry learns us.

We can have our lessons in his cell."

He'd have caused a hullabaloo locking up eleven girls. Our papas were the most powerful men on the island, next to Morrissey himself. Without merchants and planters behind him, his tribunal would have spilled to the ground. But there's no fox like an old fox with jowls.

"Case dismissed," the justice roared. "Send the prisoner to his college before he makes a damn nuisance of himself. And don't forget to charge him for the bread he ate."

We chipped in and paid the professor's bread bill, because Ovenshine didn't have a nickel in his pocket. He was skinny and frail, what with the mean vittles they give a spy. So we allowed Professor Henry a small holiday to recover from his stay in jail. Emilia would have licked him in public like a cat if we didn't hold her by the skirts. "Dummy," I hissed in her ear. "You want the tribunal seizin' him again for disturbing the peace?"

Tempers were running high, with Yankees in our harbor and all trade shot to hell, cotton turning a sickly color out on the wharves, and Morrissey becoming more and more of a dictator. It was a wicked year. The better merchants were moving off the island and setting up "war" households on the mainland. Emilia's pa closed the Salmon Emporium, and that pagoda of his sat in the dark. Emilia cried and cried when her pa took a house in Houston on Texas Avenue. The Cotton Exchange followed him there. Seems like everybody was running to Houston. That city was like a big fat bride for Galveston people.

Pa refused to go. He wouldn't let Yankees drive him out of his home. We had a houseful of colored boys for a while. Pa couldn't lease them to merchants who'd disappeared and planters who couldn't sell their cotton. So he packed them off to Houston at a cut-rate price. He was lonely without Archibald Aloysius. He couldn't talk to Ovenshine about John Locke. Professor Henry wasn't up to par on philosophical questions. His college was thinning out. He only had five pupils left. That didn't stop him from waltzing into my room at midnight. I could have screamed for mama. But it wasn't worth the trouble.

"I'll thank you to walk in somebody else's window, Doctor Ovenshine."

"Not so loud," he said. "I'm indebted to you, Sal, for saving my life."

"Well, you can keep your debts. It was nothing but a schoolgirl's prank."

"No, Morrissey would have hanged me for sure."

"Nonsense! Pa wouldn't have stood for it. You're living in his house. We only pushed the law around a little by shaming Justice Morrissey."

The skunk started smelling my hair.

"You'll be needing spectacles pretty soon. I'm not Emilia, you know. I don't have udders for you to play with."

He laughed and bit into the stem of his pipe.

"Udders aren't everything."

"Why don't you take your academy to Houston and pick up with Emilia? If she scorns you, Professor Henry, you can find a heap of other heiresses."

"You're a busy one, arranging my life. I like it fine in Galveston, honey."

And that man kissed me on the mouth! It was like a snake stinging your lips. I pushed him so hard, the pipe fell out of his hand. He bent down, scooped the tobacco coals from the floor, muttering, "Beg your pardon, Sally girl," with his twitch of a smile, and he was out on the veranda before I could cuss him again.

THAT WAS Galveston in '62. Camels growing wild in the sand hills, coming off the dunes to eat up gardens and walls. Confederate soldiers bivouacking in the Tremont Hotel. Food getting scarce. The town wrapped in its own spiderweb, with Morrissey's tribunals crashing through that web, yelling, "Spy, spy, spy." And the federal gunboats sitting out in the harbor, like mechanical frogs sunning themselves, in this war that was no war.

I'd ride pa's mare over the dunes, because Ovenshine made his own decrees and cut schooltime in half. I saw two men out on the sand hills. They looked like sailors from town, sailors in scruffy clothes. I had pity on every Galveston sailor. They were stranded in the port, with nothing to do but visit the whiskey houses and go harloting. They couldn't sail away. The Yankees had bottled them in, like the rest of Galveston.

One of these two men wore an eyepatch. He had long yellow hair, held in a knot. But I never knew sailors to carry so many pistols on them. The second man was shorter than the first. He had a small telescope in his pocket. He beckoned me to get down from my horse.

"Halloa," he said. "Harvey Beecher's the name."

He put out a bumpy hand. I wouldn't shake that dirty old mitt. Did he think I was a harlot from Postoffice Street? Whoever heard of shaking a sailor's hand?

The man with the eyepatch had more respect. But it was mighty peculiar. I'd have sworn the patch was on his right eye a minute ago. Now it was on the left.

"What's your name, little miss?"

"Salome," I said. I'm not sure why I told him that. Salome's the name I was born with. People have called me Sal ever since. But I just blurted it out. Maybe I was scared, seeing the small telescope and so many guns.

"That's a pretty name," the man with the eyepatch said.

"You believe her?" the short one said. "She's a liar, Jamey . . . if I ever saw a liar, she's it."

"Keep still," the eyepatch man said. "That's no way to treat a nice young girl. Who's your pa, miss Salome?"

"Ben Blackburn."

The short man kicked his heels. "I'll bet her pa is with the

Safety Committee. She's their little scout."

"Keep still, I said . . . how old are you, miss?"

"Fourteen," I told him.

The short man snickered over my age. "She's the fattest fourteen I ever met. Likely she's married to a Committee man."

I watched a leg shoot out. The eyepatch man had kicked Harvey Beecher in the rump. Harve rode the toe of that boot a good ten feet. He came up out of the sand clutching a dirk.

"I say we dispatch the little scout . . . send her to eternity, so she can't warn the rebs agin us."

The eyepatch man snatched the dagger away, whirled Harvey around, and held him prisoner in the sand with his boot.

"You'll have to forgive Harve, miss Salome. He's delirious sometime . . . thinks he's fighting a war, when he's a jackass sailor. You won't tell on Harve, would ye? They might put him in the home for diseased sailors."

"I won't tell. I promise . . . but what are you doing in the sand?"

"Can you hold a secret, miss? We're treasure hunters, Harve and me. Out for pirate gold."

It made sense. Unemployed sailors hunting gold. Paul Christophe and his killer band had the run of the island thirty years ago. Galveston was a savage place, unfit for quality people. Christophe moved in after the gentleman pirate, Jean Lafitte, sailed to the Yucatan, leaving his buried treasure somewhere in the sand hills. Christophe tore up the island, but he couldn't find Lafitte's gold. He started murdering off his own men. Their bones are scattered in the dunes. Pa has a proper skeleton in his library of a murdered pirate. Christophe traveled down the coast and became a hog butcher in Corpus Christi. And islanders are still wondering about Lafitte's gold.

The eyepatch man could have been a pirate himself. Only I couldn't remember one pirate with long yellow hair . . . it wasn't yellow. It was more like the color of honey.

"Where are your shovels, then?"

"Shovels?" said the eyepatch man, with his boot still in Harvey's back. "We don't need shovels. We dig with our hands."

Harve was groaning under him. "Christ Almighty, pardner, will ye let a man go? She's the bad un, not ol' Harve."

But the eyepatch man didn't pay attention to Harve's groans, except to squeeze him with the boot. He bowed to me with his honey-yellow hair and helped me onto my horse.

"Good-bye, miss Salome. Nice chatting with you."

He slapped Gussie the mare on her thigh and I rode back to the house with my heart thumping. That story of treasure was mostly cock-and-bull. They were spies, canvassing the island for fresh rifle pits and those little forts the Committee had put up. I would have gone to the justice and snitched on Harvey Beecher in no time at all. But I just couldn't bring myself to hurt the eyepatch man. I'd imagine his honey-yellow hair swinging in the sun, after Morrissey's tribunal, and my belly would ache with grief. It wasn't only that he was the handsomest spy in Texas, with a moustache that ran under the edge of his lips and that any girl, good or bad, would have been curious to touch. He was kind to me, the way King Xerxes might have been before he was corrupted by his two hundred wives. He wasn't the sort of man who'd march into your room and stare at a girl's shimmy.

But I had regrets. Ben Blackburn's daughter aiding a pair of spies. I felt like a sniveling Yankee, a Black Republican, and a Lincoln-lover. I couldn't bear to look at myself in mama's glass. It didn't do much good to shout, "Spy, spy, spy," like Justice Morrissey. The eyepatch was a secret that would have to crawl in with me, under my grave clothes.

OUR OWN army decided that Galveston was worthless to hold, and they abandoned us in October, walked right off the island.

They told Justice Morrissey to set fire to the town and stuff ashes into the wells, so the Yankees wouldn't have a drop of drinking water.

"Damnation," the justice roared. He couldn't tell which army was worse: the blues or the Galveston grays. He sneezed and ran to pa. His shoulders rumbled when he sobbed.

"I won't burn Galveston, Ben. Not for Texas. Not for all our sister states. The Confederacy can hang! We'll fight the bluebellies on our own."

The justice and his men took to the rifle pits. But they shivered in their holes, and climbed up out of the pits when it started to rain.

A floating battalion arrived. A hundred bluebellies bobbed along the channel in a fleet of rowboats, stepped onto the wharves, and took control of the island. Morrissey didn't fire a shot. He tucked in his tail and welcomed the bluebellies on behalf of the mechanics and grocers and quality people that were still around.

The blues didn't eat children or recruit colored boys and stop wives on the street. Their commandant, Captain Shirley, didn't mention rifle pits and the forts Morrissey had built in the sand. The captain was worried about yellow fever. How could he help the islanders?

Morrissey held his jaw. "The fever season's nearly gone, captain, sir. The Lord was merciful this year. Seventy dead, is all."

Morrissey reported this to pa. "Benjamin, it's a Yankee trick . . . that blah of his about the fever. You watch your silverware. That's my advice. Don't you know who that man is? 'Silver Spoon' Shirley. He robs spoons and knives wherever he goes. Collects the stuff. Have the missis bury all the spoons in the house."

Pa wasn't going to bury spoons on the justice's say-so. "Your pride is hurt, Aaron. You were wishing this Shirley was Beelzebub, and he's not. He doesn't snort fire and steal spoons. He stood in his rowboat and didn't give a damn about your rifle pits. You could have shot his head off. Why didn't you?"

"Gunboats is why. Trim one hair off Silver Spoon's scalp, and they'd blast this island to kingdom come. I had to surrender . . ."

The blues were better than that garrison of grays we'd had on the island. The grays stole our chickens. They camped in our big hotel, lazy, stinking soldiers who blabbered about killing Yanks.

The blues left our chickens alone. They put out a fire on Market Street, when our own fire company was sleeping in a whiskey house. They organized rescue parties the minute a child got lost and searched every well and rifle pit on the island.

And it took the Yankees to solve the camel problem.

They decided that camel dung on the boulevards was a nuisance to their patrols. Silver Spoon Shirley issued a proclamation, and soon the camels were roped into a field on the western part of the island, where the pirates used to live.

Pa claimed that Silver Spoon reminded him of Archibald Aloysius, because the captain could talk of John Locke. Shirley shook his head. He just couldn't understand how a man like pa could lease other human beings. "It's a business," pa told him, and he lined up six tobacco pipes to smoke with Captain Shirley. "I'd lease a white man, if he belonged to me, so why shouldn't I lease a colored? . . . captain, I had a carriage boy who was near a genius, and it broke my heart to send him away, but he got to be an awful thief."

"He might have stolen less, Mr. Blackburn, if he'd been his own man."

"Sakes, I freed the boy! And he was worse than ever."

"Then it's a conundrum," Silver Spoon said, smoking his third pipe.

Conundrum? Suckin' tobacco makes your mind go dull. Archibald was in a pickle. Anybody could see. He loved pa and hated pa, hated all of us. And thieving was his way of telling pa that.

Anyhow, Shirley opened the metal gates of the Salmon Emporium and gave that pagoda to his troops. The captain himself slept in a shack near the wharves. He owned us with his bayonets. If the blue generals told him to bomb Galveston and poison our wells, he'd have listened to them and not John Locke.

I WENT marketing with black Hannah, and the bluebellies dipped their soft caps. I got separated from Hannah near the fruit stalls, and a man pinched my rump with his claws. He wasn't in uniform. It was that sailor who liked to dig for gold with his hands. Harvey Beecher, all red-eyed and likkered up. "Howdy, miss. Salome, aint it? The girl from the sand dunes."

He lifted me right off the ground and started carrying me into the alley behind the stalls. I could smell rotting apples and spot a hill of gray turnips with warts on them while I was kicking Harvey Beecher and trying to scratch his nose. "Spy," I hissed. "You're Silver Spoon's maiden aunt . . . checking our rifle pits before the Yankees dropped in. I should have told Justice Morrissey. He'd have stretched your ears back, Mr. Beecher, or whoever you are."

I was blabbering away and kicking, and meantime the skunk had worked his elbow under my bustle. My petticoat was torn to pieces. His arms scooted like crabs. He punched me to keep me still. The blood slicked over my tongue and I started to cough. Those crab hands didn't stop. He ripped out my corset cover. He'd have had me naked in a minute, with my pantalets on that turnip hill, and him stroking me in the awfulest places, if it wasn't for the eyepatch man.

He strutted into the alley from nowhere, like he had a gift for stepping out of the fog to save a girl and her pantalets. My honey-haired friend. He started to bash Mr. Harvey Beecher over the head. The skunk crawled on his hands and knees, with his partner riding him to the end of the alley and then coming back. I had the shivers with honey-hair looking at me, and it wasn't out of fright. I got into my pantalets, and my face was red, because I'd started to swell out this year, and soon I'd have udders like Emilia Salmon if I didn't watch out and strap myself tight as the devil, with whalebone and all.

"Sorry, miss Salome . . . Harve's a pig when he's drunk."

I wouldn't have minded a long chat while I was struggling with petticoat pieces, but he was gone before I could thank him. Black Hannah found me near the turnips.

"Miss Sally, were you rasslin' with the vegetables? How'd you get so dirty and torn up? Your mama will kill you, girl."

You can't stare Hannah down, so I said, "Hannah, it was a prodigal event. The turnips started rassling with me."

She knew I was lying, but how could she contradict my story? Turnips can rise up in the middle of a Yankee occupation. Anything could happen with bluebellies around.

Four

THE BLUES spent their silver and gold in our barrelhouses and general stores. The merchants who hadn't been scared off the island were getting fat from Yankee dollars. The Confederate paper we had wasn't worth the flies on a camel's hump. People were hoarding gold. And the Yankees were the ones with gold in their pockets.

Pa welcomed Captain Shirley into the house, but he wasn't after Shirley's treasure chest. He'd smoke a pipe with the enemy, if he didn't have to betray any secrets of war. And how many secrets did pa have? The grays had abandoned us. It looked like they were never coming back.

The island was broken off from Texas.

You couldn't find a Yankee on the mainland. Houston was building streets and stretching out in the middle of a war. Even the crocodiles were growing rich. They'd sun themselves and eat the trash that civilians and soldiers tossed into the bayou. The grays were wintering up there. We had an army fifty miles from Galveston and they didn't come down to pay us a visit, or cause the blues a minute of grief.

"We might as well be Ishmael," the justice groaned. "We have Silver Spoon Shirley and camels in a Yankee corral. It's enough to give a man liver trouble."

"Things could be worse," pa said.

"I don't see how."

"The captain could have strung you up for playing provost marshal, with your spy hunts and all."

"Provost marshal? Are you insane, Ben? I'm only a judge."

And Morrissey skulked away from the house.

That broken-down hero, Nicaragua Smith, went from whiskey house to whiskey house with a plan for recapturing Galveston from the blues. The merchants wouldn't finance Nicaragua Smith. They didn't want the Yankees to run away. The Confederates would only bring more of their worthless paper dollars.

Silver Spoon could have arrested the general for preaching insurrection on a "Yankee" island. But he had pity for an old warrior who still carried around the colors of Ishmael on his chest: silver, gold, green, and red. The general had never bothered to change his uniform, but the silver was tarnished, and the gold had mixed with the green and red. People considered him a nuisance and a crank. He was a general without a horse.

Somebody listened to the general. Our chief justice. And a few stragglers from the Safety Committee that were cantankerous enough to defy Captain Shirley. But they couldn't plot war in the open, with bluebellies around. Morrissey wasn't a fool. He needed a house that Shirley wouldn't suspect. That house was pa's.

Pa said no. He wouldn't share his pipes with Captain Shirley and then go behind Shirley's back and let our house be used as a conspirators' den.

"That's treason," the justice roared. "What the hell is the matter with you? Have you lost your senses, man? The Yankees are on this island."

Pa had to give in. His feelings for Shirley didn't include the whole blue army. How could he support the Yankee occupation? He joined the Ishmaelites.

Pa would hide whenever Shirley called at the house. But the justice put a stop to that. He told pa to continue sucking tobacco with Shirley, or the captain might get suspicious. So pa smoked with Captain Shirley and talked about how they'd go fishing together after the war. You could see pa's eyes tighten up.

He was bitter at his friend the justice, but he didn't turn the Ishmaelites out. Thank God the general came on foot. We didn't have Archibald to bring him down off his saddle. He wore his military tunic that was starting to bleed silver and gold.

His followers from the "free state," the captains, majors, and lieutenants who were still alive, showed up at the house. Thirty-six tattered men. They were fine for fighting chickens and ducks. But they'd never hurl a garrison of bluebellies off the island.

The justice saw that. He wasn't about to get himself killed. Morrissey was too fond of his own fat hide.

"General Smith, the Yankees have gunboats in the harbor. They'll make short work of our little land attack."

"They won't," the general insisted. "They'll be too occupied with our navy."

"Our navy?"

"Yes, sir. The *Lorelei.*"

"That old girl?" the justice said. And his belly started to rumble from the laugh he had. The general's eyes turned mean, and the rumbling stopped.

"That old girl nearly crippled the Costa Rican fleet," the general said. "She's docked in Houston at the moment. I'm having her fitted for the campaign with nine-inch guns and muskets on her poop. So we can attack the bluebellies by land and by sea."

"Land and sea," the justice said. "That's a horse of a different color."

"But the Yankees have six 'horses' laying in the harbor," pa said.

"So what? You heard the general. The *Lorelei* has muskets on her poop."

"She's the finest cottonclad in the West," the general told his war party. "A cotton rampart can spit out Yankee cannonballs. And she'll have a pigiron tooth on her prow."

Morrissey fell in love with that. "A pigiron tooth." You could feel the victory fever hanging from his jowls. "Benjamin, do you think Captain Shirley has a pigiron tooth? The *Lorelei* will ram Yankee gunboats into hell. And she'll cover us while we chop up the bluebellies sleepin' in Bob Salmon's store. The sons of bitches, we'll learn them not to invade our island. I'm for grabbing Captain Shirley and shooting him between the eyes."

"Slow down," pa said. "You haven't had one skirmish and you're starting an execution list."

Morrissey huffed out his chest. "I can do what I like. I'll be provost marshal if we win."

The general was forgotten in the heat between pa and the new "provost marshal." He sat in that uniform of bleeding gold. He was puny and all without his scabbard and a stallion to raise him high off the ground.

The "provost marshal" didn't trust black Hannah to serve coffee to the Ishmaelites. "You can never tell which way a Negress will jump," he said. "She could run to Silver Spoon, and it'll be the end of us." He barred Hannah from the library, so I had to be the coffee girl, because pa wouldn't involve mama in the general's guerrilla army and navy. She might have a crying fit in front of Shirley. Mama had a delicate constitution.

Morrissey chewed sugar like a horse. The general spilled coffee on his britches. The guerrillas weren't so good at feeding themselves. Those veteran majors and lieutenants didn't know how to maneuver a corn cake. They talked of killing Yankees with crumbs in their lap.

It was the sorriest army and navy this island ever saw. They couldn't have attacked an empty rifle pit. Pa was hoping they'd stall until the blues and the grays stopped fighting and started up some peace. Morrissey was a swaggerer. Pa knew that man. The justice carried derringers and knives in the different pockets of his coat. But all that iron weighed Morrissey down. He couldn't swagger ten feet without taking a rest. He loved the idea of going to war. That was enough for him. He was pulling in Yankee gold, like everybody else. And then there was Nicaragua Smith.

He had his battleship with bales of cotton on the sides and a pigiron tooth. He meant to rush the Yankees with it, or die. He'd have murdered Morrissey, if the justice didn't set a date for grabbing our island back.

"New Year's Eve," the justice said. "They'll never figure on that. Silver Spoon will be celebrating, and we'll catch him while he's tipsy."

THE SKUNKS wouldn't let me into their brigade. "I can shoot a rifle, pa. Archie taught me how. We used to go across the channel and hunt for prairie chickens in the old days."

"It's not a prairie-chicken war. You'll take women and children over to the dunes. I'm counting on you, Sally Blackburn. Prepare quilts and rations. This fool battle could last a month."

That's all I was worth to the Ishmaelites. I went from coffee mistress to brevet major, in charge of quilts. It wasn't fair. I wanted to be with pa and Nicaragua Smith when the cannon balls whistled and the smoke ate into your eyes. Instead I had to knock on doors and do a lot of whispering.

I had my own brigade. I marched children and womenfolk into the sand hills with all the neutrals that didn't intend to fight. Merchants, saloonkeepers, Doctor Ovenshine, and the old men of the island. The merchants were delirious. They were thinking of the dollars they'd lose. But they couldn't betray the guerrillas once the war was about to begin. Suppose some crazy miracle happened, and the general won? They'd be branded as bluebellies and suffer the fate of Yankee spies. So they muttered to themselves on the march to the dunes, clutching their quilts.

The schoolmaster sneered at me. He had no right to sneer. I was practically the last pupil he had on the island. He'd have been a beggar without pa and me.

"Sal the marching girl," he said.

"Watch out. I have rank, Doctor Ovenshine. I'm a brevet major."

He started to laugh. "You're still a schoolgirl in my college. I could demote you for having all that sass."

"Demotions don't count for much in wartime," I said.

I made the children get into their quilts. It was long after midnight, and I stood on top of a sand hill, waiting for the guerrillas to strike. I could see clear to Water Street, but nothing was going on. Where was the *Lorelei?* The wharves were quiet as a Chinaman's ghost. The bluebellies must have been sleeping off the old year in their headquarters at pa Salmon's place. Lord, it was 1863! The new year didn't bring any battleships with it, and any Ishmaelites.

The general junked his navy.

That's what I figured. And the justice had a yellow streak inside his coat, with the derringers and the knives. The island belonged to Captain Shirley.

Just as I was despairing, the shootin' started up. The Yankee fleet was belching cannonballs. But the Ishmaelites were in town! The roof of pa Salmon's store was on fire. I heard the two armies and navies scream. *Yaaahhhh!* A rumble came up off the dunes. Galveston was shivering from the big war. You'd swear thousands were fighting in the city, and the general didn't have fifty men!

That's when I started to shake along with the dunes. *Lord, Lord, don't let pa die!* How could an old raft with cotton on her belly stand up to six Yankee gunboats?

I got all crazy-like, thinking of mama in widow weeds. I found her on the next sand hill. She was with the Women's Auxiliary, watching the cannonfire. Walls were coming down. Mama wore a blue scarf on her shoulders. She didn't look much like a widow to me.

The rumbling in the sand got louder, and I said, "Xerxes, the war is coming!" But it was only the camels. The cannons must have frightened them, and they'd escaped from their corral. They took funny, chopping steps over the dunes, screaming like Xerxes' wives. They didn't harm any of us. They were traveling to the edge of the island, where they wouldn't have to listen to the big guns and hot, battling men.

The herd got out of that crazy crossfire. And we were on the dunes with quilts and all. A man came stumbling towards us, his face streaked with gunpowder. His britches were torn up to his thighs.

It was pa.

He didn't stop and say hello to me, and I was the brevet major of our troop. I heard him tell mama that Captain Shirley was his prisoner. The blues had surrendered their garrison, and the *Lorelei* sunk half the Yankee fleet.

"Pa," I said, "how's the general?"

It took pa a minute to recognize me. Then he hugged his

daughter and gave her a kiss. "The general's alive," he said. We were a new country now, with a flag of silver, gold, green, and red.

I WENT to Justice Morrissey and Nicaragua Smith and Captain Shirley who was being "held" in pa's house; I talked to Yankee prisoners and our own lieutenants, and I still couldn't get a picture of what happened on New Year's Eve. So I had to patch together some of the story.

The *Lorelei* steamed down from Houston on the night of the war. But the general hadn't counted on the darn trees hanging over the bayou walls. The branches smashed his pilothouse and his smokestack and the artillery he had on the upper decks. That wasn't the worst of it. Panthers dropped out of the trees and parked themselves on the fo'c'sle. The general couldn't use his cannons on them. He would have woken the Yankee fleet. The panthers nearly cost us the night. They enjoyed their ride, growling at any Ishmaelites who came up close. The general had to drive them off with rifle butts. They wounded three of his men and ate part of the general's military tunic before they jumped into the water.

The battleship arrived off Bolivar Point two hours late. The general had a gelding on board named Sweet Martin. Martin was a piebald, and he was the general's new charger. The general rode him onto the island and met up with pa, the justice, and eighteen Ishmaelites. That was the land forces we had.

Pa asked the general how we were going to sneak into town and surprise the bluebellies with him clomping on a horse. "No bother," the general said. "We'll pad Martin's feet." And we lost another half hour wrapping the piebald's hoofs in swaddling clothes.

The *Lorelei* lay in hiding near Bolivar Point with her pilothouse gone and panther tracks on her fo'c'sle, while a guerrilla army and a gelding with cotton on his feet crept towards the Yankees in downtown Galveston. Our battleship wasn't supposed to move until the general surrounded pa Salmon's store and fired six warning shots.

The army had to kick that piebald into town. It was like wheeling a cannon across a broken bridge. Pa was ready to tear the general off his horse and make him lubber in the dark streets with the rest of the Ishmaelites. This time it was the justice who showed good sense. He whispered to pa. "Benjamin, you'll damage his pride if he has to walk. That man won't fight from a standing position."

So pa gnashed his teeth and slapped the piebald on the rump. "Go on, you miserable horse."

The guerrillas captured two corporals dozing outside the store. The corporals turned pale. They'd never seen a horse wear cotton shoes. Then pa himself went to the little shack on the wharves where Captain Shirley liked to sleep, away from his men. Pa shoved his revolver into that hole of a door.

"Who is it?" the captain asked. Shirley was in his long johns.

"It's Ben Blackburn . . . you're under arrest."

Pa allowed the captain to get into his pants.

"Will you surrender your garrison, for God's sake?"

The captain refused, and pa had to march him to the store with his hands in the sky.

"Benjamin, this is idiotic," the captain said. "You're not soldiers. You'll hang for this . . . and my navy will destroy your town."

The general glared at Shirley from his horse. "Prisoners should hold their tongues." He had his lieutenants light the torches they were carrying and hurl them into the windows and the roof of pa Salmon's store. He tried to fire six warning shots to his battleship, but the general's revolver jammed. It wasn't until he had a third revolver in his fist that he got out all six shots. The second revolver had exploded on him, and his uniform was full of burnt powder.

A tiny door swung open in pa Salmon's roof, and a bluebelly peeked out. "Identify yourselves, ye sons of bitches," the bluebelly screamed.

The general pranced on his clubfooted horse.

"Throw your rifles down and come on out . . . this is the loyal Galveston brigade."

The bluebelly mocked him. "Never heard of ye." He peppered the ground near Sweet Martin with rifle balls and shut his tiny door.

The general sent another dozen torches into the roof. The windows started to blaze. You could hear the Yankees scuttling inside. They couldn't get up much of a fusillade with fire in their laps. But then the gunboats got into the play. They sniffed our uprising in the smoke that curled over pa salmon's roof, and they lobbed their shells into Market Street.

The shelling turned the street black. Porches disappeared. Iron gates crumpled and fell. It was like being sucked into a whirlpool of wood and glass. The blues cheered from their burning house.

The general didn't budge from his horse. "Where the hell's the *Lorelei?*" he growled.

Pa heard this terrible boom. It felt like the island was splitting in half. It wasn't our cannons answering the Yankee fleet. No gun could make that kind of noise. It was the pigiron tooth. The *Lorelei* had come down the channel and rammed the Yankee flagship, *Harriet Lane,* putting a crack in her bow that knocked the *Harriet's* decks apart and sent her sharpshooters flying into the air, sinking the *Harriet* with all her cannons and fine musketry.

Watching their flagship go down stunned the Yankee fleet. The Yankees couldn't understand how an old "cottonboat" with an iron toothpick up front could demolish their best ship. But the blue navy recovered from the shock. It had five more gunboats in the harbor, the *Brooklyn,* the *Neptune,* the *Night Star,* the *Massachusetts,* and the *War Witch.* The fleet aimed its full battery at the *Lorelei* and fired. Cannonballs socked the *Lorelei* and landed deep in her cotton sides. She struggled in the water, with two hits in her boiler and one of her decks chewed up. But the cannons couldn't knock her out of the war. She bumped the *Neptune* and the *Massachusetts,* and now the Yankees only had half a fleet.

The *War Witch* avoided the pigiron tooth, crept up close to the enemy's stern, and decided to board her. The *Witch* had sharpshooters and marines and dismounted cavalry, and we had a phantom crew of nine men. But two panthers had forgotten to leave the boat. They'd been foraging near the boiler room, and they came out to meet the Yankees.

When the marines saw the coaly eyes of the panthers, they returned to the *Witch,* and we had the harbor to ourselves. The sea battle was over.

All the Yankees had on Galveston was a hundred men in a burning house. Some of the bluebellies jumped from the roof with their pants on fire. But the garrison wouldn't surrender itself. So the general rode Sweet Martin right into the house. He charged through the front window, the panes crashing onto his hat. That's when pa noticed the scabbard on General Smith. The general had found another gold sword. He must have paid a Mexican smith to hammer it out in secret.

The general rocked on his piebald. Not even Captain Shirley could ignore the savage blows he was delivering from inside the house, chopping off Yankee fingers and ears. He would have gone through that garrison and mutilated every man, one by one.

Captain Shirley ran to the window and told his men to give up. The gold sword distressed him a lot. He didn't want to lose so many brave men to that general on a horse. Pa remembered saying, *Nicaragua Smith.* He looked at the justice. Now they knew what a jungle warrior the general was. The search for Ishmael hadn't been a crazy scheme. The general would have taken Nicaragua and the whole damn Isthmus if a hundred armies hadn't ganged up on him.

The bluebellies ran out of pa Salmon's place. Sweet Martin pranced on the sidewalk in his cotton shoes. The general stopped thinking of his sword. He was worried about the men he had maimed. He screamed for "banditches" and rubbing alcohol. Pa and Justice Morrissey hopped to the general's words. They'd have given Galveston over to him if the island could have used a king.

Five

THE VICTORY cost us in gold. The merchants and saloonkeepers grumbled, because their best customers, Silver Spoon's men, were tucked away in the little jail under the courthouse stairs. And the merchants had to go back to using Confederate paper.

The justice didn't seem to mind this shortness of gold. He was provost marshal of an island that had freed itself of the Union and the Sister States. We were the undeclared country of Ishmael, and the justice was our dictator again. The general was sucking whiskey in the barrelhouses. His sword and his tunic were in the stable with Sweet Martin. He couldn't run an island that wasn't at war. It was up to Justice Morrissey.

He took to murdering spies.

The Ishmaelites found Harvey Beecher skulking near the wharves. They'd seen him cavorting with Yankees, wearing Navy revolvers under his belt, licking his chops at island girls, insulting the Safety Committee, and passing information to Silver Spoon, and the justice didn't waste his time with any tribunal. He summoned a squad of six sharpshooters, blindfolded Harvey Beecher, stood him next to an open coffin in the town square, and had the sharpshooters fire at his chest.

I was glad the eyepatch man got away. I wouldn't have wanted blood in his honey-colored hair.

The justice got greedy. He put Captain Shirley's name at the top of his execution bills. But pa was too smart for him. He held Captain Shirley at our house, and he wouldn't give him up to a coffin-and-blindfold party in the town square.

The justice brought his firing squad to the house to irritate pa and frighten mama and me. He read off his execution bill, declaring that Shirley was a spy as well as an army captain.

"Hogwash," pa said from his window.

"Benjamin, listen to me . . . I have affidavits in my pocket, sworn testimony—you hear?—that Captain Shirley was paying bushwhackers and Yankee scum to spy on us."

"So what?" pa said. "All captains have their spies. That's the nature of war."

"Well, sir, the man who runs spies is also a spy."

"Not in my opinion."

"I'm provost marshal," the justice shouted up to pa. "Your opinion doesn't count for much . . . will you come to your senses, or do I have to take that man by force?"

"Take him," pa said. "But you're trespassing on my property, and you'll smell some buckshot if you climb my stairs."

The justice's three chins started to shake.

"A provost marshal doesn't trespass. He has free rule wherever he steps on this island." He took out his marshal's handkerchief and wiped his nose. "It would break my heart, Ben, to shoot up this house and risk hurting your kin. But I'll have to . . . I make the law now. The mayor and the council disappeared on us, or did you forget?"

"I'm not an idiot, Mr. Chief Justice Morrissey. I know who disappeared and who did not . . . and you can disappear with your death squad."

"Benjamin, I'm warning you . . ."

"If Captain Shirley's a spy, I'm his accomplice, being as he's in my house. Hannah's a spy, Sally's a spy . . ."

"Don't be ridiculous," the justice said.

"Do you have enough blindfolds, Mr. Morrissey? Either you shoot every blamed one of us, or none at all."

Pa knew his man. Morrissey wouldn't shoot the whole tribe for a Yankee captain. He started yelling this legal talk. He was going to execute Shirley *in absentia,* he said. The captain had better not show his face. He was a dead man as far as the justice was concerned. And he went off with his firing squad.

Morrissey didn't get the chance to murder any more spies. General H. B. Nicholson, commander in chief of Texas and Louisiana, had come down from Houston with a small body of men to "open" our island for the Confederate States. He crossed the Galveston trestle bridge with his aide-de-camp, one stinking cannon, ten corporals, and his own detachment of bodyguards.

Nicholson's entrance into Galveston woke General Smith. His lieutenants helped him onto his horse, and he met Nicholson in the town square.

"Who is this man?" Nicholson asked Justice Morrisey.

"I can speak for myself," the general said from his perch on Sweet Martin. "I'm General Smith of the free state of Ishmael."

"What free state?"

"You're standing on it," the general said.

"This man is insane," Nicholson told the justice. "Who is he?"

"The hero of the Nicaraguan expedition . . . he won the island, sir, captured the blue garrison and crippled the blue fleet."

"Then we're in his debt, but we can't have a private army running around. General, you'll have to give me your sword."

"No," the general said. "You're the intruder here . . . Morrissey, are you with Ishmael, or the Confederates?"

The island state of Ishmael must have seemed slim to the justice at that moment, and he stood with the Confederacy. General Smith drew his golden sword. He would have chopped fingers and ears, but the ten corporals overpowered him and threw him from his piebald. He rolled in the dust, and the corporals put him in leg irons. The savior of Galveston had to scuffle to the courthouse like a common bandit.

THE GENERAL didn't hang. The Confederate Army confiscated his tunic and his sword and banished him from the island.

Nicholson rounded up the blues under the courthouse stairs and had them delivered to a military depot in Houston. He was going to exchange the lot of them for two of his majors that had fallen into Yankee hands. But the Yankees wouldn't give up enemy majors for the corporals and privates Nicholson had. So he tossed them into his stockade and held them there, and he took Captain Shirley away. He wouldn't tell a soul where Shirley was going. It was a secret of war. Pa liked having Shirley around, even though the captain was bitter about the role pa played in the uprising of New Year's Eve.

"I thought I was a friend. And all the time we were smoking, you plotted against me."

"Shirley, you are a friend, but you were occupying the island, and what could I do? I never asked you about your navy while you were in the house. I hope we can meet after the war is over."

"That's unlikely, Ben."

And a corporal's guard in gray uniforms spirited the captain from us in a little donkey cart. His head bobbed up and down behind the donkey's ears.

The grays moved back into the Tremont Hotel. They flooded the town with worthless money. Nicholson signed chits for his food and drink. But what were a general's chits? You couldn't spend them in Young's bacon and bagging store. They were souvenirs of the Confederate army. Galveston grew poorer and poorer with the grays around.

Young ran out of bacon, and the soldiers had to eat lard.

Nicholson let the camels run wild. He wouldn't return them to a corral the blues had built. So we had dromedaries eating our walls again.

Then the Yellow Jack arrived.

It was the worst plague in nine years. The fever struck children and the Confederate troops. The Tremont went from a barracks to a hospital ward. Army surgeons came down from Houston. They told Nicholson to shoot stray dogs and cats. The general took this to mean the camels too. He shot whatever camels he could find, saying it was the camels who brought yellow fever to Galveston and it was the camels who were wiping out his troops. Pa said it was nonsense. The camels had been on the island for years. A couple of them got away, hiding in the dunes at night, and swimming to the mainland. I started to cry, thinking of camels on the run.

The last big plague took my four little brothers. It robbed pa of the sons he could have had, and it kind of orphaned me, with no brothers to play with. And this damn plague forgot to pass our house. Pa came down with the fever.

His eyes turned yellow and he started vomiting blood into a pail. The pail was all black. Justice Morrissey ran to the house and cried into his handkerchief. He pounded his fists and said, "You rascal, Ben, you'd better not die."

Pa smiled.

"Who's the rascal? The harm you did . . . let me become chief justice for an hour, and b'God, I'd have you guillotined."

"Give me a Bible, Ben, and I'll swear you in . . ."

"Not now," pa said. "Not now." He asked for Archibald Aloysius. It wasn't the old days, when the justice could have swiped Arch from the penitentiary and given him to pa for the afternoon. A chief justice didn't count for much during the war. Morrissey had to go to Nicholson. The general signed an order putting Arch on a "holiday," so pa could talk to his old carriage boy in peace about John Locke.

Arch wore his prison clothes, a suit of brown burlap. He looked like a walking gunnysack. He had dust on his lips, and his hair wasn't groomed. I could tell what pa was thinking. He should have kept the thief at home, cured him of that habit of stealing silver and gold. Prison wasn't for Arch. The luster in his eyes was gone. Pa took two silver ingots out of his money chest and lay them in Archie's palm.

"It's not much of a patrimony, Archibald, but it might buy you extra food."

Arch returned the silver ingots.

"Thankee, Master Ben, but the turnkeys would only steal that silver out of my pocket."

"I could have the ingots sent to Warden Jones in your name."

"Then it would go into the warden's pants."

"I don't figure that," pa said. "Jones' an honest man."

"I never said he wasn't, Master Ben, but the warden wouldn't keep a separate account book for the likes of me. He'd put that silver into a general fund, and he'd dip into it from time to time and get some ribbons for his little girls."

"Archibald Aloysius, are you saying it's a world of crooks?"

"No, Master Ben. But you take honesty, and what is it? A

tradeable thing. It rises and falls in the open market. And I'd say honesty's at a low this year."

Pa started coughing that dark blood and he couldn't continue the conversation with Arch. He sat behind a curtain and tore out his lungs into the vomiting pail. And I went downstairs with Arch.

"Couldn't you have been nicer to him, Archibald? He loves you. You're the nearest thing to the sons he lost . . ."

Archibald screwed up his eyes. He was a ghost, I swear.

"How wasn't I nice, Miss Sally?"

"He gave you silver and you had to throw it back."

"It's not a question of silver," he said. "It's the foolishness that goes with it. Why should your pa contribute to the upkeep of the warden's girls?"

"That's not Archie speaking," I said. "It's his Boston education. It's made him a snob."

"A snob that the warden hires out to pick cotton. Good-bye, Miss Sally. And I'm sorry for Master Ben."

Nicholson's corporals took him in the same donkey cart they'd used for Captain Shirley. The brown burlap was shivering on his body. A ghost in a gunnysack. He never got the chance to talk about John Locke.

Pa died in the morning. His heart burst, and that terrible black blood shot out of his nose, his ears, and his mouth. The room was thick with it, the bedposts, the mosquito bar, and the quilts. And it's strange how I was all prepared for pa's dying. A voice licked at me, *Sal, he's going, your pa.* I blubbered just the same. Mama was alone, and I'd have to take care of her and be kind to black Hannah.

I remembered standing on the dunes and praying pa would survive the New Year's Eve war, and mama wouldn't have to wear widow weeds. Now mama got her weeds. We all wore black. And Pastor Johns screamed in church about good men meeting their

Maker, and it was like he was mentioning somebody else's pa. My pa was funny, and he smelled of the pipes on his mantel, and he wasn't this creature of Paster Johns' who "walked with Christ." The only time I heard of Christ in the house was when pa was cussing Hannah, Arch, or himself.

The justice nearly fainted in the churchyard, and I had to hold him up. Morrissey's a ton if you counted all his chins.

"Ben, Ben . . . damn my hide, Sally girl, if I didn't make your pa miserable trying to arrest the people in his house. I love to quarrel. It's in my blood. Damn my hide."

We stumbled around the crypt in the church wall, him with his rolling body and his little feet. He wiped the tears from his eyes with a knuckle and blew his nose. It sounded like an elephant's call. Pastor Johns said he was making a mockery of his grief with all that swaggering. But he was still chief justice of the island, and an officer of the church. Morrissey recovered his balance and frowned at Pastor Johns.

Nicholson gave his condolences to mama and me. It turned out that the general was a widowman. He'd lost his wife in the plague that struck Chattanooga last spring. He began showing up at the house. He didn't wear the dusty uniform he had on when he crossed over the trestle bridge and took Galveston away from the Ishmaelites. He had silver on his sleeves. Mama stopped wearing black after his sixth or seventh visit.

I didn't like the way Doctor Ovenshine would wink at me in the middle of a lesson. That winking had a lousy smell. I caught him with mama and the general in pa's library. They were bargaining over the rights to somebody. It wasn't black Hannah. Or mama's milking cow. What would Doctor Ovenshine want with a cow?

The justice followed me home from school one day in November. "Sal, you don't have to do it."

"Do what, Justice Morrissey?"

"Saints, didn't you know? Your mama and the general's figuring to marry you off to that idiot schoolmaster, so they can have the house to themselves . . . building a love nest with Ben gone a month."

"Pa died in June," I said.

"Well, it certainly feels like a month. I'll adopt you, child, take you from that scheming pair and the schoolmaster."

"You don't have to be alarmed," I said. "What would I do with a husband? I'm fifteen."

"There's been younger brides on this island, Sally Blackburn. I've married twelve-year-olds to one lout or another. Girls fresh from the cradle. I can't recollect their names."

"I'm no cradle girl," I said. "Professor Henry's not for me."

"Child, they've settled on the dowry and the wedding date. They left the pastor out of it, being as your mama's a widow lady. The general came to me."

I was madder'n hell, all that bargaining behind my back. I was a soldier, a veteran of the Ishmael campaign, not a marriage doll.

Mama caught me sulking at the dinner table. The general was there and my "husband," Doctor Henry Ovenshine. They were chewing potatoes with their big fat cheeks.

Mama said, "Eat your dinner, Sally dear."

She sniffled into her napkin.

"Rose," the general said, "let Miss Sally attend to her food. She's sixteen."

"Fifteen," I said, and the general got up from the table and took me into the front room. I could see why the justice was scared of him. Nicholson had the tiniest eyes. They were like pits in a pumpkin face. He could have ordered your death, or gobbled a piece of chicken, and you couldn't have told it from his eyes.

"Honey, your mama and me . . ."

"You don't have to paint up a story, General Nicholson. I'll marry that jackass tomorrow if that's what mama wants."

I could have run off to the mainland with the refugee camels, or lived like a pirate on the dunes, or just screamed and said no, no, to any husband they had in mind. But mama needed me. It was like having camouflage in the house. Mama intended to marry pumpkin-eyes, but it would be easier on her and the general if there was another wedding in the family.

I sneaked off to Hannah's room over the stable.

"You've had six husbands, Hannah, and not a single child. How did you stop your belly from growing? Did you tie it around with a string?"

She giggled at me. ". . . never met a string that could stop a man."

Hannah showed me what to do. Cotton dipped in camphor oil. You stuck it between your legs and it killed a man's seed.

"If it don't work, Miss Sally, it aint the camphor's fault . . . it's the devil's own child."

I'd trust to Hannah's cotton balls. The justice married me and Doctor Ovenshine, but he cried before he delivered the oath. I had to swear to him in private that I was marrying the professor of my own free will. Ovenshine crawled into my bed that night. It's funny how a bride behaves. I wondered if he missed Emilia Salmon. Emilia could have made him rich. And when he climbed on top and entered me, my hands reached out and took him by the ears. My "husband" felt like a rocking chair. It didn't hurt. I just let him rock. I had my cotton-and-camphor ball.

Six

M<small>Y</small> D<small>OWRY</small> brought us to Houston. It was blood money out of pa's grave, *black blood*, but it provided Henry with a new college. We lived on the college's top floor, in a house with green blinds, on Texas Avenue. Girls flocked to Henry's college. My husband didn't let a soul forget that he was almost a son-in-law to the commander in chief of Texas. He'd hint that the general owned a "quarter interest" in the school, and we prospered right away.

Merchants and speculators arrived to register their daughters. They would fight and scratch each other to guarantee a spot for their little girls. Benches had to be built. I figured the house would collapse under the weight of all those benches and girls.

Henry took to wearing ruffles on his shirts. He went around in silk waistcoats and orange pants. He "hired" me to look after the slower pupils. I had to learn them arithmetic and all. But our reputation didn't suffer. Everybody was talking about Ovenshine's college. We must have had close to forty girls.

A visitor came by. She was too young to be the mother of an Ovenshine girl. She was a beautiful lady with yellow hair, a Chinese umbrella and a dark blue shawl, skirts that took up half the stairway, and pretty galoshes for the Houston mud.

"How are you, honey?" she said, and she pecked me on the cheek like I was a lost sister of hers.

"Sakes, we went to school together! I was Emilia Salmon once. Now I'm Mrs. Thomas Brinton."

I couldn't understand how that idiot girl with udders grew up so fine.

"Where's Henry?" she said.

"With the older girls. He'll be out in a minute."

"Honey, I can't wait . . . we're feeding seventeen people tonight. But come and see my place . . . it's the big red house on Louisiana Street, with the five roofs."

Henry's class let out and I told him that Emilia had been by, but he didn't say a word.

Emilia must have had an awful lot of guests to feed, because she never came by again. And she didn't invite us to any of her soirees. She had whole orchestras come to Louisiana Street. It seemed crazy in the middle of a war, but Emilia had to keep up the morale of the South's Lone Star.

Then the soirees stopped for a while. Emilia changed her address. Louisiana Street wasn't fine enough for her. It was near the noisier saloons. But Emilia wouldn't part with her house. She let it "travel" to Carolina Street, a journey of seven blocks. She hired a master house mover for the job. It took eighteen horses and thirty mules to get the house up on giant rollers, so the master could begin. The house traveled for two weeks. It left ruts in the

road that were deep enough to bury a cannon. Three mules died.
The house groaned along the way. Pieces of slate fell from
Emilia's wonderful roofs. The slivers were sharp, and they landed
like knives that you had to avoid. Emilia was lucky it was the dry
season, or she would have had a house on Main Street, swallowed
in mud.

But she still didn't invite us after the house arrived. I guess she
wanted more quality than a schoolteacher and his bride. I didn't
care. She could keep her orchestras and her traveling house. I had
plenty to do, teaching arithmetic.

Henry began to stray from the college. He'd come home stinking of whiskey and perfume, stand there in his waistcoat and
watch me with bloody eyes. He'd climb on me before I could get
out of my shimmy. But I was ready for the skunk. I didn't forget
to soak some cotton in camphor oil. He'd raise the shimmy and
rock between my legs without taking off his orange pants.

"I'm your husband. You have to say darling to me. Say it!"

I couldn't say darling to that foul whiskey breath. I married him
to help mama along. I was the bargain that came with his new
college. I did what any bargain wife had to do. Kisses and the rest.
But I wouldn't say darling to him.

"Say it, or I'll whip your hide, you ugly little toad."

"I'm not little, husband Henry. And I'm certainly not a toad.
I'm your wife that teaches arithmetic."

He wasn't rocking in me now. He pushed in deep, and it was
like having a panther attack your body. He shoved my arms back
until my shoulders nearly tore, and he plugged his whiskey mouth
into my face. I thought I'd die from the stench, and I couldn't
get a swallow of air.

Then he pulled out of me and unplugged my face. "Witch.
Your own mother didn't want you around. I had to take the
duckling off her hands."

"The duckling paid for this college."

He went to sleep in another room. I hated him, but it kind of hurts when a husband leaves your bed. He was back the next night, after his whiskeying. And he was more of a gentleman. He removed his orange pants.

Our enrollment dropped. Merchants weren't so eager to lend us their daughters. Maybe it was on account of the war. Pockets were tightening up. We had to accept candles and bolts of cloth instead of our regular fee. So many candles for one girl. I did the tallying. I had to. Henry disappeared.

The high sheriff of Houston came around asking for Henry.

"What's he done?"

"Violated property, ma'am."

"Whose property?"

"He got himself tangled in some skirts that wasn't his'n."

This high sheriff was a riddler man.

"Professors don't have skirts," I said.

"Well, this one has quite a few, I reckon. He's the biggest fornicator in town."

I didn't feel like fainting for the sheriff, so I asked him right out. "Who did he go fornicatin' with?"

"That Galveston hussy, lawyer Brinton's wife. The woman who wouldn't let a house lie still. The streets haven't stopped shivering from the move she made."

The sheriff wasn't a riddler man after all. That "hussy" was Emilia. But it wasn't clear what the sheriff wanted with Henry. Did he come to whip him for abusing the town's most important wife? I don't think so. She could have done as much fornicatin' as she liked with some foreign prince, and Houston would have congratulated her for having so much dash, but you can't get caught in the muck with a schoolteacher. The Salmons and the Brintons were powerful folks, and they wouldn't have tolerated a public whipping and the scandal it would bring. The sheriff had come to run Henry out of town.

"Tell your man he has six hours to pack, and then I pity him. But you don't have to leave, ma'am. There's people I know who'd help support your school once the professor is gone."

I didn't like the smirk under his moustache. The sheriff must have been figuring I'd become his half-time wife. He'd make a worse "husband" than the one I already had. At least Henry didn't belong to the Salmons and the Brintons. He was only a schoolteacher who went sneaking after "quality." He should have fornicated with some lesser wife, that rat husband of mine.

I'd give him poison to eat after I rescued him from the sheriff. Was he whoring in the dark somewhere? I couldn't knock on every bawdy house window and ask for the professor with the orange pants. And I had to find the varmint before the sheriff did. Lawyer Brinton might have told the sheriff to slap Henry on the skull a little, so my husband could leave Houston with mush inside his head.

I put on my winter cape and locked the college door. I didn't have pretty galoshes like Emilia did. Mud got in my shoes. I cursed mama and the general for landing me in this place. I was an island girl. I liked the lick of salt spray, and the hump of so many dunes. I kept wishing I'd meet a camel galloping in the mud. But there were no refugee camels around. They must have followed the coast and gone down to Corpus Christi. I don't care what anybody says about Arabia. Camels love to be near the ocean. They can run in the dunes and eat salt off gates and windowsills. Houston wasn't for them.

I tried the better whiskey houses, paying a colored boy to search the front and back rooms and yell out to me if he saw Henry's orange pants. He came up with something at the fifth or sixth saloon. It wasn't Henry. It was an old bum. I recognized bits of ruined color on his sleeve. It was the prince without a country, Nicaragua Smith, the general who fell to the ground. He'd have conquered Houston if you could set him on a horse. Now he earned his whiskey running errands for gamblers in his corroded uniform. He'd heard the colored boy shout "Ovenshine," and he left his post at the gambling tables for a name he remembered from his own lost country.

That whiskey beggar bowed to me, and I was touched by all the bending he did. "Miss Sally, what in thunder are you doing here? Did that Nicholson fellow kick everybody off the island?"

The tiny general didn't know I'd married Ovenshine and that pa was dead. His fists bunched inside his sleeves.

"Dealt you off, the sons of bitches . . . sorry, Miss Sally, I didn't mean to include your mama. Go on home. I'll find Professor Henry if I have to tear out the walls of a hundred saloons."

I reached into my purse, but the general wouldn't take silver from me.

"Hell, miss Sally, we're old soldiers. Didn't I make you a brevet colonel once?"

"I was only a major, General Smith."

"We can rectify that," he said, and he sent me home to the college. I waited and waited, and those six hours the sheriff allotted to Henry was up. Then a face started sneaking in the window. If the Lord Jesus had a pair of whiskey eyes, that's how He'd have looked, with a pale forehead and different kinds of trouble twisting around His cheeks. It was Professor Henry coming out of the Houston mud, where rats like to nibble at your shoes. I didn't have to guess who was chasing him. The Salmons, the Brintons, and the sheriff's whip.

His waistcoat was in shreds, and his orange pants were black from the knee down. His tongue froze up. That man who loved to holler couldn't speak. I made him a toddy and his tongue unfroze.

"Husband Henry, where have you been?"

The toddy shook in his hands.

"You've been gone five days. I had to work with the older girls. Henry, what did you do with them all this time? They don't have the faintest notion what geography is. They couldn't even point to Prussia on the map . . . the sheriff's looking for you, Henry."

His eyes bled a dark pink.

"He says you violated one of the city codes . . . he swears you've been truckin' with Miss Emilia."

"That's a lie! I wouldn't touch pa Salmon's little girl."

"She's not so little any more. And why are you hiding from the sheriff?"

"Who's hiding? I went to Galveston, that's all . . . it's not your business what I do, Mrs. Ovenshine."

"I suppose it's Emilia's business . . . she can have the whoredog of Texas."

The toddy must have given him his strength back, because he rose up and took me by the shoulders and he started pinching me to pieces. That's when the sheriff came into the house, and I was thinking, *I hope he brought his whip.*

"Hello, good people."

I could feel the trembling under Henry's ruffled shirt. The shirt was all yellow. He must have been sleeping in it.

"Ma'am, didn't I tell you the songbird has six hours to pack? Why's he still here?"

"I'm going," Henry said.

He took a thick piece of paper out of his pocket. "You'd better read this."

The sheriff had to find his spectacles. I peeked around his shoulder and saw the military seal on that piece of paper. It was a safe-conduct pass signed by General Nicholson, commander in chief. Henry had gone to mama's "husband" to get him out of this scrape.

The sheriff was like a wounded dog. He muttered apologies. He couldn't cross the commander in chief. The sheriff was obliged to offer Henry safe-conduct to the edge of town. He waited in the street.

The husband smiled. He was Henry the conquerer now. He

shoved that piece of paper in front of my nose. "Texians," he said. "They're the dumbest race on earth."

"I'm a Galveston girl. And we belong to Texas."

"Pack, you ugly duck!"

"I'm staying . . . somebody has to run the college."

"I sold the college . . . to General Nicholson."

"Show me the bill of sale."

We stuck our bundles into the wagon Henry had. A wagon with a broken-down horse.

"There's your bill of sale," Henry said. "The whole of it."

"You gave my dowry away for a wagon and a horse?"

He chuckled to himself. "The general drives a hard bargain. What could I do? He had your mama to advise him. Get in!"

I climbed up into that wagon with mud and ice in my heart. I couldn't stay in Houston without a house, and I couldn't run home. Mama sold me into bondage. I was Ovenshine's slave. I took another look at that horse of Henry's. It was a piebald with mange on his back. A gelding, if you ask me. But I wasn't about to peek under his legs. Henry was a poor bargainer. The school was worth twenty old wagons and a mangy horse. I should have been nicer to the creature. He reminded me of Sweet Martin, Nicaragua Smith's charging horse. Martin was a piebald. Was he sold into bondage too? Martin helped us win the battle of New Year's Eve. We couldn't have taken Galveston without the piebald.

"Martin," I said. "Sweet Martin."

We drove down Texas Avenue, with the sheriff escorting us on his fat healthy mare. Rats scuttled in and out of Henry's wheels. They were big as groundhogs. They nosed against Martin's hind legs. That's my dowry. A fornicatin' husband. An old wagon. And a heap of rats.

The Two-Gun Man

Seven

WE MOVED to Palestine.

The wagon broke on us and the piebald dropped dead in the streets of that dusty town. I stood guard over Martin's body. He was a veteran of the Galveston war and he should have had a proper grave. But my husband sold him to a man from the glue factory. The man's friends dragged Martin off. They'd cook down his skin, his bones, and his hooves and turn Martin into some horrible paste.

"Why'd you give him to the glueman?" I said. "That was a war-horse."

"Will you stop your moaning? I'll give you to the glueman in half a minute."

I'd have scratched his eyes out, but Henry was the new professor of Palestine.

It didn't mean much. Palestine wasn't looking for a female academy. The town was shy of rich merchants with daughters to train. So we had to set up a college for louts and little boys. They couldn't read or write to save their hides. I unrolled the map of the world, pinned it to the college wall, and went across the different colors with my pointing stick. "Where's Tibet?"

The louts looked and looked.

I pointed to a deep purple splotch. It was a mystery to little boys that couldn't spell the word *corn*. They knew the mudholes near Palestine. They remembered Governor Sam. They could name five of the Sister States and cuss at bluebellies, Indians, and furriners. Everything else was Tibet to them. Purple and far away.

But I was going to educate the louts or join Sweet Martin in all the glue. It took me a morning to learn them how to say Egypt right.

"Egypt has a tail on it. The letter *t.*"

They went on saying "Egyp' " until I drove that *t* inside their heads.

The husband came into my class one afternoon and called me over to the door. "We're leaving this dusthole right now."

And he made me pack our bundles while the little boys sat with their spelling books. I had struggled with them, brought them out of that wilderness of dropped *t*'s, so they wouldn't be ignorant, and here I was rolling up the map of the world and running out on them with Henry-the-skunk. He'd fixed his wagon, and he had a fresh nag with more mange on him than Sweet Martin, but this was a wagon horse, not a warrior, and I didn't much care for him. Henry called him Ishmael, just to hurt me.

He had a whole lot of pluck in his wagon, with his safe-conduct from the commander in chief. He could pick up and move his college wherever he liked. But how come he couldn't settle on a place? He wasn't such a wanderer when pa was alive.

We went to Corsicana, but we didn't stay long. The husband had some secret bird sitting on his shoulder and scratching up his neck. *Move on, Henry. Move on.* I didn't have the courage to get near the children, knowing I'd have to leave them in a minute. If you asked Henry what was wrong with Corsicana, he'd say, "I'm sick of Texas."

It wasn't that. Lincoln got himself killed while the South collapsed, and an occupying army from the North marched into Texas. It was almost as if that army was chasing Henry. We traveled to Indian territory and started a school inside the Choctaw Nation. It was desolate and no armies came there, but we were hard up for pupils. The Choctaws wouldn't send their children to us.

The richer Indians allowed us to educate their body servants and slaves, colored boys that bounty hunters had kidnapped for them and would soon have to go free. The Choctaws were holding on to their slaves as long as they could. And we were hired to prepare the colored boys for Choctaw citizenship.

It was the darnedest thing. Teaching black Indians their tribal privileges. Henry couldn't speak a word of Choctaw. Neither could I. But that husband of mine was devoted to these slaves. He must have felt close to that odd territory they were in, the land of black Indians, where slaves become Choctaws and "freedmen."

He bought them winter jackets out of his own slim pay, because the colored boys were freezing in the clothes the Choctaws gave them to wear. They slept at the school, huddled around the stove. The professor learned them John Locke. And I grew bitter against Henry, because he wouldn't talk Locke with pa, or the girls of his Galveston college. He kept it for his "wives" in the Choctaw Nation.

"Children," he'd say. *Children!* A few of them were thirty-five. "Children, what the hell is in a man's color? Damn pigmentation.

An accident of birth. That pigment doesn't paint your skeleton. It's on your hide. And when you're citizens of the Nation, you remember that. You're equal to any son of a bitch."

Wish pa had heard that. It was pure John Locke. I was glad for the colored boys. Their education was going to surpass the Choctaws themselves.

But the Choctaws didn't take kindly to our college. The high sheriff of the whole Nation appeared one night with his Indian police and shot out our windows. The policemen wore Yankee uniforms. The sheriff shouted at us in Choctaw. A black Indian had to translate for Henry and me. *White teacher, if you poison our slaves with your white man's tricks, we will feed your nose and your eyes to the dogs.*

I expected the husband to hide in the shadows of the school-house. I was wrong. He was apostle to the black Indians and he went outside to face the sheriff and his men. They shook their Winchesters to scare him off. Henry wouldn't scare.

"You are the dogs and the betrayers," he said. "I have a pact with your tribe. The Nation asked me to prepare these boys for citizenship. And that's what I intend to do."

I don't think the sheriff understood a word of Henry's speech. It didn't matter. How can you shoot an apostle? Was it the melody in Henry's voice that froze the policemen to their saddles? He could have collected their Winchesters and they wouldn't have complained. He slapped the rumps of their spotted ponies.

"Giddap."

And the Choctaw police were gone.

WE HAD a graduation party. I served toddies in a great pitcher and prepared little honey cakes. The colored boys were Choctaws now, full members of the Nation. Papa Henry was proud of all his "wives." After the boys went off to live with the Choctaws,

Henry had a decline. The black Indians would come around and visit, but it wasn't the same. Henry needed them under his roof.

The Nation didn't have any more colored boys to give us. We'd seen the last of the slaves. "Henry, it's time to move the college. Maybe one of the other Nations has colored boys. We could try the Chickasaws and the Creeks."

"Keep still."

The Choctaws must have pitied Henry, because the chiefs sent us a few of their own little girls. Henry assigned them to me. They were the prettiest creatures in the Nation. They wore calico dresses, cut to a doll's size. When I told them about George Washington, they said, "Father George, Father George." I kind of wished I had a child. But not with husband Henry. Here I was, nineteen, a schoolmistress and an old-maid wife.

Citizenship was hard to bear for most of the colored boys. The sheriff would whip them for the slightest sin. The freedmen took to running away. The Choctaw police would drag them out of Seminole country and whip them harder than before. That was peculiar citizenship, if you ask me. Then the black Indians began hiding in our cellar. Henry was happy again. He had his "children" and his "wives."

But the Choctaws guessed where the colored boys had gone to hide, and they chucked us out of the Nation. We had our wagon and Ishmael the horse. Henry sat crumpled up, forlorn without his black Indians, and I had to drive the wagon. I got to like Ishmael on the trails. He was a temperate horse. He seemed to worry about Henry's condition, and he'd moan along with the husband from time to time, to keep him company.

"Henry, should we set up school in Missouri?"

"Missouri's a pile of manure."

"We could go back down to Galveston. Mama might take us in."

"And meet the bluebellies?"

"We'll meet bluebellies wherever we run. They own the world."

"Not Kansas. The people are fierce. They fight bluebellies toe to toe."

Kansas wasn't a floating island in the middle of the rocks. It had soldiers and forts, like everyplace else. I didn't care.

We went over the border and settled in Bishop Sticks. It was a street of tents and sod huts. Bishop Sticks couldn't support a coffeehouse, never mind a college. But the professor wouldn't stir from that spot. It was Kansas, where the people were fierce. I saw dirt farmers, stable boys, a pink-eyed grocer, a gambler or two, and drifters like Henry and me. We lived in the wagon, sleeping under the wagon cover, with Ishmael watching over us.

We were lucky to have him. He'd snort if a thief or a drunken soddy man came near the wagon. That's how we survived so long in Bishop Sticks. The town was dirt poor. It couldn't feed a Doctor of Philosophy, and the husband wouldn't scout for work. He'd sit in the wagon, smoking his pipe, reading Aristotle to the horse.

I tried to teach school from the wagon traces. I'd harangue everybody who passed us on the way to the grocer. "Come learn from Mrs. Ovenshine. I do spelling and geography. A poem to your sweetheart? A letter to your pa? See Mrs. Ovenshine."

That's the kind of gypsy school I ran. The town didn't have rich Choctaws with sons and daughters to spare. Children had to scratch the earth from morning to night, with their big sisters and brothers. I got the grocer's wife. Madam wanted to improve her penmanship. We traded lessons for a fistful of grub. She was the stingiest woman in the West. I had to thank her for each wormy potato. Customers were scarce.

I did have one more pupil, a gambler who paid me in gold. I'd write letters to the different sweethearts he had. Henrietta. Marguerite. He'd propose marriage to eight or ten women at a time.

And he took to whispering in my ear. "Come with me to Wichita, Sally girl."

I could tolerate the whispering and the foul noises he made with his lips. I didn't like his hand on my knee. I stopped taking his gold.

The husband noticed the loss of revenue. "What happened to that pupil of yours?"

"I dismissed him," I said. "I'm not the Whore of Babylon . . . he was taking liberties. He begged me to leave your wagon and ride with him to Wichita."

"Begging don't count," the husband said, and he went back to sucking sugar with the horse.

A CRAZINESS reached Bishop Sticks. It was called the Ten-Cent Romance. They were books you could fold and put inside your pocket. They were all about this character Wild Bill. *Wild Bill, the Indian Slayer.* Kansans were terrified of any Indian who walked. They shivered if you mentioned the Choctaw Nation. And the Pawnees were showing up in Kansas. People were scared to death. That's how come they adored Wild Bill. Wild Bill ate Indians for breakfast and lunch.

He was born James Butler Hickok, in Illinois. His pa hid runaway niggers in his house. The Ten-Cent Romance didn't have a kind word to say about the poor owners who fell into ruin when the niggers disappeared. What do you expect? *The Indian Slayer* was published in New York.

Hickok goes out onto the plains before he's eleven and gets to be an Army scout. He meets up with a black bear that's famous for murdering people. The bear stands on his hind legs and growls at Bill. Hickok growls right back. They roll through the bushes for seven hours. It's fearsome to watch. Bill escapes the death hug twice. The animal claws pieces out of him, but Hickok slits the bear's throat with an Army knife, and now he's "Wild Bill," the tamer of black bears.

After the Sister States broke with the Union, Wild Bill becomes a spy. He sneaks into the "rebel" lines, and joins a body of rangers who rob and kill Northerners—and Southerners too. Their own captains are afraid of these men. Wild Bill sticks with the "rebels" five months and leads them to their graves.

He goes to Fort Riley at the end of the war. The Indians have been massacring settlers around the fort, so Wild Bill signs up as a scout again. He grows his hair long, defying the Indians to scalp him if they can. He jumps in and out of Indian country, riding Black Nell, his favorite mare. Nell hates the "red buzzards," just like Wild Bill. She sleeps on a billiard table at the fort.

It was hokum, you ask me, all this James Butler Hickok. But I read that Ten-Cent Romance over and over, until the book tore in my hands. It seems I couldn't get enough of Wild Bill.

PAWNEES ARRIVED in Bishop Sticks. They couldn't have been on a scalping mission. They didn't have a single hatchet or a spear. The wind must have swept them off the plains.

You saw no beads or buffalo hides, just bones and hollow chests. And dust on their bodies. They had nothing to barter with. Were these the desperate characters that Wild Bill swallowed for lunch? Pawnees with hollow chests. It made me miserable to think of that Ten-Cent Romance.

The husband stopped talking to his horse.

The Pawnees must have reminded him of those colored boys in the Choctaw Nation. Henry had a fondness for outcasts. He fed them potatoes from the wagon. It would have sickened you to watch seven starving Indians chew raw potatoes like a rat.

Bishop Sticks didn't appreciate Henry turning his wagon into a Pawnee restaurant. The town couldn't afford a regular mayor, but it had a Vigilance Committee that looked out for rustlers, horse thieves, "red birds," and Southern trash. The vigilantes were shy about destroying Indians on a public street. They couldn't tell how many brothers the Pawnees had on the plains, brothers that could take revenge. So they didn't shoot or hang the hollow-chests. They invited the Pawnees to go away, and after that they threw Henry and me out of Bishop Sticks.

I was glad to leave. Ishmael perked up his ears, and we drove deeper into Kansas. We didn't last long at the next soddy town. Henry took to feeding Indians again.

We were nearly scalped twice by Kansans themselves. Vigilantes shot at us. We were Indian lovers, less than the lowest dog. It was Ish's strong back that saved us. That horse could pull a wagon through mud and fire, and blue rifle smoke.

"They'll butcher us if you go on feeding Indians."

Henry wouldn't listen. The professor had his horse and wagon, and me to drive him in and out of villages. We went to Hays. It had plenty of rich grocers. The grocers looked kindly upon a schoolmaster and schoolmistress for their little girls. We didn't have to teach out of a wagon. The grocers gave us a house on Chestnut Street. It was an old gray shoe box, with dust in the windows and spiders on the wall, but it did have a fine little gallery under the roof. I spent the morning slapping spiders with a broom while the husband showed himself to be a carpenter. He made benches and stools for the college, with Ishmael looking on.

Then he performed surgery on the house. Ishmael nickered at him, and the husband climbed up to the gallery with a big knife and cut away where the wood was rotting fast, and he plugged the holes with hot pitch. You couldn't help thinking he was a professor again, proud of his new college.

It didn't last.

He'd go drinking with the horse, take Ishmael right into the saloon with him. Horse and man would slobber up the place, and

I feared for Henry's life, because he had strong opinions, and you can never tell what a drunken horse will do. I had to drive them out with a switch, beating them on the shoulders. The whiskey-faces laughed and called me a hellish wife. I didn't care, so long as I got Henry and Ish to Chestnut Street.

But you can't have a rowdy schoolmaster, even in a rich grocers' town. Pupils began to drop out of sight after the second week. I took in lodgers. Else we would have starved. The grocers never asked for the return of their house. Maybe they were embarrassed about pulling their daughters out of the college. I had two buffalo skinners and a hunter in the back rooms. The house smelled of buffalo. I worked with the six or seven girls we still had left and ignored the stink around us.

The husband moved into the stable with Ish. He said he wasn't going to live with buffalo hunters in the house. He took to taunting me. "Little Sally, there's a friend of yours in Hays. William Severe . . . from the dime novels. He's a gambler with a pretty coat."

"Where did you see Wild Bill Hickok?"

"At the Pinto Saloon."

It was a hangout for the wild men of Hays. People had their noses bitten off in the Pinto Saloon and Faro House.

"Take me to the Pinto," I said. "I want to have a look at Wild Bill."

"The horse will take you. Ask Ish."

"Damn you, Henry, I'm not going to the Pinto with a horse."

I got mighty curious, but a schoolmistress couldn't sashay into the Pinto all by herself.

I'd hear the music coming from inside. The Pinto had a fiddler man and its own piano. *It's a lie. The husband's teasing me. There's no Wild Bill.*

I asked the buffalo hunter who lived in the house.

"The Indian Slayer, Hickok. Did you ever meet up with him?

My husband swears he's at the Pinto right now."

"Miss Sally, I've slept under every bush in Indian country, and I didn't meet that Slayer. Oh, there's lots of Wild Bills, and they're all yellowbellies. So put your mind to rest."

I stopped thinking of Hickok and his faro house. The violins got to be as familiar as the dust in my windows. I had pupils and lodgers to worry about.

And a whiskey bum. He stood near the house, in a blanket with nothing underneath. I could have chased him with a broom, but he didn't have the piggly eyes of the bums I remembered. His eyes were blue. And they didn't leak. They were the clearest blue-gray in the West.

"I suppose you're Wild Bill," I said.

"Hickok's the name."

I laughed. Soon every bum in the street would walk out of a Ten-Cent Romance. He had tiny lips and a long thin nose and matted dirty brown hair.

"I can fix you some grub, if you like."

"No, ma'am. Just a bath."

So I took the bum inside. I heated up six pails of water and filled the washtub for him and threw in some soda ash. The water bubbled up and turned milky in half a minute. That soda could take a year of filth off a mule.

"If you're Hickok, where's the Pawnee scalps you carry in your pants?"

He shook the blanket. "Sorry. I lost my pants at the saloon."

"Aren't you the Indian Slayer? Where's your six-guns and Black Nell?"

"At the Pinto, ma'am. I lost them in a card game."

He threw off the blanket, stepped into the washtub, and sat right down. He wasn't ashamed to be without a stitch of clothes. But he couldn't trick me. I wasn't going to take my eyes off him. He had gouges in his back, wider than a finger. They were marks a ferocious animal could have made.

". . . you survived that struggle with the black bear. It wasn't hokum at all."

But he turned silent on me, William Severe. He climbed out of the washtub like an Indian chief, his body painted white from that soda ash. He got into the blanket, mumbled "Thank you, ma'am," and departed from the house.

Eight

Seems we had a college in Hays that was more and more a
nursery school. I was in charge of five infant girls. They weren't
from any grocery store. The grocers' children had gone away.
These were saloonkeepers' brats, with beer and drops of whiskey
on their skirts. And we had the buffalo hunter, two skinners, a
husband in the stable, and Wild Bill.

"Anybody to home?"

The Indian Slayer was back, wearing a buckskin coat, with high
boots, butternut pants, an orange neckcloth, and two ivory-han-
dled guns in his belt. He must have had his hair washed. It was
almost yellow. It hung down to his shoulders. He was the prettiest
sight in Hays.

I looked out the door.

"Salome," he said.

"Hickok, who told you that name?"

"You did."

"That's a lie. You sat in my washtub with soda ash, and you left a half pound of dirt. I never once said 'Salome' to you."

"I wasn't thinking of yesterday, ma'am. It was another time . . . in the dunes."

"Dunes? Show me a dune in Kansas and I'll give you a dollar."

Drat that Indian Slayer! He was the eyepatch man. I remembered his honey-colored hair.

"Hickok, you've been trashing me. Pretending we never met. You're nothing but a skunk and a filthy spy."

"I needed a bath, ma'am, and I didn't want to bring up old times."

The Slayer handed me a silver dollar.

"I'm told you have rooms to let . . . would you consider taking me for a lodger, ma'am?"

I took the Slayer in. Why not? I had one more room on the second floor. I couldn't hold his spying days against him. Galveston was a dead country by now. The Yankees owned it and everything else.

"Where can I put my horse?"

"You can't have the stable. My husband's living there. But you can tie her to the back of the house."

I laughed, because Hickok didn't have a mare. Black Nell was a stallion with a missing right eye.

"How come he has a girl's name."

"It suits him."

"Does he sleep on billiard tables?"

"As often as he likes."

You couldn't argue with Hickok. He'd have told you Kansas was an island, and Hays was a ship that sat on top of a dune. And he'd have invented water, an ocean on the plains, where stallions named Nell liked to swim. It was the land of Wild Bill Hickok.

Henry moved out of the stable once he heard Hickok was in the house. "You toad," he said. "Why'd you let him in? He's a two-gun man."

"What's that mean?"

"He shoots at people. He's one of them mankillers who goes from town to town. He gambles, he gets into fights, he keeps the undertaker busy. Who'll protect you if I don't?"

The husband had his big knife. It shivered in his hand. He hid in the corners when Hickok came in and out. "I'll murder you if I ever catch you in his room. This is a pigsty for gamblers and Jezebels."

He must have got a heartworm living with Ish, and the worm went into his head. He was a Doctor of Philosophy with little red eyes.

Bill found him hiding in the corner one day, figured Henry was a thief, and threw him out the window. The husband bounced off the gallery and landed in the little garden I kept. He wasn't hurt. His hair was full of tomato leaves. I went down to him, but Henry wouldn't look at me. He brushed the leaves out of his hair and moved into the stable again.

"Hickok, that was my husband you nearly killed, Professor Ovenshine."

The Slayer wasn't sorry.

"He should have introduced himself. Why does a professor have to sneak in his own house?"

"He's afraid of you. Everybody is. You have a habit of shooting and scalping people."

"Hogwash. I'm as peaceable as a church."

"Well, you'd better wrap up your church and take it to some other rooming house."

His eyes got sad.

"You can stay. But if you throw my husband out the window one more time, you'll suffer the consequences. We have a marshal here, and he knows what to do with ruffians. You remember that."

It was a lie. Marshal Boardman had to be seventy, and he walked with a limp. He patrolled Hays with a shotgun in his arms. He held that scattergun gingerly, like a grocer's little girl. It was the thing that saved his life. The town was full of drunken soldiers from the fort a mile away. The marshal would hold them in our calaboose until some sergeant-major arrived and gathered them up. There were a lot of Negro soldiers at the fort. It seems the Cavalry was full of colored boys, and they'd have fights with the wild men of Hays. Boardman has six deputies, but they didn't like black soldiers, and they'd cheer the wild men in every scrape.

You had to pity the marshal. He had six worthless deputies, and colored boys and gamblers nosing around. He came for Wild Bill. I heard him climbing stairs. His bad leg knocked against the wood. I didn't mean to listen. But how often do you have a marshal in the house?

"Have to arrest you, Bill. I'm awful sorry."

"Which side of me are you taking? The left or the right?"

The marshal took off his hat. He was standing with Bill in the hall. He seemed ashamed of himself. He leaned the shotgun against Bill's door.

"It's the mayor and that damned council of his. They're calling you a vagrant, Bill."

"That sounds thin to me, marshal . . . saying I'm an ordinary bum. My pants alone cost fifty dollars."

"They're hoping if I arrest you, them other gamblers might go somewhere else."

Bill wouldn't scalp an old man. He got his shooters and his buckskin coat and said to me, "Save my room, missy. I'll be back." And he followed the marshal down the stairs.

Henry nickered like a crazy horse soon as he was convinced

they'd gone out. "Hickok puts one foot in this house, I'll slit his throat . . . and you, you let that mankiller abuse your husband. How do you think it feels to drop into a tomato patch? Jezebel, I'll slit your throat together with Wild Bill's."

That nickering didn't keep him out of my bed. I could have been a seesaw made of wood for all the husband cared. He rode up and down and spilled his seed into me. I didn't forget black Hannah's camphor ball cure. I wasn't going to have Henry's baby looking out from between my legs, with fat little hands, blue gums, and a bald head.

It GOT lonely without that buckskin lodger. I'd think of Bill. How is the Indian Slayer? Does he whittle Pawnee heads in the calaboose? He didn't intend to have a long sit. Else he'd have taken his stallion across the road with him. He left Black Nell with me. The horse fell in love with my garden. He'd chew tomato leaves. I'd stare into his good eye and forget he wasn't a she-horse. Nell had scars on his nostrils and holes in the skin above his ears. He'd gone through the late war with Bill. Ish was a child next to this horse. Ish could pull a wagon, and snicker like a man, but he was a dray horse, and he'd never been through enemy lines. Lord knows how many "red birds," Yanks, and "rebel" boys Black Nell had seen lying dead in the grass. Sometimes I'd swear it was Nell who wrote *The Indian Slayer*.

I'd fix an apple pie for Bill behind the husband's back and carry it hot and smoking to the calaboose at the end of Chestnut Street, on the road to Fort Hays. Bill wasn't wanting in food. The jailers provided him with ears of corn. He'd eat twenty-five to a meal. He'd send Hays to the poorhouse with his eating bills. But the marshal didn't complain. He laughed at all that corn stubble. "It's folly arresting you . . . the mayor will be the sorriest man in town."

Bill tore that smoking pie with his fingers and ate the crust and all the meat. But it couldn't soothe his appetite. The jailers had to seek out a grocer for Wild Bill. Yellow-hair burped. He was lovely in the calaboose with his orange neckcloth. His waist was slim as a girl's. *Darlin' Bill.* That's what I muttered to myself. But I didn't say a word to him.

Henry discovered the pie tins I had.

"Woman, who have you been baking for?"

"Ish," I said. "That animal's been hollering for apple pie."

"Harlot, you were fornicatin' with that mankiller inside the jail."

He went after me with his big knife and chased me up the stairs. I thought I'd die like a turkey on the plains. I wished to God I could see my pa one more time, gentle him out of the grave with a little song, because dead people don't enjoy waking up. But I didn't know the song to rouse him with.

The husband had me by the collar. My dress tore in his fist. Mercy on me. A ghost with an orange neckcloth was standing behind the professor. The ghost tapped Henry once. It was only Wild Bill.

He had the softest voice. It came up out of his throat like a piece of silk, and the purring of a giant cat.

"Doctor Ovenshine, it's agin the law to wind up on a woman, even if it's your wife."

He shoved Henry out the window with enough care so that Henry couldn't bump against the side of the house and skin his rear end.

"Did you eat yourself out of jail, Mr. Hickok? . . . I'll thank you to knock on the door when you enter this house."

"Didn't have the time. The marshal was killed an hour ago. Bushwhacked in the street. People are saying it was the nigger soldiers. I'm not so sure. It could have been one of his deputies. Or a polecat passing by. But there'll be a stink up at the fort. I left my ammo in your house."

"Are you thinking to avenge that old man?"

"No. I'm the new marshal of Hays. The council hired me from the jailhouse window. You should have heard the mayor croon. *Bill, Bill, there'll be a massacre if you don't step in.*" I didn't believe him somehow. "I don't see your badge, Mr. Hickok?"

"Have some patience. I wouldn't steal it from a corpse."

He got his percussion caps and pistol balls from inside his room. And he went down to calm the wild men of Hays. He herded them into this saloon or that, cleared the streets, and saved two colored troopers from getting lynched. The coroner and his jury met around the old marshal's body. They couldn't decide very much, except that Boardman was dead. Two pistol balls had gone in one side and gone out the other. They couldn't find the balls in the street, or figure out who had fired them.

The general arrived from Fort Hays. A sergeant had to help him dismount. The general stooped under his Cavalry cape. His left arm was a little short, and the fingers wouldn't uncurl. He had pitted marks under his moustache, like somebody had teased the skin around his jaw. But he wasn't ugly to look out. And I recognized that face. It was my father's prisoner and smoking companion, Silver Spoon Shirley, who stole Galveston for the Yanks and lost it again.

"Captain Shirley," I said, forgetting he wasn't pa's prisoner, but the commander of an Army post.

He looked north and south of me. A U.S. general didn't have to palaver with a wild woman from Hays. Then the fingers uncurled on his bad hand, and a smile broke through that pitted jaw.

He picked me up and waltzed me around.

"Sally Blackburn, or I'll be damned."

It was unbecoming for a general to waltz with a woman in the street. Silver Spoon didn't care. He had a fort to play with. And he could shut this town any time he pleased.

"How's your pa, Miss Sally? I should have hanged him and his miserable friends, but he did have good tobacco."

"Pa's dead. He got took in the plague."

That fist closed again, and the waltzing stopped.

"He was the best man on that island, squire Ben . . . Miss Sally, what are you doing in Hays?"

"I run the college for little girls . . . it's my husband's school, and I help him out. I married Doctor Ovenshine."

"You mean the professor that your pa clothed and fed?"

"That's him . . . It was mama's idea. Pa was dead when it happened, general."

"Please, miss Sally, we're old friends. You can call me Tristram."

He went to the coroner's office. He sat with the mayor and his people. No one mentioned colored boys from the fort. The mayor declared that the shooting was a mystery. Then the coroner, who was also our justice of the peace, took the dead man's badge and pinned it on Bill. Hickok was marshal since morning, but you had to have a genuine swearing-in. The council wouldn't reveal Hickok's salary. People said it was four times what the old marshal got.

Shirley invited me to Shepherd's wine room. He asked Bill to come along. I felt like trash sitting between them. They were Yankees and I was a brevet major in the rebel army of Nicaragua Smith. But the wine took most of my brooding away.

"Do you have a wife, General Tris?"

"Yes, miss Sally. But she wouldn't come out of Ohio with my daughters. She says Kansas isn't fit for raising girls. It has Indians and bad men . . . like Wild Bill."

"Tristram, that wife of yours makes a heap of sense," Bill crowed into his wine. "The savages are crazy, and there's no telling what a bad man will do."

"She can have her Ohio. It's the girls I miss."

The general excused himself, and I sat with Wild Bill.

"Hickok, how did that man get so beaten up? His body is all crooked."

"The rebels did that in their stockade. They whipped him half to death and made him eat turds for dinner."

"Go on, blame it on us. Show me another general who's crooked like that."

"I can't."

"Well, the bluebellies have funny habits, if you ask me. Mr. Shirley lost Galveston to an army of girls and old men, and he goes from captain to general in six years."

I didn't have much more to declare on Shirley's leap to general. The South was blamed for everything. You'd think the Sister States took the devil in with them, and the fiend whipped prisoners of war and gave them turds to eat and handed out crooked bodies. *I didn't torture General Tris. I didn't curl his fingers.* I got up and left the table with wine on my lips.

HICKOK SHED his buckskins and wore a Prince Albert coat. His vest came from New Orleans. It was black velvet, slashed with scarlet stripes. His pants were velvet too. He had a boiled white shirt, a gold watch, a silk sash to hold his two guns, and boots from Paris, France.

It was the same Wild Bill. He carried a jar of pickles in his pocket, he went through ears of corn, and he burped a whole lot. Babies would wipe their noses in the lining of his Prince Albert coat. But it didn't hurt his image none.

He went to the bathhouse every afternoon. The wild men cackled at first. Only a sissy-pants would bathe more than once a year. Then they started lining up at the bathhouse with Bill. They left the colored troopers alone. They wouldn't dream of angering Wild Bill.

He lived in my house.

I didn't have to worry about Henry. He was married to his horse. He'd sing duets from the stable with Ish. He'd only come out to eat or give philosophy lessons to a farmer's boy and a Cavalry officer's wife.

The Slayer was almost as invisible as husband Henry. I couldn't account for a marshal's time. He'd patrol the streets in his fancy trimmings. He'd gamble, whore with the ladies at the faro house, instruct his deputies, attend to the calaboose. He'd come and go without leaving a trace of himself, except for the pies he'd gobble when I wasn't in the kitchen.

Then, two weeks into his marshaling, I met him on the stairs. It was six in the morning. I was coming down to do up the lesson for that little nursery I had left, and he was home from his whiskeying. The sleeves of his coat were wet. He had chili sauce on his velvet pants. He rocked on the stairs like a ship gone crazy in a Galveston storm.

"How do, Salome?"

That puddlehead couldn't navigate a step on his own. I had to pull him by his scarlet vest.

"You're a pretty sight, the marshal of Hays all in a stupor."

"I'm as steady as a church," he declared.

"A church with its steeple near the ground."

I got him to his room and I undressed the Indian Slayer. His hand was clutching my shoulder. He'd have drowned on the mattress if not for me. I can't say why, but we began to roll. Hickok was clutching in a different way. He was under my flannels in a minute. And it wasn't a whiskey mouth that I kissed. The skunk was sober. And I was half naked, in the marshal's bed.

"You tricked me, Mr. Hickok."

His eyes weren't runty red. They were blue as the Gulf.

"You must be nineteen by now," he muttered.

"I'm twenty, Mr. Hickok. And you remember that."

But I wouldn't climb into my flannels and disappoint Bill. He could exhaust a girl with his kissing. His tongue could be rough and smooth, like a porpoise's back. He'd stop to eat a pickle. And then the marshal entered me. I had to let out a moan. It was like carrying an angel in your body with yellow hair. You didn't feel the weight of a man on you. Hickok wasn't an elephant. He'd push awful slow, with that angel's lightness that terrified you, and then his rocking went fast. I couldn't think of Henry. Pa, pa, it was the first time I took pleasure in a man.

Nine

ALL THAT rocking must have put me to sleep. I woke to the look of his eyes, that ocean blue. It was a happy color. He'd been through the house making breakfast, and he burnt his thumb on the coffeepot.

"Hickok, should I fix a banditch for you?"

"No," he said. "She'll heal." And he lay his thumb in the butter jar.

We had crackers and jam. I tasted the coffee on his mouth.

I wished all of Chestnut Street would go away. I had the Slayer in my arms. I could sniff his long yellow hair.

I wondered when he had time to marshal. He didn't ask for corn and sweet rolls. He ate every pickle in the house. He'd put on that sash of his and go downstairs to gamble a bit. But he wouldn't be gone long. I'd hear him leap on the stairs.

"Been thinking about you in that gambler's hall."

And he'd just about smother me with a kiss. He'd have posies in his hand, or chocolate from the sweet shop. He'd lick that chocolate out of my fingers, and I'd rub his goatee.

"Bill, couldn't we take a walk together? . . . I know, I'm a married woman, but you're the marshal here. Who'd ever question Wild Bill?"

"Your husband might."

"That Henry, he's occupied with a horse."

"Well, I wouldn't want men staring at you . . . I'd be obligated to shoot out their eyes."

It was fancy talk, if you ask me. But I wouldn't go and argue with Bill. I went on being his indoor woman.

"Bill, let's take a little trip . . . they have an opera house in Topeka."

"Marshals can't go on holidays," he said.

"Bill, we could make it short."

He wouldn't stir from Chestnut Street. He'd gamble and expect Salome to be waiting for him in his bed. I waited. He was sweet with me, once he climbed the stairs. But he took to leaving in the middle of the night.

"Where you going, Bill?"

"To the jailhouse."

He'd be back in the morning, with chocolate and posies, and the posies were like a bribe. *Calm the indoor woman with a bunch of flowers.* The kissing and smothering didn't stop. But I got the feeling I was Hickok's doll. I hadn't come out of Texas to live in a dollhouse.

"There's a dancing party at the fort. Will you take me, Bill?"

"Salome, I'd step all over your feet."

I moved upstairs.

Bill came knocking at my door.

"Honey, come on down to my room . . ."

"I won't," I said. "Not until you walk with me in the street."

So Bill took me walking. Once around the square, with China-men sweeping the sidewalks, and we went on home. I got out of my petticoats, and Sally became Bill's doll again.

Something rubbed at the Slayer. The marshal wanted me, but he wouldn't stay put. He had his whores and all. He was Wild Bill Hickok, and the ladies wouldn't leave his sash alone. I got to live with his harloting, long as he'd climb the stairs to me. Hickok's doll and harem girl, with posies in the morning. But he stopped climbing.

I had to truck my petticoats out of his room. I'd catch him in town, during one of his patrols. "Busy," he'd say, looking at his feet, but his eyes wouldn't break with that ocean color. He wouldn't even whisper "Salome" in my ear. I was the schoolmas-ter's wife.

He was the yellow-haired plague.

I wouldn't send him notes. It would have poisoned my heart to beg invitations from Bill. He'd come to me at any old hour, stand by the door until I could smell him in my sleep. My eyes would open, and he'd take my hand and lead me down to his room.

I won't reveal my pleasure to that skunk.

I'd be one of them mummy women of Egypt who know how to lay dead for hundreds of years. But my body rolled into Bill's. And I couldn't cough away those little whimpers of delight.

He brought me a valentine in the beginning of September. It was a gold neck chain.

"I won it at the Pinto," he said.

"And if I wear it, some woman will come and scratch out my eyes. She'll remember it as the chain her husband used to gamble with."

"That's no bother, Salome. You can wear it around the house."

Drat the Slayer! I wore his valentine. And I wasn't sorry. But the marshal jilted me. He had a "wife" who worked inside the Leavenworth Hotel. Her name was Indian Lorraine. She scrubbed pots, she boiled gentlemen's shirtfronts, told fortunes, and lived in a shack behind the hotel. People said she had a baby daughter, a yellow-haired beauty that was Bill's child. I had to see for myself.

I snuck over to the Leavenworth and kept my eye on this Lorraine. She wasn't a kitchen hag with dirty hands. She had a powerful mix of blood. Indian Lorraine could have been Irish and Pawnee. Her skin was pinker than mine, but she had hair with such a deep burning color, it would have made the plumage on a crow look sickly and pale. I went into a shiver and walked out of the hotel.

I didn't want to meet Lorraine's little girl. I might have strangled the child. I was like an old scheming dog that licks the new puppies in the house and then leads them to the river and drowns them all. A "wife" was one thing, but I couldn't bear to think of Bill with a child that didn't come from between my legs.

I wouldn't scold the Slayer, or discourage that "appetite" he had for me, his morning calls that took me down to his room twice in September so far.

He fingered the chain on my throat. And it was like a trigger being pulled, because the bile I had exploded onto Bill.

"Hickok, do you have a neck chain for your Indian wife? I hear you took a kitchen girl from the Leavenworth . . . a half blood called Lorraine."

"You believe every whore who goes around saying she's my wife?"

"Not unless she had a child with yellow hair."

The finger went away from my throat. "I must be a pa to millions if you're blaming the whole yellow-haired population on me."

"I wasn't thinking of populations, Bill . . . only a little girl who lives in a shack."

Bill got into his velvet pants, wound up his sash, with the six-guns inside, and told me to dress. We went out into the morning, Bill and me, and he marched up to the shack behind the hotel. He didn't care how many people saw him with the schoolmaster's wife. He carried a girl of six or seven out of the shack. She didn't have a particle of yellow. Her hair was all twisted into dead brown tails. She wasn't Bill's.

I felt the fool, trying to pawn an Indian child on Bill. But I had a better map of Hickok's nights. I could picture where he was when he didn't come home to Chestnut Street. He'd whore, gamble, whiskey up, and bunk with Indian Lorraine.

He trotted into the shack with the little girl and closed the door. The chimney coughed. The sun was slanting high on the roof, and I had to remember who I was. Salome Ovenshine, with a husband in the stable and a lodger who took you twice a month.

THE TOWN grew quiet. We didn't have more than one killing a week. They'd find a colored trooper under his pony, with a dent in his skull. The coroner would rule it an accident. *Kicked to the dickens by a drunken horse.* But there was hardly any pistol play. Bill wouldn't allow it. The wild men had to settle a grudge with their fists, or Bill would run them out of Hays.

I'd watch Bill do his morning and evening rounds. He didn't have to cradle a shotgun, like the old dead marshal. His yellow hair was enough. Bushwhackers and rattlesnakes crawled into the dust at the first sight of Bill. They wouldn't waltz with a two-gun man. The wild men took to wearing vests from New Orleans. They'd smile and say, "Howdy, marshal," when Bill pranced in the street with that catlike walk of his. A panther in a Prince Albert coat.

He'd spring up onto the sidewalk and shove a meanmouthed

bum into the calaboose. He'd run down a breakaway horse. He'd carry sick old men to the barbershop on his back. He'd chase rats to their death, his yellow hair showing through big swirls of dust. His blue eyes would fall on you for a minute, and you'd have this spooky feeling. It was like being blessed by the vicar of Kansas. No bad could come to you then.

But a drifter arrived at the Pinto Saloon, a bully from Canada who swore up and down the streets that he'd kill every longhaired marshal on the plains, beginning with Wild Bill. His name was Saskatchewan. He was another two-gun man. He wore nasty little gloves of the smoothest brown skin. His guns were holstered in sparkling leather strapped to his thighs. He had a moustache that was bleached white. People said he could make a rooster shed hair.

He drank his whiskey, belched in front of the wild men, destroyed a billiard table, and went out of the saloon. "Where are you, Willy boy, you longhaired son of a bitch?"

Bill showed up in the street. He'd just been chasing rats, and he was a little tired.

"Mister, what asylum are you from?"

"Shucks," the bully said. " 'Tis the great man himself, Marshal Hickok. Longhair, no asylum ever housed me. I'm Saskatchewan, and I've a mind to kill you."

Hickok called to a young boy. "Bub, will you come over here? I have a gnat in my eye."

He gave the boy a handkerchief and stooped until the gnat came out.

"This aint no operetta, longhair. You have ten minutes to saddle your blind nag and cross over to the next county."

"I think I'll stay put."

The bully went for both guns. He crouched, and his right leg moved forward a bit. I heard three short pops, and the dueling was over. Bill's elbow made the slightest curve. It was like he was going to caress a baby. Saskatchewan's guns got caught in his suspenders. Bill's three balls spun him around. He was so close to Bill, his chest was on fire from the bursts of black powder. Bitter smoke crept between Saskatchewan and Bill; they stood in a blue cloud. When it lifted, the bully was dead. He lay at Bill's feet, his jaw in the dust. Hickok hadn't touched his second gun. It was still in his sash. He'd pulled with his right hand. It was a puzzle to me. Why did they call him the two-gun man?

The bully was wrapped in a blanket and buried in a pauper's mound on Boot Hill. The Slayer was so popular now, we figured him to be marshal until the new century arrived in Kansas. The elders didn't have it planned that way. Bill was too expensive for them. The council asked him to take a cut in salary. Bill refused. He wasn't their ten-cent marshal. He told the elders to bring in a dog from the street. The elders found a candidate. He was a retired Pinkerton man, Roger Straws. They put him into the Democrats, and offered him up to the people of Hays.

Bill ran as an Independent. He didn't bother to electioneer. He was the Indian Slayer. Straws lectured in the saloons and on the streets about the value of a Pinkerton man. He'd been a detective thirty years, "wiping out Pawnees, rebels, and crooks."

Bill tickled his goatee, played monte and stud, slept with his Indian "wife," went on killing rats and carrying old men to the barbershop, and when November came he lost. James Butler Hickok, Independent, got less than ninety votes. The Pinkerton man had a hundred and five. How'd he gather in so many?

Hickok's term wasn't up until January. He wouldn't quit. But his eyes weren't so blue in Hays. The town suffered because of it. We had rats on the sidewalks. The grocers hired the Pinkerton man to club them, or the creatures would have gotten into the grocers' bins. Straws clubbed rats half the day, and he wasn't even marshal yet.

Bill slapped down his badge on the first of January and made room for Roger Straws. He'd been marshal under five months. I waited for the Democrats to feel sorry. But they never did.

Straws was a clever marshal. He fired his deputies and brought in retired Pinkertons like himself. Hays was policed by a bunch of old men. They didn't wear sashes and neckcloths. They didn't duel in the street. They didn't have one shooter between the six of them. They were a shotgun army. What lunatic would stand up to so many scatterguns? The grocers congratulated themselves. The mayor sucked on black cigars. And Bill was with the rats.

He gambled away his beautiful coat. His little beard got wispy on one side. And I'd think, *fool, why don't you leave Hays?* But I didn't want him to leave.

I'd bake a pie and remember his panther walks through town. Then I'd have an itch to look at his face. The high cheeks, the honey-yellow hair, the lips that could have gone to a girl. I'd dream, and the monster would be at my door, without his pretty coat.

He was nothing but a philandering marshal who had to give up his badge. And I was his harem girl. It could have come out of an old, old book. A love story that got off to a crooked start. Him and his "wives." A woman in every shack. Salome and Indian Lorraine.

I was mending my corset, and I threw the straps at Bill, pieces of whalebone that knocked off his hat.

"Howdy," he said, with a finger in his little blond beard.

"Get on out, Wild Bill Hickok . . . go where you belong. With your half blood and her Indian brat . . . and all those other wives you have."

"Salome," he said. "I'd divorce them wives, every one, but I can't find a lawyer who'll handle the case."

Curse my blood. I couldn't stay angry at him very long. He was a liar, but I went downstairs with Hickok. He started biting my face, gentle and harsh, and soon I had his teeth all over. But never mind his bites. I took Bill into politics.

"The Democrats stole the election. They invite old men marshals to Hays. It would be fine if Saskatchewan had a brother, and the brother came here. The Pinkertons would wet their pants."

"So what? They'd shoot the brother before he shot me."

"You'd kill him with your left hand."

Bill looked at me as if I was the wildest, dumbest woman in Hays.

"Hickok, why don't you get out? Hays is grocers and old men. Hays is hair balls. Hays is rats."

"If it's so rotten, missy, why don't *you* go?"

"That's what I mean. We could go together."

"You're a married woman."

"You call that married? Henry hasn't said a word to me in a month."

"He might say more if you were a better wife."

It was like a bear had marked me, hearing that from Bill.

But he must have smelled the harm he did.

"Truth, he aint much of a husband . . . jiggering with a horse. But it would be happier all around if he didn't come chasing me."

"Chase you? What for?"

"Woman stealing. Why do you think 'Katchewan was in Hays?"

"To earn some glory as a two-gun man."

"He was a jealous husband, I'll bet. Someone must have told him I'd jiggered his wife. And he come down from Canada to fix my tail. Only a farmer would pull with both hands."

"Why'd you kill him then?"

"He talked such a heavy song, he fooled me with it. I should have nicked his ears and sent him home."

He must have liked the wool on my shimmy, because the Slayer wasn't in a rush. He went slow with me this morning. I could trace the ruts in his shoulder, the knife wounds in his kneecap, the peppered dents of buckshot on his thigh. He was a factory of holes and marks, like he was wearing Egyptian letters, and you could read the different wars on his body. We ate pickles from his jar. The Slayer smoked a pipe. He didn't dress and run to his Indian gal or the gambling tables. He oiled his guns and walked down into the garden and had his shooting practice in the snow.

He'd fill a rag with wood chips, bundle it up, tie it to a tree, and pull at it with the two guns. That stuffed rag looked like a human head hanging from the tree. It had little eyes and ears. The Slayer knocked it all to pieces when he pulled. His left-hand gun wasn't any slower than the right. It "kissed" the rag head just as often.

Then he did a funny thing. He stood in the garden with that ruptured head and blew on his hands. The Slayer blew and blew. It was like his hands were a woman he was aiming to please. He didn't favor one hand or the other. Hickok blew right and left. He wiggled his fingers and started blowing again. Bill, the two-gun man.

HE GAMBLED during most of the January frost. It was an unreliable season for Bill. He'd lose and win his pants. He had his Prince Albert coat for a day, then I caught one of the monte men wearing it. The coat suffered as it moved back and forth between Bill and the faro house. He staked Black Nell and lost his one-eyed stallion. "Good," he said. "Now I won't have to stable him for the winter." He lost his sash and his boots. He was making himself light in January, when he should have been storing some fat. He lived on pickles, Salome's hot pies, and whatever the Indian woman gave him to eat.

He'd have gambled his moustache if he could, and played for his ears. He got into trouble with the Cavalry. He had a shoving war at the Pinto. Not with colored troopers. These men were pink. Loutish boys, I'm told. Lazy with fort life. They gambled with Bill and tried to cheat him. He slapped at their heads with his old slouch hat. The troopers must have pulled on Bill. One had his cheek shot off, and another lay dead near the stove. The live troopers parted company with Bill, fleeing to their Cavalry wagon.

I heard a hullabaloo in the street. The troopers rocked their wagon and yelled for a lynching party. Bill climbed the stairs to his room. He'd cut an eyebrow in the scuffle. His mouth was swollen and his face was scratched. He told me the troopers had tried to jump on him. "Salome, I kicked back a few . . . but I left a corpse in the saloon."

"What did the marshal have to say?"

"Dunno. I didn't see Straws. I'm going to the cemetery."

"Bill, you aren't thinking to wrap yourself in a blanket and die?"

"Hell no. I can fight off a hundred Pinkertons from the top of the hill."

"But Shirley could help you. You could go to General Tris."

"The Cavalry would skin me alive."

He took his rifle and his ammunition bags and I gave him every shawl I had in the house, so he wouldn't freeze on Boot Hill. Then he kissed me on the mouth. It was a long, sucking kiss, like he was trying to push our whole history into it, and it was also good-bye. It hurt his face to kiss, but he wouldn't stop on account of that. I touched his yellow hair and said darlin' to him, Darlin' Bill. He caught me crying. I didn't mean to sniffle so loud.

"Let me come with you, Bill. I can live in the snow. I'll put some turnips in with your ammunition bags . . . we'll have a feast."

"And Straws will shoot you in the nose. You stay here."

He ran to the boneyard west of town.

Straws knew better than to march up into a hill of snow, looking for Wild Bill. Once a day he'd wear a kerchief over his mouth and stand with his Pinkerton men at the bottom of the hill. It satisfied the mayor. He said, "Justice is being done."

The elders patted Straws on the back. He was their man. "Roger, you'll arrest Wild Bill soon as his rump starts to break with the cold. He'll come down off his mighty hill and beg us to hold him in the calaboose."

I hated Marshal Straws. I hated the elders. I wanted to be up on the mountain with Bill.

I got cans of gooseberries at the grocers and baked eleven pies, put them in a sack, and started for the cemetery. A blizzard began to fall. The snow blew me and my sack of pies. Straws' men must have heard the pies clink, or I would have gotten through to Bill.

"Sally Ovenshine, you're under arrest."

"What for?"

"Aiding and abetting a murderer is what we'd call it."

"Bill's no murderer. And how am I abettin' him?"

"With apple pies."

"Gooseberries," I said, but I wouldn't argue with Pinkerton men. They stripped me of the pies and brought me to the calaboose, shoving me along with their shotguns. I'd misjudged the marshal. Straws was mad as hell. He yelled holy murder at the Pinkertons.

"You must be growing teats in the snow . . . arresting miss Sally for having an 'arsenal' of pies."

"She was going up there to feed him, Rog."

"Get out of my sight."

The Pinkertons went off to the saloon with their shotguns, and the marshal set me free.

"He'll starve, Mr. Straws. How long can he live on a jar of pickles?"

"About a week," the old man said.

"Well, he's been up on the mountain ten days."

"Don't you think I know?"

The marshal went into the blizzard and carried the sack of pies up the hill.

I'D HAVE dreams of the Slayer right in the middle of the afternoon. A piece of my head would spin out and be up there with Bill. It was spooky to live in both places. Boot Hill and Chestnut Street. I could feel the rough edge of his clothes, the shawls he wrapped around his face, the rips in his skin, the hands he'd have to keep warm. I could tell you how he rationed the pies. He'd draw quadrants in the crust with a fingernail, and scoop out each quarter pie with his fist. He'd have to bite on his hunger, because this was the same Bill who could eat twenty-five ears of corn.

Then my dreaming took me to the stable, and I was with Henry and Ish. I wondered about them two. Henry had the ague in my dream. He was shivering and sweating under a horse blanket. I put on my coat and went out to see. Ish snorted when he heard my trampling in the snow. Henry didn't stir.

"Husband, are you sick?"

"I'm excellent," he growled. "Go away."

I peeked through the partitions. He was lying with a Cavalry officer's wife. The husband had set up a commissary in the stable for himself and the horse. Henry was stinking rich. He had a cookstove, sausages, condiments, and China tea. I didn't have a turnip left. He must have been hoarding his pupils behind my back. I was angry at Ish. The horse had betrayed me somehow.

I had a mind to slap that military wife out of the stable, destroy the little house of sausages and tea, kick Ovenshine and Ishmael into the snow. Then I'd have to provide for man and horse, keep them in the parlor. No. Ish could dance on the ceiling for all I cared. I had the Slayer to think about.

THIRTY NIGHTS and days. Hickok lived between blizzards and sunshine. You didn't see smoke coming from the mountain. Was he afraid a little fire would draw the Pinkertons to him? The Slayer had to survive on gooseberry flesh. Was William breathing or not? He could have been defunct, like Saskatchewan, wrapped in a grave of shawls.

A rumor spread from the fort. People were saying that Tristram Shirley had put out a "dead or alive" notice on Bill. The military was showing its displeasure with Marshal Straws. Hickok was on the mountain, and the military wanted him off. He was fair game to scalphunters now. Disgusting men had come to Hays. They were expecting a big prize for carrying bits of Hickok down the hill. They had long rifles, knives, and sacks for Bill's head. The Pinkertons wouldn't let them go and hunt. The marshal issued an order and posted it on a dozen trees. It puzzled the scalpers, who couldn't spell. So the Pinkertons had to read it aloud: *Hear ye, gallivanting in the graveyard is strictly forbidden without the consent of Roger Straws.*

A wagonload of troopers arrived. They stood like mean little birds at the bottom of the hill. They had whiskey and sausage pies. They broke the pies with red fingers and stuffed them into their faces. One trooper offered me a pull from his bottle. "Do you likker, ma'am?"

He must have figured I was a sporting woman from the faro house. Because he lumbered over for a kiss. Straws nudged his shotgun into the trooper's belly.

"That's our schoolmarm. She doesn't talk to strangers, and she doesn't likker on the street."

The trooper scuttled away, but a second wagonload arrived. They wanted to go up the mountain and shoot Wild Bill. They mixed with the scalphunters, cursing the marshal and his old men. Other troopers were coming on foot. Soon we'd have a war in Hays. You couldn't fight the Cavalry with seven shotguns.

The mayor begged Straws to resign.

Straws wouldn't do it. He'd take on the whole United States before he'd give Bill up to these drunken troopers.

"You're out of your mind," the mayor told him. "Hickok's a corpse by now. The son of a bitch has been up there fifty-one days."

"Fifty-two," I said. "And don't you call Bill a son of a bitch."

The mayor rubbed his moustache. "Pardon, Mrs. Ovenshine. I didn't mean to slander an old lodger of yours."

He returned to the council of elders. The elders washed their hands of us. They couldn't hold themselves responsible for any massacre that took place on the hill.

The sons of bitches were running away from the law. It figures. They deserted Bill and us to save their grocery stores. But there wasn't any massacre at the edge of Hays, thanks to Tristram Shirley.

The hill could have been on fire. That's how the troopers ran. They'd discovered a dog sled rocking in the snow. The general didn't need a driver. He'd come out of the fort with his two white huskies and a wooden boat with runners at the bottom. That boat could tear through snow faster than a team of devils.

He didn't pause to chat with the mayor. He scowled at the elders, and he might have reserved a tiny smile for me, but I'm not so sure. The huskies whisked him up into the mountain, and you could see that sled ride into crevices and continue going. It would have made the damnedest war machine. Nothing could crack its hull. And his white dogs could have gotten the general up any mountain face. The sled shrank to the size of a bowling pin. The pin wiggled. And that disappeared. Shirley was in the boneyard with Bill. But all you could do was look at snow. When Shirley didn't come back down, the marshal said to his Pinkertons, "Cover me, boys. I'm going up the hill."

He didn't track more than ten feet. That crazy pin was jumping along the snowline at the head of the mountain. We waited, and the muzzles of Shirley's white dogs landed in front of our eyes like a miracle out of Tibet. That's how far it seemed from here to the cemetery.

The Slayer wore the general's overcoat. He had rags around his head. The rags looked like the tropical hat of an old Galveston pirate. But these weren't the tropics. His mouth was bitten dry. His nose was thick as a broom handle. Hickok had the chilblains. Shirley cut him out of his boots. The Slayer's hands and feet had swelled to twice their size. I thought he was wearing fat red mittens.

The general screamed for the mayor. "Where's Black Nell?"

"What, sir? I don't understand."

"Get Bill his horse."

"Hickok doesn't have one. He gave the critter up at Pinto's Saloon."

"Get me the horse, I said."

"It belongs to the saloon now."

"Then borrow it."

"What about a bill of sale?"

"Hang your bill of sale. I need the horse."

So the mayor's people rounded up Black Nell, and the Pinkertons lifted Bill out of the sled and put him on the horse. The Slayer's body could hardly bend. The Pinkertons had to tie him to the saddle, else Bill would have fallen on his face.

A frozen man and a one-eyed horse. The huskies should have taken Bill to the Army surgeon. Why'd the general bring him down from the boneyard to stick him on a horse?

Somebody had to speak for Bill. "Tristram Shirley, do you expect him to ride to China in his condition?"

"Quiet, Sal . . . please."

Shirley patted Nell's rump, and the stallion rode off with Bill.

Ten

THERE WAS barking out my window, *wuff, wuff, wuff.* The house shivered. It had to be the general's white dogs. Huskies can move a house with the bellering they do. It's no lie.

Shirley knocked on the door.

"Sal, will you let a man in?"

"No. I'd have to murder you for what you did to Bill . . . making him ride away."

"Murder me indoors. It's freezin' out here."

"Then slide in with your huskies, general. They'll keep you warm."

I showed him mercy out of respect for pa. It was because of Galveston that Tris suffered terrible wounds. I let him into the house. But I didn't offer the general a biscuit, or a spoonful of tea. We sat in the parlor, with snow stuck in the spurs of his Cavalry boots.

"You're the great white father of this town, Tristram Shirley. Are you sending me into exile too? Or do I have to rassle with one of your troopers first?"

"This isn't New Jersey, Sal, where the generals row on the Hackensack River. It's the plains."

"Why didn't you have a surgeon look at Bill?"

"I couldn't. If I drove him onto the fort, it would have meant good-bye Bill. My own tribunal would have hanged him."

"Maybe hanging's better than rotting on a horse."

"He won't rot. I arranged for some wood choppers to meet him at the North Fork. They'll look after Bill."

I was smiling now, because Bill wouldn't have to clomp to China on a half-blind horse.

We had the last piece of turnip pie in the house. The general left with his husky dogs, and I stole Ish out of Henry's stable. I harnessed up that good-for-nothing horse, and we went into the snow. "Traitor," I said, and Ish wiggled his ears. I found the wood choppers' camp below the North Fork. These wood choppers weren't a bit too friendly. I had to ask them twice about Bill. Goldilocks is what they called him. Goldilocks had some of their cabbage and left.

"Which road did he take?"

The wood choppers shrugged. "The road to Floridy."

"You can't get to Florida from Hays. That road doesn't exist."

They got angry and tossed wood chips at me and the animal, and I had to get out of their camp.

I PASSED the Leavenworth Hotel and saw Indian Lorraine. The hotel had let her go. She wouldn't boil men's shirts or wash the hotel silver. She was wild with grief over Bill. "I'm Mrs. James Butler Hickok," she mumbled. "I'm Madam Bill. My husband was murdered by the United States."

"Where's your daughter, Madam Bill?"

"Mind your business," she said.

I went to Marshal Straws. He told me the little girl had become a street gypsy that chewed on cow pies.

"Can't you help her and Lorraine?"

"Sure. I could throw them in the calaboose. They'd have grub. But the mayor wouldn't allow it."

The marshal took up a collection. He harangued the Pinkertons and squeezed a few nickels from those miserly old men, and he pulled a dollar out of his own pants.

I couldn't contribute much. The hunters and skinners who lodged with me had moved out of Hays. I stole some sausage from Henry, but I couldn't continue sneaking into the stable. Ish would have squealed. I drove that animal to the Army camp. Never saw so many blues in one place. They were having a great sport of killing chickens in the snow. A hundred and fifty white men with hatchets in their hands. The colored troopers stood off by themselves, spitting tobacco into a pail. The chicken hunt was a piece of foolishness. The Cavalry had nothing to do.

The general's aide barked at me about calendars and appointment books when I tried to go in and see Tris. "Tell him it's Sal from Chestnut Street."

Tris came out of the commandant's office. His tunic was unbuttoned, and that bad left arm of his hung at his side like the limb a doll would have. Then the fingers tightened at the end of his cuff. I couldn't be sure if he'd been whiskeying or dreaming in his office. He looked wilder than those horseless Cavalry men running down chickens in the snow.

The general had a book on his desk. He must have been reading before I broke into headquarters of the Seventh Cavalry. And that book made me jealous somehow. The general could whiskey with words on a page. The book had ravaged him. There was a girlish man on the cover with beautiful cheeks and eyes. I'd swear it was Bill without his goatee. This man had a hairless face. "Who's that?"

"Lord Byron."

I wasn't a Kansas hussy without an education.

"Didn't he swim a river and have a clubfoot?"

"Byron was the most adored man in the world. Shame on you. Haven't you read *Childe Harold?* What did you ever learn from Doctor Ovenshine?"

"Lots of things." I couldn't let him insult all those years of schooling I had. "Tristram, did you know that vermicelli comes from the East? Marco Polo brought it back from China."

He wasn't interested.

"General, I didn't come here to discuss books. We have a woman starving in town, a half blood and her little girl. What are you going to do about it? You have a quartermaster. Get him to feed Indian Lorraine."

"The quartermaster doesn't truck with starving women."

"Would Byron have fed Lorraine?"

"I suppose he would."

"Then your quartermaster can."

And I marched out of the Seventh Cavalry.

WHATEVER YOU think about Tris, the general wasn't lazy. An Army bus drove out of that lunatic fort with provisions for Lorraine. The Leavenworth had dispossessed "Madam Bill," so the quartermaster's men put up a tent for her. Tris had twenty troopers search the town for Lorraine's gypsy daughter. She was eating mud in a well. They took her on one of their ponies to her mama's tent.

But Lorraine didn't prosper without Bill. The provisions would rot in the tent, while she clucked, "I'm Mrs. Hickok, I'm Mrs. Hickok." She took to stealing from the grocers. The Army had to pay her bill.

That bus would be in town twice a week. I heard a clamor in front of the house. I thought the Army had come for a visit. "Who's there?"

"Lord Byron."

I let him in.

He had sausages and a slab of beef from the post.

"General, I'm not a charity case."

"It's not charity, Sal. It's simple affection."

"Bill was my sweetheart. You'd better know."

Lord Byron didn't take the sausages back.

"Bill told me about you and him."

I'm glad Hickok was so free with his mouth! I ought to have put a billboard up: SALLY OVENSHINE, SOMETIMES MISTRESS, SOMETIMES WIFE. It might bring a little business my way.

Did Hickok sign me over to the general while they were up on the mountain together? I warned General Tris.

"I don't care how many other women he had."

"That shouldn't stop you from riding in my sled."

"You're right. I'd love a ride in the snow."

I had a fondness for the general's white dogs. They'd climbed a mountain to get Wild Bill. Tris wouldn't burden them each with a name. Dogs were dogs to the general. Their blue tongues put a shock of color around all that white hair. They had slanted eyes, and their snouts were like two wet buttons.

That hand at the general's side wasn't so dead. He could pull on the reins with it.

"Which direction, Sal?"

"The boneyard," I said.

We bobbed along Chestnut Street in that wooden boat, with

me sitting behind the general. Town folks stared at us. I didn't worry. I was with the commander in chief. The plains belonged to Tristram Shirley. His troopers needed their chicken hunts. They probably didn't see another face for a hundred miles on their scouting missions, except a few Pawnees.

We went to the west, through Grocery Lane, and into the outlands of the city. I could see the dogs' necks rise above the general's shoulder. The necks didn't puff out with strain. It was like the sled and all was a part of them, and the huskies could have carried us across the United States. Into Florida, I imagine. I heard the rip of ice. But the runners never sank in. The huskies glided us over soft spots. Then they tilted their necks, and we were going up the hill. Snow churned and spit at our sides. The bump of a rock shook the braces and sent a dizzy sound into my ears. Our bodies rumbled with the boat. Once we dipped so far, the dogs vanished on us, and I figured we'd overturn. I held tight to the general. The huskies appeared ahead of us in the snow, and we swam with the sled, dipping and bumping to the mountaintop.

The cemetery was flat and grim. It didn't have more than five tombstones on it. The tombs had been put up by the grocers to remember children and wives. The rest of Hays didn't have a single marker for their dead. Just paupers' mounds on Boot Hill that the wind had lashed into a level pie.

It wasn't much of a mountain, and here I'd called it Tibet. We went on past the boneyard, to the rumpside of the hill. The dogs pulled to a stop. The wind roared under the sled, and it rocked us sweetly. The boat was a cradle now, and we sat on the mountain's tail. The general turned, and I can't figure why, but we started to kiss. It wasn't that hungry gnawing I did with Bill. The general kissed my eyes, and I could feel the little holes under his moustache. I had to keep telling myself it was nothing but blue lips on a mountain. *Salome's in love with Bill.*

HE'D COME every day. Mostly in the afternoons. He must have had a sausage factory in his sleeve. But I didn't endure him on account of his Army provisions. I could have scratched through winter with a hatful of turnips. He took my mind off Bill.

He'd have chocolate babies in his pocket that some lieutenant's wife had molded with her hands. He brought me a plucked chicken in a box filled with snow.

"General, I can't eat that bird, knowing your men chased it around with a hatchet."

He'd pretend to be all sad. "I sat with the women and plucked it myself."

"Liar, you never plucked a chicken in your life."

His moustache would go wicked at the ends.

"Tristram, what's inside your head?"

"I'll be right back. It'll only take a minute to shoot Doctor Ovenshine."

"What's the worth of it? You still have a wife."

"I'll strangle a divorce out of her and kidnap my two little girls."

"It would do wonderful things for your career."

The wickedness had gone out of his moustache. It was trembling. "I'd quit the service, Sal, if you'd come away with me."

"Don't talk like a lunatic. I'm in love with Bill."

He promised not to jabber any more. I lay down with him, and I wasn't sorry. I didn't love the general, but I was awful fond of him. And it wasn't like stealing from Bill. The Slayer had a wagonload of "wives."

The general wasn't shy about taking off his tunic.

The wounds I remembered on Bill seemed tamer now. The general didn't have bear marks. He didn't carry buckshot around. I couldn't read Tristram's scars. It was the strangest encyclopedia you ever saw. Hair wouldn't grow on his bad arm. His belly was mottled and brown. It was as if he'd been put to boil in a pot, and his numerous parts had registered their own color, leaving him all a sad puzzle of flesh.

He wasn't unappealing. I took to his patchwork chest. It was cozy, sleeping inside a crazy quilt.

He didn't go off to shoot his guns at the side of the house, like Wild Bill. He'd tell me stories about Byron's baby hero, Don Juan of Seville. Juan was always getting into trouble. Women seduced him before he was ten. He'd have to hide under their skirts when their husbands were around. He was the best solution for a barren wife. A few minutes with Juan and their bellies would grow. The husbands couldn't duel with a child. They'd have murdered his pa, but he was long dead. So they petitioned his mama to drown the boy or get him out of Seville.

I laughed and laughed over the magical boy who had all that power riding in his pants. But I felt sorry for Juan. "Byron must have been an awful sinner . . . endowing a boy of ten like that. What other child swelled the population of Seville?"

That rascal Tris was wooing me with a story. I didn't care. I'd shut the house and move into Tristram's sled, live between him and his white dogs, but he'd have to promise me more Juan.

I HAD to wait a while for Juan to grow up.

Madam Bill disappeared from her tent with the little girl. We figured she was on a drunk. But she didn't turn sober in a week. The Pinkertons said it was too cold to bother with Lorraine. Straws cursed them, and we knocked in the bushes behind every house. It's funny, but the grocers provided us with lamps. You can't tell out of what corner pity will come.

The United States didn't fall asleep. The troopers were out on their ponies, looking for Lorraine. Tristram was there. He led the search with his white dogs. People were saying that Madam Bill had been scalped. And now we had a new Pawnee scare.

A Pinkerton discovered red spots on a handkerchief.

"That's chicken blood," the general said, and told the Pinkerton to stick his eyes in a whiskey bottle and forget the Pawnees. "They're freezing on the plains. Why in hell would they kidnap a crazy woman?"

It seemed as if Madam Bill and her little girl had been chewed into the sky. Even the ponies turned sad. They trundled home to the fort with the troopers dozing on their necks. But you couldn't beat down the general's white dogs. They would have sucked all of Kansas into their green eyes.

"Tris, let me run the dogs. I have a feeling about Lorraine."

I got into the sled with Tris, and I was the general's driver. The dogs didn't pull away from me. I could have been tied to them with a silk string. That's how smooth they were to my touch. We started up the hill. The huskies had been that way before. I didn't have to lead them to the boneyard. They knew that bumpy trail. The March wind nearly drove us from the mountaintop. The howling was fierce. The five tombs shivered in the snow like soft teeth. We didn't topple. The dogs pushed down with their knees and held us to the earth. Tris never complained. He swallowed wind with me and the dogs. I gave that silk line just a tickle, and the dogs got out of the boneyard. We went into the hollow on the rumpside of the hill.

We saw them perfectly, Lorraine and the girl, frozen into the mountain. They hadn't fallen. They stood half buried, like ducks caught in Galveston Bay at the beginning of a freeze. Pa would chop them out of the ice with a look of wonder in their eyes.

We worked on Lorraine, clawing with our hands. The girl was easier to budge. We dug them out of that icy hollow and lay them on the back of the sled. Their clothes had stiffened to cardboard. The girl's face wasn't grim. She and her mama hadn't been surprised by the ice. They'd gone up the mountain on a stroll to Bill.

I was their personal undertaker. I wouldn't put them with grocers' wives and paupers, in a patty-cake of frozen dirt. I gave them to Tris. He declared Lorraine and the girl dependents of the fort, and they were buried on Army ground. But we had one more puzzle. Nobody could tell us the girl's name. I asked the owners of the Leavenworth. They must have heard Lorraine whisper to her daughter hundreds of times. The owners couldn't remember.

"It was some Indian name, honey. Bright Eyes or Kiss-on-the-Tongue."

I wasn't going to have the Army stonecutter fool with Kiss-on-the-Tongue. He wrote: BELOVED DAUGHTER OF INDIAN LORRAINE, SEVEN YEARS OLD, DIED IN WINTER, THE YEAR OF OUR LORD, 1870.

Eleven

I HAD Lord Byron into April and May.

The snow melted from the ground with Don Juan in my ears. Juan runs from Spain to Britain, and the British ladies flock to him. He grows a beard at twelve. The British lords would love to kill the boy, but Juan comes to America. He doesn't care for New York. He leaves for the West and becomes a scout.

I was getting suspicious of the general's tale. Juan was beginning to sound like a two-gun man.

"Is this Byron, or Shirley's adventures of Don Juan?"

"A little of both," he said.

I was a licentious woman. You could win me with any old song if it had the right pluck. Tris would arrive with cuckooflowers,

sing of Don Juan in the West, and we'd go upstairs to my room.
I didn't have to lock the door. Who'd have bothered us with the
general's white dogs in the yard? We had all the liberties of
husband and wife.

He didn't moan about the creases on his body. He didn't curse
the rebels who'd tortured him in the stockade. He had Byron's
heroes to think about, stories to tell. I couldn't keep up with them,
Tris had so many songs. If *he'd* been my teacher, and not that
awful Henry, I wouldn't be such an ignorant girl.

But after he'd come out of my quilt, and strap his sword on,
he'd turn a little sour. "I'm tired of soldiering. It's a silly business,
plotting wars out on the plains. It's like we were expecting Costa
Rica to ride up the boot of Mexico and steal Kansas from us. I'd
give them the plains. Let the Costa Rican Army patrol the district
and capture a few starving Pawnees. Sal, we could take the dogs
and go. I'm due a pension from the government."

"Your wife would eat it up."

"Then we'll rob banks, and retire to San Francisco."

"Tristram Shirley, we'd make a rotten pair of thieves. You
wouldn't be able to look your dogs in the eye."

A MAN in dark glasses showed up at the house. His hair was tucked
in under his hat. But he couldn't fool me. One piece of glass had
fallen out. The other piece was like an eyepatch.

He let that yellow hair flow down from his hat. And he put the
spectacles into his shirt pocket. His face was all healed. That
winter bite was gone. His hands were long and thin. "Are you
looking for a room, Wild Bill?"

"No, ma'am. I was snifting around the hotel. Lorrainey wasn't
in her shack. They hired a new Indian woman."

"I wouldn't know about the Leavenworth. But Lorraine is
dead."

A tooth peeked out of his mouth, or you couldn't have told the difference in Bill.

"She have man trouble?"

"It wasn't that. She was devoted to you. She kind of went insane after the general put you on your horse."

"How insane?"

"She wouldn't wash a spoon and she told me to call her Madam Bill. She took a walk in the mountain and froze to death. I think she was looking for you."

You could see the muscles knot around his eyes, like he had a woodchuck under the skin, and it was starting to chew from inside out. That's the way with mankillers. They slaughter people, and end up swallowing their own hide.

"What about Lorrainey's girl? Where's little Arlene?"

So the girl did have a name, and it wasn't Kiss-on-the-Tongue.

"She died with her mama," I said.

His face darkened, and his temples were shot through with purple blood. "Salome, are they up on the hill?"

"I wouldn't bury them with horse thieves. General Tris took them in. He got the Army to set up two graves at the fort. Bill, you lied to me. Arlene wasn't an Indian brat . . . she was your little girl."

I shouldn't have deviled him in his grief. What harm could it be whose girl she was? She wasn't there to sit on Bill's lap. Couldn't I let him have a dead child?

He put on his crazy spectacles and walked down the stairs. I tried to hold him.

"Bill, what happened to Nell?"

"That horse got bronchitis. He didn't survive. We were in a cave on the Stinking River . . . wintering like two papa bears. But the cave was damp. And you know Nell . . . old war wounds and the whooping cough."

"I thought you said bronchitis."

"It's the same thing."

Bill fled from the house, but he didn't go sneaking onto the plains. He went to the Pinto and started beating up wild men. It wasn't a drunken brawl. The wild men didn't say one bad thing to Bill. He blamed the town for letting his little girl die. Hays had killed the half blood and Arlene. He swore to destroy the town and all its wild men. That's the word that came out of the saloon.

I heard the moan of furniture from my window.

The Pinkertons arrived with Roger Straws and seven shotguns to aim at Bill. They could have blasted him into the roof of the faro house. They'd have caught half the Pinto in their fire, but it wouldn't have bothered the Pinkertons much. They weren't fond of wild men. Something else was holding Straws back. I could smell that after I'd gone into the street. The old man didn't want to scatter Bill's guts. He was feeling low about little Arlene.

"Hickok, will you come out of there?"

Bill stopped wrecking wild men to say howdy to the marshal. "I'm not finished, Mr. Straws."

The old man was wiser than a pack of Hebrew judges. He didn't recite the law to Bill. He didn't talk mush about saloon-keepers and wild men's privileges. "We neglected Lorrainey and the girl, Bill. But I couldn't watch them every minute and hold Lorrainey in her tent. Like it or not, she'd have found a way to the hill. She had it in her head to walk on ice."

Bill came out of the saloon.

His hair was knotted with glass. He had the wild men's blood on his pants. He'd given up the thought of murdering Hays. The marshal's voice must have put some of that bitterness to rest. He had the secret look of a cave animal. He wasn't part of us.

He had a pony in place of Nell. He climbed onto the pony's back, and I wondered if he was going to leave human company behind and become Wild Bill of the Caves. Would he make peace with the black bear, hunt with squirrels? He rode away from us.

I REMEMBERED the rag face with little ears and eyes that Bill would hang from a tree and shoot at in the garden. The face would explode, and Bill had to fill a new rag with wood chips. The devil must have been hiding in the bushes, because the rag grew into little Arlene. I kept seeing her face on the tree, hanging there like an evil lantern. *Salome, it's the devil doing tricks. Don't let the devil win.*

Who had turned the fiend against me? Ishmael, I figured. He's the devil horse. I went to the stable. Ishmael wasn't in. His side of the stable had been cleared. It was a parlor now, with a settee for entertaining officers' wives.

I asked the professor where Ishmael was. He wouldn't say. I had to worm it out of him. He'd sold the horse.

"Husband, that animal was dearer to you than a wife."

"Well, me and Ish weren't getting along. I didn't enjoy the way he was looking at me."

"How will we ever leave this country without a horse?"

"I'm not leaving," he said. "I'm satisfied."

Henry bragged about the selling price. He gave Ish to the town newspaper for a "nickel." What would a newspaper want with Ishmael? A horse can't cry the news. I walked in on the *Citizen Gazette.* They'd fashioned a rag around Ishmael's eyes and put him on a treadmill to drive their printing machine.

It embittered me.

I took that blinder off Ish and freed him from those steps that went round and round to nowhere.

The editor and his flunkies came running out of their office.

"Ma'am, what are you doing with our horse?"

The editor's name was Jorrid, and he was the grocers' man.
He'd never been kind to Bill.

"Jorrid, you have no right to the horse. My husband shouldn't
have sold him. Ishmael's half mine."

It was a big lie, but I wouldn't abandon the horse, even if Ish
was a traitor to me. Jorrid didn't care a bean about Henry or Ish.
He must have noticed the dogs outside my house every afternoon.
I was the general's "lady."

"You can have that freak, Mrs. Ovenshine. He's not much
good as a power horse. He dreams too much on the treadle."

Ish followed me home. I'd saved him from traveling to China
on a treading machine, but I still wasn't talking to him. He'd give
me love bites on the shoulder. "That's enough. You're the Whore
of Babylon, Ish. I suppose you'd fall in love with any man or
woman who took a rag out of your eyes . . . go on now." And I
left him to muddle in the yard.

I had my caller to reckon with. Shirley had slipped into the
house. His huskies sat on a nubble of grass. They were snow dogs,
and they looked strange in June, like circus animals that didn't
belong in the street. Their whiteness flew out at you from a
different season. I couldn't imagine the sled chomping on dirt and
grass. The runners left scars wherever the dogs would go.

I didn't mention that to the general.

He waltzed me around the front room. "Sal, climb into your
silks. We're having a hop at the fort tonight. A regular soldiers'
ball."

"You sure give a girl a lot of notice. Tristram, I have nothing
to wear . . . and the Army wives will point at me. They'll say I'm
your little whore."

"They'll say no such thing. I'll discharge them and their husbands, shove them out on the plains for the Pawnees to eat."

"The news will get to your wife."

"Damn my wife. I'm taking you to the hop."

I had to search and search in my trunk for suitable clothes. I found a crushed hoopskirt and a satin bodice that had gone a little wormy at the ends. This was the land of calico, and the good women of Hays wouldn't be caught in satin frills. I put on my satins for Tris, tucking in the wormiest places, and mended the wires in the skirt. I had five crinolines made of horsehair. They were half my trousseau.

It was murder sitting in a sled with all those hoops. I was a bundle of wires. The hoops couldn't settle in. They'd curl or get crushed near the bottom and billow out at the sides until the sled had its own sail. We flew along, a China clipper on the open plain, our runners leaving two deep ribbons in the grass. Wild chickens and birds scattered in our wake. We were a marvelous company. Two dogs, a general, and a schoolmistress in a crazy skirt.

I couldn't find a ballroom anywhere on the post. Just stables and chicken houses, tents and low buildings for the troopers, Army headquarters and officers' homes. The "hop" was going to be in the cooking house, which had a canvas roof and smelled of burnt coffee and cabbage on the boil. Everybody was waiting for the general.

I had the only hoop in the cooking house. The other five ladies wore skirts without bustles or wires. There were two hundred men. Some of them tied handkerchiefs on their sleeves. The handkerchiefs made them extra women. That was your Cavalry ball.

I kept thinking the canvas house would drop. The wind decided to be ugly in June. The roof swayed, but nothing happened. I danced the mazurka with the general. My hoopskirt kept knocking into things. I spilled five cuspidors. I bumped two of the Army wives and six "handkerchief" women. "My goodness," I muttered. "Beg your pardon." People couldn't be unkind to the general's whore.

I knew there'd be trouble with the "handkerchief" women.

They looked at you with slinky eyes. They felt ridiculous at the hop. The provost had chosen them with numbers out of a hat. They were touchy about who would get their favors and who they should ignore. They despised themselves and didn't want to dance.

Colored troopers nearly battled with the "handkerchief" women, most of whom were white. The provost would have flung troopers and "handkerchief" women out the door and whipped them all tomorrow, if not for Tris. He put a handkerchief on and danced with colored troopers and with the whites. It shamed the "handkerchief" women. Their own general didn't mind mazurkaing with a man.

I drank a salty punch between mazurkas and chatted with the Army wives. I wondered if the fort was starving them. They had gouges in their cheeks, like pilfering Indians, and no middle at all, nothing but the pinched waists of polite little girls. I was a fat hen around these wives, a hen in a hoopskirt. I grieved over the flesh on my arms. I'd have to wear an iron stomacher or stay a hen.

The Army wives let me in on their little secrets. Kansas was less to them than the dust under their feet. "We all wish we were back in the States." I suppose they meant Connecticut or some other part of civilization. "It's one thing to beat the rebels, dear. Now that was a war. But this Indian trouble. It shouldn't concern a decent man." And it didn't concern the wives. They had fashions to consider. They followed the ways of European women, who were growing leaner every year. "Lord Byron says a lady of distinction should exist without an appetite."

Byron, Byron, Byron.

The ladies of the fort lived on crackers and jam. They sampled different teas at their poetry circle. They knew Byron by heart. *Roll on, thou deep and dark blue Ocean—roll!* They played tennis on the plains, like the best wives of Europe. They had nothing to do with Army life. They were five queens with little to queen about. They couldn't rule in a cooking house, with troopers and "handkerchief" women as their only subjects. They saw Byron's blue Ocean in front of their eyes. Fort Hays was swallowed up in all that blue.

I could have been the sixth queen. Why not? The wives were eager for another woman. They would have taken the general's concubine into their poetry circle. But I'd rather get my Byron from Tris.

Which of the queens had started up with Henry? They wouldn't say. Was he tutoring the five of them, or only four? What could have interested these Byronic ladies in Doctor Ovenshine? He must have had a charm I couldn't see. Were they bored Cavalry wives under all the shellac, and Henry was a relief from their own men? What kind of sorcery did he practice behind the house?

Maybe it was Tristram who was the devil.

He'd steal my clothes while we were in the sled. We'd rock in that cradle with the dogs looking on.

"Won't you live with me, Sal? . . . please."

I was tempted, tell you the truth. I didn't have Bill. The Slayer wasn't coming home.

He kissed me hard enough to break a girl's mouth.

"I'm a general. I could keep you in my rooms if I like. I have the Cavalry at my disposal. It wouldn't be difficult to capture one schoolmistress."

"What should I do with Henry and Ishmael?"

"Hang it, I'll give them a room at the fort!"

The professor wouldn't go to any fort when he had his stable.

I packed a few things, tied Ish to the sled, and we sailed out to the fort. I had trepidations. The grocers' wives could have hissed at me. I wouldn't care. But what would the United States think of a general living with his whore on Government land?

Tris wasn't afraid. He wanted me. His soldiers carried my trunk into the general's bedroom. I wasn't the schoolmistress from town any more. I was Mrs. Shirley to them. It was fine. They'd never seen the general's other wife.

I didn't turn my nose up at the five queens. We'd sit together in the cooking house with their husbands and all. They wouldn't touch the beef at the general's table. They had their crackers and jam. I'd chew and burp into my military napkin. I wasn't going to starve myself on account of Lord Byron.

The soldiers would exercise Ish, but they couldn't understand how Mrs. Shirley could have such a mangy horse. They offered to lend me a palomino from the stables, "a real Indian pony" that I could be proud to ride. I thanked them for their kindness and said I'd stay with Ish.

The general didn't have that sad face he used to carry around with him. He seemed happier at the fort. We'd stroll onto the parade grounds and he'd smile and talk with the soldiers about their families "back in the States."

I didn't burn for the general the way I had for Bill. It might not be the kind of love that Byron would have bothered with. It didn't roll like that ocean of his. It was more like the rocking of a sled.

It lasted about a month.

I woke in the sweat of August, went outside, and found two young girls. They wore bonnets in all that heat. But I couldn't mistake what was behind the bonnet strings. The girls had the general's dark brown eyes. I had a craving to disappear, step out of my body and run. I didn't have to look very far for the woman who was with the general's daughters. I'd say she was a thick and ugly toad with warts everywhere. It wasn't true. She was much slimmer than I could ever be. She had a handsome mouth and a nose that was clean of warts. What was the purpose of shouting

hello? I had a trooper saddle up my horse. Me and Ish broke out
of there in our own hot wind.

WE WEREN'T two orphans returning to Hays. I had a house on
Chestnut Street. The house was mine. I had work to do. Half the
dust of Kansas had come in off the plains. I swept and swept,
promising myself I wouldn't think of Tris. But girls in bonnets are
powerful things. I couldn't sweep them out of the front room.
They were trying to strangle me with their bonnet strings. I shook
them off. *Salome, you didn't have much luck as a concubine, and
you didn't have much luck as a wife.* The earth stops still wherever
I lay my foot. And I have to stand on some dead spot.

Dogs were barking in my head. I ran to the window. There
were no huskies waiting in the yard. A week went by without that
sled. I stopped looking at the calendar. I crawled from night to
night. *Wuff, wuff, wuff.* I ate pickles out of a jar to end my sorrow.
Burping was all the relief I got.

I couldn't get rid of that barking sound. I begged to God my
ears would break. I was a mad creature in that house. My one
companion was a horse. Ishmael would nicker from the garden.
I'd nicker right back. *Neeeeawww, neeeeawww.* The wild woman
who had to keep her throat out of bonnet strings.

Wuff, wuff, wuff. I wouldn't go to the window. There was a
knocking downstairs. Was it the devil and his brother? They
could knock until the doom arrived in Kansas and the plains fell
off the map. Salome squeezed her two eyes shut. An eye opened
and landed on the windowpane to catch a pair of white necks.
The huskies had come for a visit. I hobbled downstairs and let the
general into the house.

It was Shirley all right, and not an October shadow I'd manufactured in my sleep. He had his saber and his spurs. Only his eyes
had shrunk. They were pits in a Halloween mask.

"I'll have to do my toilette, Tris. I haven't washed in six weeks."

His chin jumped. "Miss Sally, you look god-awful."

"That's what you get for eating pickles. Byron would approve. He likes his women without a drop of fat . . . Tristram, I can't offer you much in the way of food. I have nothing but pickles in the house. I could send Ish to the grocer. The horse does the marketing for me. He bargains like the best Hebrew trader. He bangs out the price with his foot."

Tris touched his hand to my mouth. He wasn't trying to gag me. He was caressing my face with a general's fingertips. He started to cry. I'd never seen a grown man blubber like that. His eyes broke out of his Halloween mask, and it was the same Shirley I remembered, with big brown eyes.

I'd have eaten his face from loneliness.

"It's good-bye to generals, Sal. I'm a turd. She's holding me prisoner at the fort."

"What she?" I asked. "Who she?" I was talking like a China-woman. I knew what she it was. Tristram's wife.

"I had to sneak out of the fort like a jackass to see you . . . Alice has her lawyers in Ohio. They're ready to pounce. Hell, I could sit through a hundred divorces. But she'll take the girls from me . . . how in God's name did she learn about us? I was sure she wouldn't come out here. Alice hates the dust."

"A woman's instinct," I said. "She could smell me all the way from Ohio."

"No, no . . . the officer ladies must have scribbled a note. I'd have shot the five of them a year ago if I kept my wits."

"You and your wits! You shouldn't have moved me onto the fort. It was like a slap to the missis. Parading a harlot in front of the men."

"You're my wife. Why shouldn't I have you next to me?"

"Because there's another Mrs. Shirley . . . and she runs on the side of the law."

"I'll bundle the girls, Sally, and we'll go out of Kansas."

"That's good news. We'll have marshals and sheriffs following us with lawyer papers . . . go on home before Alice finds you missing."

He wouldn't hear what I said. He hugged me in my rotten clothes and we rolled around and made our cradle on the floor. I shivered against his heat. And then he was gone. *The frost will come and go, Sally girl, and you won't see that man again.*

I was wrong.

There was barking in an hour and the scratch of blades on the grass. The lunatic was back. He'd stole his daughters from Captain Alice and had them in the sled. Two sunbonnets peeked out from the rear. I saw fright in the missies' brown eyes. They didn't want to go bumping around with their pa. Tris barked to me from the sled.

"Will you hurry up and pack!"

I would have kissed him and the dogs and dug my face into the missies' bonnets and soothed them with a nursery rhyme. And Ish. I wouldn't forget the horse. I'd bring him with us, traitor that he was. That's the feeling I had. To leave this town and run with Tris. Wasn't I like an aunt to Ishmael? I could mama Tristram's girls. If only they'd smiled at me once from the sled. I might have been brave and whispered, Damn, we'll be fugitives together. But I had this filthy tick of caution in my head. *Sally, he'll lose his girls on account of you. And the bluebellies will hang him for abandoning a fort.*

"I'm not going. You think I want your wife and the Army hounding me? Good-bye."

I waved to Tris and the little Miss Shirleys.

Ish watched me from the garden. The huskies had blue

tongues. I went into the house and bolted the door. It felt like half a century until the sled took sail. Then the runners squealed. I spied out the window. Tris didn't pull the huskies west, toward the boneyard and the final bit of Hays. He went east to the fort. The girls' bonnets bumped up and down with the nose of the sled. The cold was settling in. The dogs' hot breath curled along Chestnut Street.

EYES

Twelve

I was a woman with howling in my ears. I mourned three men. Pa had the ocean to rock around his crypt in the churchyard wall. Bill slept with the black bears, and Tristram had his fort. I was buried in a house. I saw a witch in the looking glass. Her skin was rough as paper. She had a tiger's moustache.

I was a hag at twenty. I belonged in a spinsters' hospital. I ate my turnips with two claws. People were coming to have their fortunes told. Your ablest fortunetellers were Indians, widows, brokenbacks, and wild women like me.

I read the mayor's hand. He must have figured I was whoring on the side. He burrowed into my skirts with his knee.

"Mayor, you'll win the next five elections, but will you leave my skirts alone?"

"I suppose I'm not good enough," he snarled. The mayor had brown teeth. "You open your skirts for generals and mankillers, and nobody else can get in."

I slapped his jowly face.

"I could arrest you for that," he said, rubbing his cheek.

"Go on. Run to Straws and tell him how I slap mayors for a living. Don't forget to bring your wife to my jury trial."

He got his hat and left my front room, cursing his way to the door. "Viper woman, Lorrainey had better manners than you. You're sucking blood since Mrs. Alice arrived at the fort. She put you in your place."

I threw my comb at the mayor. The metal bounced off his neck.

"That's aggravated assault," he said. "You'll rot in the calaboose."

But no one lifted the fortuneteller from her house. I had a fresh client. Jorrid the newspaperman. I told him the *Gazette* would prosper in 1871. He might even find himself a wife. I got my nickel fee, and Jorrid stuck his rotten newspaper in my lap. "Read it, Mrs. Ovenshine."

I had to unroll it first.

He was smiling hard, like the world lay right between his legs. "It's a special edition . . . I inked it just for you."

I saw a sketch of Bill on the front page. It was scratchy and dark, and somebody gave him a hat to wear that was too small for his head. The printing jumped in your face.

WILD BILL THE NOTORIOUS IS DEAD

I didn't reach for my handkerchief and go blubbering through the house. It was a newspaperman's filth. *Tempestuous William was killed last Monday on Kansas Avenue in Topeka. The news is sweet. Our late marshal was a vicious destroyer of property and lives. He had a fitting end, gunned down by two mad-dog gamblers in the street.*

I cackled at the news, and Jorrid must have been thinking I had that special craziness of the witch, being her inability to cry. But I had nothing to cry about. Jorrid could chew on his Topeka stories. Bill was in the caves.

It didn't stop me from reading the *Gazette.* The editor retracted his story after a week. *We regret to say that the William murdered in Topeka was not our own Wild Bill. Hickok lives and breathes in another part of the country, much to our chagrin.*

The louse began printing up more of his lies. He said Bill appeared in Junction City, showing off his marksmanship to a band of English dukes. Then he had Bill freeze to death in Lawrence and come alive to swallow Indians on the plains. *It seems William can't sit still. Our hero has a spotted history. He dies on you, and just when you think William's gone for good, he's risen again. I wish that untamed boy would settle his affairs once and for all. Alive or dead, William. Take your pick.*

I WOKE one morning with a rumble in my chest. I'd lost the smell of black bears. Bill had gone out of his cave. Then that lying Jorrid suspicioned what was in my bones. The editor swore up and down that he'd located Bill. *William has finally elected one spot. He's moved to Abilene. Doubters needn't take my word. They can write to James Butler Hickok, care of the marshal's office, Abilene, Kansas, and see what happens. Let's hope William lives out the month of April and doesn't perish right away.*

Half of Kansas was heading for Abilene. It was the biggest cattle town in the world. The Kansas Pacific had gotten to Abilene. Why shouldn't everybody else? Cattlemen would drive their herds up from Texas over Chisholm's Trail, sell cows at a fat price, so the Kansas Pacific railroad could take the cattle to slaughter in Chicago.

Abilene was the shipping place. People said the traffic was so hot, you could hear cows moo from Topeka to Hays. I listened. I didn't hear one cow. It never discouraged the wild men. They got on their ponies and went to Abilene to look for work. Jorrid went with them. He sniffed where his readers were and took the *Gazette* along.

It was like living inside a whale. The cattle business was swallowing all of us. I wouldn't budge from Chestnut Street even if that mooing could eat a whole country. I had some pride. I wouldn't run to Bill, much as I'd love to see his yellow hair. Let him make more children with his Indian girls. I'd think of the general. Stuck in his fort with Captain Alice of the Ohio grenadiers.

The lady captain would come to town. She didn't bother with a pony from the stables. She liked to drive Tristram's white dogs. She'd deliver little acts of grace wherever she stopped. Candy to the pauper children in their mamas' shacks. Indian dolls to the grocers' girls, who were getting bigger every season. Did they suck molasses off the top of grocery barrels? Why else would they have such brown chins?

Alice was their tutor. She taught them etiquette right in the grocery stores. Alice learned them how to put silver on a table. I'd hear her blabber while I went in to buy coffee and beans. She told them that proper wives drank tea straight from the saucer. I never knew that.

I sneaked home, got out a saucer, and slurped China tea in the dark. Some of it spilled on my leg.

Next morning I heard that familiar wuffing of the dogs. I put my nose in the window. It wasn't Tris. The huskies had brought Captain Alice to the house. The lady knocked. By Jesus, I didn't have to let her in. But I turned coward after the sixth knock. She'd get the troopers to attack, and I'd be left without a wall. I opened up for the lady.

She came in with her parasol. Byron would have loved her. She had the slimmest waist in Kansas.

"Are you the fortuneteller, Mrs. Ovenshine?"

"Yes'm."

"I'd be grateful if you'd read my hand."

We went into the front room.

"Would you care for some tea?" I said.

"That's a lovely idea. I'm parched."

I prepared two saucers, but the captain looked at me like I was the town fool.

"Did you break your teacups, dear? I can let you borrow a couple. Good china's a little scarce at the fort. The savages steal them from our kitchens . . . I'm sorry. I forgot to introduce myself. I'm Mrs. Shirley, the general's wife."

I was ashamed to admit that I'd seen her and her sun bonnet girls at the fort while I was living in Tristram's bed. So I played ignorant with Captain Alice. "How do?" She had a strange etiquette, you ask me. Damn her, should you slurp from a saucer, or sip from a cup?

I took her hand and started to read. I wasn't a palmistry woman. I couldn't read the future in the hills and marks on a hand. I wouldn't jabber about Mercury, Venus, and the Plain of Mars. Those figures were nothing to me. I felt the captain's wedding ring. It made me shudder, because the heft she had, the weight of her hand with the golden ring, told me that she could teach saucer tricks to grocer girls and feed candy to the poor and drive Tris' huskies around and she'd still have a broken life.

"Mrs. Shirley, I think you ought to consider leaving Hays."

"What on earth for?"

"Savages," I said. "They get mean in the summer . . ."

"You silly woman," the captain said, and her hand snaked out of mine. "You're not much of a fortuneteller."

"If you're worried about that nickel fee, I wouldn't charge the general's wife."

She clapped a nickel into my hand. Then she grabbed her parasol and twirled it in my front room. It was like a folded shield with lots of silk mouths on it.

"You're a whore, Mrs. Ovenshine. If you bother my husband again, I'll have you thrown in jail."

She marched out, climbed aboard the sled, and drove away.

I HEARD Ish snort under my window. He couldn't have been serenading me. It was long past midnight. I looked out. The stable was on fire. I ran to Henry. He'd been smacked over the head. The Pinkertons arrived with pails of water. They shucked the water into the stable, and then beat at the fire with old wet brooms. They were the best firemen in town. The roof was gone, and every wall, but the Pinkertons had hopped around and saved Henry's wagon.

"Who put you out of business, son?"

"Bluebellies," the husband muttered in his fog.

"Soldiers, you mean?"

"Bluebellies."

And the Pinkertons didn't pursue it. They weren't blind. The huskies had stopped coming to the house. Shirley wasn't my protector this year. And it wouldn't have mattered. It was Captain Alice who made the law.

I took Henry into the house and rubbed his blue head with some butter in a cloth. He blinked, but the fog didn't clear. I could guess what was behind the "bluebelly" story. *Captain Alice.* She must have told the husbands of those Byronic ladies at the fort about the lessons Henry was giving. She'd do it in whispers.

She wouldn't want officers murdering their wives. People might think the Cavalry was filled with bluebeards. *Don't kill him. Just burn him out.*

You can never tell. It might have been drunken soldiers who put the stable on fire. But I'd swear the lady had a hand in it. Will I be the next one to sit in smoke? *Pyromaniac.* I read that word in the husband's dictionary. Alice was a pyromaniac. She had an uncontrollable itch to watch people burn.

Henry wasn't much good. He walked in that blue fog of his and felt homeless without his stable. He wasn't surly to me. He couldn't piece two sentences together, but he'd developed a magical eye after that knock on the head.

"Who gave you the neck bracelet?"

"That trinket," I said. "It's only junk. I found it in the street."

The bracelet left his mind and he started to whimper. It was like an animal heaving, a horse's sigh, and not the sound of a man. He hugged me, weeping into my shirt waist. "I'm a sinner and a thief. Sal, I lied to your pa. I'm no Connecticuter. I'm from New York City. And I've never been near a Doctor of Philosophy."

"I knew that. Ages ago. I don't think you fooled pa for a minute. He smelled a hungry bird and he took you in."

"And he allowed that bird to start a college?"

"Why not? Would you believe how many Doctors of Philosophy we had before you got to Galveston? Five or six. And they were dullards, all. Pa had to keep Justice Morrissey from whipping them. You were the first schoolmaster that didn't run away."

"I'm a victim," he said, laughing now. "Your pa and the justice swindled me . . . they couldn't get another person to teach you girls. So they picked on Ovenshine."

"How'd you ever get to Galveston, Henry?"

He started pinching the clothes on his chest. "I had to go South. Folks were bothering me."

"What folks?"

It was the same old Henry, frightened of shadows on the wall.

"Woman, we can't stay here. The bluebellies are coming . . . we'll try Abilene."

"It's a city of cows."

"Cows can make you rich," he said, scratching his face.

"Sure, we'll go and sell the pies they drop in the street."

Abilene. I didn't care. I had that awful desire to peek at Bill. Sakes, I'd have become his harem girl again if Bill would consent. That's the kind of creature I was. But it hurt me. I couldn't say good-bye to Tris. The Army shoots concubines that venture near the fort. That's how it is with Alice around.

I HAD plenty of peeks at Bill. The Indian Slayer without a scalp in his pocket, the two-gun man from the Ten-Cent Romance. He didn't step like a panther in Abilene. Bill had slowed. He'd gotten a little jowly since Hays. His hair didn't shine. The honey had gone out of it. It was a dirty yellow. The marshal wasn't so fastidious about the way he dressed. His silk sash had aged and his boots were awful dusty.

I stopped him on Texas Street.

"You don't have to pretend we're strangers, Wild Bill."

"Who's a stranger?" he said.

"Can't you say howdy to a woman you know?"

"Howdy," he muttered, plucking the brim of his hat. "Where's General Tris?"

"At his fort, where do you think?"

"Aint you married to him?"

"You are the most peculiar man. Tristram has a wife. Her name's Alice. She moved to Kansas with her two little girls."

"Is that why you come to Abilene . . . because you couldn't have Tris?"

"Oh, you can talk," I said. "Living in the caves . . . you didn't send me one darn letter."

"My spelling's not so perfect, missy . . . and I'd be embarrassed, writin' to a schoolmarm. You might correct my stuff with a pencil and all."

"I wouldn't lay a pencil to your words."

"That's kind of you, Salome . . . so long. I've got to patrol this goddamn village."

And he continued down Texas Street. Was he jealous of Tris? Drat the Slayer! I wish it was so. But you couldn't tell anything in Abilene. It was the oddest "village" you ever saw. Cattle hollered from their pens. A great big *moooooooo* shook the back of your head. That was Abilene, 1871, an open barn cut down the middle by railroad tracks, and a dusty marshal named Bill.

I almost fell in love with that railroad line. The engine cars had fire pots on them that could spew a mountain of steam and kill cattle noises for half an hour. You couldn't have survived without the *huff-huff* of the trains. It kept a girl from mooing along with the cows.

I rented a shack from Leopold, Abilene's Hebrew trader. He was fierce when it came to a price, but I learned how to bargain with Leopold. I tossed the Book at him. "Would Ezra live in such a hovel? Would Amos? Would Jonathan? You ought to let it out for free."

Leopold touched his derby. "What can you pay me, miss?"

"How should I know. I haven't started working yet. I'm a fortuneteller."

"Ah," he said, with a trader's grin. "Wonderful. Every half blood for miles around is a fortuneteller. You can't go a hundred yards without meeting one. What does your husband do?"

"He's opening a college for the best young girls in town."

"Marvelous," Leopold said. "We have whores and babies, but no young girls."

"Then we'll have to bide our time until the babies grow. Henry isn't in a hurry."

He let me have the shack on speculation. Leopold was a twenty-percent man. He wanted a fifth of what I took in. It was robbery. But we couldn't live out in the street. So I signed a contract with Leopold that made me his mule.

The shack was pitiful on the inside. It didn't have a piece of lining anywhere. The wind blew into my drawers. And when it rained, it rained on your head. Henry tarred the roof and I tacked muslin to the walls. Then I took some lampblack and wrote on a square of cloth:

CONSULTATIONS WITH SALOME
HAVE YOUR FORTUNE READ BY THE QUEEN OF HEARTS

It was fancy business, Salome and all, but I had to compete with a nation of half bloods, and I wasn't going to give them an edge over me. I'd play the white witch. It didn't work a whole lot. There was a lean line to my door. Something had to be wrong. The half bloods didn't suffer. Cattle boys would come in and out of different huts. The Hebrew explained. "Indian Annie tells fortunes on her blanket. She rolls over twenty times a day. Gives each of her fellas a little weddin' ring. That's why they're devoted to her."

"I read hands," I said. "I'm not in the rolling game."

He took his twenty percent and dropped it into his hat.

"You'll suck air, miss. That's the way it is in Abilene."

I'd show the Hebrew who I was. I had Henry drum for me. I can't say how many saloons and boardinghouses he drummed. He'd bring back old men without a nickel in their pockets. The old men didn't slobber and leer. Henry must have sold them on my witching powers. They had raw noses and rabbity red eyes. Could I recite the whiskey graves I felt in their hands? Most of them wouldn't last out the cattle season. They'd die on their pallets of sweet straw. So I hedged a bit. No one likes a fortune that stinks of death.

"You'll dream of your mama tonight." And they did.

I had to stop asking Henry to be my drummer, or the Queen of Hearts would have a field of raw noses rise up like onions in her shack. Leopold sent his collectors around. They were the meanest boys you could imagine. Pups with derbies on their skulls and shooters inside their vests.

"Do you have the cush, miss?"

"What cush?"

"Leo's share."

I didn't have a nickel for the boys. They tore the muslin from my walls. They cuffed Henry with the brims of their hats. Henry had blood on both sides of his face. What kind of derby could do such a thing? Then they unbuttoned themselves and pissed on my wedding trunk like a gang of horses.

I'd had enough. I swatted the boys with my one good broom. Their derbies sailed across the shack. But they wouldn't get out after the sprinkling they did. They dug into their vests, and the shack got silvery blue from the gun barrels in their hands. They meant to blow Henry and me out the front wall.

Another derby appeared. I understood why the brim was sharp. A razor had been sewn into Leopold's hat. He cut through the boys' vests with it and turned their clothes to ribbons in front of my eyes. They begged the trader to stop.

"Leo, didn't you tell us to collect the lady's cush?"

"Cush is cush. I didn't say hurt."

The boys ran from Leopold. He took Henry outside to the Maple Street well and washed the blood off. He came back alone.

"They're eager, you know. They like to please their grandad."

"You a grandad? Pah! You're not more than twenty-five. How did you get such a brood?"

"Like everything else . . . on the open market."

"You bought those boys? Not one of them is black! Where did you find so many slaves?"

"Who's a slave? They're orphans from Chicago. They work for me. I made a deal with the man from the orphanage. He was happy to be rid of them . . . ten less mouths to feed."

"That's monstrous. Turning boys to cattle."

"You're crazy, miss. Do cattle wear shoes? I outfitted the boys from head to toe."

"Head to toe is right. You put razors in their hats."

"They have to have protection. There's rough people around."

"Like Henry and me, I suppose. Five more minutes with your darlings, and the two of us would have been dead."

"It's not my fault, miss. I should have told them not to come here. They get excited when they can't find money to collect."

"Leopold, I'm not doing so well as the Queen of Hearts."

"It's no surprise. You're not made for a shack. Why don't we work out something more convenient?"

I didn't care for that dimple growing under his derby. Twenty percent was all he'd ever get from me.

"I'm building a hotel on 'A' Street," he said, like he was Jehovah mapping out the world.

"Good, less cattle boys will have to sleep on the prairie."

"It won't be a dosshouse, miss. Nothing but the best. For cattle buyers and railroad agents. I'll need a hostess, a lady with a good figure and manners to go with it."

"Hire a half blood," I said.

He pushed up the crown of his hat. "I can't have a broken Indian in a premier hotel. You're underselling yourself, miss. Quality women are hard to find. They don't stop in Abilene . . . all you have to do is entertain the cattle buyers once or twice a week. I'll give you a room with first-class paper on the walls."

I was burning inside. "What will you do with my husband?"

"Let me worry about that."

I threw turnips and pie tins at the trader.

"Quality woman, huh? You mean a high-stepping whore. You can have your shack, Mr. Leopold. I'll dig a hole and live in it."

"The shack is yours," he said, wiping turnip dust off his sleeve. He went out and I waited for Henry. I was boiling mad. Did Leopold bribe Henry to sit on the lip of the well? I couldn't scream at him. His face was covered with razor bites. The man from New York City. I'd had him six years. He was more of a puzzle than Leopold, a trader prince at twenty-five with a brood of orphans under him. He'd charge you blood and money for a paper of needles. No one else had needles in this town. He'd have you whoring for him if he could. But Henry? What was driving that lunatic? All we did was wander the minute I was his bride.

He'd talk to me in the pinched light of the shack. It was mostly jumbled words. I tried to imagine his life in New York. Was he a carpenter? He'd have had rough hands. A baker? Bakers don't talk of Marco Polo. They have burnt wrists from shoveling bread into the oven. Was he gentle born? He wouldn't have picked his teeth and walked on pa's balcony without a shirt. He had something of the high in him, something of the low. I'll be damned if I could figure it out.

And Bill? I could have been in Florida for all he cared. He'd have nothing to do with pilgrims from Hays. We'd murdered his child, let her become a mummy in the snow. I wasn't any more innocent than the grocers, the Pinkertons, and the wild men, who were pilgrims here, like Henry and me. *I wanted to save Lorrainey and little Arlene. I tried.*

You think Bill would listen? He'd tramp down Texas Street in his dusty boots. That's men for you. There's something criminal about the whole population. It doesn't matter if they're generals, schoolmasters, or itinerant marshals. You haven't a notion of what's in their heads. They marry you, they bed you with a song, they spill their seed and vanish to some pony, sled, or cave. It's lucky I had black Hannah's camphor cure, or you'd see me with a bellyful of infants hanging from my skirts, struggling to find their own pa.

Thirteen

I was walking down Maple when I had to pee. I opened the privy, and there was Bill.

He didn't growl, or shut the door.

"Will you read my hand?"

"Hell, I'd be embarrassed . . . knowing you the way I do."

"Lorrainey did my hand," he said.

"What'd she tell you, Bill?"

"That I'd die a lonesome man."

"That's not much of a read . . . everybody's lonesome when the devil takes you."

He held out that girl's hand of his, with the beautiful fingers, and I had to show him that I was at least as good a witch as Lorraine.

"You'll marry," I said.

Bill cawed from his potty chair.

"What's her name?"

"Who?"

"The little woman I'm going to marry."

"Sakes, Bill, I can't read everything."

"Where'll we live?"

"How should I know? . . . in some hut or a tent."

He tried to pull a dollar out of his pants. I wouldn't take money from Bill.

He closed the door.

And I had to stare at the privy, with Bill inside. I could smell the devil somewhere on the roof. It didn't surprise me any. This was Abilene. The devil must have followed Bill from privy to privy.

Beelzebub.

He ate cow pies for lunch and liked to mock the Slayer. He'd reach around like a girl from the saloons, hook his little finger in Hickok's sash, and tear at the silk.

Bill had more enemies in Abilene than one stinking devil who lived on cow pies. The cattle boys couldn't stomach that marshal in the privy. They drove their herds up from Texas, on miserable ground for three hard months, sucking coffee and a fistful of beans, drinking dirty water, with dust caked around their eyes, losing arms and legs in a stampede, paying a special tax to the Indians so they wouldn't get scalped, and when they arrived in Abilene, with cattle creating dust storms in the streets, they expected whiskey and women and a wide open town. Their reward was Wild Bill.

Hickok put up notices against the wearing of guns. He warned the cattle boys not to ride their ponies into the saloons or chase married women on the street. He forced them into Little Texas on the south side of the railroad tracks. It was a gully of streets near the Smoky Hill River. The cattle boys renamed it Mud Creek, because the river wasn't worth a toad, dead or alive. You couldn't wash your long johns in the river, and drink the sour mud that dried in early June to a bumpy cake with cracks in it. Little Texas had the ugliest whores on earth. It had Chinamen, whiskey bums, pitiful saloons.

The Texans didn't have much choice. They could stick to their mud, or leave their holsters behind and cross the railroad tracks into civilization. There were three thousand of them, and Bill had to police them all with a few ancient deputies and one good boy, Robby Dykes. He was a Texan who'd given up the cattle trails to become Bill's left hand. He was known on Mud Creek as Corporal Rob. The cattle boys despised him, because he'd gone over to Hickok and the law. Rob didn't have the long smooth fingers of a two-gun man. His hands were swollen from his cattle days. But he could club an ornery Texan and cover Bill on his walks through Abilene.

It was two against three thousand.

The cattle boys didn't have the spunk to pull on Bill. He would have shot their hearts out before their hands left their sides. So they appeared on Texas Street without their gun belts, mumbling harsh words against Hickok and his corporal. Sometimes they'd get courageous and sneak a gun across the tracks. They hoped to murder Bill.

The Slayer was shot at once a week. Licks of fire would come out of the dark, and Bill would have to roll on the ground. Is it any wonder he was so dusty-looking?

LEOPOLD'S HOTEL was rising up on 'A' Street. It was like a Swedish castle on a prairie of tents and huts. He named his fortress Noah's House. He'd built an ark to outlast Abilene, when we're washed away in the next flood. Noah's House would unmoor itself from the wet ground and sail to the nearest ocean.

The chandeliers had come by the end of June. The ark was complete. The Hebrew arrived at my door without his vicious brood. He'd sent the orphans out to prey on other folks. The Queen of Hearts had nothing to give him. No nickels for the Hebrew. He laughed. Leopold had a proposition.

"I could hire an English couple with recommendations long as my arm. The best people. The wife sews and keeps the books. The husband ladles soup like the queen of England. But why should I hire English when I have you and Mr. Henry around? Cancel the fortunetelling act. You have to become respectable in a week."

"What are you driving at, Leopold?"

"I want you to be the landlady of Noah's House . . . stop frowning, miss. You'll get wallpaper in your room and you won't have to entertain a soul. Just be nice and curtsy to the customers. Mr. Henry has to come along. I need a man and wife. I'm offering ten percent of the take."

"Twenty," I told him.

"Twelve, miss. Not a penny more."

"Then wire your English couple. I'm a twenty-percent woman, Leopold, or did you forget?"

He sidled to the door. I had a suspicion he wouldn't run very far. There was no English couple. All he had was Henry and the Queen of Hearts.

The trader sidled back. ". . . bloodsucker, you can have your twenty percent."

WE OPENED on July the Fourth.

The mayor was there with his council of wise men. We had a hundred rooms. Nabobs from the railroad line explored Noah's

House, admiring the canopied beds and the crystal pieces that hung from the ceiling like tangles of clear blue rope. I fondled the cherubs in the wallpaper while no one was looking. The cherubs had fat little wrists.

The trader shot off roman candles from the roof. The candles drove into the sky like long, twisting birds with wings that could melt away and tails that could explode and spill red and blue fire. Leopold's orphans ran under the roof, holding out their derbies to catch whatever sparks they could. Leopold came down from the roof looking disgruntled. He'd burnt his sleeves. The nabobs never even noticed. They were delighted with the hundred rooms. Wild horses couldn't get them to stop at any other place. The Noah was *their* hotel in Abilene.

Bill was at the fireworks. He watched the smoking candles with Robby Dykes. He stood with the council of wise men. He tasted our lager beer and gingerbread snaps. He wore a fresh sash. He shook hands with Henry and the trader. His blue eyes fell on this and that. He hardly said a word to me.

I had a hotel to run. Waitresses, washerwomen, Chinese cooks. A wine room, a restaurant, a meeting place for buyers and sellers of cattle. Lounges where the nabobs could smoke and dream of engine cars with the power to lug a city across the plains. The nabobs had the whole future to play with. Abilene would be all crystal by 1905. You'd have nothing but cities of glass. Crystal sidewalks, crystal hotels. Would the cows be crystal too?

The hotel was short of hands.

I had Henry out scratching for Chinamen, but the railroad had swallowed them up. I complained to Leopold. "Damn your hundred rooms. You can't find one extra Chinaman around here . . . looks like I'll have to borrow those orphans from you."

"That's impossible, miss. It would embarrass them. They're not page boys, they're bill collectors."

"If they're that precious to you, Leopold, *you* stop the cooks from having a tong war in the kitchen. *You* look under the waitresses' skirts for mustard pots and silver. I quit."

Leopold gave in to my fury and let me have the boys. They wanted to work in their razor hats. I said no. I didn't need bullies at the hotel. I dressed the boys in blue. I wasn't thinking of the Cavalry. I had oceans in my head. Salt and blue spray. Camels sucking wood.

The boys would bring out glasses of sherry to the nabobs in blue serving coats, blue neckcloths, blue collars and pants. They rattled their throats at me, threatened to burn down the hotel, cut up Henry's face again, and pour sherry in the nabob's eyes. It was a rotten bluff. They wouldn't disappoint their old "grandad," Prince Leo of Abilene. They did their collecting on the side, ducking out of the hotel in their derby hats to squeeze rent from some hard-up woman in a shack. If they returned with blood on their neckcloths, I'd howl murder and go at them with a broom. So they learned to wash after their pillaging. The nabobs had gotten used to the boys. They wouldn't have their sherry from anyone but an orphan in blue.

The orphans' character began to invade the hotel. You could feel their presence in the lounges and the wine room. Blue boys creeping everywhere. They could have been the cherubs in the wallpaper, only their wrists weren't fat enough. They were in love with Robby Dykes. You'd think they would have waltzed around a deputy marshal, run from his shadow as fast as they could. It wasn't true. They'd collect nickels and dimes for Leo, but they didn't want to become a merchant prince. They'd rather fight "Texians" with Robby Dykes. They wouldn't have flocked to William Severe. They didn't like Bill's goatee. He smelled of mayors and councilmen. And they had to keep "trick" guns hidden in their vests because of Bill. He was the man who disarmed Abilene. He wouldn't show mercy to Leo's boys. But the orphans could do anything with Robby Dykes. Rob would never snitch. He played broom ball with the boys. They'd roll up a newspaper, wrap it in wire, and sock the newspaper ball into the clotheslines at the side of the hotel. The wires would loosen, and "flesh" would come out of the ball after thirty knocks.

That deputy didn't hog the broom. He let the boys have lots of swipes. He'd gallop between the clotheslines and reach out with both paws, cutting his fingers on the wires when he made a hard catch. "You're gonna cripple uncle Robby one of these days." He'd laugh at his bloody thumbs, tie them with rags and continue the play. He didn't watch over his fingers, like Bill. He'd have galloped until his arms fell off.

"How's William?"

"Who, ma'am?"

"The liontamer."

"We don't have lions, ma'am . . . you'll have to wait until the circus comes to town."

"Silly," I said. "The circus is right across the tracks . . . in Little Texas. And the tamer's Wild Bill."

It was useless poking Robby. I had to ask him outright.

"Why doesn't Bill take his dinners at the hotel? There isn't another establishment that serves gooseberry pie."

"Bill's not hungry much. He eats a boiled egg."

"One boiled egg for Bill? He'd gobble a hundred ears of corn. Bill was my lodger in Hays. Does he mention me to you?"

"No, ma'am."

"Doesn't he call me the witch who murdered Arlene?"

"I'm not sure. Who is she, ma'am? I never knew an Arlene in my life."

What was Bill doing with this dull boy? Robby belonged in Mud Creek. Did he play the fiddle for Hickok? Sing while Bill lunched on an egg? Was this the only backup the marshal had?

Hickok needed all the Robs he could get. A ghoul rode into town. He bit people on the leg. He tore hatpins out of women's hair. The ghoul attacked mostly in the dark. His victims swore he had one green eye and one milky blue. People heard him groan at night. They said he rolled under the sidewalks, and had a beard of dust. He wore purple on his middle, and devoured young girls. We didn't have young girls in Abilene. Just whores and babies, like the Hebrew said.

It was a fish tale. Jorrid, that rotten scribbler who'd come from Hays with the wild men, puffed out the story in his Abilene *Star*.

PRAIRIE MONSTER ON THE LOOSE
RAVAGES TEXAS STREET

The wolfman visited us again last night. Mrs. R. N. Bernham of 21 Maple lost a tooth to the critter. He leapt on the good lady while she was coming home from the laundry where she worked and repeatedly punched her in the face. "He's hairy all over," Mrs. Bernham told the *Star*. "And ten feet high. He doesn't have peepers. He has two white holes in his head."

Readers, it's an outrage when a wife can't walk in her own town. What does the mayor and his celebrated marshal intend to do? I say kill the no-gun rule and arm Abilene! Let's have a chance to go up even against the critter. The *Star* is offering a hundred dollars to any man or woman who captures the two white holes in his head.

Wolfman! White holes in the head! It was Jorrid's dream. He loves to stir up the town with hundred-dollar rewards.

I bought a milk cow for the hotel, and the cow went dry in a week. It was a cursed life, landlady of the Noah. I didn't have a minute to myself. Waitresses clucked at you. Chinamen wrestled over the soup. I could have been a commandant under some terrible siege. I had Cavalry in the kitchen, foot soldiers bumping on every floor. If I didn't bark and slap at different people, the Noah would have caved in like a hoopskirt that was sick.

And all the time I was thinking of menus. Roast duck. Partridge under glass. Corn, corn, corn. I tried to lure Hickok into the hotel with the menu we had posted outside. That monster could have come along and held hands with Hickok. I'd give them any table in the house. But the menu didn't work on Bill. He wouldn't eat partridge under glass.

Maybe he was out looking for the ghoul.

Jorrid badgered the mayor each morning in the *Star.* "Arm the Texians! Arm the Texians!" The mayor had to listen. Folks believed it was perilous to step away from their houses. The wine room was empty after dark. The "wolfman" was ruining our hotel. The mayor declared a crisis in Abilene. He repealed the no-gun rule "until such further time when the monster is apprehended and sits before man and God."

The "Texians" didn't catch any ghouls. They shot at every lamp in the whorehouses along Maple Street. William and Robby Dykes herded them into the lockup. There were too many cattle boys to keep. They tore out the front wall of the calaboose and carried it back to Little Texas.

The mayor's council of wise men preferred the ghoul. They scratched a sentence in the town's Minute Book and posted a new ordinance. "From this day forward all Texians residing in the area known as Mud Creek are forbidden to bear arms north of the Kansas Pacific line."

It was like playing broom ball in a big dark closet. Everybody was liable to get banged on the head. Each ordinance would contradict the last. And no one could tell us who the "wolfman" was. I'd swear he was a starving Pawnee, or some other wretch shivering in the dust.

But he wouldn't go away.

More and more women were hearing him groan.

The orphans searched for him with their razor hats.

The vigilance committee smothered Abilene with torches and

tried to smoke him out of the dark. The wolfman escaped. Jute and burning wood drifted into the hotel. The nabobs had bits of ash in their sherry. There was talk of hiring Pinkertons to seize that ghoul. The mayor said it was ridiculous. "Abilene can handle her own affairs."

Then we had a quiet spell. Women didn't scream at white holes in a hairy head. A milky blue eye didn't roll out of the sidewalks. I was glad. If there was a "wolfman," I'd have seen him. Bossing a hotel didn't make me less of a witch.

Somebody came howling up to my room in the August heat. I had ears. It was the Hebrew barking for help. I let him in. His left sleeve was gone. The buttons were twisted on his coat, like a hand had been there a short while back.

"Tried to kill me, miss . . . the ghoulie man."

I gave him a lick of sherry to quiet his nerves.

"Leopold, you have your razor hat . . . why didn't you fling it at him?"

"I did. It bounced off his head."

"Well, what did he look like? . . . you're the first witness I can trust."

He gulped two more fingers of sherry.

"Leopold, does he have eyes and ears? . . . or is it some wild animal?"

"Ah, miss, I saw one blue eye . . . if you can call it that. It was more like a milky hole with a blue circle in the middle. And the hole ate up the blue."

"A cannibal eye," I said, not knowing what to think. "And the other one?"

"Plain milk."

"What about the rest of him?"

"Hair," he said. "Lots of hair."

"You mean he had some kind of pelt in the way of skin?"

"Exactly," the trader announced. "You should have been a Pinkerton, miss."

"Sit here," I said. "And don't move . . . mark down what you drink. That sherry costs fifty cents a pull."

"I won't pay. I own the joint."

"Listen, Leopold, I get twenty percent of whatever you swallow. Mark it down."

I went into the street. The orphans came running after me with their hats on. They'd heard what happened to Leo, and they wanted to follow the witch.

"I'll take him alone," I said. "And don't you wear those hats in my hotel. It's impolite."

I was sick of monsters. I'll bite his leg before he bites mine. I'll eat through that pelt of hair and see what nation I come to. I'll bite to the end of the world if the "wolfman" doesn't say quits.

He wasn't on Texas Street.

He wasn't on First.

He wasn't on Cedar.

I passed the row of shacks on Maple Street, pinking up my ears for that enemy. The leaves could have been feathers trying to breathe in slow, slow air. The marigolds were out. Their yellow brains drooped in the yards. I couldn't believe a monster would traffic in such weather.

Where was old milky eyes?

The Hebrew must have boxed with some big fat bird gone mad with the heat. And the bird reminded him of a hairy fellow. I was ready to go back and soak my feet in a pan of cool water and count the fingers of sherry the trader had in my room. And that's when I heard the groan. It wasn't any sound you'd expect humans to make. It was more like a sick bear, or a camel with a wound in his throat, praying to die in the Galveston sand hills. The sound had come from an old barn at the end of Maple. Another one of

Leopold's properties? Abilene was on loan to the trader. He could flourish anywhere, with his brood of razor hats. Kansas. Indian country. Tibet.

The groans got louder, and then grew soft, and it was quiet again. But the quiet couldn't cheer you. It tasted like holes in a mushy head. I wouldn't run for the marshal. You think I'd stand behind Hickok's sash while he showed the wolfman how eternity looked from the eyes of a shotgun? I didn't need Bill.

The groaning started up. The barn shivered once. The veins jumped along my wrist. I should have had my broom to swat the monster. The barn was a groaning tunnel, black inside. There was a blue eye waiting for me. I couldn't talk to it. The eye ran away. A hand swept out of the dark. The fingers clutched and unclutched. They caught nothing but barn air.

"Can I bring you fresh water, sir?"

The groaning was fierce. It boomed between the walls until I figured the earth under my toes would split all the way to China, and I'd disappear from Abilene without a mark.

The fingers opened. They did have a strange pelt around the knuckles. It was only dust packed high. The ghoul didn't have one callus. His fingers were girlish under the dust.

He tried to ram me with his head. The wolfman missed. Both his eyes were milky. He had a monstrous crop of hair. The hair swung out like knotted yellow rope. It was Hickok, the Indian Slayer, and he was blind.

I touched his face. I stroked the dusty pelt behind his ears. Goddamn if he didn't try and bite my wrist!

"Hold off. I'm not a Texian. I'm Salome Ovenshine."

Wolfman Bill grunted at me. "The fortuneteller who took to hotelkeeping . . ."

He laughed until a groan tore out of him. He rode back into the dark, a writhing hump of a man who could hiss from between the white holes in his head.

"Get me Robby Dykes."

I ran to the calaboose and had to wake Rob. He was snoring with a whore under Hickok's desk.

"Robby Dykes, will you come out of there?"

He showed his ruddy head. "Yes'm."

"The marshal's in trouble. He has that rolling sickness of his. Do you understand me, Rob?"

He got into his boots and pants, collected some handkerchiefs and a pail of water, and followed me to the barn. We found the "wolfman" humped up near the door. His eyes were bleeding that horrible milk. The blue irises had gone way into his skull, and it was hard to believe the irises would ever come back.

Rob wet a handkerchief in his pail of water and put it over Bill's eyes. The wetness was able to draw out some of the milk. He kept changing handkerchiefs. I couldn't tell if it was the gentle lay of Robby's hands, or the hum in his throat, or the magic in his pail, but when he took off the last handkerchief, Bill's eyes were blue as they'd ever been. The white holes were gone. He could see from here to the Choctaw Nation.

Robby slapped the dust out of Bill's hair and washed the Slayer's hands and goatee. We had a marshal again. He could throw terror into a cattle boy's heart, knock heads with a black bear, walk down Texas Street. And he was chattier with the blue in his eyes.

"I'm sorry I was mean to you, Salome. It aint much fun, twitchin' in a dead barn."

"What's wrong with you, Hickok? Did you catch some unholy disease when you were living in the caves? Bat fever?"

"It's snow blindness."

You couldn't figure that Slayer. "August isn't much of a month for snow. We're in the middle of a boil. You sure it's not the heat that's ailing you?"

William insisted on the snow.

"It's from that time I was laying up in the boneyard . . . having nothing to look at but winter sky and the snowline, and the weather beating on my face. The attacks started right then. That's how come I went to the caves. I was hoping the cool dark would cure me. It did for a while. But the blindness come back. It's the darn light that gets into my eyes. I'd be in my glory if I could walk up and down Abilene with a mask on in the early afternoon. But masked marshals aint appreciated around here."

"Why don't you visit an eye surgeon?"

"What if the surgeon talked? The Texians would love to hear how Hickok has blind fits. They'd dog my tracks until that pain bit me, and then they'd jump on my head. Damn cowboys."

"Don't look at me. I wouldn't lead Texians to the barn."

"You're a Texian."

"Hell I am. I'm from Galveston. We had camels, remember? Did you ever meet a cowboy in the dunes when you were spying for the Yankee soldiers?"

The marshal couldn't twist out of that.

"And how come you and Robby never feed at the hotel? Is the menu insufficient? I'll give you all the corn you can chew."

"Suppose I have a fit at the tables?" Hickok said.

"I'll cover you with a big cloth and tell the other diners to go on with the meal."

"Will you stuff sugar under my tongue to keep me from moaning too loud?"

"I'll do better than that. Sing to the customers. You can moan your heart away. They'll never hear a word."

William went off with Robby Dykes.

I stopped thinking about partridge under glass. What's the use? Bill wouldn't come. But he did show up for dinner. Bill and that sweet boy, Robby Dykes. The dust had come off Bill. His long hair was almost honey yellow. His little beard had plenty of nap. Rob must have shined him up in the calaboose.

William's eyes weren't milky tonight. He spotted a man at the
end of the dining room, eating with his face to the wall. "Who's
that?"

"Melvin Brown, the man with eczema."

"Why's he in the corner?"

"Shush," I said. "The regulars won't eat with him . . . they
can't bear to look at his face."

"Well, this aint much of a restaurant," Bill said. "Banishin'
people like that . . . it's undemocratic."

He invited Brown over to the table. Customers got up and left.
I couldn't blame them much. The man with eczema stole your
appetite. His face was raw as uncooked beef. It didn't bother
William. He had his partridge and wild duck. The Chinamen had
to bring him a whole pot of corn. He ate the stumps and everything. He had nine dishes of berries and cream.

Rob picked at a partridge bone.

I rolled a berry in my mouth.

"Eat, will ye?" Hickok said, standing up to scowl at Rob, me,
and the restaurant. We had to listen to the democrat. You could
hear the cracking of bones all around the tables. Hickok burped
and took another dish of berries and cream.

Fourteen

You couldn't read the Slayer's mind. He sent Robby around with a railroad ticket to Topeka. "Bill wants you to meet him on Tuesday at the Miriam Hotel."

"What Tuesday?" I said in a whisper. Chinamen were about the place. And I didn't want them squealing my business.

"Robby Dykes, I have the Noah to run . . . I can't traipse to a foreign town."

"Tuesday. At the Miriam. Bill says you should register as Mrs. Axelmire. And wear the right clothes."

Tuesday it was. I asked the Hebe to take charge of the hotel. I told him I had to shop for curtains in Topeka.

"I can get you curtains, miss."

165

"I won't have bargain goods hanging in the dining room. It needs a woman's eye. And you can't do better than Topeka silk."

I bought myself a parasol like Captain Alice had, and a bustle skirt. I put my night things in a linen bag and rode the train to Topeka. The Miriam had verandas front and back and three separate roofs. It was painted a chocolate color, with pillars and lamps and awnings on every window in the house.

I was Mrs. Axelmire.

But I couldn't find Bill.

I had a dish of ice cream.

I scribbled a postcard to the Hebe.

I had a second dish. I watched the gracious wives of Topeka merchants and railroad men walk in their bustles. They were lady frogs with cotton on their rumps. I went upstairs. Did Bill send me to Topeka out of wickedness? Did he mean to show?

I fell asleep on the chaise. I dreamt that Bill and me were man and wife. His eyes had healed. We strolled on the carpets inside the Miriam, with a page announcing us to all the Topeka royalty as "the Hickoks of Abilene, Mr. and Mrs. Wild Bill."

We had an infant with us, by Jesus! Young Willie with blond hair. I was the happiest mama in the West. I could throw away the camphor balls. I'd have a brood of Willies with Wild Bill. And then I cried. Because I knew right in the dream it was only a dream I was having. There weren't any Willies around. Not a one.

I could feel two arms hugging me. Bill. He was wearing a silk shirt and a cravat that could have come off the Prince of Wales.

"Why are you bawling, honey? It's me."

"I know who you are," I said. "Mr. Axelmire . . . I thought you were a black bear for a second, on account of that dark coat you have."

"Well, I'm not a bear. I'm only William."

And he took me down to the Miriam's restaurant. We sat on chairs with enough wood for a king. The tablecloth could have supplied six whole skirts. The silver was heavy in your hand. Somebody brought a rose for the table. We had the Miriam's best pink wine, stored in caves under the hotel.

William danced with me, and we went to the opera house. We saw an acrobat on a wire near the roof, doing the devil's own tricks. William yawned.

He took me back to the Miriam, holding my hand in the street. People stared at him. They knew it was Wild Bill. He was famous wherever he walked.

We burped a lot, getting out of our clothes. Bill unwound his cravat, and I'd swear it was six feet long. We did such loving at the hotel, I'm ashamed to say how. William kissed my ankles and worked his way up. I thought the chandeliers would break.

"Bill, can we hold the room for a week?"

"I'll tell you tomorrow."

I slept against the old bear-wounds in his shoulder, but I didn't wake to Bill. He was gone with his cravat and his silk shirt. That was the Indian Fighter. He never sits in one spot.

A page knocked on the door. Goodness, I had to dress before I could let him in.

"Your husband's gone back to Abilene. Urgent business, ma'am. Will you be finishing out the week? Mr. Axelmire paid the bill."

"I'm leaving," I said. "You can send him a refund at the Abilene jail."

I DIDN'T go chasing him with my parasol. What was the use of poking Bill? He'd have said the mayor wired him that bandits were coming. And the bandits got lost on the road to Abilene. There was always a story to tell. Besides, we did have a problem.

Cows.

We had more cows in Abilene than a whole population of

turkeys, pigs, and men. The stubborn ones broke from their stockyards and mixed with everybody on Texas Street. Twenty or thirty of them occupied the Noah's front lawn. Chinamen from the kitchen beat their hides with sticks, but the cows wouldn't go. People looked to the railroad. The Kansas Pacific wasn't moving a single cow. The price of beef had dropped in Chicago, and Abilene was sitting tight. Buyers and sellers wouldn't hold hands at the Noah until the market jumped back to July. Their cattle bellowed on my lawn.

Meantime more herds would arrive, and with the cattle you had cattle boys. The mayor got scared. Abilene was becoming a "Texian city." A regiment of gamblers, whores, and fancy men followed the cattle boys into town and grew fat on Texas Street. Churchwomen complained that you could find nothing but whores and "Texians" in the heart of Abilene. Texas Street was the devil's hole. Mulberry and Maple would soon be filthy sinks.

The mayor spoke from the town's Minute Book. Sharps and prostitutes couldn't keep open house on Texas Street any more. They had to move into the flat stinking land behind Mud Creek. Hickok did all the moving. He walked the gamblers and whores to the far side of the creek. The whores wept. Their new home didn't have one tree. It could have been the moon. Dried mud with little footprints. The gamblers scratched their chins. No longhaired marshal and eggsucking mayor could destroy their industry. They put up a shantytown in that mudhole on the moon and called it "The Devil's Addition."

Cattle boys flocked to the gambling dens. All you had on Texas Street was churchwomen, cows, and a few saloons. The mayor had to revise his Minute Book. The town would starve to death if he didn't allow a casino here and there. The whores began to travel both sides of the creek. They stepped in cow pies. The price of beef kept falling.

While the cow pies collected and Abilene swam in dust, The

Devil's Addition prospered. You could hear the fiddles scraping from the moonland of cracked mud. The mayor smarted with jealousy. He'd made war on the gamblers, and the gamblers won. He'd never scribble that in the Minute Book. "We've pushed the sharpers out," he wrote. Then he shut the Minute Book and tried to wheedle the gamblers back from the moon. The gamblers were happy sitting behind the creek, bleeding whiskey and stripping cattle boys of pants, boots, and money belts.

The mayor sent for Bill. Hickok and Rob had to cross Mud Creek with their shotguns high and close The Devil's Addition. The gamblers picked up and went south of the moon. The mayor ordered Bill to fence them in like cattle. The gamblers built "Heaven's Delight" in their enclosed hump of ground. You couldn't keep the "Texians" out. They preferred that hump to Abilene.

The mayor mulled and mulled over the gamblers' enterprise. How far could he exile them before they'd build a new city of tents and shacks? He was through with those rotten men. He imported fresh gamblers from Topeka and helped them put up the Alamo, "a grand house of mischief" on Mulberry Street. A share of the profits went into the city's chests. The Alamo had three orchestras, its own calaboose, a fleet of gambling tables, the tallest mirrors in the West, double glass doors, a row of bottles with enough firewater in them to drown an army of sailors, an indoor gallery where the whores could circulate and be seen from the bottom of the Alamo, a billiard parlor, a ten-pin alley, and a stage for any performance the Alamo cared to put on.

The exiled gamblers couldn't compete with such finery. The Alamo was wooing some of the cattle boys away. The town was growing rich into September. And then we had the last big cattle drive of the season. There was a dust storm over Abilene. Knives and forks shivered on our tables at the Noah. The ground seemed to shift. The teeth chattered in your head. That's what a herd could do.

The cattle boys whooped as they came in on their spotted ponies. Pony and rider were lacquered down with dust. Their eyes were slim gray pockets. It didn't take the cattle boys long to see how unwelcome their herd was. Another store of cows. Each herd was like a great swollen belly added on to Abilene.

The cattle boys didn't bother with a trip to the bathhouse. They walked into the Alamo with their gun belts on. "Where's the marshal?" They'd been told on every damn trail that *Hickok's down on Southern boys.* The barkeeps couldn't produce Wild Bill. So the cattle boys made them collect whiskey bottles from the wall and lay them in the dust outside the Alamo. Then they shot the legs off gambling tables. They tore pieces of crystal from the chandeliers. They destroyed one of the three orchestras, ripping the strings off every fiddle they could find. They clucked at the whores and forced the gamblers to undress. They still weren't satisfied. They smashed the mirrors and created webs of silver on the walls. It couldn't get them to smile. They broke through the double glass doors and stumbled onto the street and into a dozen cows. They searched between the cattle. "Come on out, Billy boy . . ."

William was standing on a balcony over their heads.

He'd gone in the back way, climbed the Alamo's stairs, and went out to the veranda. His guns were in his fists. "Any cowboys asking for Hickok?"

The cattle boys twisted their necks to look up at Bill. They started to pull. Bill shot once or twice at their hats. He shaved their crowns and said, "Would you like some more of these pills?"

One stupid cattle boy fired at Hickok. The ball slapped the side of his coat. It didn't harm him any. Bill fired back. Robby Dykes had come running around the corner to help Wild Bill and got in the way of the ball. It struck him in the ear. Robby shivered

once and fell dead. Bill groaned at Rob's body on the ground. The
cattle boys wouldn't face a maddened Wild Bill. They got on
their ponies and ran for shelter in the deadlands behind Mud
Creek. Bill jumped down from the veranda. His knees began to
rock near Robby Dykes. I'd heard the shooting over at the hotel
and I scampered to Mulberry Street. Rob lay in the blood that
was spilling out of his ear. Bill stooped and tried to catch the blood
in his palm. His eyes weren't so blue.

He wiped the blood on his coat and went after the cattle boys.

People have different stories about what happened next.

Some say he swallowed Little Texas with one slap of his tongue.
He liked corn, I know, but even Bill couldn't eat all the dust and
wood of Little Texas. He trampled through Mud Creek, banging
into outhouses, Indian orphans, and old men. It wasn't like Bill.
He wouldn't bully the weakest part of the population just because
the cattle boys had disappeared. His eyes must have gone milky
on him and he couldn't tell an orphan from an outhouse. So he
grabbed at whatever was close. Teeth, hair, and cracker barrels.
He lopped tin chimneys off the low roofs. He carried a tail of
clotheslines with him. That's how I read the devastation. It was
a blind man's wind.

Bill recovered while crossing over the creek. He would have
been stuck in that moonland forever without his eyes. He reached
the gamblers' city of Heaven's Delight, and here he didn't attack
old men. He left the chimneys on the roofs. But that rage was in
him. He picked a spotted pony off the ground and hurled the pony
into a gambler's tent. He wasn't chasing shadows. He wanted the
dusty cattle boys who'd come off their drive to heckle at him on
Mulberry Street. Hickok poked through the tents. Whores ran
out onto the prairie rather than look at the blue twitch in Hickok's
face. Gamblers packed their money bags and figured it was time
for a new territory. One Chinaman says that Hickok found his
cattle boys, shoved their hats into their mouths, and made them

chew. Another one swears the cattle boys got away with the gamblers and the whores. Whatever happened, Hickok didn't bring anybody out of Heaven's Delight. But it couldn't survive Hickok's visit. That tent city fell to the ground.

DON'T BOTHER me with your tents and blackjack money! I was worried for Bill. Rob hadn't been Hickok's left hand. Hickok had his own left hand. Rob was Bill's eyes. He'd lead him out of a barn or an empty shack when Bill had his fits of blindness. He'd wash Bill's goatee with that pail of water. There was no one to carry the pail now but me.

I went to the calaboose.

Bill was drinking rum out of an old jelly jar.

One side of his face was darker than the other. It was like half of him was in a hateful dream. He couldn't forgive himself for shooting Robby Dykes. He'd be gulping jelly jars until a cow knocked on his window and sang him to sleep if I hadn't come along.

"Hell, Bill, it wasn't your fault that Rob flew around the corner. That was a freak shot."

"I'd have spotted Rob two years ago, felt his boot tops, the blur of his neckerchief. I'm moon blind, and it's getting worse."

"Why don't you come and live at the hotel? I'll look after you, Bill?"

"I couldn't afford the Noah," Bill said. "It's a cattleman's paradise."

"I'll tell Leopold to give you a special rate."

"It's bad luck to have the same landlady twice."

He filled his jelly jar. I shouted at him.

"My Topeka husband, Mr. Axelmire . . . you think I murdered Lorraine and little Arlene. You have an unforgiving nature, Wild Bill. I would have saved your little girl if I knew how."

"Arlene wasn't my natural daughter. I told you that. She didn't have one pa that Lorrainey could remember. It rubbed me bad. A child with a million papas running loose, and she couldn't claim one."

"But why were you so vicious? You were ready to kill all the white men and women of Hays."

"I left some gold in five saloons for Lorrainey and the girl. Lorrainey didn't get a drop of it. They figured, *Wild Bill's dead somewhere, so why waste gold on a half blood and a little Indian bitch?*"

I heard the clomp of hoofs on the sidewalk. Holy Jerusalem, a cow did look in the window! She was licking the sash with her tongue. Hickok didn't need a soul. He had his jelly jar, his calaboose, and Miss Emilia at the window, the cow who was in love with Bill. I dipped my head good-bye, but Bill asked me not to go. "I have a present for you."

He put a silver locket in my hand. It had his likeness inside. A miniature, painted with rosy cheeks and a blue sky over his head. I was awful glad to have that locket from Bill. It had to mean something. Was William a little fond of his old landlady?

The cow slickered up the window.

Bill took me down into his cot.

"Woman, why's your face so red?"

It was Henry talking. I blinked to make sure. I'd been pondering ghouls and hairy Texans so long, that man disappeared from my head. His voice was like a buzz in my ear. He could have strolled into the wallpaper and I wouldn't have been able to tell. I was growing blind to Henry. Jorrid had the answer. It was the "fate" of a Western town for husbands to lose their wives. That's what he wrote in the *Star*.

The plague is upon us. In the East they moan of abandoned wives. Rotters desert their families and run out West. We, sir, are the West, where the ratio is one woman to each hundred men. I'm not speaking of those bawdyhouse brides from the Alamo and other places. Whores abound in Abilene. But I wouldn't consider a whore any man's wife. The heart of the issue is that husbands are abandoned out here. Women have their pick. I don't mean bawds. I mean quality women. They float from husband to husband, while the devil laughs at this mockery of the vows of marriage. Western morals, sir? The parson's cry is of no avail. We are the town of abandoned men.

That Jorrid could bleed on every page. I was Salome the sorceress, if you listened to him. Devouring husbands the first chance I had. Sure, some wives ran from their men. What can you expect in moo town? Men hummed at you from morning to night. I can't recollect all the "marriage proposals" I had in a month. But I didn't abandon Henry. He just dropped out of view.

"Answer me. Why's your face so red?"

Because I have Bill's locket under my gown. I can feel his miniature press into my heart every time I swallow a bit of air. It puts a blush on my cheeks, Henry Ovenshine.

"I'm red from laboring in this hotel. I'm red from screaming at Chinamen. I'm red from living with you."

He must have known I had a piece of silver from another man near my skin. But he wouldn't mention Wild Bill Hickok. He started babbling about his sins. I tried to paste some sense to his story. Was he a printer in Manhattan? He kept talking of ink. "I inked him," he said. "I inked him proper."

"Who, Henry? Who did you ink?"

"Doctor Ovenshine."

"That's yourself."

"No, no, I was Ovenshine's clerk."

"Then, by Jesus, who are you?"

"Your own little Henry, the college master with a school he left behind. I'm in the hotel game . . . with you and the Hebe."

And he trundled away with a Chinaman's smile on his lips. Let Jorrid lament the evil wife. I don't care. I couldn't see Henry from the cherubs in the wall. The husband was swimming in ink. I didn't idle. The sorceress became Bill's eyes.

I made my rounds of Abilene like any marshal. If Bill wasn't back at the calaboose by ten o'clock, I knew he was stuck in some barn, moon blind now. He'd thrash in the dark until I came for him. I had a bowl of water and strips of muslin for his eyes. I'd put his head in my lap and rinse him like a baby, caress him where he bumped his face in that blind fit, make up little nursery songs to suck the blue into his eyes.

> The fat cow jumped
> The fat cow jumped . . .

"Salome, why didn't you bring a mandolin?"

"Shush," I told him, and the Slayer was too weak to rebel.

THE CATTLE season was coming to an end. I didn't have to worry about that great shiver of dust that could smash china and splinter a roof whenever a herd arrived. The herds had stopped. But what were we going to do with the cows we already had? It got so that you couldn't step into the street without running into a cow or a steer. The sweethearts had captured Abilene. Soon they'd sit at the gambling tables and sign themselves into the hotel. But the cattle boys were gone. Mud Creek had become a home for Chinese cooks.

A new population drifted into Abilene, a guerrilla band that lived on the prairie, grabbing whatever they could. They were scavengers, chased from town to town by the Cavalry. A handful of them were "unreconstructed rebels" who'd entered the late war on the losing side. Others were just scoundrels who attached themselves to any band that happened to come along. But you couldn't mistake their leader. He was a pirate in tangled silver, gold, green, and red. Nicaragua Smith, worn with age and the dream of so many different armies. I invited him into the Noah without his men.

He blubbered when he saw my face, holding me like he'd just stepped out of some doom in the countryside.

"Awful nice to look at you, miss Sally. I'm a prairie tramp . . . we don't get to see Galveston girls in our line of business."

"General, what is your business?"

"Plunderin'," he said.

"That's a far cry from Ishmael."

He wasn't the same general who rode his piebald into a burning house to cut off Yankee noses and force the Union Army to surrender Galveston, so we could have our island country, free of bluebellies and butternut pants. These beggars didn't have Ishmael in their heads. They were more like murderers and thieves.

"Times are different, miss Sally. Texas is filled with scalawags. We fought the skunks. Not with Ishmael. We joined that other nation."

"What nation?" I asked.

"Ku Kluck Klan . . . we had a glorious year hunting scalawags. I was a cyclops with ten secret provinces. I had a throne and all, miss Sally. But the federals came and stole my chair. Texas is hateful to me now. It's scalawag heaven, with scum from the North country and niggers in tall hats. Lord knows how long my boys have been out on the plains . . . we'll wander til we drop."

The general swore he didn't take lunch in the afternoons. The prairie had destroyed his appetite for a sit-down meal. But he still sat down and ate an apple pie with his fingers, the way a guerrilla would. The general was a cyclops, I swear. Old age and the

Cavalry couldn't harm him. He'd have his Ishmael on the plains.

"Any news of Galveston, general?"

"Nothing that isn't three years old. Your mama's alive, far as I remember. Morrissey caved in. He's crippled with the gout. That robber doesn't leave his room . . . but I have something else. A chunk of your father's house is riding with us."

"A house can't get up on a horse."

"We'll see." He called out to his followers who were picking their teeth near the front porch. "Bring me the black Wild Bill."

I tittered in that roll of skin around my heart. Desperate people loved to play Wild Bill. You had Wild Bill of the Mountains, Wild Bill of the Plains, Blue William, Billy Thunder, and now the black Wild Bill of the Cyclops Guerrilla Circus.

"Don't smile, daughter," the general said, with pie crust on his fingernails.

Archibald Aloysius walked in. He wasn't wearing a convict's burlap rags. He had a neck handkerchief, a flannel shirt, and two six-guns. The cyclops hadn't lied. Archibald Aloysius Blackburn was my one surviving brother.

I didn't care if he was a colored boy. I hugged him harder than Jesus. I could have crushed his bones with happiness, but Archibald was so stiff. It was like hugging a mountain of ice.

I asked the general if Archie had also been a cyclops with the Ku Kluck Klan. The general said no.

"I picked up Wild Bill after the Yanks took my throne away."

"He stormed the penitentiary," Archibald said. "He stole twenty of us right out of the warden's lap."

"I wouldn't forget Archibald."

The cyclops tore open another apple pie and chewed on the meat. He was proud of his assault on the prison. It was the craziest thing. Archie just couldn't escape that old cyclops. It was the general who swiped Archie from the Galveston wharves when Arch was a freeman and a sailor out of Boston. The general needed money for his Nicaragua expedition, and he sold Arch to pa with the justice's help. And now Archibald was riding with that guerrilla circus.

"Why don't you stop being a guerrilla, Archibald, and go on home to Massachusetts?"

"I can't," Arch said. "Too many sheriffs have my picture on the wall . . ."

"Those pictures couldn't travel to Boston. Boston's too big."

"And what would I do when I got there? Teach in a kindygarten? I'll stay with the general."

"Don't discourage him, daughter. He's the black Wild Bill. He can pull on a man like bats winging out of hell."

"Pull on your tooth," I said. "There's only one Wild Bill. And he's marshal of this town."

The general winked at Archibald. "We know that."

I had this dreadful feeling the guerrillas had come to Abilene for gunplay. I shouted at the general. "Hickok's my friend."

"You're not too picky, are you, daughter? We hear he's been shooting Texians down like prairie buzzards."

"You heard wrong."

"Then where are your cattle boys?"

"Gone to Topeka, I suppose. The season's finished."

"Finished? What's been making me deaf? All you have is cattle in the streets."

"That's on account of the big price war. Abilene won't sell a cow to Chicago."

"Is that so?" the general said. And I wondered if the cyclops intended to shoot Hickok all to pieces and steal our cows. I wouldn't furnish the rascal with any more pies.

Old cyclops didn't get the chance to jump on Bill. Hickok arrived on the porch with his shotgun. He shoved guerrillas aside with the neck of his gun and walked up to old cyclops and me.

"Bill, this is Nicaragua Smith, and that's my brother Archibald Aloysius . . . they're Galveston people."

"Tell them they'd better stroll to the far side of the tracks. They're breaking the no-gun rule."

"We'll stroll," the general said. "In a minute. Hickok, shake hands with Mr. Aloysius. We call him the black Wild Bill. He's getting famous. Our Bill is a poke of thunder. That's how quick he is on the pull."

William wouldn't shake hands with Archibald.

"There's lots of thunder lying in the ground. The cemetery is long with pull artists, Mr. Smith."

"I'm a general, sir," the old cyclops said.

"Then I'll ring the town bell for you and celebrate your coming . . . now you stroll on out of here with your tin men."

Archibald's fist started to curl close to his gun belt, but the cyclops scowled at him, and Arch lowered his eyes. They left the Noah, collecting ruffians from the porch.

"Bill, I didn't invite them to Abilene . . . the general was the biggest warrior Galveston ever had. Lord's sake, you were there when he drove the Yankees from our island. I don't know how he got to be such a terrible scamp . . . and Arch belonged to us. My other brothers died of the Yellow Jack when I was a little thing. I can't remember one. Archie was our carriage boy. You wouldn't think he has a Boston education. He can chirp in French and argue like a magistrate. He got wicked on us and pa had to lend him to the warden and all, but I wouldn't have a living brother without Archibald."

"Slow down," Bill said. "I won't hurt your brother. Hell, he can become marshal if he likes. I ain't fooling . . . the black Bill's all right. But I have a mind to run that general into the cottonwood breaks. Those tin men might get lost in that little stack of trees, and it's the last we'll hear of Mr. Smith."

I broke crockery on my way to the kitchen and screamed at the Chinamen. You could say everything was the Chinamen's fault. Dust, wind, old cyclops, the man in the moon, Chicago beef. The cyclops didn't get lost in the cottonwoods behind the cemetery.

He took over Mud Creek. You could hear the crack of pistols from morning to night. The ruffians weren't killing themselves. The *crack, crack* wouldn't have been so regular in a brawl. Archibald was airing his guns.

Damned Sally mashed her teeth.

One of the Bills would make me a widowwoman. How could I win? Sooner or later I'd have to cry for William or Archibald Aloysius. I wanted to disappear into the cottonwood breaks and eat bark off the trees.

I didn't have time for chewing bark. Bill didn't get back from his evening tour of Abilene. I had to chase down his blind man's groans with a bowl of water. He picked a barn near Mulberry Street. He was shivering in the dust and biting on a piece of wood. I had to force that stick from his mouth. It was half twisted from the crunch of his teeth. The pain must have been impossible, or you wouldn't catch him biting wood like that. He had blood on his mouth. I cradled his head and washed his eyes but the milk wouldn't go away. I rocked him in my lap and sang every nursery song I knew. I changed the muslin "banditches."

"Salome, you'll have to give me a begging cup. I'm finished."

"Then we'll beg on the same street . . ."

"You beg? The Noah's your house. I'm finished with this game of blind man's bluff."

I shushed him and rocked his head. *What kind of sorceress are you that can't chase milk?* I kissed his bloody mouth. *The fat cow jumped . . .* I'd stay in that barn and work a month on Bill. I'd grow a beard to merry him. I'd sing to the man in the moon. Maybe that son of a bitch can help Bill with his moon blindness. I didn't have to sing. Bill's eyes fluttered like a swallowtail against the muslin in my hand. I could feel the color strike. That milky web broke into a blue twitch. We were able to leave the barn.

I WENT to Mud Creek in the morning. Old men squatted on the railroad tracks. The guerrillas had pushed them out of their tents. I found the cyclops shaving in the creek.

"Halloa, daughter, what brings you to our little neck?"

I was blunt with the cyclops.

"Go on out of here. Do your plundering someplace else."

"Daughter, I haven't bled a soul in Abilene."

"You've come to kill Hickok, haven't you?"

"He needs killing." The cyclops rolled his eyes. ". . . calling us tin men."

"He could have kissed your heels and called you Kublai Khan and it wouldn't mean a toad to you . . . not the way you are now. General Smith, I once served under you. I was your brevet major and I still have some rights. Don't send Arch across the tracks."

"I'm no magician, Major Sally. You speak to Archibald. If he wants to pull on Hickok, how can I prevail on him not to pull?"

I let that lying cyclops scratch his beard in the creek.

Blue pistol smoke took me to Archibald Aloysius. He was shooting cans off a dry-goods box. I shivered for the "wolfman," for sorry-eyed Bill. Archibald wasn't the cyclops' pet bear. He had two holsters, but he didn't pull with both hands like that dead farmer, Saskatchewan. The right was his pulling gun. The left gun didn't leave his side. He put his back to the dry-goods box, twisted his body around in a move that was so soft, you could hardly see it, and pulled with his killing hand. He shaved five cans off the box, spilling tin into the air with a loud rattle. He could have shot cherries off a tree, splintered the *o*'s and *q*'s on the mayor's ordinance board. He was the black Wild Bill. But how did he become a two-gun man in the penitentiary?

"Arch, did the warden run a shooting club?"

"I had my own schooling," Arch said. "Years and years of it. I taught myself to pull on a wooden gun. The turnkeys wouldn't donate powder and balls to a nigger convict."

I didn't know how much to tell Archibald. But I had to trust him a little.

"Arch, we played together once upon a time . . . I got extra tarts for you from mama, and you gave me piggyback rides on the ice. Doesn't that count for something?"

"It counts," Arch said with whistling teeth. "You're my little white sister who couldn't tell a camel from a dromedary. But I've changed, or haven't you noticed? I stopped driving carriages ten years ago."

"But you don't have to set yourself to murdering Bill."

"Murder?" And he started to laugh. "The marshal's the quickest thing alive. I'm just a poor boy from the wooden-gun school."

"He's going blind," I said.

The bitterness went out of Arch. "He didn't look blind at the hotel."

"It's moon sickness . . . it comes and goes."

"I thought mooneye only happens to horses and cows."

"Well, it's happened to Bill. What's the point of shooting at him?"

"If he has mooneye, he should sit in a rocking chair without his guns."

"Drat your rocking chair! Will you promise not to go near Bill?"

"I'll promise you Kentucky and Alabama if he retires before tomorrow."

Arch was a bandit like the other tin men. He belonged in the cyclops' circus. But I couldn't help it. I loved Arch. He was more family to me than my own mama. I left him with his target pieces and walked on up to the tracks.

THE GUERRILLAS came out of Mud Creek in the morning. They didn't have a gun on them except for Archibald Aloysius. The black Wild Bill wore a polkadot neckerchief and a spangled shirt. They weren't holiday clothes. The different spangles and dots were supposed to blind a man in the sun. People stood on the sidewalks. Even the cows had big eyes.

The mayor was there to watch the fun. He rocked lightly on the wooden boards. The whole sidewalk creaked.

He combed his silky moustache, delighted with himself. I ran up to that jackass in the long-tailed coat and shouted in his ear.

"Mayor Tom, stop those guerrillas. Your Minute Book is filled with laws against dueling in the street."

He flicked his moustache comb. "Hickok's our peace officer. Go to him."

"What if the black cowboy ruins your peace? . . . those bandits will ride hog over the town, and you won't have Wild Bill."

"Haw! The marshal will say *boo,* and that nigger will drop his pants and run."

The jackass wouldn't listen. I was standing in his way. He couldn't see the Alamo's double glass doors. Bill liked to gamble all night and come out for his breakfast around noon. If his eyes went back on him, he could crouch under a table and pretend to have a drunken fit. No one cared. The Alamo was used to a dusty marshal.

I crossed in front of the guerrillas.

The cyclops bowed and smiled. "Just a picnic, daughter, just a picnic."

It was too late to tug at Arch. The guerrillas would have sent me off to live with the cows on the other side of the street.

The cyclops cawed into the Alamo like a rooster with a big red hat. "Wild Bill . . . we're the tin men from over the creek and we've come to wish you a hearty appetite."

Hickok stepped through the glass doors. His sash was crooked. He had dust on his knees. His guns hung near his belly, and one of his boot tips had broken off. A dirty yellow stocking poked out

of the boot. He squinted at all the cows and men in the street.
"Are you some kind of troubadour, Mr. Smith? I didn't ask for
a breakfast song . . . it's too early."

He was on the sidewalk, leaning over the guerrillas. One hand
went behind his back and dug at something. Hickok had straightened his sash. He could see the brown dots at Archibald's throat,
the spangles, the shirt cuffs, the holsters with leather beards at the
bottom. The marshal wiggled that patch of yellow stocking and
stood with his boots and shoulders against the doors, his body
framed in glass.

The cyclops spread the wings of his coat. He signaled to the
tin men, and they did the same. It was to tell Hickok that they
didn't have a hideout gun in their coats. But Bill wouldn't move
from the doors.

"Hickok, I think you're a puny little snake, and Mr. Aloysius
agrees. He's the real Wild Bill. You're a scumsucking gambler.
You steal aces and eggs. You grease pigs and donkeys for a dime.
You're the town chimney boy. You have soot on your tongue. You
rob pilgrims and simple people . . . you had no cause to insult my
men."

"Tin is tin," the marshal told him.

The cyclops knocked his ankles into the dust. "Should we learn
you how tin can pull? . . . why don't you speak to Mr. Aloysius,
chimney boy?"

"I wouldn't want to rile him," Bill said. "I like his neckerchief
. . . and he doesn't have so much tin in his mouth."

Hickok turned to go inside, but Archie had to squawk.

"You do steal aces and eggs."

Bill faced around again. "We ought to steal a few eggs together, Mr. Aloysius. That could bring us a nice breakfast."

"We can have your breakfast out here, Hickok."

Archie dipped his right knee, and I knew what would happen
next. I could have closed my eyes and screamed down, down

inside my head, where guns don't bark and blood didn't explode through a man's shirt and sashes didn't matter. But I never screamed. I looked with all the other folks and fat mooing cows. It wasn't much of a bark. The guns spit a crazy blue fire. The doors shattered behind Bill. Archie walked in a slow circle and shot five times. The balls didn't touch Bill. Archie's eyes seemed to go out of his head. He'd dance and fire, dance and fire, and the balls would break wood and glass. Hickok only pulled once. The ball ripped into Archie's spangled shirt and the spangles went gray with smoke and a red ink burst out everywhere.

The cyclops tried to catch Arch. But Archie kept on walking in a circle that got shorter and shorter until he dropped. Bill wouldn't let the tin man take Archibald to Mud Creek.

"Go on, skedoodle."

The cyclops banged himself on the chest with white knuckles. "He killed Arch, he killed Arch . . ." His eyes were raw. He began to follow the steps that Archie made. His walk narrowed to a tiny line. The guerrillas grabbed his arms and carried him over the tracks.

Arch lay on the ground, holding his bloody shirt where the ball had gone through. His knees kicked out. Fishy white holes swam in his head. Bill didn't climb down from the sidewalk to examine Mr. Aloysius. Archibald was the coroner's property. Bill went into the Alamo. He'd sit with the coroner after Archibald shed his ghost. But the coroner wasn't there. He never got up before noon, no matter how many niggers were dying in the street.

The crowd had already begun to thin. The mayor walked away with his council of wise men. They'd come for the shooting, that's all. The mayor had different things on his mind. He had to do additions and subtractions in the town's Minute Book.

The black Wild Bill had a few orphans and the undertaker at his death watch. And that scribbler from the *Star*. Jorrid Ferguson. The cows and us were the only mourners. Jorrid made a pillow with his coat and put it under Arch. I ran into the Alamo and borrowed a pitcher of water from the barkeep. The bad women were parading their skirts. Bill sat in a corner, scooping up cards. He scooped with a dull smile on his face.

I brought the pitcher out to Arch. He couldn't take water into his mouth. I wiped his forehead with the end of my skirts. He didn't recognize me. He was in that moonland where the dead like to sleep. Jorrid sat on his knees near Arch's body. He pulled the eyelids down on those two fish holes. He left a smear of ink on Archibald.

I didn't cry.

Sally'll get herself a live brother from someplace else. He won't be a two-gun man that you can kill so easy. I'll make him a merchant prince. Traders don't get shot to pieces. They buy hotels.

The town wouldn't pay for Archie's dying. I should have studied the Minute Book. You couldn't find one nigger bandit in any of the chapters the mayor had written. He put up a notice on the town board. *Mad dog shot outside the Alamo, October the 2nd.* That was it. No Archibald Aloysius Blackburn had ever come to Abilene.

The undertaker wanted twenty dollars before he'd consider moving Arch. I only had ten in my pocket. He cursed me and took the money with a crabbed fist. He dug a hole near the cottonwood breaks. We didn't have a regular service. The deacon wouldn't climb up the hill for Archibald. To hell with the whole lot. I sang the songs Arch had learned me from the Boston Freeman's School. About junipers and onions and the savage bounty of the soul. The undertaker had gone, and I could sing my head off. The words echoed down from the breaks.

> The Lord's a Massachusetts man.
> He brings onions and glory

To the miserable and the weak.
He sits Himself under a juniper
And He waits for us.
Onions sting the eye
But the soul's too strong for onion fire.
The Lord's a Massachusetts man.

I wouldn't forget Archie's songs. But I might have confused the words a little. A man walked out of the cottonwood trees. It was Wild Bill. He had bits of cheese in his beard.

"I'm sorry 'bout your brother. I meant to scratch him in the side . . . but I wouldn't have been in the play if I had to stand around and pick the spot. He had a gorgeous pull. Where did he get his shooting habits?"

"In the penitentiary."

"Then I ought to convict for a while . . . something was wrong with your brother. A boy that quick shouldn't have come up slow . . . why was he watching my beard?"

Beard, beard, I told him you were blind.

Arch was looking for the moon sickness in Bill. I was the girl who slowed his arm. He went dueling with my stories in his head. Salome, the murdering witch. I dropped the poison in Archie's ear. Whatever I did, I'd have some dirt on me.

It was the bitterest pickle a girl could chew. *Archie dead is Bill alive. Bill alive is Archie dead.*

I felt like that bird in the Swiss clock that cuckoos at the beginning of every hour. Hickok took my hand and we climbed down the hill. The cuckoo girl and Wild Bill the Victorious, with cheese in his beard.

Fifteen

THE SLAYER didn't abandon me at the bottom of the hill. He brought me to a little house on Maple. Did he rent it from the Hebe? It had cardboard windows and rolls of flypaper, like nooses hanging from the wall. I snuck out to borrow eggs from the Noah and I cooked a jelly omelette on Bill's stove.

That stove belched fire on everything. I'd have thrown the omelette out the window, but the Slayer wouldn't let me.

"I'm fond of black omelettes."

He chewed a pickle with his eggs. Then he pulled on his goatee. He looked into this tiny mirror he kept for trimming his beard.

"Who's handsomer?" he asked, with a miserable face. "The general or me?"

"You are, Bill," I purred to him, like a fat lady cat.

Bill was happy now. That miserableness went away.

Men have more vanity inside them than a truckload of women. I didn't care. I'd go on purring to Bill. But the cyclops put us in a fright.

We figured him to come riding out of Mud Creek in his coat of four colors. Bill had to rush to the jail and recruit barbers and gravediggers to defend the town.

A whore died in the icehouse. A smithy hacked his finger off by mistake. But nothing seemed to happen on the other side of the tracks. An orphan or two shouted in the night. Grandpas carried tents on their backs up to the railroad station. The tin men stared and stared into their campfire. The cyclops never stirred.

Leopold knocked on my door. He had his army of boys with razor hats. The boys stopped working for me. They had to protect the Hebrew from guerrillas and all. The mayor wouldn't telegraph the Cavalry. "I'll be a dead man before I'll cry to the United States."

I thought the Hebrew would ask me to go down to Mud Creek with a spoon and fork under my waist and murder the cyclops' men. That's the kind of propositions Leopold liked to make. *A hundred dollars in gold for each tin man I could deliver.* But he hadn't come with any proposition.

"Salome, we have a Pinkerton at the hotel . . . Melvin Brown."

"The man with eczema?"

"The beef face is just a disguise. It's a special cream he uses in the morning. It gets his cheeks to swell."

"Is he after Nicaragua Smith?"

"The Pinkerton's from New York City. Our bandit problems don't concern him. He's out to arrest your husband, I think."

"Lord, what did Henry ever do?"

"Nothing special . . . Brown swears the professor's going to hang."

"Well, why didn't you kick him out of the hotel?"

"And start a fight with the Pinkerton Agency? We'll have detectives chewing off our hands and feet . . ."

I went up to Henry's room. I couldn't live with him. He'd become an inky person, like Jorrid the scribbler. Henry did the hotel's books. He drew a column for every towel at the Noah. It was awful pretty. But you couldn't tell if you were making money or losing it from Henry's columns. The Hebrew didn't care, long as he had columns to show. That was the hotel business.

Henry had a little hermitage near the roof. He wasn't happy about another creature invading it. He loved to pull his room of secrets around himself and shut it tight. But I was landlady of the house, and I had the key to Henry's room.

He was sitting in the dark. His lamp could have gone out a month ago. He wouldn't have bothered to light it.

"Have you been talking to the eczema man?" I whispered into that dark hole.

An echo sprang from the corner. "Why not? Doesn't the Hebe pay me to entertain his guests?"

"Smith's a Pinkerton from New York."

The lamp sparked up, and the room hissed with the smell of oil. Chips of light fell over us. Henry had the look of a startled herring, all puffy and silverfaced. He swooned in his chair, making little noises with his mouth. He was bending and crying like a baby girl.

"How can I help you if you blubber and won't speak?"

"Ovenshine," he mumbled with his fat lips.

"By Jesus, are you Henry Ovenshine, or some other man's ghost?"

"I'm Lyle Aldridge, from Trenton, New Jersey."

"Now you're a Jersey man! How many homes have you had?"

"A hundred and five, with Abilene . . . if you count this cattle circus a home."

"It's small wonder that you sang to us of Xerxes and Marco Polo . . . What did you do, Lyle Aldridge, that a Pinkerton should scrub the whole country for you?"

The professor pitched into this long tale that could have been the adventures of a damaged Marco Polo. He came out of Trenton to be a scribe in a banking house on Nassau Street in lower New York. His chief at the bank was a Doctor of Divinity who'd given up his calling to play with other people's cash. This lapsed churchman was bitter about it. Doctor Henry Ovenshine made a hell for his scribes and clerks. He accused them of being the devil's helpmate. The tiniest ink blot was a sign of their damnation. One clerk went mad under Doctor Ovenshine. A second clerk struck him on the face and was carried off to the Tombs. My husband Lyle-Henry endured the doctor's insults. "Ink on your cuffs again, Mr. Aldridge?"

Lyle started to embezzle. He stole copper pennies from the bank to keep from going insane. The pennies grew. Lyle put away sack after sack in the drawer where he had his pen holders. He couldn't think of how to get rid of the money.

The churchman discovered Lyle's hidey-hole. He didn't scream to the bank. He took Lyle and his penny sacks into a closet with the other clerks. He'd captured the devil's accomplice, and he had to show the clerks how Doctor Henry Ovenshine could beat the devil. "Chew your rotten gains," he said. "You won't step out of this closet until you eat every penny, Lyle Aldridge."

Lyle reached into a sack. He grabbed a fistful of coppers and swallowed one, two, three, four . . . the pennies tasted like hot green slime from the Delaware River. He'd been pushed into that slime once by a gang of bullies on a frog hunt. He wasn't going to suck copper any more.

"Had enough?" Ovenshine shouted at him. "Eat, you devil boy!"

Lyle seized the ink pot in that closet and stuffed it into the churchman's mouth. Then he walloped Ovenshine about the head with a sack of coppers. Once, twice . . . the doctor's brains started to balloon. The clerks whimpered in the closet. It was filled with ink, blood, and copper pennies. Marco Polo ran out of the closet. He's been running ever since.

"Was he dead or alive when you disappeared?"

"Half and half . . . he had a big blue peach on his dome. He'll remember that hit wherever the hell he is."

"Why did you steal his name?"

"It has character to it . . . somebody had to be Doctor Ovenshine."

"Fool, you left a perfect trail for the Pinkertons . . . it puzzles me why it took them so long. They must have forgotten you during the war. Else they couldn't believe a runaway clerk would have the boldness to call himself Doctor Ovenshine."

I packed a bundle of meats for Henry and had him go hide in the cottonwood breaks. I could waltz with an army of Pinkertons. I was Ishmael, the land of one girl.

Old beef-pie visited me in the afternoon. I chortled to myself at his eczema cream. "Are you hungry, Melvin Brown? I can fix you an early dinner." I'd put chalk in his cabbage, chalk and glue.

I had this horrible desire to scratch the red pudding off his face. Was there another eczema man under the pudding? You couldn't tell with a Pinkerton.

"I haven't seen the doctor at breakfast or lunch?"

"Try the Alamo. He might be gambling with Wild Bill."

"He don't gamble. I'd say your husband is missing."

But the eczema man wouldn't admit he was a detective from New York. He was sly with his pudding on, that sneaky son of a bitch.

I WENT into the breaks with another bundle of meat. Henry's eyes lit up through the trees like a forest bird. The cottonwoods had changed him. He wasn't the inky person I remembered from the

Noah's roof. He had little feathery things all over. Burrs fell out of his pockets. He chewed his meat and never asked about the eczema man in the house. I developed a sudden admiration for Henry. I would have shed all my skirts if he hadn't been so busy with the meat.

I'd judged him too harsh. He was a poor boy from Trenton who could have stayed a clerk for fifty years until he died with black ink running out of his heart. But he struck his banking master on the head and broke with Nassau Street. He was cursed as a wanderer from that day. He'd come out of nowhere to start a college for Galveston's best young girls. I shouldn't have complained about his teaching.

I had a wanderer's education, good for the bitterest times. I inherited colored Indians, cows on the lawn, a dead brother, a marshal with moon blindness, and Ishmael the horse, who stood in the shade behind the hotel with nothing in the world to do but stare out at the bushes and suffer the flies on his back.

I left Henry with his bundle of meat. Brown might get suspicious if I was away too long. He didn't have cabbage in his usual corner. And he didn't come down for breakfast. Old beef-pie was gone. He'd given his soiled shirtfronts to our washerman, and that was the last of Mr. Brown.

A new customer arrived at the hotel. Jacob Traugott. He was the first man to sign our book since Archibald got killed and people grew scared of the guerrillas' revenge. He was as handsome a fellow as you'll ever meet. With a silver watch fob and a waxed moustache. He never picked his teeth at the table. His eyes were china blue. His linen was so white, you'd swear he left nothing but pink shadows in a room. He couldn't fool Major Sally.

"Mr. Traugott, where's your eczema cream? I'll hang myself from the mayor's window if you're not Melvin Brown."

He smiled, and the devil take him, he was much more handsome with wrinkles on his chin.

"Forget Brown . . . your husband belongs to me. Marshal Hickok has a suppeany on his desk. He'll be fined and jailed if he doesn't help me in my search."

"What's the charge on Henry?"

"He's no Henry. That's Lyle Aldridge, a notorious bully boy and a sneak. He's done robbery and assault."

"Pah!" I said. "Your bully boy was a clerk who took pennies from his bank . . ."

"Seven thousand pennies, ma'am, if you care to be exact. And he just about killed one of the managers."

"That manager deserved the thrashing he got . . . and my Henry immortalized him. He borrowed his name and title and everything."

"He's a robber. I told you that. Now where is your Henry, ma'am?"

"He shoved out with the wind," I said. "But you can find him. When the cows get to mooing hard in the mornin', that's Henry."

The pretty smile went from Traugott's face. His nose was fat all of a sudden, and his linen didn't look so white. "Take care, Mrs. Aldridge. I can drop a suppeany on you that'll lay heavier than all the cows in Abilene. It's not a laughing matter. A suppeany's worse than prison. It's like carrying a child that never gets born. Hear me. You'll answer to twenty judges before I'm through."

Nobody delivered a suppeany to the hotel. It must have gotten lost. The town had other troubles than a clerk and his silent wife. It was a busy season for the undertaker. Ten holes were dug in a week. A special plague visited Abilene. It started with the guerrillas. Two of them died one afternoon, and it wouldn't stop. They were found in the creek with their heads kicked in. At first we thought a feud was going on, that the rabble across the tracks were fighting themselves. We weren't sorry. At this rate the whole darn guerrilla circus would disappear inside of a month. But then the cyclops walked up to the tracks with an armed guard and hollered for mayor Tom. Somebody was entering his camp, he said, and killing off his men. The little general was haggard and pale in his old war coat. "That somebody isn't human, or we'd have captured him by now."

The mayor turned to his wise men and whispered *wolfman.* The ghoul was out running again. I didn't believe it. I'd been watching over Bill, rinsing his eyes in empty barns. What reason would he have to jump across the tracks and murder tin bandits with his rotting boots? This "wolfman" wasn't Bill. There had to be a second ghoul in town.

Holy Jerusalem, has Henry gone wild? Did the cottonwoods turn him into a killer? You couldn't be sure with Henry. The professor was full of surprises. I went into the breaks. Would I meet a "wolfman" who was all feathers and burrs? "Lyle-Henry?"

A growl came from the trees. "Don't call me that . . ."

Henry paddled to the edge of the breaks.

He brought a wind of feathers out with him. The feathers dropped away, and twigs cracked under his feet, but he didn't look murderous to me. He was a scribbler whose shoulders had straightened in the cottonwoods.

"I'm hungry," he said.

Lord, I forgot his bundle of meat!

"Be careful, Henry. A lunatic's on the prowl. He's been murdering guerrillas like flies."

"I'm hungry," he said.

"Can't you listen? You're in danger . . . nothing but trees to cover you. Henry, you're all alone."

"I'll come down and swallow the Hebe and his hotel. I'll bite on the calaboose door. I'll roast a cow . . . woman, I'm starving up here."

"Then you wait."

I returned with ham, pickles, and cheese, but the fool had gone off. I shouted after him. "Henry Ovenshine, you come back and eat your grub!"

The breaks were still. I didn't hear a body run or fall in the cottonwoods. It was just like the professor to ask for grub and then ride on his feathers to some faraway tree where he could suck a twig half the night and pretend it was a chicken bone.

He wasn't riding feathers that night. He was in Mud Creek. The guerrillas fished him out of the creek next morning and laid him on our side of the tracks with one of their own murdered men. You wouldn't have recognized Henry if not for his wool shirt and the scribblings in his pocket. He'd been kicked to pieces. The marshal let me have his scribblings. They were addressed to "Mrs. Ovenshine of the Noah House Hotel."

Darling, will we ever leave this land of cows? I long to suck your ten fingers and fly out of Kansas with you. It has been three whole years now since I heard the thump of your heart . . .

He was Lord Byron near the end, scribbling love poems in the breaks. But I didn't get to see a word until I was a widowlady.

I put the poems in my wedding box.

We had two burials in the same afternoon. The undertaker wouldn't stick Henry near the murdered tin man. "Ma'am, we don't want one of our own sleepin' with the devil." So the graves were far apart.

One side of the boneyard went to the guerrillas. They grieved in their corner, while most of Abilene was at Henry's grave. We had the mayor, the pastor, and his deacons. None of the deacons would cross to the other side, and the guerrillas had to bury their man without a decent prayer. It was pitiful to watch. If Henry had been closer, their dead man might have had some kind of grace.

The little general brushed his war coat, and Ishmael's four colors burned on that hill. The deacons could rot! He marched across the boneyard to comfort Henry's widow.

"Daughter, it's a desperate month . . . I was fond of brother Henry. I'd have made him foreign minister if my country survived."

Oh, it was a big lie. He never liked Henry. But it was nice to think of my dead husband as the new Talleyrand. Aldridge-Ovenshine. He would have collected the black Choctaws and Cherokees and put them up for citizenship in our little nation. Then he'd declare war on New York City and free all the clerks. He'd give the Hebrew a license to build hotels to his heart's desire, and he'd find a place for Hickok, so Bill wouldn't have to stroll Abilene in the dark. I don't care what Talleyrand had in mind for his wife. I'd grow fur on my back and two storage humps, and be Aunt Sally, the wise camel of Ishmael, and the first dromedary to ever become chief justice. I'd nicker out my decisions with a camel's laugh. You couldn't escape Aunt Sally. I'd bite evildoers on the tongue. I'd argue with the Lord about the living and the dead. I wouldn't ask him to raise up pa. I'd plead Archibald's case.

"The cyclops and Justice Morrisey stole him, sir. And it twists a freeman when he becomes a slave. It turned Archie bad. He taught himself to shoot in the penitentiary. But he wasn't a bandit, sir. He was like the boy in the children's book who cuts off parts of himself with a scissor knife until he's nothing at all. That's how hateful his own body was. Sir, you ought to give Arch another chance."

I MISSED Henry now he was gone. I'd visit his hermitage in the roof. I'd smell his inky lines, the crazy towel lists, and recite his poem about sucking my fingers. I must have been reciting too loud. The Pinkerton climbed up to the roof.

"I know," he said. "It's hard to be a widow . . . I have a confession to make. I didn't hang around this dumb village two months with birdcrap on my face because of Lyle. I recognized him the first night I got to Abilene . . . calling himself Henry Ovenshine. I could have socked him to the ground, tied his hands and feet, rolled him out to the choochoo train, and let my associates deliver him right into Manhattan."

"Well, why didn't you?"

His fingers went to his moustache. He stroked the wax. Then he took his hand away.

"Damn it all. I was interested in you . . ."

"You have an odd way of showing your interest, Mr. Traugott . . . poking into corners like a rat."

"I'm a detective, Mrs. Sally. That's my job."

"And I'm a widow."

"I didn't mean any disrespect. I'll get out of here when I catch your husband's killer."

"That lunatic isn't Pinkerton business."

"Then I'll hide my badge. I'm not leaving without the son of a bitch."

Traugott stalked the boneyard and the cottonwood breaks. He stepped into Mud Creek and wandered in that moonland beyond the guerrillas' shacks. He mocked the town's theory of wolfmen and ghouls. He didn't have confidence in creatures that were only part human. "It's a bear or a man, but nothing in between."

His palaver was fine, but it couldn't save guerrillas from having their heads kicked in. The lunatic crossed the tracks. He murdered two gamblers and three of the wild men who'd come from Hays. Then a whiskey bum and two more wild men. A thought nagged in my ear. How come the lunatic turned to wild men? Was he carrying the same grudge as Wild Bill. Did he have a daughter that froze? And a half blood wife?

I gnashed my teeth until my chin was ready to fall. Was Bill impersonating a lunatic to have his revenge on Hays? Then I was his accomplice, the lunatic's own little girl.

I took off that dunce cap I was wearing.

While Jacob stalked the lunatic, I stalked Bill. I washed his eyes, fingered his boot heels for signs of blood, followed him to the Alamo, spied on him from the back door. But I had a hotel to run. The Slayer was shrewd enough to get up from his card game after I'd gone to the Noah, stomp on a wild man, and wipe his heels in a drinking trough . . . if he wanted to. He'd been a scout and a Yankee spy. He could shake off a widowlady, to do his rotten work.

The longer I stalked him, the less I could decide about Bill.

I wish the Pinkertons had a school in town. I'd go to that detective college. Traugott could learn me to slap pudding on my cheeks, and I'd get to the heart of it. But Jacob didn't have time to start a college. He was off searching down clues that took him to every street and little garden. He had samples of clay and dust bulging out of sacks in his pockets. He'd put a sample of dust under the microscope he kept in his room and squint at it for half an hour. I couldn't understand his contraption of metal and glass. I'd look into the peephole. Traugott would turn a screw and the dust would blow up into an apple. The apple had blue and red warts.

"Jacob Traugott, any circus performer can accomplish that . . . dust into apples. It's a stupid trick."

Jacob unhooked the body of his microscope and stuck it in a special shoe box that was cushioned with green felt.

"It has nothing to do with apples . . . I can tell the tread of a man's foot. The bluer the color, the deeper the heel mark is."

"And if the lunatic happens to be a bear?"

"Bears have heels, Mrs. Sally . . . they'd leave the darkest sort of blue."

"So far you haven't trapped a thing. If you're Jacob the magician, tell me who the lunatic is?"

"There's more than one."

"By Jesus, how many do we have in town?"

"I don't know . . . two." He picked at the wax on his moustache. "Maybe as high as four."

"Four lunatics? We'll all be dead."

"No. I'll catch them by tomorrow."

The wild men decided not to wait. They got on their ponies and skedaddled to Topeka. Without wild men, the four lunatics had *us* to kill. But I didn't believe Jacob's notion of colors. *Bears and heavy men were blue* . . . we'd have spotted four lunatics.

The Chinese cooks stuttered in the kitchen. The maids hugged the walls. A murderer could be crouching in the stairwell. Thank the Lord we only had one mouth to feed. The dining room was empty but for Jacob. The cattlemen left their cows and took the train to Kansas City.

The Hebrew wouldn't shut the Noah. "No wolfman's scaring me out of business." He had his razor hat and two hideout guns, twin derringers in waxed pockets. His orphan army tried to run away. Leopold had to beat them down with his hat. The boys loped from room to room with clenched teeth. They'd rather dig for potatoes in their Chicago orphanage than die in Abilene.

Leopold called them dopes.

"The monster aint killed an orphan yet."

They smoothed the crowns of their own razor hats and said, "Leo, put the hotel on wheels and we'll move onto the prairie. This place is haunted. Abilene's down to the mayor and Mrs. Ovenshine."

"Keep your birdsongs," the Hebrew told them. "We have a marshal, whores, and plenty of Chineemen. We aint wanting in people."

But he wouldn't go anywhere without the boys. They guarded the outhouse when he was inside. They slept on bundles of straw near his bed. They chewed cabbage with him. Every whore Leo took had to stare into ten wolfish faces. It spooked them to have so many eyes about, and they began to insist that Leo hold the boys behind their curtain. They were like ten little wives. Leo should have been a Mormon. Then he could have married all ten.

JACOB'S MICROSCOPE didn't amount to much. He couldn't produce his four assassins by the first tomorrow. *Bears are blue, cows are blue, pigs are blue, and so are men, women, and boys.* I caught him in the dining room, eating the milk out of an egg. He was still the prettiest man alive, even with egg white on his moustache. He didn't talk about killers and blue footprints.

"Mrs. Sally, you'd do me a terrible favor if you'd dance with me."

"Jacob, the orchestra's over at the Alamo . . . and widows can't dance in saloons."

"Hang their fiddler man," he said, holding out his hands to me. "I can cluck better than a fiddle."

And we waltzed in the dining room, around tables and chairs, with the Chinamen looking at us and Jacob providing an orchestra with his throat. Never heard a man warble like that. Then he grew quiet, but that orchestra of his lay in the room. His warbling wouldn't leave my head.

"That was kind of you, ma'am."

"It wasn't at all . . . I haven't done that much hopping in quite a while . . . I used to dance with a general over at Fort Hays. But his wife arrived in an Army ambulance and cut off his dancing boots."

"I have a wife, Mrs. Sally."

"I figured as much . . . Pinkertons make the best husbands. They can do all their cooking under a microscope."

He scrubbed his moustache with a wet finger. The wax appeared from under the egg white. His eyes went dark as gun metal.

"I know who the killers are . . . just wanted to dance with you before I pick them up."

"Can't you tell me, Jacob?"

"Not until I give them to the marshal. It could be dangerous with murderers about, knowing that you know . . ."

I had a chill after Jacob left the dining room. All he believed in was blue and red warts. He couldn't take his eyes out from under the microscope.

I drank cups of China tea.

I didn't hear a word from Jacob or the marshal.

The sun poured down into the dining room and lit the sideboard with a red and yellow fever. Every knob could have been a burning tulip. I had my second pot of tea. I didn't have to shake the tea leaves in my cup. The bitterness in my mouth wasn't from those red leaves.

Jacob was kicked to death somewhere between the dining room and a deserted garden in back of the hotel. One of Leo's boys tripped over him while Leo was in the outhouse. The boy screamed *murder, murder,* and Leo broke the privy door and came running with his derringers, his razor hat, and his blue-red behind.

WE HAD armed patrols after that. You couldn't trust yourself walking in the street. Jorrid blamed the marshal. "William is good at bowling colored boys into heaven," Jorrid scribbled in the *Star,* "but he can't seem to find one simple lunatic that's destroying the town. We'll have more ghosts than men, if William doesn't act."

Bill looked and looked for the lunatic. He marched everywhere with his own two feet. When the mooneye hit, he had to crawl into a dark hole and wait for Salome to come with muslin and water.

"Bill, Jacob said there's four assassins. He was going to arrest them . . . and then he got killed."

"Why four assassins and not six?"

"He didn't say."

Bill stumbled out of that dark hole with only one eye working. I chased after him.

"Where do you think you're going, Mr. Hickok?"

"To catch the four assassins."

Bill came up with the usual dust on his knees.

The mayor had his own small posse. Men would creep with shotguns into every seventh bush. Two of them were found with half their faces gone.

People learned to sit at home. They did all their marketing in a gang. The Pinkertons wired us for Jacob's body. We had to dig Jacob out of the earth and ship him to their Chicago office in a bed of ice. He was such a pretty man. His face was pink against the ice. I wish I could have danced with him one more time.

The Pinkertons forgot to ask about his microscope. I brought it to my room in that special shoe box. I pieced it together and looked at cotton balls and bootlaces under the glass. You'd swear worms were crawling in the cotton. And the laces grinned like vermicelli. But I couldn't find Jacob's color. I packed the microscope. The four assassins weren't under any glass.

Leo knocked on my door. A crop of razor hats rose up behind him. The air turned blue from orphans' breath. They all tried to squeeze through the door, afraid that one of them might be left stranded in the hall. They got stuck in the doorway, eleven frightened imbeciles, counting Leopold. I hauled them in.

"Salome, it's not safe here . . . you should live down in the cellar with us."

I couldn't help laughing at their proposal.

"You have enough trouble as it is . . . add another party, and the whole ship will sink."

"I'm serious," Leo said, and he took off his hat. The boys started taking off their hats too, but their elbows got in the way.

The hats flew up to the ceiling and bumped along the floor. I kind of liked the Hebrew's menagerie.

"Listen, we could get married . . . I'm not poor."

"We're already partners," I said. "I didn't advertise for a husband in the *Star.*"

His brow tightened. I'd hurt him with my witch's tongue.

"I'm in mourning, Leo. I couldn't get married now."

"We had an election," he said. "Salome, you won. The boys want you for a mama."

I kissed them all on the left eye. Lord, I was tempted to marry the Hebe. The only family I had was a horse in the yard.

"Maybe next year . . ."

Leo put on his hat and the eleven of them managed to wiggle out of the room. But people didn't get lucky after proposing to me. The orphans shrieked up at my window that same night. I couldn't understand their wailing at first. Then I knew. Leo snuck away from the boys. He had to declare his independence for five minutes. He went to the outhouse and forgot to come back. He was lying near the pit, his head torn to pieces.

It was awful lonesome without that little Hebe around the house. He was like a godmother and a good witch. If not for Leo, I would have stayed a fortuneteller and starved to death. He took the Queen of Hearts from a shack on Maple Street and turned her into a hotel lady. And what did I know about the Hebe? I couldn't say if he was born in Chicago or was a furriner. He didn't seem to have many roots. He could have stitched himself together with that paper of needles he once sold to me. Is that why he always had spools of thread in his pockets? To put another stitch where the seam was breaking? And now the lunatic broke his head.

I shouldn't snivel. The boys had it worse than the Queen of Hearts. They'd lost their grandad in the privy. If I couldn't marry Leopold, I could still be a mama to the boys. I fed them, combed the jiggers out of their scalps, and they guarded me with their razor hats.

"Aunt Sally, Aunt Sally, let's get out of here."

"Not until I capture the man that killed my husband and my two friends . . . it's me or the lunatic. One of us is going to die."

We went to lawyer Calvin for the reading of Leopold's will. The papers were in Leo's hand. He'd written them up with the lawyer's help.

I, Leopold the Trader, being of sound mind and body, make this last testament to dispose of my properties and provide for my loved ones in the event of my decease. To my dear partner, Salome Ovenshine, who has been a blessing to us since the day she arrived, I bequeath my holdings on Maple, Texas, and Mulberry, to wit, three outbuildings, nine fortunetellers' shacks, the barn next to where Jannings keeps grocery, two dugouts, six tents, a fighting bird who goes by the name of Rooster, twenty percent of the Abilene *Star*, held in secret, five percent of the Alamo, an eighty percent share of the whores Molly, Ginger, and Calamity Jane, a pound of gold dust in lawyer Calvin's safe, thirteen hundred dollars in the Bank of Abilene, the silver pieces sewn into my mattress, my two prize derringers, my hats, shirts, and silk neckcloths, my boots, my pants, my coats, and other garments I have neglected to count; and I also release outright to Mrs. Ovenshine her share in the Noah, held in trust by Trader Leopold, namely me, and whatever belongings that come with the Noah, including John the Chinaman cook, who is twenty percent mine. Mrs. Ovenshine may do whatsoever she pleases with twenty percent of John.

To my beloved associates, Alfred, Gabriel, Valentine, Joseph, Spencer, Nicholas, Jeremiah, Timothy, Weldon, and Charles, who have been like sons to me, and more, I bequeath my share of the Noah, to be held in trust for them by lawyer Calvin until they come of age, and two hundred dollars cash for each, also held in trust, with the hope that some or all of them will take advantage of the dollar and secure a first-class education for themselves.

I wept to hear the trader's will, and how generous he was with the particulars of his property, but the orphans grumbled behind my back. "Leo swindled us. Where's our cush? We want something now."

They would have marked up the lawyer with their razor hats if I hadn't consoled them. "Dumbbells, we're rich . . . say you're sorry to Leo and thank him for what he left you in his will."

"Thank you, grandpa Leo . . . thank you for the cush we'll never see."

I swept them out of the office, like a prairie hen with her brood, thinking how ungrateful they were. Leo loved the boys, and I meant to fix it so they could have a "first-class education," and not be orphans with razor hats, collecting a dead man's rent.

I located Rooster, Leo's fighting bird. He was a chicken with one eye slashed out of his head. His beak had splinters on top and bottom. You could count the feathers between the bald spots on his back. Rooster was retired from the pits. It cost me out of my pocket to keep that bird alive. But I wouldn't destroy Leopold's favorite chicken.

His three whores weren't bringing in much rent. It was a slow month without cattle boys, and the whores ate up twice what they could earn. The least of them was two hundred pounds. I had to sell the girls to the Alamo, or get stuck with their eating and face powder bills.

I visited Jorrid Ferguson at the *Star*. I owned twenty percent of the scribbler. But I couldn't gather a dime. The *Star* was a losing proposition. Jorrid had just about enough to pay for his ink. I wondered if the orphans would ever get to college. I'd have to dress Rooster in a coat of shellac and send that chicken out to war.

I had other grief with Jorrid.

"If you can't deliver cash, you might change your policies some."

"How's that?"

"Go softer on Bill . . . you blame him for each calamity that drops from the sky."

Jorrid's mouth began to tremble.

"I don't bend to the mayor. Why should I bend to you? I'll damn Hickok if damning's what he deserves. Look at us! You have to take your shotgun into the privy. Abilene's disappearing, and the marshal goes around in velvet pants."

"Bill doesn't wear velvet any more."

"Never mind. Nobody dictates what I write."

I went home to the boys. The first thing I did was free John. I wouldn't keep twenty percent of a Chinaman. John wasn't a cow or a whore or the Abilene *Star.* I gave back the part of him that belonged to me. John wasn't a bit joyous. He started to cry.

"John, we don't have a soul to cook for. The hotel is dead."

It took me twenty minutes to explain that John was his own property now. He packed his one paper satchel and, sniffling harder than before, he crossed the railroad tracks into bandit country.

I was in the kitchen boiling cabbage for the boys. They could have moved to the top of the house. But they wouldn't stir from the cellar, where they'd lived with the Hebe since that Fourth of July when the Noah opened its doors to cattlemen and quality people as the premier inn of the West. The Noah lasted a hundred and thirty days.

"Jeremiah, Gabriel, Valentine . . . come on upstairs and eat."

We had a dining room to ourselves, with cuspidors and gold curtain rods, crockery to feed a village, and tablecloths that could have rolled into small tents. The boys gobbled their cabbage, but you couldn't get all ten to sit down and share a meal. They'd come and go in bunches of four, five, and six. They always had some business to do in the cellar.

Once, when they were out on a spree, with their razor hats of course, I decided to venture down into the cellar and clean the big old dungeon that had been Leo's part of the house. Not even the maids went there. I had to dust with a candle in my fist. The rooms were very small. I found a closet with a lock on it. I couldn't get in.

"Auntie, what are you doing?"

It was Jeremiah. He'd come up behind me with his derby on. The candle licked at his eyebrows. He'd grown in six months. He was tall as Aunt Sally in his razor hat.

"Jeremiah, whose closet is this?"

"Grandpa's," he said.

"Why's it locked?"

"Grandpa lost the key."

The candle jumped, and Jeremiah's hair went from coal to honey. The flame was on his nose. His teeth were silver knuckles in a line. He shrank into the black walls. "Jeremiah, where are you?"

A voice shot from the other side.

"Auntie, don't get scared."

I turned the candle on him. He was holding a featherbroom. He slapped it against the wall and wiped the broom on his hat. He was a prize featherduster.

"Who learned you that?"

"Orphans have to dust their rooms same as everybody. We did it in Chicago . . . and we did it in grandpa's room."

Jeremiah worked by candlelight and we cleaned up the place, two featherdusters in a hole.

He became my helper, chopping cabbage in the kitchen with Weldon and Gabriel. The boys didn't have family names. They'd come from a foundling hospital, and Leo was the first grandpa they'd ever had. I can't imagine who their mamas were. The Hebe "lifted" them from Chicago and showed the boys how to wear a razor hat.

They slept in their dungeon, but they liked to play upstairs.

They would whip their hats around, and you could see a derby float across the dining room and catch itself in a candelabra's ears. They gambled on the steps, laying silver on the carpet and grumbling over a missing queen. The hotel was like a great toy house. They'd pull knobs out of dressers in the upstairs rooms. They'd drape comforters on their shoulders and pretend to be lords and kings of their own estates. They'd growl and hiss a lot, but no two of them ever seemed to fight. They didn't have much interest in outside company. The orphans were happy with their comforters and the Queen of Hearts.

We'd winter here, and open up the hotel for the next cattle drive if Abilene could get rid of this season's cows. The Hebe had taken care of us. We had flour and firewood and dollars in the bank, and Rooster to bring us luck. I ought to have been happy as Gabriel and Nicholas and Charles. Only I felt this scratch, scratch in my side, like a featherbroom with razors at the top. We hadn't had a murder since the Hebe was found dead. It bothered me. Was the lunatic taking a rest? I listened to that featherbroom in my side and took John's cabbage knife down into the dungeon and chopped off the lock to Leo's closet. The shelves were packed. A hundred papers of needles. A hundred spools of thread. But there were things stuffed behind all this trading stock. Six pairs of bloody boots. Neckerchiefs that the guerrillas loved to wear. A gambler's money pouch. Piles of silver. Jacob's gold watch . . .

I wanted to nail that closet shut and run out to the flatlands behind Mud Creek and become a moonlady that howled and barked and lived on prairie grass, and never see another human face. If I didn't turn wild this minute and hide on the moon, I'd have to go upstairs and meet the boys. Four assassins? Six? Ten was the number. Ten was just right.

I shouldn't have scorned that machine in the shoe box, with its knobs and peephole and metal heel. Jacob understood his colors. Blue was for bears, and for the blood that dried on a leather boot.

I was the rottenest detective.

Who could have gone spooking in the streets but orphan boys familiar as pie? Say howdy, turn their featherbrooms into bats and hit you over the head, walk on you with their fat shoes, pick at your body like scavenger birds, cut away your money belt and clutch whatever souvenirs they liked, put the shoes and all in paper sacks, and get on home in their children's stockings. They couldn't leave orphan's tracks on a tin man. The town would have solved the riddle of tiny heel marks in a skull.

Who saw them stumble around in fat shoes? None of us. Maybe the boys didn't stumble so much.

I picked a boot out of the closet, dug my fist in up to the sole. My elbow was lost in that fat shoe. Then I puzzled it out. They didn't have to traipse in a heavy boot. They held the thing, cuffed you with it, made it into a socking shoe. That's why Jacob couldn't find monster prints in the dust. The monster kicked you all to pieces, but his feet never touched the ground.

I went up out of the cellar, with my fist curled inside the shoe. Alfred, Joseph, Weldon, Timothy, and Valentine were playing cards. Jeremiah and Nicholas were shooting their hats into the ceiling. Gabriel, Charles, and Spencer must have been near the roof. Valentine looked up from the deck of cards. He didn't have to point at the shoe. The others could tell what was in his face. Swollen eyes. A sadness for the mama they'd have to kill.

Nicholas jumped up and freed his hat from a candelabra. Alfred fingered his silver on the stairs. It was Jeremiah who opened his mouth.

"You shouldn't have gone into the closet, Aunt Sally."

"And you shouldn't have murdered so many men."

"Nineteen aint that many."

"And your own grandpa . . ."

Jeremiah could have been pleading over flour and eggs. That's how calm his voice was, with the softest music.

"It was Leo's fault . . . he wouldn't give us any cush."

"He was saving for your education, monster boy."

"Who's a monster?" Jeremiah said, and there was a lick of anger in his voice. Gabriel, Charles, and Spencer could hear that corrosive melody from the roof. They'd come down a floor and stood with the card players. I wasn't their mama at all. They were a family of ten that knew how to sing to themselves, and smell trouble in the simplest turning of a song.

"Grandpa can fiddle with his education . . . and fiddle with your head."

The boys didn't seem in a hurry to mess up the house. I wasn't any tin man. They'd have the devil of a time murdering me. I was Rooster, the fighting chicken. I was Ishmael and Major Sally. I was the Queen of Hearts.

We were like armies on rocking horses. None of the horses would rock. We'd pass the winter that way, on an idle horse.

Jeremiah broke through that idleness. "Auntie, swear you won't peach on us and we'll let you live."

"I'll peach . . . I'll peach to Hickok soon as I can."

I thought they'd go for my neck, but I heard a thick cackle in the house. The boys didn't need horses to rock, they were laughing so hard.

"The blindie man," Nicholas said. "Jerry, look who's gonna chase us!"

"We could have kilt him every Tuesday of the week," Valentine said, and he rolled on the floor, mocking Bill, and made a horrible flutter with his eyes. And then I knew how they got the notion to murder and collect souvenirs and blame it all on the "wolfman." The little sons of bitches had seen one of Bill's attacks.

"Quiet, Val," Jeremiah said. "You're insulting auntie's favorite man. She moos with him in the jailhouse."

Drat those orphans! They followed everybody's business.

I was the cackler now. "I don't need Bill to do my fighting . . . come on. Jeremiah, Nicholas, are you ready?"

I went for the boys with my shoe. It kind of stunned them. They figured me to beg. *Spare me, Gabriel . . . oh please.* But Sally was on the stairs and she cuffed Valentine in the chest with her fat shoe. He dropped down to his pieces of silver. I'd have made him eat his money if I had more time.

"That's for Leo . . . the cruelest murder you ever did."

Valentine was out of the war. He lay with his head on a baluster knob, his tongue rolling in his mouth. He grabbed at his chest as if a rock had bounced on it. That's how I struck with a shoe.

The other nine collected their hats. They rubbed the sharp edges. Nicholas brayed how he'd cut me off at the throat and use my head for Halloween night. He danced on his skinny boots, but he didn't throw the hat. Gabriel smiled. He took Leo's derringers out of his coat, cocked the silver hammers with his thumbs, and aimed both short barrels at Sally's heart. I walked up the stairs. The derringer boy pulled away from me. I grabbed hold of Charles and smacked him on the right side of his face. His cheek blew up. He had a mushroom over his jaw from Aunt Sally. I hit him again. He fell under the stairs, moaning with the memory of my shoe.

"Be still," Jeremiah said. "She aint nothin' but a mad lady. She'll wear herself thin."

A door opened at the front of the house. It wasn't the right season for guests. We were having our winter, and who was disturbing the peace?

"Anybody to home?"

It was Wild Bill. He'd come out of the blue. It wasn't like him to stroll here on his rounds of the city. What had pulled him to the Noah? We didn't have a public kitchen without John the cook. Had William dreamt of gooseberry pie? I had no pies to give him.

The boys stopped backing away from their aunt with the shoe. Seeing Bill had put the fury in them. Auntie was forgotten. Sakes, we didn't even have a proper fight. I did all the socking. The shoe must have waxed their heads. But William woke them out of that strange sleep. "The blindie man." They pushed aside auntie and her shoe and flung their razor hats at Bill.

The hats cut into Bill's arms and legs, but he didn't fall down. He'd come to the Noah with dust on him in the midafternoon. The razors brought him out of his own muddy sleep. "Assassins," he said. "Four and six . . . ." He didn't have to look at that bloody shoe on my hand. He sensed all the murderers we had in the house.

"Off the stairs, chilrun, one at a time."

The darlings wouldn't surrender to Bill. Gabriel had his two pocket guns. Weldon had a Bowie knife. Timothy had a dirk. They flew at Wild Bill, sailing down like bats with terrible wings, headed for Bill's throat. He shot them out of the air. The bat wings exploded with blood and smacked into tables, candelabras, and walls. The ceiling started to drop. We all went white and gray with burnt powder and ceiling dust.

I punched through that gray storm, passing scalps, lips, and eyes. You couldn't see a whole face. The storm cleared. Bill walked from Gabriel to Weldon to Timothy. The boys lay quietly dying in different parts of the floor. I crept over to Tim and put down that awful shoe I was carrying.

"Auntie, my tongue is dry."

I fetched a bowl of water. Tim was gone. His spirit had fled to some orphans' home we'd never heard about. Bill helped me shut Tim's eyes.

Sixteen

I visited a while with Bill. I was scared of ghosts running through the hotel. I didn't want to think of Gabriel dying with Weldon and Tim. The marshal boiled China tea in his old pot. We drank it with rum until our eyes turned red.

Bill waltzed between the curls of flypaper with heavy feet. He wasn't proud of having to shoot at little boys. Journalists from other parts of the country came to William's shack. They wanted to interview the Slayer.

"Wild Bill, tell us how you captured the fiends?"

He emptied the pot of tea on their heads, and the journalists disappeared.

I was no darn journalist, but I had to ask Bill why he'd come to the Noah that particular day.

"I was looking for you, Salome . . ."

"Was it my petticoats you were after?"

The Slayer frowned. "I was worried, is all . . ."

"Didn't you have an inkling about Jeremiah and his gang?"

"No," Bill said. "I wouldn't suspect chilrun to go around stomping people."

"Who did you think the killers were?"

"Pawnees . . . or rattlesnakes."

He'd never be a Pinkerton. But I'd rather have him than any old detective. I lived with Hickok three days. He was gentle and quiet. He slept a lot and sucked on this mouth harp he had. He could only make the saddest music.

"Where did you find those songs?"

"In the caves," he said. "I learned them myself . . . it calmed the bats. They liked my tunes."

We drank coffee and kissed. And I'd wonder about Bill. He just couldn't decide if he wanted a woman in the house. He was like a groundhog that burrowed out of its hole for a little light. But the groundhog had to go under again. Wild Bill. He'd buy me a ticket to Topeka, spend his night with me at the Miriam, and then he was gone.

Why ask more of Bill? He couldn't give what he didn't have. He was a longhair from the plains, a two-gun man.

"Bill," I said, "I think I'll go on home. I'm not frightened now."

He took me back to the hotel. I didn't catch a ghost on the stairs.

"Thank you, Bill, for keeping me . . ."

He touched his hat and marched to the calaboose, where he was holding the boys.

WE HAD seven live orphans to lend the hangman.

The mayor was pleased. He built a tiny zoo for the town. He put the orphans in wire cages and had the cages stacked to the ceiling of the calaboose. Folks arrived from everywhere to look at the Seven Beasts. No one bothered to remember Gabriel, Weldon, and Tim. Dead boys didn't count for much.

Abilene was making money on the orphans.

We had a November jubilee. The mayor charged ten cents a look. Lines stretched from the Alamo to the jailhouse door. The mayor wrote to the cattlemen in K.C. "Sirs, get rid of your goddamn cows. Shoot them, sell them, give the animals away. You're spoiling our jubilee."

The cattlemen never wrote back, and our vigilantes walloped the straying cows with broomsticks and returned them to the stockyards at the east end of town.

The hangman's name was George. He was an expensive son of a bitch. The mayor had to give up a fortune to bring him here. He came with his own pile of hanging ropes, curled up in a dozen baskets. He waxed the ropes morning and night. He sat in the calaboose, waxing rope like he was petting a snake. He had candy for the boys and stories of ferocious criminals that he'd "knotted." I can't tell you why, but it calmed the boys, having him around with his ropes. They grew attached to hangman George.

The mayor didn't have a notion about the job of hanging Alfred, Valentine, Joseph, Spencer, Nicholas, Jeremiah, and Charles. A small gallows couldn't hold seven boys. The hangman had to rescue him. George asked for three carpenters and designed the gallows himself. The scaffolding would be higher than the courthouse. He meant to hang all seven with one pull of the trapdoor.

We listened a whole week to hammers and saws. The gallows rose out of the ground and spread north and south until it occupied most of the mayor's square. Spectators would have to stand right under the gallows during the jubilee.

I prayed the gallows would fall, but that hangman was a master builder. His darn scaffold tree wouldn't shiver once in rain or wind.

"George," I said, "aren't you the least bit ashamed? . . . coming to rope seven orphans."

" 'Taint my business. I don't beggar with the law."

"Then what is your business?"

"Hanging, ma'am. Pure and simple."

"I suppose it's fine with you that judge and jury were the mayor's own men."

" 'Taint much different up in Topeka."

"Then take your business over there."

"I will when the time's ripe. But why are you bellering so much? The boys stomped around and made twenty ghosts."

"Nineteen," I said. "And I have a right to beller. I'm their aunt."

"Pshaw! Seven orphans with a single aunt." And the hangman turned his back on me.

I borrowed John from bandit country and we baked a heap of pies. I delivered them to the calaboose in a handcart. Folks thought I was vending hot pies in the street. Puffs of gooseberry smoke traveled with the cart. Bill had to unscrew every cage to shove the pies in to the boys. Jeremiah bit him on the hand. "If it aint his nibs," Valentine spoke from the chicken wire. "Conquering Bill." But they devoured the pies, gooseberries splashing on their shirts. Bill wrapped his hand in an old neckerchief and walked outside.

"Your big teeth will get you into trouble," I warned Jeremiah.

"Auntie, did you save a pie for George?"

"Hangmen don't get free pies . . ."

"He's our friend. George explains us things . . . a rope can rot if it aint rubbed good. And it can split just like a man."

"You shush!" I didn't want to hear of hangman's rope. That scaffold tree was in my head all night. I had dreams of it growing and growing until it cracked into some angel's hut, and wood rained down over Abilene. It was a sign for the hangman to pack his ropes and ride the hell out of here.

Jeremiah was pondering over a slip of paper, a handbill of the Seven Beasts and their nineteen victims, designed for the jubilee, with skulls for the boys and a coffin under each victim's name.

"Jeremiah, will you put down that trash?"

"It's a tally sheet. Mayor Tom lemme have it . . . what's Doctor Ovenshine doin' on the list?"

"Sakes alive, you socked Henry to pieces with your shoes . . ."

"Auntie, it wasn't us. Wouldn't we remember if we kilt him?"

I took my handcart and wheeled it home. Who murdered Henry if it wasn't the boys? Another set of orphans? Chinaman John?

FAMILIES RODE in to watch the hangman work. George would climb to the top of the scaffold and run across it to test the frame. The hangman had the littlest feet. He wouldn't wear boots on the scaffold. He ran in his stockings to preserve the wood. He had seven ropes in place. He'd shinny down the sidebar to the gallows landing while children clapped. But their mamas and daddies hadn't come from Topeka just for gallows tricks. Any fool can go up and down a pole. They expected more from a hangman.

He opened his baskets and took out seven dummies that were liver than most horses, cows, and men. They were sacks filled with straw, but the son of a bitch had tailored his dummies with hands and feet and clothed them in derbies, pants, and vests. He straightened the derbies, kicked a lever with his toes, and the dummies dropped through the big trapdoor and jibbered on their lengths of rope. George wasn't satisfied. He dove through the trap, riding a dummy to the ground. He pranced under the gallows, going from dummy to dummy and grabbing their legs, pulling as hard as he could. The scaffold held. The roof of the gallows wouldn't sway for the hangman. Nothing twitched but the dummies themselves.

It was cruel. Dummies dressed like orphan boys. George was a crowdpleaser. He worked a hanging for whatever he could get. But this was Abilene, at the prairie's edge. It was moon country. You couldn't predict much from cows and men. He had a sorceress not far from his side. Salome, Queen of Hearts.

I was helpless against George. I couldn't lay that gallows low. The hangman had too much art around him.

He'd get likkered and go to the boys and begin to weep. It wasn't the thought of hanging them that bothered George. It got lonesome carrying his art from town to town. Who wanted to look at a hangman after his work was done? He had to disappear with his ropes.

He strummed on the cages with a finger, whiskey in his mouth.

"Jerry, Nick, Val . . . goddamn, you're the only family a hangman's got."

"You faker," I said. "Building dummies of children you mean to hang."

"Aw, auntie, that's fer the people . . . they're a fickle lot. They don't give a heck about the plumb line of a rope. My ropes don't twirl an inch off target. But they adore the frills and the curlycues. A hangman can't command a salary in such mean times if he don't produce some magic. Hell, I wouldn't throw dirt on the boys."

His bawling got so fierce, Nicholas had to hold George's finger through the wire.

"Aunt Sally," Valentine said, "stop making Georgie cry."

" 'Taint her fault, Val . . . I'll jump in the river if I can't find a new profession."

"Our creek's too shallow," I said.

"Then I'll cut my throat." He took out his braiding knife that he used to mend the ropes. It was a sharp hook with a handle on it. But he didn't plunge it into his hangman's neck. He hopped on the jailhouse floor and slashed holes in the chicken wire. The jailors subdued him, knocked him twice in the head, and the hangman turned sober. He repaired the chicken wire with his braiding knife. He sobbed just as loud.

"Lordy, I'm afraid," he said.

And the boys had to quiet that fool hangman, hum to him from their mended cages. "Georgie, you can't help it what you are . . . God made you a hangman."

The rascal sucked on his whiskey bottle and sniveled some more.

THE TOWN had buglers and fifers and a drummer boy. Ladies brought their picnic baskets. Kites flew over the square. They were like lazy bats leaving shadows on the hangman's carpentered tree. Children ate rock candy on a string. They cracked the hard sugar in their mouths and swallowed the string until you thought you were in the land of goats.

We had thousands at the jubilee.

The mayor didn't know where to put them all. He sent his wise men to comb me up and down with sweet words. They wanted the widow Sally to open her hotel.

"You can say to Tom to soak his head in a barrel of dishwater . . . I'm not putting ghouls up at the Noah."

"Where's a ghoul? We have fine, 'spectable citizens fer the jubilee."

"To cheer when orphan boys swing on a rope . . . if that's not ghoulish, what is?"

"It's the ghouls what murdered your husband, ma'am."

"I'm not so sure. Lord knows where Henry is."

Rooming houses were already filled with local vermin, and the "furriners" from Topeka and Leavenworth had to stay in wagons and tents and the ditch behind the gallows. The furriners hadn't come for kites and rock candy. They grunted and milled about while the Seven Beasts had their last breakfast. Cobbler pie and a little tea.

The hangman took his breakfast with the boys. He wouldn't perform on gallows day. He didn't have to climb the scaffold in stocking feet. The furriners could go to hell. He ate a cobbler with the boys.

"Wash your throats," he said. The hangman knew. Your neck burned more if your mouth was dry. So the orphans threw back their heads and guzzled tea.

The mayor looked in. "What's holding things up?" he roared. "Town's waitin' for the Beasts."

"Let the town wait!" the hangman rasped. "The boys haven't finished their tea."

"You'd think they was having champagne at the 'Frisco Palace . . . this aint a tea party. It's a hanging, George. Hurry up. Tie their hands and gimme the seven rats."

George refused. "I'm in charge on gallows day."

"I'll arrest you, George, and hang the boys myself."

" 'Taint legal. And you couldn't hang a chicken anyhow."

The mayor turned to Bill. "Marshal, arrest that man!"

"He's right, Tom. You'll wreck your jubilee."

"Then hurry him, for pity's sake."

And Tom went out to the furriners. The boys drank more tea. We heard thick screaming from the square.

The hangman punched a jailor.

"Nobody's tying up the boys. They'll walk to the gallows with their hands free."

Hickok wouldn't fend for his jailors. "Listen to George."

The hangman led the boys into the street. He was holding a satin box. Furriners and town folk jeered at him and the Seven Beasts. I walked behind Bill. The cyclops was in the crowd. The orphans had killed his men, robbed them and beaten them with their socking shoes, but he wouldn't jeer at children. He'd have whipped the boys until their backs fell off, and shaved their heads, branded them on the mouth as little murderers, but he wouldn't have had a jubilee.

Charles tripped on a kite string. The hangman told us not to help. "He can stand. Charles aint a cripple."

Charles kicked at the string and got his ankles all wound up. He would have remained a prisoner of the kite, but the hangman grumbled and cut him loose with that sharp hook of his.

The furriners wedged around us to hiss. We were stranded a hundred yards from the gallows. We bumped against their shoulders and fell back upon ourselves. It was like bobbing in a small ocean. I didn't mind the bumps, but that ocean shrank and shrank. We wouldn't need a hanging soon. The furriners were squeezing us to bits.

The hangman had been stuck before. He put the satin box under a shoulder and slashed at the air with his hook. It turned perilous for the furriners' cheeks and eyes. And we got to the gallows with that hook going in the air.

Children hung on the steps, but George flicked them away. No one could mount his gallows but the hangman and his seven boys. The mayor was furious. He couldn't deliver his jubilee talk on the gallows landing.

"You hold to the ground," George said. "You can't come upstairs with us."

"That man's a criminal," the mayor barked in a weak voice.

"He belongs with the insane . . . will ye do something, Wild Bill?"

It was too late to argue with George. He hopped on the gallows and stationed the boys near a particular rope. It was Valentine, Spencer, Charles, with Alfred in the middle. Joseph, Nicholas, and Jeremiah at the end. The orphans got out of their boots and stockings. That's how it was in Abilene. You always hung a man in bare feet.

Tom signaled for some music. The drummer boy was slow. He must have felt a chill. He knocked on his drum with beady eyes. The fifers whistled a death song. The buglers spit. George had no time to listen. He removed seven hoods from his box and slipped them over the boys' heads and then laid on the hangman's knot. He mumbled to the boys. Their lips moved under the hoods. Then he bound their knees and ankles with bandages.

I asked Bill what the "banditches" were for.

"They won't dance on the wire if their knees are tight."

I hated the hangman's art. "Banditches" and hoods. I begged the Lord to bandage up my eyes. He wouldn't do it. George went from boy to boy, purring under the hoods. He wouldn't play to the furriners. He kicked the trap, and the boys dropped through. They weren't plain sacks. They were orphans with spines on them. Six went down perfect, but the seventh rope split. Jeremiah fell to the ground. His head was covered. He didn't have to look at that awful twitching on the gallows tree. The six boys shivered once, twice, like it was a pack of animals invading their bodies and going out again. Their necks dropped to the side and their toes didn't jiggle.

The furriners enjoyed the hangman's mistake. Now they could see another boy twitch. George had to get onto the roof of the gallows and lay a fresh rope for Jeremiah. He gritted and slapped his chest. A rope had never failed him.

While George sat miserable on the roof, the jailors took the dead boys from under the gallows and carted them off, one by one, in a wheelbarrow. The mayor had coffins prepared, rosewood "beauties" polished and rubbed by Tom himself. They stood against the courthouse.

The furriners weren't interested in boys on a wheelbarrow trip. They crowded near Jeremiah and touched the boy who ought to be dead. Bill had to shove them away. I whispered to that hood lying on the ground. "Jeremiah, are you there?"

The hood didn't answer.

The hangman scrambled down to us. He had his hook. "Don't tetch him!"

He picked Jeremiah off the ground.

Jeremiah stuttered in his bandaged ankles and his bare feet. He couldn't grip a thing with his toes. He was like a boy on the moon.

A scratchy voice came from under the hood. "Where are we, George?"

"In Abilene," the hangman said. "With the monkey people."

"And Val?"

"Val's daid."

George climbed up the gallows steps, with Jeremiah making little hops in his "banditches." The hangman knotted him tight and kicked the trapdoor. The rope split again, and Jeremiah landed in the dust at the bottom of the hangman's tree.

Children laughed and laughed, thinking it was a hangman's game. Mothers fed them jelly doughnuts. The furriners were getting bored watching the same boy die. The pastor appeared with his crew of deacons. They hadn't visited the calaboose once.

"That's enough," the pastor warned, with his church collar high on his neck. "Thomas," he told the mayor, "you will not hang a boy three times. No, no, no." He shook his neck and the collar burst. The deacons had to button him closed.

"There has to be something in your Minute Book about the Lord's will working out of a rope."

"That's plum crazy, Pastor Hind. The hangman's a bungler, is all."

"Thomas, you listen . . . the boy Jeremiah won't hang while I can breathe."

He stood guard over Jerry with his walking stick.

"Hickok, arrest the pastor!" mayor Tom squealed.

Bill wasn't the mayor's fool. How can you put a church collar in jail? The deacons would have to come along. They didn't go anywhere without pastor Hind. We'd have a mess of holy people in the caboose.

The hangman jumped in. He knocked the pastor down and snatched Jerry from the deacons. He'd already fixed another noose for Jeremiah. He carried him up the steps. Jeremiah was in a muddle from being "kilt" twice, and twice falling to the ground alive. George wouldn't knot the "kilt" boy so fast. He swung on his rope, testing it with a hangman's full weight. His skinny legs rifled in the air. You had the feeling he was about to hang himself. But then he slipped the noose on Jeremiah. He stayed there talking to the hood.

Tom shouted up at him.

"Hangman, you'll never work Kansas in your life. Ye hear me, George? . . . you're finished. You're the pigs' hangman, is what you are . . . Jesus, will ye do up that murdering boy?"

"I'll do yer fat head," George bellowed from the landing. But he danced away from Jeremiah on his skinny legs, howled at pastor, deacons, mayor, Bill, the furriners, and me, kicked the door, and Jeremiah plunged toes first. He seemed to rise up to the door again as he twitched on the rope. A little tongue of spit showed through the neck of his hood.

The furriners had lost their interest. The hanging went on too long. They'd grown mean now that the novelty was gone. They pinched the drummer boy, broke a fife, cursed Tom and his gallows day, and walked out of the square.

The hangman cut Jerry down from the scaffold with his hook. Jerry plopped onto the pastor's leg.

"He's alive, he's alive," one of the deacons jabbered.

The coroner said, "That's silly." He'd come from his morning nap to check the hangman and find out what was cooking here. He'd show the deacons who was dead. He had to keep jerking the hood to get it off.

Jerry's face was a swollen blue. He'd swallowed half his tongue on the gallows. The cyclops tossed the coroner aside and covered Jerry with his war coat. "If you're planning a resurrection party, come back tomorrow . . . he won't wake up before that. Damn fools, leave the boy alone."

Something gray crept over us. It was George. He stood on the gallows with seven pairs of boots. He could have been an angel or a flying fish. Nobody would have cared. His art was used up. All I could remember was his skinny legs.

I found Bill stumbling along Cedar Street. He wasn't heading for the barns with mooneye. He was in the middle of a long drunk. The fool started hopping with me in the dust.

"I'll marry you one day, missy. Just you wait . . . you have the prettiest eyes."

"What color are they, you whiskey bum?"

"Amber yellow with flakes of green."

He wasn't drunk as all that.

"Hell with the plains . . . we'll go to the high country."

"And what will we do there, Mr. Bill?"

"We'll plant potatoes in the rocks and nibble on the skins."

"I didn't know you were a farmer . . ."

"I aint. But I'd rather eat potatoes than be a sheriff . . . where's George?"

"At the Noah."

"Tell him we ought to switch professions . . . there's a few in town I'd like to hang if I had George's ropes."

He hiccupped, finished his dance, and stumbled down the street. It was no use chasing after him. If he had one more pull of whiskey, he might forget the color of my eyes. I went on home to George.

The hangman stayed with me. He wouldn't go out of Abilene. I let him have the whole top floor to himself. Telegraph boys arrived from the railroad station with messages for the hangman. Some mayor was offering him work. The messages began to pile up. All of Kansas could have heard about the frailty of his waxed ropes, and it wouldn't have mattered one bean. No other hangman but hangman George had a satin box and big tailored dummy dolls. But he wouldn't go to work. He drank whiskey from the Alamo and lived on my top floor. He'd given up waxing ropes. He climbed the stairs, blew his nose, and didn't seek the company of women or men.

I pitied George, having only that art of hanging people. He wasn't much good for anything else. Hangmen shouldn't take holidays. He was like an infant without his rope.

"George, there's a circus in town . . . we could pay it a visit."

"Whose circus is that?"

"Mrs. Lake's."

I read to George from the handbill. "Mrs. Agnes Lake, danseuse, tightrope walker, and daredevil of world renown, will bring her Hippo-Olympiad and Menagerie to Abilene, beginning the thirtieth of November. This noted artiste has played before emperors and kings. She will give twelve performances of the tragic 'Mazeppa,' during which she is strapped to a wild horse and rides up a special mountain constructed for her at the Alamo Saloon."

The hangman laughed into his whiskey bottle.

"Mountains in a saloon . . . that'll be jolly."

"You are an ignoramus, George. Everybody knows of Lord Byron's 'Mazeppa.' "

"Who's Lordy Byron?"

"The English poet with a clubfoot. He died in the ocean, swimming to save the Greeks."

"No wonder. A cripplefoot can't swim. And what's this 'Mazeppa' about?"

"Hangman, don't you have a morsel of history in your blood? Mazeppa was a Mongol prince. He married a Russian girl. And the Mongols decided to punish him. They banditched Mazeppa to a horse and sent him into the mountains to starve."

"That is tragical," the hangman said, closing his whiskey eyes. "But who's playing the prince?"

"Madam Lake, of course."

"Then let's go to the circus."

The hangman combed his hair and we got in line for tickets. "Mazeppa" was sold out. You had to scream and fight if you wanted to catch Madam at the Alamo. The ticket people wouldn't meddle with a hangman and his hook. They found a place for us in the saloon. We sat against the wall. Half of Abilene was sitting close to our laps.

The Alamo did have a mountain on her stage, and the mountain went up to the roof. Different crags and teeth had been sawed into the wood. It had snow painted on it and Mongolian bushes and trees. The hangman couldn't help but locate this mountain according to his art. "Miss Sally, you could knot twenty men on that piece of furniture . . ."

But then he thought of his own gallows tree and Jeremiah, and he hunched deeper into the wall, trying to make his body disappear. He wouldn't even whisper to me.

We waited for "Mazeppa" to begin.

The actors were having an evil time. The curtain had a wooden pole on the bottom, and it took three men to shove the damn thing up and down. A tragedian got socked in the head, and he was out of service for the night. The other tragedians squawked and danced with one eye on the pole. Nobody listened. Mazeppa wasn't in the first act. Just Mongols with long beards. The stage men pulled on their ropes, and the curtain crashed to the floor. We could hear the mountain shake. People were sick of Mongols. They hollered, "Mazeppa, come on out!"

The curtain rose up with a great rumble of noise.

We had Mazeppa now, the Mongol tribesmen, and Mazeppa's Russian wife. The wife was played by a boy in a wig. It was troublesome, because he was prettier than most of the wives in town. And Mazeppa made a lovely man. Madam had her hair bunched under a Mongolian hat. She wore boots and colored scarfs. The Mongol chief pointed at her in a tremendous rage. "Prince Mazeppa, you have married this harlot behind our back. She is a Rooshun slut, and you will suffer for it."

The tribesman brought a pony out, and Mazeppa was lashed to the pony with ribbons, belts, and scarfs. The Rooshin wife blubbered. The tribesmen beat her with sticks. "Slut, slut, slut."

They finished with her soon as the curtain started to creak. The tribesman wanted to run. Mazeppa frowned at them from the pony's back.

People were disgusted with tragedians from a circus. They tossed a mess of sunflower seeds onto the stage. The seeds upset the pony. The Rooshun wife had to stroke his neck, and the pony began his climb. His hoofs clopped on the mountain. The audience ran out of seeds and had nothing left to throw. But they turned quiet as the clopping brought Mazeppa up the mountain crags. Women swooned. The pony looked like he was going to smash his feet and sail into the audience with Mazeppa.

The hangman suddenly spoke. "If that aint the cleverest little horse!"

Crags were flying off the mountain. The pony broke more and

more wooden teeth. The mountain shivered. It was so steep near the top, that pony could have been riding up a wall. Mazeppa's ribbons and scarfs were loose, and she slid down to the pony's tail. The hangman clutched my hand. "Lordy, she's gonna die . . ." Husbands were swooning with their wives. I didn't scare so easy. I could smell a sorceress. Mazeppa was singing to the pony in the softest voice. The pony got her to the roof.

"Prince Mazeppa, don't you hurt yourself," the audience crooned.

She wiggled up the tail like a swimming dog and reached the pony's neck. We clapped in a fury over Mazeppa.

No one bothered with the tragedians at the bottom of the mountain. They had slivers of wood on their Mongolian capes. They'd have to repair the mountain right after the prince and her pony descended from the roof, or you wouldn't have a mountain for tomorrow.

A husband woke out of his swoon. "Will ye marry me, Mazeppa darlin'?"

Mazeppa waved to him with one of her "banditches." It was a green and yellow scarf.

WE FELL into a kind of sloth with Mazeppa in town, watching the pony night after night. The tragedians canceled the first act. The tribesmen took themselves off the stage, and you had Mazeppa, the little horse, and the Rooshun wife. The pony was a circus animal named Emperor Charles. Madam would ride him bareback in the afternoon, sit down with a family of tigers in her circus tent, and walk above Mulberry Street on a long clothesline. But these were only advertisements for "Mazeppa," ticklers, I'd say. And ticklers weren't necessary. We'd hooked ourselves to the Mongol prince.

Madam was supposed to play in Topeka, but she didn't move

on with her circus after the twelfth night. She abandoned her other engagements to live with us, and I had to wonder why. Abilene wasn't big enough to hold a perpetual circus. I stopped guessing so hard after Mazeppa stuck all the tigers in her tent behind the calaboose. Madam was in love with Bill.

She'd sulk on that clothesline of hers. She barely could sing to the horse. She fell off the pony in the middle of her circus act and had to wear a sling on her arm. She'd still do "Mazeppa" at night. She'd ride up the mountain in her sling, while the audience went crazy with fear. She wouldn't purr to Emperor Charles. She'd lie stretched out in her "banditches," like somebody's sick cow, with pale sockets in her head. But George was right about the pony. He was the cleverest thing. He'd go on up the mountain, kicking teeth, and he wouldn't let Mazeppa spill. Even the pony was sorry for her.

How did she get so stuck on Bill? She must have read about him in the Ten-Cent Romance. Is that why she stopped in Abilene? To meet the Slayer? She wouldn't have been disappointed by a little dust. Did she have hopes of marrying William, and leading him to Cincinnati, where her people were? I knew Bill. He'd gamble his last shirt away before he'd retire to a tentful of tigers in Cincinnati or anyplace else. But it troubled me. Mazeppa was the darling of the West. She'd had lambchops and ale with the biggest kings in Europe. Her Mammoth Circus had gone to Berlin. And she gave us "Mazeppa" every night with her arm in a sling.

I was just a widow with a piecemeal education. I didn't wear tights on a clothesline. I couldn't sing to a horse and do daredevil tricks. I could only watch over Bill when his eyes went bad.

He wasn't Wild Bill of the Barns this December. His attacks must have let up a little. I couldn't find him at his house. I had to visit him at the calaboose. I heard the tigers meowing from their tent.

"You have lots of company, Bill. A family of tigers and an acrobat . . . people say Mazeppa's out to marry you."

Bill tugged on his goatee. "When the lady's done with Kansas, she'll go East to Cincinnati. I don't want any paper collars on. I'd be lost back in the States. Have to trim my whiskers and get into a goddamn cravat. I'd choke to death."

That William. He wouldn't remember the cravat he wore at the Miriam Hotel. He had a tune for every occasion. Mazeppa or her tigers didn't stop him from kissing me. The ladykiller wouldn't seek you out. But if you stood near his door, he'd be searching under your petticoats in a while. What was that coolness of his? Was Bill a little scared of the ladies that he "kilt?"

"Don't you love me, Bill?"

He could have been a China mask with blue porcelain eyes. His smile didn't tell you a thing. Was he punishing me for the weeks I had with Tris?

"Like you, like you a whole lot, but I aint much on lovin' people."

"I know . . . you prefer tigers and acrobats."

"Who says? I'm a drifter, is all."

Yes, he'd drift in and out of your life, like some ghost ship hiding off Galveston, covered with sargasso weeds. He'd love you the best way he could. You'd catch him one year, lose him the next. He had his mouth harp and his Navy guns. What else did he need? He was a widower now. With no Black Nell.

He put on his hat and borrowed a dollar. The Slayer was short of cash.

"Been having dreams," he said. "About the chilrun."

"So have I, Bill. The awfulest dreams. With Jerry biting my nose . . . like Rooster, the Hebe's warrior chicken."

"Maybe the boys needed hanging, but I shouldn't have helped Tom with his jubilee."

"You're the marshal. You have to follow what's inside the Minute Book."

"That son of a bitch fills up the pages to suit himself."

"Tom's justice is as good as most. He doesn't murder or steal."

Bill went on to the Alamo.

The hangman was inside the house. He must have found his art somewhere on the top floor. He didn't creep near the roof. He was waxing his ropes in the dining room. It was a hangman's way of telling me good-bye.

"What do I owe ye, Miss Sally?"

"Not a dime. It was my pleasure, George. I liked having you here. But I can't say I'm fond of your profession."

"It's all I know. My pa apprenticed me to a hangman when I was little. I been roping people these thirty years. I get double what any hangman gets. Oh, I run off and likker for a spell, and then I go back on the circuit . . . like a judge."

The rascal kissed my mouth and gave me a hug that was near indecent, and he packed his ropes and his dummies and he was gone.

I'd gotten used to his skinny legs. I liked his silences in the house. And the putter of his feet. Maybe he'll do his likkering at the Noah next year. I could live with a hangman on the top floor. But I don't think he'll come. George wouldn't "play" Abilene a second time. It's unlucky for a hangman to follow himself. Ropes have memories . . . just like a man.

The artiste came to the house. She was wearing her sling, but she didn't have her Mongol hat. Mazeppa was Madam Lake this afternoon. You could have hid tents and tigers underneath the hoops in her skirt. She had lots of gray in her hair. Lord, she was older than Bill! But she was kind of pretty for a grandma.

"Are you the Queen of Hearts?"

"Yes'm."

"I'm Agnes Lake. The Hippo-Olympiad belongs to me."

"Madam Lake, you're the best Mazeppa in the whole darn world."

"Thank you, child."

Who's a child? I was twenty-four. A widow with a live husband sneaking around. I'll wax his ears when I find him.

"Are you a white woman?" Madam asked.

"Yes'm."

"I'm shopping for a witch, but I wouldn't go to a half blood. I am not very fond of Indians."

"I'm from Galveston. I don't have an ounce of Indian blood."

"I'm told seven murderous orphans widowed you. That's a shame. I'm a widow. My late husband was Mr. Thatcher, the circus entrepreneur. Did you ever hear of Thatcher's Olympiad and Animal Park? That was a while ago . . . before Mr. Lincoln was shot. I played for Mr. Lincoln at the Hippodrome. He was such a kindly man. He visited with me backstage. He was fearsome tired, having to fire his generals every other week. It was the rebellion that killed him, not that awful John Wilkes Booth. Seeing his nation split . . . pardon me. You are a daughter of the South."

How many other Black Republicans did she have in her circus itinerary? Couldn't she shut up and be Mazeppa for a while? She was fine, long as she was on a mountain.

"I'll need a special favor, child . . . one of your brews."

"Is it for palpitations, ma'am? Or lumbago? Is something the matter with Emperor Charles?"

"No," Madam said. "I want a love potion."

I wasn't that good a witch. Hickok could swallow the strongest tar, tobacco, and tea, and he still wouldn't marry Mazeppa. Let her choose another darling, and maybe I'd help the acrobat.

She took out a tiny handkerchief and touched the corners of her eyes.

"It's hopeless," she said. "You're a woman, child. You understand the fickleness of men . . . I met an Army scout during the late rebellion. I won't lie. We had what you might call an attachment."

"A what, ma'am?"

"A liaison . . . we were practically engaged. It was wartime, and understandings between men and women didn't mean that much. But he broke his promise to me . . . he swore he'd come to my circus after the fighting was over, and he never did."

"Who is that critter?" I asked, with an anger in my heart.

"Oh, I couldn't say, child. It might be libelous for him. But he's here in Abilene. And if you could mix me up a love potion, I'd be more than grateful to you . . . I'm offering twenty dollars to the witch that bends that fickle man over to my side."

Mazeppa could keep her twenty dollars. I'd brew a pot of arsenic for Wild Bill, and present him with the loudest bellyache he ever had. Then he could romance the tigers in grandma's tent. Poor Indian Lorraine. She'd had a "husband" whose nose went everywhere. But I wouldn't poison Bill. I put China tea and ketchup in a pickle jar and gave it to the acrobat.

"Try that on your Army scout. It'll bend him quick. It's the meanest potion in America."

She left with the pickle jar under her sling.

I walked the town, boiling with a fever against Bill. I should have asked Mazeppa how many valentines she got.

Tigers padded in the skunk grass near Mazeppa's tent. They were so skillful, they could hunt without ripping up the grass. A weasel hissed at them, and the tigers ran back to their tent.

People were tiring of ponies on a mountaintop. They wanted a saloon with less wooden teeth. They couldn't snort whiskey and gamble after eight o'clock, when the tragedians arrived with the prince and Emperor Charles. The lamps were turned out. The tragedians wouldn't play under gas light. "Mazeppa" required torches in the dark. The tragedy would be ruined if you didn't have the proper streaks on Madam and her pony. It took a quarter hour for the curtain to move, and sometimes Madam didn't get off her mountaintop until near midnight. Charles had to dawdle at every crag to do the tragedy right. People snored while the pony slapped on wood. They were wishing to themselves that Mazeppa would have a great spill. That was a tragedy worth talking about.

Madam climbed. The pony clopped. They went under and out of the torch light. Mazeppa's "banditches" put zebra stripes on Emperor Charles. Folks tittered and scratched.

I looked at her face under the next lick of the torch. It troubled me. Her mouth curled into itself until she had a mummy's lips. Her eyes swam in her head. She didn't see mountain, roof, or Charles' ears. Drat the Queen of Hearts! Mazeppa tried the potion, and it didn't work. That old suitor, Wild Bill, wouldn't go under the tent with her. I shouldn't have tricked Mazeppa with ketchup and China tea. I had a suspicion she'd do us a tragedy that even Abilene could admire.

It wasn't the upclimb I was afraid of. A tragedian wouldn't bungle the first part of her act. It was the downclimb. Tigers couldn't console her. The downclimb was perfect for a jump.

But we didn't have a downclimb. Madam arrived at the top, and that horse wouldn't stir from the mountain. He stood like a sergeant on the highest crag. People could only think to yawn. Soon we had a general stamping of feet, and then a hollering that grew murderous loud. Mazeppa would vanish and come back to us in that uneven light.

A fury ripped through the Alamo. People wouldn't consider leaving until Mazeppa finished the show.

"Ye hear me, Mazeppa, get off that stupid hill!"

They called her a whore and a circus hag with sissy tigers. They said the awfulest things about Emperor Charles, that he was an "unnatural horse," a wife to Mazeppa and a husband to the tigers.

"Marshal, arrest the horse. Criminals like him shouldn't run free . . . it's a disgrace to the womenfolk."

Bill was there, but he wouldn't listen to that mob. Angry men climbed the stage and chopped at the mountain with their heels. Wood began to splinter off, and the mountain swayed a little, but you couldn't get the pony to budge.

Women shrieked. "Oh, Mazeppa, oh honey . . . please come down." They were painted ladies from the Alamo.

Bill hurled the angry men into the audience. Then he started up the mountain for Mazeppa. He didn't have that pony's sense of things. His boots stuttered on the crags. He tripped and had to hold the mountain with both hands. That fool marshal would break his neck.

His hands were bloody from the cracks in the wood.

You saw his hat, a bit of shirt, and no more Bill. The mountain rained a little dust, a crag broke off and fell on a tragedian, throwing him into the pit, and then Bill tunneled up out of the dark. He took the wrong turn, and you could watch his hat descend the mountain. Hickok was lost on that Mongolian hill. People howled at the marshal's blunder.

"William, find any gold up there? Send us a picture card from Alasky."

His hat was on the rise again. He hopped from crag to crag. He was getting smaller by the minute. But the mountain couldn't swallow Bill. He'd travel behind a tooth, invisible for a while, and then a hand would reach out, and it was William at the top. He tore Mazeppa's "banditches," picked her off the pony's back, and carried her in one arm, like a papa bear holding a toy. The tragedians' fire lit his moustache and whatever hollows he had left in his cheeks. Mazeppa clung to Bill. She purred to Charles and he started the climb down. Bill didn't have to touch a crag. He

had his guide. He held Mazeppa and followed the horse's clopping in the dark.

A CLOWN yelled in my window. *Hey, hey, Sally the witch!* When
I got downstairs I discovered twenty dollars in a nose rag outside
my door. The clown laughed and I threw the nose rag at him.
"Tell your missy I haven't earned my fee . . ."

The clown stood on his head. He was still laughing.

"What's so funny?"

"Mama says you are the most worthwhile witch."

"I haven't done a thing. William climbed a mountain, is all."

The clown kicked his legs out and stood up again.

"Mama says it was your potion that got to Wild Bill."

"Fiddlesticks! Bill won't leave this town. He hates the thought
of Cincinnati."

"Mama'll feed him more of the brew."

"It's ketchup and tea in a pickle jar."

"Don't matter," the clown said, "long as it works."

"Are you deaf? Hickok's drinking plain old tea."

"Tea's powerful if'n it comes from a witch."

He sure was a nervy clown.

"Go on, take the twenty dollars back to your missy. The Queen
of Hearts is closing shop."

He reached into his clown suit and wagged the pickle jar at me.
"Mama wants a refill."

I took the jar out of his hand and smashed it against the side
of the house. Never heard such an explosion in my life.

The clown looked at the smashed jar and had the boldness to
weep and twitch on my lawn. "Mama's gonna kill me now."

I didn't need a clown on my conscience. I had enough hurt.
"Stop that bawling."

I found me a pickle jar and brewed Mazeppa another dose of tea. The clown stood on his head with joy. You could mash your brains living like that. The clown didn't care. He bumped over the lawn. He could have been a giant Easter egg, or a land turtle. Mazeppa raised some curious men and beasts at the circus. Tragedians that ate and slept in Mongol clothes. Tigers that were afraid of anything that moved. Clowns that didn't bother walking with their feet.

Now Mazeppa had my magic tea.

She didn't have to tempt Bill with it. The marshal lost his place in town. He had a rumpus with Tom. The mayor called a meeting to write up the next year in his Minute Book. "No more cows," he said.

> Mayor Tom McFarlen begs all men who had contemplated driving Texas cattle to Abilene the coming season, to seek some other point for shipment, as McFarlen and his officers will no longer submit to the evils of that trade. Cattle and cattle boys are not welcome in Abilene.

He told Bill to begin slaughtering every cow in the stockyards.

"I helped ye slaughter seven boys," Bill said. "That's the last goddamn slaughter you'll get from me."

"You're good at rescuing circus sluts, I suppose. Wild Bill Hickok, will you or will you not commence slaughtering cows?"

Bill threw Tom over the meeting table. The wise men hid behind their own chairs. Tom sat still for half an hour, then he crawled away from the room, woke the judge, and had a warrant prepared for the "search, seizure, and arrest of Mr. Hickok."

"But we'll need a marshal to arrest a marshal," the wise men crowed.

"Don't you worry," Tom said. "I can wear two hats." And he swore himself in as marshal of Abilene. Tom collected his vigilantes and went for Mr. Hickok. He was too late. Bill sneaked out of Abilene with the tigers and all. Was it the tea that got him to revolt against Tom? How'll I know? Bill joined grandma's circus without saying good-bye to the Queen of Hearts.

I was the fool.

Bill grew fond of that grandma again while he was rescuing her from the mountain. It was just like Bill to do his courting on mountain crags. Did she smile at him from the roof of the Alamo? Love potions be damned! Mazeppa winked at her old Army scout. And the scout winked right back.

Seventeen

I BROUGHT Rooster into the house. The chicken had gone bald in captivity. I took him back from the farmer who was supposed to feed him. That rotten man had let the bird starve. I yelled at farmer Gwynne. "I put Rooster in your boardinghouse, and all he did was swallow dust."

"Hell with that bird, and hell with you. He's dying on his feet."

"Then you can return the boarding money I gave you."

"No returns," the farmer said. "I did surgery on your chicken. Spent two afternoons pasting up his beak. He has more cracks in him than a target box."

"You'll hear from my lawyer, sir."

Gwynne went for his shotgun, and I got out with the bird.

I fed him barley soup, and he began to develop a winter coat. Feathers grew in around his neck. He pushed through the house with his one good eye. He was the only companion I had in the world. I was down to taking my meals with a chicken.

"Would you like a drop of honey on your bean pie?"

He cockled out a little song and raised his comb. Then he dug his beak into the food.

Give him a month, and he'll learn me table manners. But how long can you gossip with a one-eyed bird? Rooster didn't know the boys or the hangman who'd lived in this house.

"Sure is lonely around here . . ."

And he answered with a shake of his neck.

That's when the stairs turned into a gallows tree, and I found the boys hanging from the top floor. Nicholas, Jeremiah, Joseph, Valentine, Alfred, Spencer, and Charles, their necks twisting to the hangman's ropes, their tongues long in their mouths, their faces pinched and black, with no hood to cover the gruesome work.

I scolded the boys. "Haunt me all you like . . . see if you'll get me to cry!"

But I couldn't help blubbering. Being a widowlady was the least of it. I'll catch Lyle-Henry and give him a slap with the broom. He won't forget his wife . . . I was a witch without luck. Having different families, and losing them each time. Tristram. The trader. Archie. George. Traugott, the Pinkerton man. The boys and Wild Bill. If the chicken left me, I'd have nothing but orphans with broken necks around the house, up from the devil to eat hollow spaces into my heart. You couldn't go and talk to Nicholas. He was with Beelzebub now. That was his dummy on the hotel's mizzenmast. I wish we had a flood, and the Noah could sail onto the prairie and leave this land of cows and bitter men. Rooster would protect me if wild Indians attacked. You could paste his beak a dozen times over. He was still a fighting bird. He'd peck an enemy to pieces.

I sprinkled mouse droppings under the mizzenmast. I put flies' tails next to the dummies' toes. I picked a worm out of the cabbage leaves and painted him red. Nothing happened. I gave the darn house to the ghouls, told the chicken to mind the silver and all, and took a stroll. I'd pass a barn and think of Bill. I missed nursing that Slayer, rocking him on a dusty floor until the milk went out of his eyes. Darlin' Bill. He left me for an acrobat. Shush! All he ever did was collect ladyfriends and fiancées, and give out hundreds of valentines. My "late" husband wasn't the only scribbler. I'd do an inventory for William, month by month.

VALENTINES DELIVERED, 1860–1871

November	....	80
December	....	51
January	....	26
February	....	3
March	....	17
April	....	97
May	....	135

Bill got his ardor up as the summer came along.

June	....	211
July	....	422

I couldn't finish. I wasn't his tallyman. I hoped the tigers had a jealous fit and chewed off his tongue.

I arrived at the edge of town, where the stockyards were. The cows had long sickly faces. No one tended to them. They had to graze on patches of dead grass. Their mouths were black from eating so much dirt. Some of their noses had begun to peel. They were skeletons in loose bags of skin.

I climbed over the wood gate to be with the cows. Their hoofs seemed soft as jelly. It must have hurt the cows to take a step on those jelly hoofs. They'd never reach Chicago. Tom had built a graveyard for them in Abilene.

I rubbed against their prickly hides. It startled the cows, feeling a woman's body and all. They gathered up their skeletons to give a push. I was thrown from cow to cow. But they didn't try to trample the witch. The cows had a nicer game than that. They shoved closer and closer until I was left without an inch. The skeletons could squeeze me into a pound or two of bone dust. I didn't cry murder. I'd make my boneyard with the cows.

Bubbly air whipped from their mouths. They blew the devil's own heat in my face. It was like a baker's oven, living between the cows. I had a fiery wax in my ears. My lungs couldn't suck for anything in that rotten furnace. But a fist came down on one of their noses. Blood shot out. That fist whacked again and again. The cow was horrified. She stood there blinking, with her nostrils ripped apart, and crashed into the lady behind her. Something was at my collar and the rump of my skirt. Rude hands. I'd felt them many a time. In my own bed. He had a sombrero over his eyes, but you can't fool me. My husband had arisen. It was Lyle-Henry. He tossed me over the gate. I landed with my petticoats in my mouth.

"You're a bully and a coward, Lyle . . . making a false widow out of your wife. Are you going to die again in the creek . . . or will you pick a new place?"

I said all that with the sombrero swimming over me, and then I closed my eyes and fainted in the grass.

Rooster woke me with a gentle caw. I was in my nightgown at the Noah, under a quilt. Rooster was on my bed. He strutted south to the footboard. That chicken had the strangest feet. The webbing touched on the quilt and sank down like it was a child's hand sitting on my leg.

Somebody was cussing him. "Scoot on out of here, you goddamn crow." I recognized the little general, Nicaragua Smith.

"That's not a crow, general. It's my bantam chicken. He was once the best fighting bird in town."

"Sure. When Richard the Lion Heart visited Kansas on his Ninth Crusade. Daughter, that crow is fairly ancient."

"General, who let you into this house?"

"Never you mind." And he fed me beef tea out of his own guerrilla cup.

"Where's the Chicken Heart?"

"Who's that?"

"My husband, the resurrectionist."

"He's with us."

"Oh, he switched costumes with one of your dead guerrillas and now he's just another tin man."

"Don't be unkind," the cyclops muttered. "The Pinkertons are after him. He has to stay underground."

"Couldn't he have sent me a message, so I could stop mourning him?"

"I told him not to. You can't make exceptions when you're dead."

So the dead man with the sombrero hat saved me from Beelzebub and his herd of sickly cattle, and now I had the cyclops for a nanny. I was doing fine.

"Sakes, general, will you at least thank the dead man for me?"

The general was huffy about it. "Daughter, Lyle doesn't exist."

"Well, did he have a christening at your camp? What name is he carrying?"

"The Nacogdoches Kid."

I laughed in bed. "Why Nacogdoches?"

"He wanted a Texian name."

"He's no more a Texian than Wild Bill."

"There's no harm in it. He was fond of Galveston, where he had his college and lived in your father's house."

"And learned me dribble, so that I'll always be an ignorant girl."

"What's ignorant about you? You're a manageress here. You have the Noah."

"A windy barn without paying customers. And a chicken to guard over me."

"That's a crow," the cyclops said, looking at Rooster one more time.

I wouldn't argue with a guerrilla chief. "Is Nacogdoches replacing Archibald? Are you turning my husband into a two-gun man?"

The cyclops went sad in the shoulders. He shriveled up in my room. If I waited long enough he'd go to Rooster's size, and I'd have two birds in the hotel.

"I'm to blame, miss Sally. I should have discouraged Archibald. But I wanted to winter in Abilene, and I figured the marshal would do us bad."

"So you gave him a boy who learned to shoot with a wooden gun."

"He was lightning, I tell you. The black Wild Bill. And I'd heard Hickok was going spotty in the eyes. I didn't say that to Arch. Because he wouldn't put the drop on a blind man . . . I was sure he'd kill the marshal. He had the faster pull. But something must have been irritating him. He was a touch slow that afternoon."

I'm the murderer. _I_ told Arch about Bill's mooneye.

"Daughter, why are you sniffling into your soup? You won't find much nourishment in tears."

"General, I'm just salting the beef tea."

The cyclops blew his nose.

"Be back tomorrow," he said. But it didn't work out that way. The bandits lost their roost in Mud Creek. Now that Tom was his own marshal, he decided to rid Abilene of that old warlord,

Nicaragua Smith. He didn't strike with his vigilantes. He could have hurt himself, and there'd be nobody to put down Abilene's future in the Minute Book. It would have been a blow to Tom. A town with blank pages. We might as well perish and rot. He telegraphed Fort Hays and told where the guerrillas were.

The horse soldiers arrived, white and black troopers of the Seventh Cavalry. Where were Tristram's dogs? I didn't see a sled bump into town. A colonel sat with his troopers in a long pony line. He wore a cape and a soft blue hat. But he wasn't Tristram Shirley.

The troopers got ready for their surprise attack. The colonel and his two majors had a little drinking party with Tom. Then they rode across the tracks with the clatter of swords and guns. The tin men shot them off their ponies. The Cavalry scampered to our side of the tracks. Half the ponies were missing, and the two majors were dead.

The cyclops rolled up his blankets, collected saucers and spoons, packed each guerrilla on a horse, and let the prairie swallow him.

I scoured the creek for wounded men. Lord knows, one of them might be Nacogdoches. But the cyclops didn't leave any wounded behind. He disappeared without a hint of blood. It was the Cavalry that lay groaning. Tom had to lend the courthouse to the soldiers as a little hospital. I became a courthouse nurse. I didn't love the Cavalry all that much. But I was good with bandages. And it was a shame to watch men die and not do a thing. The surgeon was a lout. He cut men to pieces and sewed them with a crooked stitch. He chomped on a cigar in the middle of his surgery, and left ashes in the wounds that he closed. He'd come to us without morphine in his surgical kit. Soldiers screamed to death. I gave them tea and honey and held their hands. The surgeon's stitching needles were filthy as his tunic. I ran to the colonel, who was convalescing in the mayor's room. He had a "banditch" on his head. His name was Ibbetson. He must have been new at the fort.

"That surgeon you have is the worst sort of butcher."

"It's no secret," Ibbetson said, snorting from a whiskey bottle under the mayor's personal sofa.

"Well, why don't you take him out and shoot him? It might save a couple of lives."

"You can't go into the field without a surgeon. The Army wouldn't have it."

"Then give up your whiskey . . . men are dying downstairs."

The colonel apologized. "Didn't mean to be selfish, ma'am."

I fed whiskey to the dying in little tin cups. The surgeon put his hand on my backside. "Meet me in an hour, will ye, honey girl?"

I socked him with a tin cup. He sent two corporals after me. The corporals marched me up to Ibbetson with bayonets.

"Punching an officer, ma'am. That's a hanging offense."

"Well, hang me then."

Ibbetson smiled with that banditch on his head.

"You're too valuable to hang in wartime . . . I'd make the peace if I could grab hold of the guerrilla general. Who is that man?"

"Nicaragua Smith."

"Didn't he take Galveston from us with two cannons and a cotton boat?"

"Colonel, he took whole empires. But he's kind of old. And he's gone into banditry . . . where's General Tris?"

The colonel stroked his moustache.

". . . Did you happen to notice a sled lying around, and a pair of beautiful huskies?"

The colonel let his moustache go and looked up at me. "We had to shoot the dogs, ma'am. They were miserable without Mr. Shirley. You must be Mrs. Ovenshine. Tristram never stopped talking about you."

"Colonel, will you tell me where he is?"

"It's hush-hush. The Army's housing him at Fort Leavenworth. They don't know what else to do with a general who strangled his wife. They didn't dare call a tribunal. It could have ruined the Army. Notes kept coming from the Secretary of War. It was unthinkable. They just wouldn't countenance it, ma'am. You *can't* have a general murdering his wife . . ."

I couldn't listen any more.

"What about the girls?"

"They're with an uncle in Ohio . . . I don't understand it. Tris wasn't the violent sort. Something broke in him . . ."

Ibbetson saw me reach behind my back. I was undoing the ribbons to my nurse's apron. "Where are you going, ma'am?"

"Fort Leavenworth."

He leapt up from the sofa.

"Are you a crazy woman? They won't let you in. And if you mention me to them, I'll deny we ever spoke."

"I wouldn't betray you, colonel. You know me."

"Mrs. Ovenshine, I don't know you at all."

I GATHERED up Rooster and that old workhorse, Ish, and we set out for Leavenworth in Henry's wagon.

When we got to the fort, the guard wouldn't let our wagon through.

"State your business. Are ye merchandising?"

"No. I'm looking for General Tris."

He waved a booklet at me. "I have the fort roster, and there aint no General Tris."

"He's in the dungeon," I said.

The guard was angry. "We don't put generals in the sink. Will ye get out of here?"

"I'm not moving until I see Tristram Shirley."

He hollered to another guard. And that guard hollered to a
third. A lieutenant from the provost marshal's office arrived at the
gate.

"Ma'am, we have no Tristram Shirleys. I promise you."

"What did I tell ye?" the first guard said.

"Liars! Shall I go and write the Secretary of War?"

The lieutenant took me to the provost marshal. They sat me
in a chair. "What country's employing you? Are you a foreign
agent, stirring up Indian trouble? Who sent you to our fort? We'll
put you in irons, you goddamn witch."

"I'm a second cousin to Ulysses S. Grant. My daddy plays poker
with the president . . . hang it all, I'm Salome Ovenshine of
Galveston, Abilene, and Fort Hays."

The two of them whispered like old wives. "Damn it," the
provost marshal said. "This is highly irregular."

"She'll be a nuisance, sir," the other one said.

"Suppose it leaks out that Shirley's living with us, a *strangler*
and he's not even in the stockade."

"It won't leak, sir. She wouldn't want to hurt that no-account
general."

"You're responsible, Fischer. I wash my hands of it. Far as I'm
concerned, this woman isn't here. What in thunder do they
expect from us? . . . hiding generals, behaving like cutthroats and
mercenaries. Let them throw bricks around us, so we can all be
secret men . . ."

"It's an insignificant detail, sir. Nothing. A visitor for the man
in compound nine. She can pose as a washerwoman."

I'll wash their heads, cackling bluebellies. The provost marshal
squinted at me. "You are never, never to give your right name
while you're with us."

"You can call me Diana of the moon if you like."

"Don't be impertinent," the lieutenant said. He brought me
down from the provost's rooms, and we went across different

yards until my feet ached with weariness. Into one building and out the next, through corridors and latrines, where I had to close my eyes, because bluebellies were squatting on the pit. They laughed at the washerwoman, and we still weren't finished with that hike. It was a barracksland that wouldn't end, only these barracks weren't filled with soldier boys. They were damp and frozen dead. It must have been a part of the fort that was up for sale. But it didn't look like many buyers were around. I had the spooks in this vacant Army village. Chimneys that didn't smoke. A mile of buildings without a face.

We stopped in front of a long barn. The lieutenant knocked, and a shutter opened near the door. A growl came through. "Speak up. Who are ye and what authorization do ye have?"

"John Fischer and a guest . . . from group sixteen to compound number nine."

I wasn't any hangman's doll. Group sixteen had to be the provost's office, and compound nine was this barracks barn. Did they talk like that in the Ku Kluck Klan? A bunch of lively parrots.

The parrot inside the barn shoved on a bolt, and I was let in the house. Seems like the lieutenant wasn't "authorized" to come in. I stood alone with the parrot. He leered at me.

"You his concubine?"

He pointed to a man in the middle of the barn. It was too dark to catch much of him. I didn't have to guess. Tristram Shirley.

The parrot wore two guns. But he didn't have a military coat. He came in a helter-skelter of rags. He stank of a damp barn in early winter.

"I'm Meyers," he said. "That's his lordship over there. He's a poet. I bring him his gravy and I watch him when he sleeps. Group sixteen can count on ol' Meyers. I'm up twenty-four hours, miss. Meyers goes round the clock. You won't catch him blinking . . ."

Wish I knew what the jailor was blabbering about?

Tris walked in the shadows that dropped from the roof. He wasn't dressed in rags. He had the blue boy's cape that generals and colonels love to wear. I listened to the sound of his boots. They squeaked on the barracks floor. It was a barracks with only one bed. For Tristram Shirley. That man Meyers didn't have to sleep. He was more ghoul than jailor, in my opinion.

He didn't prevent me from going to Tris.

We met under the shadows, with Tris so pale. He couldn't believe the eyes in his head. "Sal?" Then he rushed over and picked me up in his arms. We whirled about in that cape of his. "God, I'm happy," he said.

His old prison scars shivered on his cheek. I wasn't blind. He had little to show under the cape. His Yankee brothers had stripped him clean. His gold braids and general's stripes were gone. He could have been any dog soldier.

I heard terrible weeping behind me, like a man having to part with his soul. It was two-gun Meyers.

"They tricked me, group sixteen . . . Lord Byron, this gal aint a concubine they got for you by the hour."

"She's miss Sally, my sweetheart from Hays."

Meyers shook his head. "It's a mystification. Compound nine is closed to the rest of the world. It's me and you, aint it, my lord? How'd she get to us?"

"God knows," Tristram said.

"You mean she's real company?" Meyers wept louder than before. "A sweetheart . . ." And he disappeared to the ends of the barn.

"That's the damnedest jailor," I said.

"They couldn't trust an ordinary soldier to stay with me . . . someone with family and friends, who might ask about the man in the isolation house. So they got Meyers. He was a mess-boy. He shined officers' boots, he fed slops to the dogs, he dug the graves. He fits perfectly. I'm Byron to him. And he doesn't ask another blessed thing. But how did you find me? I thought I'd never see your brown hair . . . Meyers can tell you how I pace. I go to the center of the room, scratch with my feet, and conjure you out of the wall. It's been keeping me alive."

"Well, you are the right magician, 'cause I'm here."

Damned if we didn't kiss, with Meyers loping in the dark.

"Your troopers came to Abilene with Colonel Ibbetson," I said. "We had a bandit problem. Nicaragua Smith. He shot the pants off your men. It was a grizzly war. Ibbetson pretended he didn't know you, but I squeezed the truth out of him. He's not so bad for an Army colonel."

Tristram's eyes wandered to the roof. His lips curled into a quarter smile. "You're a widow now, aren't you? Some children murdered Doctor Henry. There are no more impediments to marrying me. I'll shout like the devil if the provost doesn't sneak a chaplain into compound nine . . ."

"I can't marry you, Tris. That rascal Henry faked his own death . . . he's on the Pinkerton list for assaulting a banker in New York."

"Then we'll switch our marriage plans," Tris said, "and have a long engagement." I couldn't get him to talk about his wife. He wouldn't mention Captain Alice or his little girls.

Meyers appeared from the grayer side of the barn. "The lieutenant's barking for the missy."

"Let him bark," Tris said.

"I can't, my lord. They'll whip the two of us."

"I wouldn't mind the whipping."

"Then think of me . . . they'll whip her also. Group sixteen don't have much of a heart."

Tristram touched my hand. "You'll come again, Sal? To Lord Byron's house . . . promise me you'll come."

Meyers was the one with the most sense. "Lord, what's the good of a promise when there's group sixteen to fight?"

"I'll come."

The lieutenant stood whistling against the barn door.

"Once a month," he said. "And don't you bargain with me, you little witch. If you show up oftener than that, we'll give you and your pathetic horse a private home. Compound seventeen. You won't see the strangler or anybody else."

I saluted the son of a bitch.

"The fourth Wednesday of each month. And if you breathe a word, we'll put a coffin box in the compound. Just for you."

That darlin' man accompanied me to the fort's main wall. I wish I had a pony to ride. My feet were bloody from the marching we did. I wondered how many other forts were inside Leavenworth, with missing soldiers and all.

IT WAS holy murder to stretch out that month between visits to Mr. Shirley. I had a chicken to entertain me and the antics of mad Tom. In January he slaughtered every cow. He enlisted all men in Abilene under the age of seventy-five, armed them with sledgehammers, and advanced upon the stockyards. The slaughtering took two days. You could hear the moaning and the plunge of the hammers from any side of town. With that socking, you'd think the hammers fell on stone. It wasn't stone. There was a traffic of blood in the streets. It got to the walls of the candy shop, reached into the dry goods stores and the undertaker's front room. Every one of us had stepped in cow blood.

A mule train arrived from Topeka to collect the slaughtered cows and cart them away. The collecting was a week long. The mule drivers hid in the Alamo. The stink of blood and sour entrails went everywhere. It dizzied you to walk in the street. But Tom was stubborn through the hammering and the hauling of cows. "It's a lesson," he wrote in the Minute Book. "We sell tools. We grow tomatoes and corn. We are not some station in a cattleman's paradise. The yards and holding pens will be knocked down and destroyed. Cows are anathema in Abilene."

The blood stayed with us. It left a pink jelly in mud and snow. It was still there on my second trip to the fort. Ish clopped along that jelly road. It was a mile before the pinkness disappeared from the ground.

I'd baked a dozen pies for Tris and that funny two-gun man. The guard wouldn't let me bring them into the fort. "No packages, no fruit stuff."

Lieutenant Fischer arrived at the gate. He was surly with me. "Goddamn you, woman . . . making yourself conspicuous. You'll come emptyhanded, or you won't come at all. We don't run charity wards at Leavenworth. Save your pies for that bald duck in the wagon."

"Rooster's not a duck," I told him. But the lieutenant wouldn't listen to me. I had to go hiking with him again. It was a fearsome trip. The wind blew us into the sides of buildings. Nobody had shoveled the walks, and we sank into snowdrifts that were tall as a roof. I lost Fischer three times. That vacant Army village in back of the latrines was a white field with chimney pots. We'd gone a mile into the fort, and it felt like a march to nowhere. I'd see the same chimney pots. Was the trickster leading me in circles, like a blind horse?

Then we bumped into a wall of snow. A piece of the wall opened up. I didn't have to wait for Meyers' growl. Fischer got us to compound nine. I went through the wall, and it shut behind me, leaving Fisher out in the cold. My whole face chattered in that barn. It was icier inside than out. Meyers couldn't keep the chimneys going. They might call suspicion to compound nine. Meyers was wearing two Army coats, and Lord Byron had his cape bunched around his ears. But they didn't look to be suffering. They'd set a table for my visit, with wine and winter greens. Meyers had cooked a stew over a nest of twigs. We ate and drank as if we'd been doing this all our lives, meeting in an empty barn. That month in Abilene shot away. Cows and blood were gone from my head. I had a home in a barracks house, with a keeper named Meyers and a general that the Army had banished to a fort inside a fort. Men had a way of going invisible on me. But Tristram was visible as hell. Lord Byron smiling at me out of his cape. Send for the chaplain. I'll marry Tris as often as he likes.

I WAS the hermit of Abilene.

I got my vittles and that was all.

A gray barn was the only season I could remember. Tom turned empty lots into fields of corn. "The corn's in ear, the corn's in ear," folks would say, proud of Tom and themselves. Husks grew up outside the Noah. I walked through them, but I didn't see. My summer and winter were miles away, in Leavenworth.

It was more than a year. Thirteen visits, and he still wouldn't talk of Alice. "Tristram, won't you tell me what happened with the wife?"

"You're my wife," he said, sloshing the wine in his cup.

I'd have strangled Alice myself, but I couldn't let go of asking.

"I wanted you," he muttered, his eyes rolling from the wine he had. "I'd ready the dogs, throw a blanket into the sled, and start my midnight crawl to Abilene. She'd follow me on a pony, with a lantern in her hand. I could feel that light shaking on my neck. *Idiot,* she'd say. *Go to your whore . . . but don't bother coming back. It'll make a lovely story, Tris. The commandant locked out of his house. They'll laugh. How many generals lose a fort?* Damn my feeble hide. I turned the sled around, and the dogs did the rest. They followed the eye of her lantern . . . she started mocking me at dinner. *Go on, run to that fortuneteller. She doesn't need you. She has her Billy boy and a hundred others by now."*

"It's a lie," I said. "I did love William, but you always knew that."

Wine spilled out of the cup. His head jerked inside the cape. I put my fingers over his mouth.

"Tristram, you don't have to explain . . ."

He kissed the fingers one by one and took them away from his mouth.

"I didn't plan anything. I was soaping the dogs' bridle straps, and shaving the leather down to get rid of all the mildew. And she was chipping at me in front of the girls. *Your daddy has a paramour. Your daddy has a paramour. He's a bad, bad man.* I threw the straps around her neck, knotted them twice, and pulled . . . the girls saw. They didn't yell *mama* once."

MERCURY COULD have bumped into Venus, and I wouldn't have known. Were we at war with China? Was the queen of England coming to the States? Victoria Regina. Didn't she lose a husband somewhere back? I'd have to ask Tris . . .

I scribbled a calling card for myself with a grocer's pencil:

Mrs. Salome Ovenshine Shirley
c/o Group Sixteen
Leavenworth, Kansas
Lord Byron's House

That's all the identification I'd ever need. I didn't show my card to Fischer. He'd have put me in the doghouse. But Mr. Shirley laughed at the scribbling I did.

"Then you are my wife . . . it says so on the paper."

"Lemme have a look," Meyers squealed. He put on his spectacles and stared at the card. He was furious. He trampled the card with his boots. The echo shot across the barn. It was like bowling ten pins in a closet. The boom was so loud.

"Missy, if you write *group sixteen* on anything, paper, stone, or wood, they'll tear your heart out with an iron fist."

"How'll they ever see it?"

"They got spies. Group sixteen'll jump into your petticoats if they have to."

"It's just Fischer and an old marshal. They couldn't track a bleeding hen."

"Missy, they could track you to the equator."

Meyers huffed out his chest. His guns came unholstered with all that huffing, and he had to load himself up again with his twin metal pieces. He had gun oil on his pants.

"Meyers, we're a family, me, you, and Lord Byron. I don't care what group owns us."

I promised him I wouldn't scribble calling cards. I wouldn't tell a soul about Lord Byron's house.

"It aint fer myself. The group can beat the stuffing out of me. It's dangerous fer his lordship . . . any words what points to him."

Meyers dropped his shoulders all of a sudden and went mum. Lord Byron had to finish. "He's trying to tell you that the group has its own parlance. We're all nonpersons in sixteen's eyes."

"That's it," Meyers said. "Nonpersons. Nobodies."

"Well, three nobodies is better than one . . ."

Tristram laughed and ate his stew.

I asked him about England's midget queen. "I hear she won't have her picture taken with any man or woman who isn't her size. They're raising a whole empire of midgets for Queen Victoria."

"Who told you such a monstrous thing?"

"Doctor Ovenshine."

"She's not so small as that."

"She has to stand on a box to decorate her admirals. It's lined with velvet, to cushion her royal feet. But a box is a box."

"She could stand on two boxes and she'd still be a woman
. . . she loved a man, Prince Albert. And she proposed to him."

"Wasn't he a furriner?" I said.

Lord Byron stopped eating his stew.

"A queen oughtn't marry a furriner. She should take one of her
own kind. Otherwise you'll have an empire of imbeciles."

"He was her cousin, for God's sake."

"That's different," I said. "Did the queen know Byron?"

"How could she? The queen was three or four when Byron
died."

"Byron could have gone into the royal nursery and played with
her."

"You're a venomous arguer, Mrs. Shirley. I give up."

The jailor brought out another bottle of wine. He wouldn't let
Tristram drink from it until he tasted a drop. Meyers sampled
everything first. That way "sixteen" couldn't poison his lordship.
We drank until the roof started to swim.

"Little drunkard," Tris said, and we hugged under his cape a
mighty long time.

I WONDERED about Tris, how he slept when I was away from him,
how he could survive without smelling the sun. "Sixteen"
wouldn't let him out of the barn, not for the littlest exercise. Some
stray soldier might spot him and ask who the man in the cape was.
Son, he's the strangler without a country.

I'd store up a month of questions for Tris, and forget them all
the moment I was with him. We'd jabber about the darnedest
things. Princes and turtles and Meyers' stew . . .

And then we couldn't jabber any more.

The guard came out of his hut in the wall. It was winter, I'd
say. He was freezing. He had an old fur muff for his hands, but
the wind ate into his collar. He knew me. I was the hag of Fort

Leavenworth, twenty-seven by the Christian calendar, if we were approaching the Lord's year of 1876. I'd gone through his gate a couple of centuries in a row.

"Who are ye?"

"Sally the washerwoman," I said.

"Fort's closed. Move yer goddamn truck."

"I will not. I come through on Wednesdays."

"Cap'n changed the day on ye. It's the Monday after the Thursday of the second night of Halloween."

"Halloween doesn't have a second night," I told him. "You get me Lieutenant Fischer, before I knock your gate down with my horse."

He frowned at Ishmael and lowered his fur muff, like he was the King of Siam. "That nag couldn't knock butter in a jar . . . the cap'n left instructions. *Lordy Byron is dead.*"

I threw him to the ground and drove a dozen yards into the fort. Soldiers rushed at me with bayonets. Rooster pecked one on the arm with his splintered beak. But the sons of bitches held Ishmael by the ears and pulled me off the wagon. They stuck me in the guardhouse for riotous washerwomen. It was an abandoned officers' privy. Fischer walked in. The fool at the gate hadn't lied. The lieutenant was a captain now. I'd been ignorant of his rise in the Army all these months.

"You are the most infernal woman in the land. I believe you could overcome this fort if you had the proper ammunition."

"Where's Tris?"

"The boy at the gate told you . . . Mr. Shirley dropped dead."

"Of natural causes, I presume."

"Don't blame us. The rebs had Mr. Shirley two years. You must have noticed the scars on him."

"It's strange he picked this month to die in . . . was it a present from group sixteen?"

Fischer slapped my face. "You'll not mention that again if you value living . . . the rebs killed your man."

"Take me to Meyers. I want to hear it from him."

"Meyers is out shoveling. We can't pester that boy. You'll frighten the worms away."

"Did you put the worms on top of Meyers?"

"Stupid witch," he said, dragging me through the privy and banging my shoulders into the wall. He let me out and we hiked over the grounds of his precious fort. We didn't pass any vacant Army villages. We weren't in the hidden part of Leavenworth. We climbed a tiny hill. I heard a man sing with a growl.

Merry is the grave where a soldier falls . . .

Meyers wasn't digging a grave. He was on his knees, scooping for worms with a bucket. Was it bait for some general's fishing party? Or were the cooks preparing a special worm soup?

Fischer went down the hill and I had Meyers to myself. He was weeping the minute he saw me. He abandoned all his worms.

"Meyers, did they poison Tris? . . . was it *sixteen?*"

"No, missy." He wiped his eyes on a filthy sleeve. "I was the taster. You couldn't poison him and not poison me. Aw, he loved you so much. Lord Byron was on his bench . . . every poet has to have a bench. He said, *Meyers, Valentine's Day is coming. I'll have to do up a poem for Mrs. Shirley.*"

"Valentine?" I said, shuddering a little. "Is it February?"

"It aint March," Meyers said. "And it aint October. So what month could it be?"

"Meyers, do you have the poem?"

"His lordship didn't get that far . . . he whistled and said, *Twenty-two days to miss Sally.* It's the last he spoke. He dipped his pen into the well. He scratched a couple of times and slumped over. When I got to him he was through. I had my best years with Lord Byron. It aint often ye live with a poet . . . don't you cry, miss. He said he was lucky having you for his sweetheart. Compound nine meant nothin' to him. He wished for you, and he got his wish."

Meyers went back to his worms. The captain had come up the hill. He had a package under his arm. I said good-bye to the jailor, but he didn't answer. He was busy scooping worms.

The captain accompanied me down the hill. "Here," he said, shoving the package into my chest. "It's Mr. Shirley's cape. I had one heck of a time retrieving it. The general's ambiguous status didn't entitle him to any clothes. I had to steal it behind the quartermaster's back . . . we're not so efficient as you think. We created group sixteen to handle Mr. Shirley, and we dissolved it after his death. I'm with the provost marshal, is all."

He shook my hand at the gate, and I still couldn't figure if group sixteen was bad or good.

Eighteen

The hermit came out of her hole.

She stepped on Mulberry Street. She put down a dime for an old Ten-Cent Romance. *Hickok, Marshal of Abilene.* The clerk stopped me. "Just a second, Mrs. Ovenshine." The romances had gone up to fifteen cents. I gave him his nickel and left Harkness' book store and circulation library. Old as it was, I could smell the book's ink. That was peculiar, because the cover told you: *McCandle's Ten-Cent Romances, Printed at 18 Spruce Street, N.Y.* I'd swear the printing shop was closer than that.

I read into the book. *Marshal of Abilene* had mayor Tom, the wolfman, the Seven Beasts, the war between Bill and the cattle boys, and a widow named Mrs. Ovenbright, who ran the hotel where "those murdering orphans lived."

Even the hangman was mentioned.

> "Fastidious George. A worthless drunk away from his ropes, he was the nonpareil of gallows builders. There weren't enough trapdoors in the whole of creation to satisfy him. He would venture up and down Kansas and all the odd territories with his hanging supplies. Officials favored George over every other hangman. He was thorough, he was quick. He was the only executioner with lifesize dolls to measure the exact drop of a man. But George had a malady common to many hangmen. He would grow attached to certain of his 'clients' and found it difficult to part with them. Such was the case with the Seven Beasts. He was known to cry in their presence. He ate pickles with them. He browned peanuts on the prison stove . . ."

McCandle wasn't from Spruce Street in New York. He was a flatlander from the plains. I wouldn't be surprised if McCandle was our mayor, mad Tom. Tom scribbled a lot. Maybe he wrote his romances on the backside of the Minute Book. I went to the courthouse to put the question to him: was he McCandle of Spruce Street, the author and manufacturer of the Ten-Cent Romance?

Poor Tom. He was squirreled in his office with paper cuffs on his sleeves to spare his shirts from all that scribbler's ink. He was setting down our history, writing our laws, so that people a hundred years from now would remember our jubilee and the corn Tom picked over the cows. I'd have scribbled a different story. A town that was cursed with sleep.

I frightened Tom. The cuffs sprang open and fell off his sleeves. He hadn't expected a visitor during his writing hours.

"Miss Sally? Didn't you marry an Army man up in Leavenworth?"

"No, I've been living in retirement . . . don't you ever stop scribbling, Tom?"

"Can't," he said. "I have to get it down on paper . . . people forget you in a minute. And they tell lies."

"But you're the mayor, Tom. You hired the hangman . . . and you fired Wild Bill."

"Hell," he said. "You could lay all of me in a bottle of ink."

I asked him if he was writing Ten-Cent Romances on the side.

Tom looked bewildered. "I'm no dime novelist. I don't have the appetite for it . . . haven't you seen the posters? We're offering money for McCandle, dead or alive."

He tightened his paper cuffs and went back to scribbling our immortality.

I left the courthouse and paid my penny for the Abilene *Star*. It was the usual drivel. Jorrid Ferguson hadn't let go of hating Wild Bill.

Pray, where is that killer of boys?

We at the *Star* hope he lives and moves, a terror to bad men and little boys. When last heard from he was in the lockup at Kansas City, after being pulled out of a Missouri Avenue saloon as a pauper and itinerant cardshark. But that wasn't the only complaint against our Bill. He's been battling Texians again. At the Kansas City Exposition he told the band not to play "Dixie," insulting a group of pilgrims from Laredo. He entered into a shoving match with the pilgrims and had to be gagged and bodily removed from the Exhibition. Thus Hickok is a credit to us all . . .

We have been in correspondence with the shootist, but I'm afraid his letter is months old. He writes lovingly of his old bailiwick. "I'm Hickok. I wear my hair long as usual. If I ever pass through your pigtown, I will step on your liver and feed your lungs to the sparrows and the hawks."

Fine literary stuff from Wild Bill, Indian Fighter and Vagrant.

Rumors abound. The latest word has it that William is out of the lockup and has gone to Cheyenne with our dear Mrs. Lake and her circus people. Some even say that William married her, and that man and wife are honeymooning in Cincinnati. Congratulations, Bill. Better married than dead . . .

It wasn't a shock to me. I always figured Bill would end up in a circus. That's where he belonged. Inside the acrobat's tent. Would he give Mazeppa a brood of tiger babies? Something troubled me about that chatter in the *Star*. Jorrid's voice had a creak to it. I'd heard that creak before. In the new Fifteen-Cent Romance. The son of a bitch was blessing Bill and cussing him in different publications.

I trapped the author, like a mouse. He yammered this and that, but his face was rotten with the lie of it.

"McCandle, what's your next issue about? . . . Hickok goes to Washington? Or Wild Bill meets Kublai Khan?"

"Where's the harm?" he said, miserable as hell. "Everybody enjoys seeing his name in print. Hate him or love him, it comes to the same thing. Wild Bill."

I didn't bring Rooster along to peck at the journalist. I had to sock him with a woman's paws. Blood dribbled from his mouth. Two inky boys looked in from another room.

"Close the door," he screamed at the boys, and they disappeared.

It was hard labor socking a man.

"Don't you ever write novels on Bill . . . if you do another Fifteen-Cent Romance, I'll set your hair on fire."

"You would," he said, wiping his bloody mouth with a handkerchief. "You're rotten enough. I suppose it irks you that our William's a married man. He picked a bride over you."

I socked him one more time and went on home after his mouth started to bubble up with blood.

THE TIN men returned for a visit.

They drove their ponies through store windows. They took whatever spoils they could get. They carried off whiskey, whores, and chandeliers from the Alamo. They pranced on Mulberry Street with sausages around their necks. They tore up the sidewalks with their ponies' shoes. They captured baby pigs and threw them on top of awnings. The piglets squealed for their mamas, and the guerrillas laughed. They held up the railroad office, they robbed the bank, they ripped away the calaboose walls.

When they had their fill of sausages and chandeliers, the tin men got to me. They rode up and down my lawn, waiting for their leader. He had a kerchief knotted around his head, like a Galveston pirate, and a sombrero on top of that. Nacogdoches.

He sat high on his pony and waved his sombrero at the house.

"Aren't you going to invite me in?"

I had Leopold's little single-shot. I danced onto the porch with it. "I'll blow your head off, Nacogdoches."

"Honey," he said, "you're embarrassing me in front of the boys . . . they're kind of old-fashioned. They expect a wife to behave."

"I'm not your wife. I'm a widow," I told him.

"That's a goddamn sophistry. A widow with a live husband isn't a widow at all."

The guerrillas agreed.

"I married again while you were playing dead."

"Who's the lucky man?"

"Tristram Shirley. I'm his widow now."

"I know the law," Nacogdoches said. "The first husband gets title if the second one is gone . . ."

He began to climb down from his pony. I aimed the derringer at his ear.

Nacogdoches had a narrow smile. "One pull is all you have."

"That's sufficient to crease the side of your head."

"The boys wouldn't like that. They're liable to do you to hell."

"But you won't be here to see it, Mr. Nacogdoches."

He thought about my argument and crept high on the pony again. "Didn't I save you in that cattle yard? You'd have been a mess of dirt and blood without Nacogdoches."

"It wasn't your business anyhow . . . where's Nicaragua Smith?"

"The federals shot him down."

"He was too old to be a bandit," I said.

"Nonsense! It was a filthy sneak attack . . . sidewinders. They wouldn't have got the general any other way. Now will you let me in? I'll whip you, girl. I was your schoolmaster."

"Just try."

He promised to kidnap me some night.

I didn't let on how I admired the change in him. He wasn't a stooped clerk. He was the Kublai Khan of Kansas. Nacogdoches rode off with his men.

I didn't want to be a pirate lady. I was Lord Byron's widow, even if no chaplain had bothered to marry us. I could pick my gray hairs soon as they arrived. I started up crowing to Rooster. I poured oil on Ish's mange. Don't you worry. I had things to do.

The novelist banged on my door.

"Jorrid Ferguson, get on home to your printing shop. I'm not in the mood for a scribbler."

"Open up. There's bandits about."

I set the latch free and the dime novelist entered the house.

"Who is that sombrero? . . . he busted us to pieces."

I wasn't going to snitch on Lyle, not to this legendmaker. He'd do up a whole line of romances on the Nacogdoches Kid.

"He's probably some cattle boy from west of the Pecos."

"A Texian? That explains it. He was having his revenge on Hickok's town . . . they're mean west of the Pecos."

Mention anything to a dime novelist, and he'll build you a song in half a minute. You couldn't trust a romancer in your house.

"Jorrid, why'd you come?"

The novelist had an injured look. "I'm a swine, miss Sally . . . I've swindled Wild Bill all these years, living off those novels. I'm not jealous of his long hair. And I don't have the least ambition to be a two-gun man . . . with every bum in the West popping at you, thinking they'll become William the Remarkable once they murder him. I'll hold on to my nom de plumes. I'm McCandle today. I'll be McGregor tomorrow. But the truth of it, miss Sally, there isn't much fat in writing novels. Bookmen lie and cheat. I didn't clear a hundred dollars from *Marshal of Abilene,* counting paper and ink."

"That puts me to tears, knowing your paper costs . . ."

"Let me finish! I hate the ease of him . . . how he strolls along like a cat. That's what unnerves me. Thin lips under his moustache. And those blue eyes . . ."

"You're blind," I said. "The blue's gone out of him."

"Missy, I know. That's why I risked meeting bandits to come here. We got a few particulars on William from the telegraph machine. Our boy's gone on an expedition to the Black Hills. He's hunting gold in Dakota, and he didn't take his wife."

"It's not my concern where William goes."

"Will you keep quiet! That stuff on Bill stinks to heaven. There's a rah-rah about him taking off from St. Louis. They discuss the train fare and all. Bill will make his camp in Deadwood Gulch. He'll turn the Hills upside down for precious metal. He'll mine more gold than any other man. Yes, he's married. Yes, he'll be rich in a month . . . it's been silent ever since St. Louis. I'd say he's starving in Deadwood. The prospecting is over with. He's hard up, I tell you. He's lost his money and most of his eyes."

My paws were at Jorrid's throat. "Where'd you get that about Bill?"

"I'm a newsman. I can interpret a kettle of fish. Half the world knows Hickok is going blind."

I took the three hundred dollars I had in a shoe box upstairs. I grabbed whatever pickles and turnips I could find. I stuffed blankets and warm clothes into the wagon and shut the hotel. I harnessed Ish, gave Rooster his territory on the tailboard, and we got out of Abilene. I didn't have to say good-bye.

Abilene would have the same future, cows or corn. I was going to Deadwood.

NEBRASKA WAS filled with highwaymen. I had to drop the horse's straps and shove both of Leo's derringers into their eyes. "I don't bother maiming people . . . I shoot to kill."

Word of me must have spread through Nebraska. Highwaymen would bow in the slush and warn their friends. "Darn fool, that's Nebrasky Jane . . . Hickok's country woman."

I guess legends grow in crooked ways, like a mouthful of teeth, with soft spots, missing roots, and a jagged edge here and there. I couldn't blame Jorrid for the coming of Nebrasky Jane. Now I had a nom de plume.

NOM DE plumes weren't much good in Dakota. Highwaymen up there had never heard of Nebrasky Jane. I had to pull on them. They scratched their whiskers and snickered at my single-shots, but they left us in peace.

We ran into a grasshopper storm. The critters sat on us for a whole afternoon and just about ate us alive. Rooster was covered from head to toe with hopping green legs. He pecked at the air and killed five hundred, but it couldn't even throw a dent in the storm. The sky was brown with them. Then the world went black.

I screamed and shook my arms.

I learned to close my mouth, or I would have had a grasshopper party under my tongue. I couldn't see more than the bump on Ish's tail. The hoppers made little mashing sounds that were worse than the devil. They could eat my calico dress and kick at my eyes, but Beelzebub wasn't going to crazy me. I crawled to the front of the wagon and pulled Tristram's cape out of my wedding chest. I sat under the cape, cussing the devil, with the hoppers smacking against Tris' blue skirts, and their serenade gnawing in my ears, louder and louder, until you believed the pests were saying, *Die, Sally, die.* I wouldn't die for the devil's satisfaction. The mashing stopped. The storm didn't wind down. It just went away.

The sky was pure silver. There wasn't a green leg in the air. Nothing but a carpet of broken grasshoppers next to the wagon. Thousands and thousands of the pests. They'd beaten into the wagon boards and their bodies had come apart.

Rooster was a mess of sores. His tail and his red comb were gone. The horse had bald lines on his back. The pests had run off with Ish's hair. And the wagon had valleys in it, where the hoppers had nibbled right through the wood. But they couldn't seem to hurt Army wool. Tristram's cape didn't have a single hole in it. I brushed the grasshoppers out of its skirts and put the cape with the rest of my trousseau.

We could have been wounded men home from the wars. We didn't have a home. We had to cross the Dakota Badlands to reach the Black Hills. The roads disappeared. I got in front of the horse and led that wagon through gulleys and crazy divides. The ground had sharp teeth. We inched against a mesa wall. Ish pulled for his life. I tore up blankets and "banditched" the horse's feet. Our turnip barrel was empty, so we ate corn meal and pickles, and the pickles made me think of Bill.

We'd end up sucking stones. We found the narrowest road that could have been a coyote trail, or running ground for jackrabbits.

We followed it. Hairy creatures came jumping out of the mesa wall. They knocked me down, slapped at Rooster with sticks, and seized the horse. I recognized them under their rough clothes. They didn't carry sausages round their necks. But they were the same guerrillas who sacked Abilene. They dragged us to their leader. Nacogdoches didn't have his pirate hat. He was scarred and bitten. He wore a moustache in the Badlands, and he slept in a tent.

"Sally of the desert," he hissed. "My old, reluctant wife. Where are you going?"

"Deadwood," I told him.

"Ah, that other husband of yours, Buckaroo Bill. You are a fickle thing. Weren't you mourning General Shirley a couple of weeks ago?"

"I still am."

"Then why the rush to Bill?"

"He's sick," I said.

Nacogdoches barked out loud. "You hear, boys, the great gold miner is ill. And nurse Sally is coming to the rescue . . . she performs miracles on her men . . ."

"Did the Cavalry chase you here, Lyle?"

"What Cavalry? It's the goddamn Pinkertons. The federals hired them to track us. And you can't get loose of those little men with the funny hats. Paid killers is what they are."

"And what are you, Lyle?"

"We're the last quality folks, me and the boys . . . we'll get even with the bluebellies for bringing in carpetbaggers and pissing on the South."

"Did you forget, Lyle? You're the man from Trenton, New Jersey. You scribbled in a bank."

"I'm Nacogdoches. Texas is my home state. We'll turn her into a republic again . . . I'll show you who I am."

He pushed me into his tent, dug his filthy hands under my

calico rags, and wrestled me to the dirt floor. I could hear the guerrillas chuckling outside. It was like grasshopper talk. They poked their rabbity heads into the mouth of the tent. Nacogdoches tossed his boots at them. "Will you give a fella some privacy?"

Then he buttoned up.

The guerrillas were so busy watching me and Nacogdoches, they never did molest the wagon. We left that robbers' den and took the next coyote trail.

IT WAS more a pothole than a mining camp. One dizzy street that dipped into a canyon wall. The houses of Deadwood leaned this way and that, like chimneys preparing to slide off a roof. It was dusty here, at the end of the world. You could lose sight of your ankles, walking in Deadwood Gulch. The wind picked up a horrible roar, bumping down the canyon. You'd think an Indian god was hammering on top of your head. These hills belonged to the Sioux. The town was filled with squaw men, whites who had married into that Indian nation, and had abandoned their Sioux brides to look for gold. Some of them had Sioux markings, others weren't the least bit Sioux. But you could always tell a squaw man. They just didn't fit around most whites.

I went up to a bunch of squaw men in the street.

"Cousins, can you tell me where Wild Bill Hickok's mining expedition is?"

They had a most bitter laugh for squaw men.

"Ma'am, Billy aint mining this month . . . you see that shack yonder? He's crawling in there."

They pointed to a hovel that was half in Deadwood and half out. It was at the deepest edge of town. One shove, and it would have gone over the canyon wall. THE ST. LOUIS MINING COMPANY. J.B. HICKOK, SOLE PROPRIETOR. The hovel had a curtain in place of a door. I passed through the curtain. You had to squint hard, or you would have missed William Severe. He sat in the corner, gazing out at nothing.

"Hickok," I said. "It's Salome Ovenshine."

He let a gob of tobacco juice fly from his mouth. I didn't see one mining tool on the premises. His company had gone to rot.

"Damn you, Hickok, the reports I've heard are true. You're starving."

I went out to the wagon and returned with those pickles he liked to gobble up. I wasn't so alarmed after he started to burp.

"I know about that honeymoon of yours. I'll feed you and help you make your fortune, and you can go back to Cincinnati and wear the finest paper collars. What happened to the bravoes in your expedition?"

"They took to the hills when they saw me with the mooneye. They have their own company now. That's no bother. I'm a gambling man. That's how I make my gold."

"How much have you won in Deadwood so far?"

". . . you can't hold cards if your eyes are missing."

I moved closer into that hovel. My shadow fell on Bill. He never noticed it. Hickok couldn't see eighteen inches in front of him. He wouldn't have known I was Sally from his curtain door. But William was used to the dark. He'd gone into the caves one winter and come out with a bat's "ear." You didn't have to worry. He had his Navy guns. He'd shoot your belly off if you were the wrong man.

The first thing I did was fumigate the shack. I sprinkled William's house with camphor balls from my wedding chest. Then I got in line with harlots, gamblers, and squaw men at the town well and came back to William with a bucket of water.

"Don't be bashful now," I said, helping the Slayer off with his clothes. "Mazeppa won't hear a thing . . ." I scrubbed the dirt off Bill with a cake of lye soap I had with me in the wagon.

"Trust the old witch."

Next I trimmed his moustache and washed his long hair in the bucket. William had his honey color. He was "goldilocks" again. But you wouldn't believe the elephant flies he left in the bucket. Lord knows who'd been living in William's hair. It was a regular boardinghouse for big and little pests.

I dusted William's coat and pants in back of the hovel. Then we dressed the Slayer.

You'd think it was the old Bill. Hunger had eaten up his jowls. He had that narrow jawline of a mankiller. He put on his slouch hat and stuck the Navies in his sash. "Darlin'," he said, "how much money do ye have?"

"Two hundred dollars."

Lord, I had to keep a hundred in reserve! I knew he'd gamble our fortune away soon as he was able.

"Come on, girl," he said. "And if you spot a man cheatin' on us, touch my elbow and I'll take over."

He didn't walk like a man without eyes. You wouldn't catch him stumbling. He was as sure of foot as a circus trainer. I had to rush along to keep him company. We traveled up the road to a saloon that wasn't much bigger than William's hovel. It was in a line of saloons. This one was called the Number Ten.

Mouths hung loose when the Slayer walked in. People were expecting a prickly ghost, and there he was, smooth as silver in his Prince Albert coat. His face was washed. His ears were clean. His moustache didn't have a trace of shaggy fur.

"Gents," he said, "meet my new pardner, Mrs. Ovenshine."

The gamblers stroked their hatbands. "How do?"

Bill sat down with them, taking the stool against the wall, and he motioned for me to come sit beside him. The gamblers fumed under their hats. They took fierce bites of tobacco. They ground their jaws and spit juice between their legs. They considered it an

injury to have a woman at the table. Women were for sporting, not for cards. But they couldn't go against Bill. His hair was combed today. His Navies were up above his knees. They had to let his "pardner" sit.

They shouldn't have troubled themselves. Bill lost our money in five minutes. I looked for cheaters. There weren't any. Bill had a gambler's knack. He could growl with his eyes and make you think he was holding a fistful of jacks. I'd swear he couldn't see half his cards.

He was ready to sign a pocket check for his coat, his hat, and his boots. I stole the pocket check out of his hand. "Time to go, Bill. We have beans on the boil."

He got up, and we marched out of the Number Ten. William stormed once we were in the street.

"Don't you ever contradic' my play."

"I'll contradic'," I said. "We'll be in the poorhouse with your winnings, Mr. Wild Bill. They have to be robbers at the general store . . . else they wouldn't be here. How will we find you another coat after you gamble it to pieces?"

"I'll wear the same dirt I was wearing before you come."

"And they'll shovel you onto the junk pile . . . with all the smelly things."

"Bull. I'll win tomorry. Just you watch."

I watched. He gave our last hundred to the gamblers, and I had to pull him out of the Number Ten. William screamed at me. I didn't care. Cabbage cost eight dollars a head in this darn gulch. It was worse than robbery. The grocers were waiting to fleece you blind. I had to go back into the fortunetelling business. I painted a fresh sign near William's curtain.

COME TO DAKOTA SALLY
THE QUEEN OF HEARTS
FUTURES AND PASTS
A DOLLAR A READ

I had to keep up with the crazy prices or we couldn't have bought a cabbage leaf. Dakota Sally bloomed in no time at all. Fortunetellers were scarce in Deadwood. The gamblers stayed away. They wouldn't have their futures read by Hickok's "pard." It might offer Bill an advantage at the table. Sure, blind man's bluff. But I didn't need those cardsharks. I had enough squaw men and miners coming through the curtain to supply us with food and gambling money.

Everybody paid with tiny pinches of gold dust. The littlest pinch was worth a dollar. But they built up in the palm of your hand. I'd stir the dust and shape it into a mountain before Bill carried most of it away in his hat to the Number Ten saloon. He was like a child that just couldn't grip the value of money. I managed to hoard a little. I found a hiding place under a loose plank in the wall. Only it was Bill's hiding place too. He'd scratched out a letter with his crooked penmanship, a letter he forgot to mail. I shouldn't have unfolded it.

DEAD WOOD BLACK HILLS, DACOTA July, 14th 1876
AGNES DARLING,
   I have given up Prospecting there's not much gold as I can see All this talk about sitting on a tub of Yellow rocks forget the Yellow you would laugh to look at your husband in Prospecting shoes but never mind Pet we will have a house one day and be so happy
   I have my shooters and Dacota Sol he is the best pard a man could have Sol will save me if he can

J B HICKOK
WILD BILL

I put the letter back into the wall.

DACOTA SOL. What was I doing here? I was less than dirt to Bill. The fortuneteller who wiped his nose. He could feel me sulking in the shack.

"What's wrong with you?"

"When are you planning to leave these Hills and return to your darlin' wife?"

"I'm stuck, you little fool. I couldn't crawl to the privy without you . . . I'm the name what scares. *Wild Bill.* But folks aint shivering so hard."

"We'll make them shiver," I said.

"Where's the satisfaction? It aint much enjoyment bloodying people. It never was. The hokum they write about you. Might as well be a wooden Indian outside a tobaccy shop."

"I caught the legendmaker, Bill. It's Jorrid Ferguson. He won't write another romance. He promised."

"There's ten of him. Wild Bill's got so many faces, I can count forty-five moustaches on myself . . ."

"We'll hire a lawyer and sue. It's called an injunction. It means they can't print lies about you."

"They'll print them anyhow. You'd have to banish ink from the country . . . and then they'd do their inking abroad."

A whole stack of novels appeared in the gulch. *Deadwood Bill.* Jorrid shipped his new line of Fifteen-Cent Romances to the Dakota territory. But it was Deadwood, and the prices were marked up to a dollar. I'll strangle that author soon as I can.

Bill had a terrible curiosity over the book. I had to go out and buy a copy. He'd sit in his corner, and he'd ask Dacota Sol to read him from *Deadwood Bill.* It hurt me, knowing what a ghoul Jorrid was, feeding off a blind man's reputation.

I found a passage that was tolerable and I delivered it in the spookiest voice I could.

"Hickok, yer a dead man," shouted Cherokee Tom, that mad killer dog. Cherokee and his gang murdered, kidnapped, sodomized, and maimed two hundred or more women and men. Cherokee's boys had hatchets, spikes, and six-guns. They'd already

robbed every miner in camp, raped the women, and tossed the cardplayers into the ravine. Hickok was the only man they hadn't sullied, and they meant to do him a powerful harm.

It was twenty-four of them to one Wild Bill . . .

"Hogwash," I said. "It's what they call hyperbole in school . . . a lowdown exaggeration."

"Will you continue?" William harped. "What happened to Wild Bill?"

"Sakes, whatever can happen in a Fifteen-Cent Romance? He'll kill the twenty-four . . ."

"Don't jabber so much. Let me hear it from the book."

"Cherokee Bob," said Wild Bill, dressed in buckskin for his Dakota travels. "You couldn't hurt a gentleman frog in a dry lake."

The halfbreed didn't rush at Bill with his band of deplorable men. He commenced to sniff the air around Bill's shoulders. "What's that? . . . hey, Hickok's totin' parfume."

"It's pomade," Wild William said. "I'm partial to shiny hair."

"Pomade?" Cherokee muttered. "It has the ripest smell. I believe I will cut off every lock behind your ears."

He moved on Bill with his hatchet . . .

"Will you read?" William said. "Don't stop now."

Deadwood Bill took the halfbreed by his scruffy hair and hurled him and the hatchet into his twenty-four men. He bowled half of them to the ground. The other half charged the Indian Fighter. He would never pull his six-guns on a gang of rats. He slapped them to hell, going from one face to the next, until the tribe of them turned and ran into the Black Hills.

"Trash," I told him.

"But it's pretty," Bill said. "Even if it is a filthy lie. You'd need twelve arms to slap twenty-four men . . ."

MET AN old neighbor while I was at the well. Roger Straws, the retired Pinkerton who won Bill's job as marshal of Hays. Straws had become a Pinkerton again. He was the man who'd chased Nacogdoches into the rocks. He had his shotgun army of little old deputies. He was using Deadwood as a station.

The Pinkertons had captured five guerrillas. Straws was holding them in a shack behind the saloons. That shack began to fill. He had everybody but Nacogdoches by the end of the month. He'd visit with me and Bill.

He saw the state of Bill's eyes.

"Sally, there's not a physician, nurse, or toothpuller a hundred miles of here . . . and this damn place is lousy with jackals and thieves. Do they know how eyeless he is?"

"He can still pull on a shadow, Mr. Straws. The jackals won't disturb him while he has his Navies on."

The old man scratched behind his ear with a gnarled thumb. "Say, have you head of this Nacogdoches? . . . not a soul in our Dallas bureau can speak a word of him. I'm inclined to think he's no Texian at all."

"Beats me, uncle Roger. He's probably a half blood, like one of those villains in the Fifteen-Cent Romance . . . Cherokee Tom."

I hated lying to the old man, but I couldn't spill on Nacogdoches, even after the harm he did, shaming me in front of those rascals, inviting tin men to stick their noses into the tent while he was on top of me, like it was a goddamn circus act. *The Famous Coupling Tigers, Mr. and Mrs. Nacogdoches.* Only I wasn't Lyle's tiger wife. Not any more.

We were lucky to have uncle Roger around. He noised it through the gulch that it would be intolerable to him if anything "unrefined" should happen to Hickok. Folks grew gentler to us. Merchants let me have their cheaper rate. They dropped their

cabbages down to six dollars a head. They figured the whole Pinkerton Agency stood behind Bill.

The biggest roughnecks curtsied to us on our walks to the Number Ten. "Morning, Salome. Morning, Bill." And the gamblers stopped pawing at William's gold. They were worried that uncle Rog might come in with his shotgun army and blow them into the Hills. Suddenly Hickok was bringing back gold dust from the saloon.

"Didn't I tell you I'd win tomorry . . . I never said which tomorry it was."

He liked to have me read to him. We bumped through the legend of Wild Bill in McCandle's books. Scalp-taker, two-gun man, circus star, and actor in Buffalo Bill's Combine.

"That man's a liar who says I couldn't get along with Buffalo Bill. I got along fine with Bill Cody. It's just that I didn't care for all that playacting in his Wild West Show. I had to work up a routine with them spotlights in my face. A footlight exploded and near burned my eyebrows off. The Combine had me jump up on stage and drink colored water out of a jar. I hollered into the audience, *Either I get real whiskey or I aint tellin' no stories.* People laughed. But where was the fun of it? Playing dead while actors in Indian paint ran at you with rubber tomahawks and socked you on the cheek. I told the audience, *Adios, m'friends,* and I left the Combine. Cody was away and the Combine did him dirt. They hired a man in a blond wig to play Wild Bill . . . I got to the theatre and slapped that wig off his ears. They dragged me to the police station and they locked me inside this fortress, the Tombs. The rats sucked on your shoelaces. The jailors were scared to come in. That's how many murderers you had in the Tombs. But they weren't troublesome. They said, *Aint that Wild Bill?* And they begged me to put my signature on their cuffs . . . Cody dropped by. He'd been visiting with the mayor. He laughed and said, *Find your coat, William. You are a bothersome fellow.* But I was reluctant to get out of that hole. I didn't mind the rats on my prison shoes . . . and I'd be lonesome without my murderer friends."

I watched his face for a twisted smile. "Are you sure that isn't a whopper you're telling me? *Rats living on your shoes.*"

"Salome," he said, "it's the godawful truth."

I was curious about the Slayer's travels.

"What's it like?" I asked. "Cincinnati and New York . . . are they bigger than Topeka?"

William frowned. "You could fit most of Topeka into a Manhattan restaurant."

"Then why didn't you stay in Manhattan?"

"Hell, they would have turned me into an author . . . made me write up a book . . . or put me in enamel and advertised me as the man of the West. I'd have to ride a pony in the street."

"You'd have had your fortune, Wild Bill . . . and a house for your bride."

He wouldn't talk of Mazeppa. Did he come to Deadwood on a little holiday from the acrobat and her tigers? You'd never know with Bill. He'd run from women, earthquakes, and fires.

He played a tune on his mouth harp and knocked away the spit. "What would a fortune do me? . . . people asking for free lunches, pointing at you. I can't walk in the goddamn city. You have to watch the trolley cars. You could get run over by a horse on a rail. Folks pissing everywhere . . . squatting in the worst sort of filth."

"Deadwood isn't exactly clean, you know. It's a town that can use a bath."

"I'd rather live in the gulch," Bill said. "And not have to look at cement. A building could fall on you and crack your brain . . . that's New York and Cincinnati."

He had the silliest notions, Wild Bill. Give him a frog pond and a gambling tent and he'd be satisfied. But not for long. He was restless as a Persian camel. He'd chew on walls and ladyfriends.

But I'm a shameless woman.

I was happier in this hovel, with a blind man, than I'd ever been.

I'd pretend to be Hickok sometimes in my sleep. What was it like? Wearing Navies under a sash. I could have been a millionaire, offering my signature to everybody. Acted with Cody or another Combine. Curled up my moustache and become the man of Manhattan. Visited beer gardens with all the ladyfriends I could carry. Wild Bill Ovenshine. Who'd ever pull on me? I could smell a hideout gun in a snake's hat. I'd fight any strongman they had around. What's a strongman when you've wrestled a killer bear and won?

BILL REACHED out for me one night with his beautiful fingers.

"How long have I known you, girl?"

"More than half my life."

All the Slayer did was abandon me. He was too sick to go anywhere, or he'd step into his slouch hat and start a mining company in Colorado and gamble his shirt away.

"Salome," he whispered, "have a look under the bed."

I dug out a gold locket in the shape of a heart. I lit a candle and turned the locket over in my palm. It had writing on the back: TO MY DARLING ALICE, WITH THE SIMPLEST AFFECTION, FROM YOUR BOB. MINERAL WELLS, 1867. He'd won it at the saloon.

"Will you put it on?"

"You and your valentines."

Bill took me close to him on the bed, and we kissed until the candle blew out.

I WASN'T Sally the widow now. And I was more than Dacota Sol. We lay down in that hovel at night, with the Navies under the pillow, and my own derringers in the mattress somewhere, but it wasn't a bed of iron and gun oil. We had our loving on that bumpy straw. He'd touch my face in the dark and whisper, "I liked ye when you was a little girl . . . on the dunes and all. Harvey Beecher was set to cut your throat."

"Yankee spies," I hissed.

"Harve couldn't murder you. His knife would have bent."

"Hickok, you and your hundred wives . . . I wouldn't think you'd noticed a schoolgirl on a horse."

"I noticed," he said.

And we fell asleep with my hand under his jaw.

I'd traveled with a bird and a broken wagon to be with Bill. It was almost like an ocean voyage. A twenty-year trip. The geography I'd been studying was my own darn life. Tibet was in this hovel. I could stop marching to China.

"Love ye," he'd say in the morning, with straw from the mattress in his beard. He'd pluck that goatee of his, and we'd get to kissing. I'd fry up some bacon for him, and his new friend would come through the curtain, a drifter named Jack McCall. He hardly had a beard on him, McCall was such a boy. He was a miner who couldn't hold a shovel right, and Bill sort of adopted him. He would feed the boy pickles at the Number Ten. He was luckless as a gambler, this McCall, and Bill fed him money too. But Jack was a crazy boy. He'd bark at Bill sometimes. "I don't need you, longhair."

The boy would sneak out of the shack, and I'd tell Bill, "He could use a spanking. I have half a mind to lay it on him."

"Salome," Bill said. "He'd whimper. And you'd hate yourself for it."

So I would. But I didn't like him barking at Bill.

The boy would come in, guilty and all, with dirt on his face and some wild flower he'd pulled out of the rocks.

"That's for you, miss Salome . . . I'm sorry if I was troublesome."

Bill could sense that bitterness in me.

"Take his flower, will ye?"

I shoved it in a book. "Thank you, Jack."

The boy would go out again.

"You hurt his feelings," Bill said. But he'd stroke my hair, and we'd forget about Jack McCall. I played checkers with Bill, read to him from McCandle's novel, cleaned his mouth harp, helped him wind his sash.

I heard the push of dust in the street.

Boots poked under the hem of Bill's curtain door. I reached around for my derringers, but Bill told me to put them away. It was the squaw men, waiting for an audience with Bill. "Come on in."

They crouched inside the shack, six bashful squirrels, asking protection from a blind man. The gamblers and the roughs had threatened to burn them alive if the squaw men didn't contribute some gold to the Deadwood Gamblers' Club.

"We knowed you did a lot of scalping, Bill, but we heard you wasn't agin us. Hickok don't hate squaw men. That's the tell of it."

"It's extortion," Bill said. "There aint no Deadwood Gamblers' Club." He got his Navies. "I'll be right back."

He wouldn't let me go with him. "We have guests, Salome. Boil 'em up a little tea."

I had an anger for these squaw men from the day I arrived. I remembered how they'd laughed at Bill. And I wouldn't feed them a bit of cabbage and tea. I hated to think of Bill going up against the gamblers without me and my pocket guns. But he was home before the shack fell down with all my shivering. He went among the squaw men and dropped little packets into their fists. "Here's your gold, m'friends."

They wouldn't give up worshiping Bill.

I had to bump them through the curtain, or they would have

thanked Bill until the moon came out.

"Hickok," I said, "how did you convince the gamblers to give up so much dust?"

"It didn't take convincing. I beat their pants in a poker game."

Deadwood Bill. The scribbler knew his man. Jorrid could go on writing novels even after doomsday arrived at the gulch. What the hell was a hero anyhow? A blind man in a purple sash.

HAD TO go to the privy.

I took a candle along. You couldn't tell what lizards you'd meet in the dark. I stepped over a man outside the privy door. I shone the candle in his face. It was the boy, with whiskey on his shirt and a yellow chin. He was the drunkenest thing alive.

"What do you want, grandma?"

"Who's a grandma?" I said. The boy was right. I was near thirty, and that's a grandma's age.

"I'd like to use the privy, if you please."

"Go on in."

But I couldn't make water knowing that boy was there.

"How's the marshal?" he asked.

"Why aren't you nice to Bill? He feels you're a son to him . . ."

McCall cackled like a Chinaman. "When I need a daddy, I'll shout, *Bill, Bill, Bill.* "

I couldn't help it, but I kicked that rattlesnake.

He cried like a baby. His tears were green against the candle-light. He crawled into the bushes. I wasn't sorry. I was able to make water in peace.

I THREW the camphor balls away. I wanted a child with Bill, not a dream child I'd had in a Topeka hotel. But a genuine Willie.

I didn't tell the Slayer. He'd worry how a blind man could support an infant in the gulch. I'd figure a way to feed another mouth. I'd do fortunes at five dollars a read. I'd open a whiskey house. I'd buy a string of whores . . . I bought one, a girl of skin and bones. The barkeep at the Shovelers Saloon let me have her for eighty dollars. A good cow was worth more than that.

I hid her from Bill. He'd have hollered to see me own a whore. But I had to prepare for Willie. It wasn't much of an enterprise. The whore couldn't draw company in a town that was starving for women. She had just about the saddest face. Men wouldn't ask her to lift her skirts so often.

"Honey, what's your name?"

She was "Oklahoma" on the bill of sale.

"I'm Molly," she said.

It was curious, that voice she had. I'd heard it a hundred years ago, when I was a child in the dunes.

"You're no Molly. I'll bet you you're Emilia."

And she started to cry. It was the same Emilia Salmon whose pa was the dry goods king. She'd married lawyer Brinton and was the belle of Houston's Carolina Street, having her house moved by a million donkeys and all.

"Emilia, what ever did happen to you?"

"My husband threw me out."

"I'd think your pa would have offered to kill him for that . . . he was the richest man alive."

"Pa put him up to it . . . he said I had a wickedness for men, and it couldn't be cured . . . he'd clap me in the asylum if I didn't get on out of Texas."

Well, I wasn't going to have Emilia Salmon whore for me. It would have been indecent. She wasn't family, but she was near enough. I scraped together all the gold I could for Emilia, and I put her on the mule car that left this hole once a week.

"You get on the train at Cheyenne and buy a new dress."

"What good will it do me?" she said, still crying.

"You go to California and pretend you're a widowlady . . . and don't you whore on the next husband you have."

She hugged me from the mule car and I handed her the bill of sale and watched her ride out of the gulch.

I guess my Willie would have to wait.

CABBAGE WAS at three dollars a head. That was the pull William had in his Prince Albert coat. He would strut with his hands parked under the skirts. The blinking he did was like a miner bothered with sun spots. There was an awful lot of blinking in the gulch. The miners would come down from their claims in the Hills, twitching with sun fever after a morning of shovels, picks, and mules. They'd hold their pay dirt in sacks tied to a mule's neck.

Men of the old St. Louis Mining Company would slink past Hickok. He wouldn't begrudge the gold they were carrying. "Howdy, pardner," he'd say, recognizing them only by their shadow.

We walked into the Number Ten. Jack McCall was inside, with his drunken yellow chin. He glared at me and Bill. It irked McCall that he couldn't pay for his own suppers. He was too poor to wear a gun.

William sat down to play. The beggar asked him for gambling money. Bill let him have a few pinches of gold. I heard a buzzing in my ear, like grasshoppers going into a storm. I didn't stop to search what that buzzing was about. I figured grandma Sally was growing deaf.

McCall lost his gold.

Bill said, "Jack, did you eat?"

"None of your business, longhair."

Bill smiled and asked the barkeep to fix Jack a meal of pickles and beets.

I couldn't get rid of the grasshoppers. It was McCall's own craziness I was listening to. That whiskey fever he had. If Bill had slapped him like a dog, the beggar would have whimpered and ate his beets. But he couldn't abide the least bit of charity on this rotten day. He reached into a holster lying on a stool, gritted his monkey teeth, said, "Jack McCall aint nobody's servant," and fired at William's head.

I didn't scream. I didn't bark a word. I could have been a wooden pony with my feet stuck in the ground. I forgot to cup William's head after it started to fall. I was wood. I was nothing. A grandma and a girl.

I was dancing with Beelzebub.

In William's shack. I remember. Only I heard the slap of water outside. Our hovel had moved near the sea. Camels were nibbling the walls. Beelzebub wasn't a two-gun man. He had the smell of oleander leaves. He was my own pa. Out of the grave to dance with his daughter.

"Pa," I told him, "how did you get to be the devil?"

He had water on his moustache. He flicked it off with the blade of his hand. His hair was black as Jesus.

Pa kissed me on the neck.

The camels beat the walls with their heavy mouths.

Pa wouldn't answer me.

"Are you angry? . . . is it for the husbands I had? . . . I didn't love but one or two . . . a general, pa. You know. He was a captain in the old days. Silverspoon Shirley. He died of grief and rebel wounds. He strangled a hateful woman and lost his little girls on account of me . . . and then there was Bill. He was the roughest man and the gentlest, pa."

Pa wouldn't listen to his girl. My throat was leaking from the devil's tongue. His face crawled down my chest. I struck him a blow, pa or not. I wouldn't have relations with the devil.

"Beelzebub," I said, "go on home . . . you have no business in this house."

His chin was where it shouldn't be.

I whacked him with every knuckle I had. It was like falling on leather mush. Pieces of him came away on my fist. The fiend bled a dry juice. My knuckles were sticky with him. I was a lunatic striking the devil who was my pa. I wish he'd stop that awful kissing. My chest was going to glue. My knuckles were powerful sore.

Then pa was gone. The shack fell down. I was wearing Navies. It wasn't a kindergarten story. I was Wild Bill. I didn't have to curl my moustache, or pretend a thing. I was the Slayer, and I wasn't blind at all. I had eyes on me to kill a man. I was lustful too. I knocked on the door of the Number Ten and took the six whores they had, women with bellies like an ocean, and I spilled my seed into every one. Then I sucked on my mouth harp. I had corn for breakfast. I filled a barrel with the stubs. I chewed and chewed until my teeth ached with the swell of corn. The whores were sleeping, but I had them again. And they begged me to leave them alone for an hour. I got into my boots and my sash.

There was a horse trolley outside. I climbed on, but I wouldn't pay the trolleyman his nickel. This poor boy's trolley bumped in the dirt. It didn't even have a trolley track.

The trolleyman saw my Navies and he shied off.

"I wouldn't charge you, Wild Bill."

The horsecar rode up out of the gulch. I pulled on jackrabbits and trees. I shot branches and rocks to hell.

A woman was lying in the road.

The trolleyman wouldn't stop. "She aint nothin but a whore, Bill."

I jumped out and carried her onto the trolley. She didn't weigh more than a sack of feathers would. Highwaymen had beaten her and robbed her gold.

"I was going to California, sir."

"I'm William," I said. "I'm no sir."

I had to ask the trolleyman where the hell we were heading for.

"Oklahoma, Bill."

"We'll take you to Oklahoma, honey."

She didn't complain. She dug her fingers under my sash. The Navies dropped to the floor of the trolley. I lay down with the little woman. The trolleyman looked at us. I told him to mind his goddamn horse.

"I have some business back here, bub."

The little woman was warm enough to marry.

"I could never love another man," she said, winding that sash around the awful swelling I had.

"You," I shouted to the trolleyman, "tell us when we come to Oklahoma," and I picked up my mouth harp and played.

I heard a cackle. It wasn't the horse. I looked at the trolleyman. His head was riding with this crazy laugh. I'd have shot the son of a bitch, but I couldn't find the Navies on the floor. He was no trolleyman. That was pa with the crazy laugh.

I threw him off the trolley.

I wasn't his daughter now. I was Wild Bill of the Navies, and I didn't have to shovel the devil's shit. The little woman must have slid down somewhere. She was gone. And I had to kick that trolley horse, or he wouldn't stir. "Oklahoma, ye hear?"

We got along fine after that.

I sang to him with my harp, and the spit cooled his neck. I found my Navies under a trolley chair. We drove for a week without passengers or the sight of cow, man, or bird. Then we hit upon smoke and city lights. It wasn't Manhattan. It was a town by the name of Chalk.

Folks tee-heed at the trolleyman with dust on his back.

"That aint Abner," they said. "That aint Abraham."

Then they looked under my hat and they ran for shelter. "It's the other Bill."

What the hell were they blabbering about?

"Chilrun, where can I get me a bath?"

Those that hadn't run all the way home pointed to the Broken Finger saloon. I got down from the car, went inside the saloon, walked upstairs, and hollered blue and loud until every whore at the Broken Finger was occupied with fixing my bath. I didn't have teats and a nest of whorehair. I had that jumping black thing between my legs that could draw in like a snail or shoot out. It was a goddamn pizzle, and I used it on all the girls.

The barkeep stole up on me while I was naked.

I took him by his scalp and threw him into the wallpaper.

"I didn't mean no harm," he groaned.

"Bub, you don't address a man when he aint inside his boots."

"We heard you was a marshal, Bill . . . and we need a marshal in Chalk. We need him bad."

"I gave it up," I said. "I aint in that line of work."

"People are getting kilt . . . we have the rottenest two-gun man living here . . . a nigger he is, escaped from the penitentiary and all."

I had a fat goose in my neck. "Does he go by the name of the black Wild Bill?"

I wouldn't kill a man twice. It was the worst sort of luck. But he was downstairs waiting for me.

I had to wind up my sash and drop the Navies in. It was a town of piss the trolley had brought me to. It was the devil's place. Chalk.

Black Bill was standing near the stovepipe. He had his fancy neckcloth and his starry shirt. He slapped me with a glove.

"How are your eyes, killer man?"

"Twinkling," I told him.

He took three short steps and pulled.

I couldn't play on my mouth harp while a nigger shot me all to pieces. I went into my sash for a Navy. He had a bellyache where my ball hit. He banged into the stovepipe and twisted it around.

He dropped, holding his belly, and died.

"Mama's turds," I said to the wall. "Goddamn . . . kill a man twice and anything can happen."

I looked out the window. The trolley wasn't there.

"Who's been stealing from me?"

The barkeep wiggled a shoulder. "That trolley belongs to the trolley line, Bill . . . it aint yours."

I had his whiskey. I was stuck in Chalk, with a dead man at my feet.

I played my mouth harp.

I took a whore and undressed her in my lap. I'd run, I'm telling you, but I was shy a horse.

I'd have to wait until the next trolleyman showed.

That whore was eating at my underpants.

Her head was right between my Navies.

I yawned.

I'll catch the trolley that comes tomorrow.

The trolleyman didn't come but his trolley did. The horse rode into the saloon. I told that whore to go gentle on my pants. I stood up, climbed into the car, and shoved out of there.

I must have gone to sleep in that trolley.

I woke with the worst din in my ears.

You couldn't crawl a step without another trolley car getting in your way. People climbed on and off the trolleys. Some of them went into my own little car.

I had to ask the next trolleyman, "Bub, what town is this?"

He roared at me. "You're in Manhattan, you country fool."

I pulled out a Navy and the roaring stopped.

I had the damnedest trolley horse. He took me right into town. A man hollered up at me. He was in a city hat and city shoes.

"Hickok, is that one of your games . . . posing as a trolley driver? . . . get on down. The Wild West is starting in an hour . . . you'll be late, man."

The city hat came up into the trolley. I couldn't pull on him.

*Supposing he was my friend? He dragged me over to this goddamn
hotel, carried me up two floors, put me in a linen shirt, powdered
my face, combed my hair, dusted off my chin.*

"Who are you anyhow?"

"I'm Chuggers, your valet."

"I didn't know I had a valet."

"I'm Cody's man. He lent me to you."

*This Chuggers rushed me down the stairs. Folks pointed to us.
Grandmas asked me to sign their little souvenir books. I got me
a pencil from the hotel clerk and scratched, "Happiness to one and
all, Wild Bill."*

*Chuggers took the pencil out of my hand. He snuck me around
to the back door of the Bowery Theatre. The whole troupe was
waiting. Boys in leather pants and Indian bonnets, and Cody with
his silver beard.*

*He has the fat of it. He gets to shoot the Indians after they shout
and dance and wallop me.*

*He took out his pocket watch. "William, ten minutes late
. . . it's your turn to die. Don't forget the ketchup."*

*Chuggers stuck a pig's bladder filled with tomato sauce under
my coat. I had to stab it with a whale's tooth while Cody's Indians
were walloping me, so I could be bloody and all.*

"I aint dying tonight."

*"You'll die," Cody said, "if we have to hold you down and do
you into a pudding."*

They shoved me onto the stage.

There were thousands in the theatre.

"Sing us a song, Billy . . . give us the Wild West."

*I wouldn't sing. Let Cody come with his Indians. They can chop
at my face and I'll bleed for everybody.*

*"Lord," Cody whispered from the curtain. "Sing something
. . . they love you, William."*

I wouldn't sing.

Cody threw his Indians at me. They did the walloping, but I wouldn't stab the bladder and I wouldn't lie down. I took out a Navy and shot the feathers off a few Indian bonnets.

Cody let the curtain drop.

Spit flew from his beard. "I'll kill you myself, Wild Bill Hickok." He jumped out from the curtain, and we rassled like twin bears. I had him by the beard and I would have bit it off at the roots if Chuggers hadn't rescued him.

The troupe climbed on me and kicked me across that theatre and into the street. I hopped back to the hotel. I signed grandmas' memory books. I had three of the best Manhattan whores you could beg or borrow. I took the three of them together. You could swim in that wetness we made. But it left me feeling sour. What the hell could a man want? I called out the window to my trolley horse.

"Don't you move, son . . . I'm coming."

I got out of that hotel. I climbed onto the trolley and spoke to the horse.

"Take me to Oklahoma, will you?"

The traffic had cleared. There wasn't a second or third trolley in the street. The horse pushed along slow. It was useless kicking him. He knew the trolley line. We couldn't get to Oklahoma without going through Chalk.

I took out my mouth harp and sucked on it.

An old man was sitting there. He wasn't being frivolous. He was putting "banditches" on my throat.

"Miss Sally, you were boiling up . . . it's ten days now. But we crippled that fever of yours."

It was uncle Roger. He shouted at another man. "Will you hurry up?" The man was Lyle-Henry. He'd shaved off his guerrilla moustache. He was tearing muslin strips for Roger Straws. *Nacog-doches.*

"Where's Bill?"

"Gone," Roger said.

"To Oklahoma?"

"Gone is gone . . . we buried him and got hold of that crazy boy. He's locked in with Nacogdoches' men. He'll hang, I suppose. Aren't that many who can survive a miner's court. And Bill was getting damn popular . . . don't you recognize your husband, Henry Ovenshine?"

I recognized him enough.

"He wandered out of the wilderness the day Hickok was shot. It was queer and all. Nacogdoches had kidnapped him . . . he's the best damn nurse in the territory. That fever wouldn't have lifted without his help. I'll leave you for a minute . . ."

Straws went out into the street to smoke his pipe.

"Nacogdoches," I said.

"Not so loud," Lyle whispered to me.

"You fool, he knows who you are . . . he's taking pity on us, is all. You think plucking the hairs from under your nose could trick Roger Straws? He's a Pinkerton man. He wasn't born the day before last . . . besides, you're still on the Pinkerton list for assaulting that banker . . ."

"Hush up!"

Roger walked in, tapping his pipe against his heel.

"I can't repay you, uncle, for being so nice."

The old man started to blush. "What the heck . . . you're no stranger to me, little girl."

Little girl. With a grandma's constitution.

"I'll visit tomorrow," he said. And there I was, alone with Lyle. I wanted that dark country where William was. I'd sit and play with him and Beelzebub.

"Woman, what are you bawling about? . . . I worked my backside raw to save you."

"Thank you, Lyle, but the truth is, I'd prefer to be dead."

"Dead? I'll give you dead." He took the collars of my shimmy shirt and twisted them around until I really thought I'd gone to Beelzebub. Then he started to blubber. "What about me? . . . running half my life. You had an education. Where'd it come from? Doctor Ovenshine. I learned you all those antiquities. Adulterers and kings . . . and I had to jump from town to town, with detectives on my tail . . . hide with lizards, go in and out of banditry, crawl on my nose, while you picked up with any man you pleased."

"Any man?" I would have thrown the water jug at him if I'd had the strength. "Lyle-Henry, you're just about the most unfaithful husband in the world, barring your lecherous kings."

"I was faithful," he said.

"So faithful you had to molest me in front of an army of tin men."

"That was Nacogdoches," he had the nerve to say. He was blubbering less. "I'm Lyle again."

I turned to the wall and faked a couple of snores. Lyle strolled out of the shack.

I got up and looked for pickles.

I was leaving this dusty camp. It was a dunghole without Bill. I cried to think of him out-pulling the most vicious mankillers there was, even with his sore eyes, and getting dropped by a boy he was trying to give supper to.

I found the pickles. I gobbled a few, burped, and I was fine.

I hitched up the wagon, stuck Rooster inside, packed whatever I could . . . Straws must have taken William's pistols and slouch hat for the miner's jury. But I had Bill's valentines in my wedding chest.

I climbed onto the wagon's lip. It creaked like hell. Poor Ishmael didn't have but the memory of a tail. He was still a good wagon pony, hairless and all. I heard this funny whimpering behind me. It was Lyle, standing in the road, the biggest tears you ever saw running down his cheeks. I just hardened myself to that boohooing of his.

"What about me?"

"Oh, you can play Nacogdoches in another part of the country . . . but do me the kindness of saying good-bye to uncle Roger."

"Where are you going?"

"I'll let Ish decide. Between him and the bird, they'll get me to some darn place. I'd like to smell the ocean once a year."

"What about me?"

I clucked at Ish, reined him a little, and he moved along. We didn't go but fifteen or twenty feet when that horse stopped of his own volition. He was a stubborn thing. I turned to look at Lyle.

He was standing in the same spot, like a lost child would be.

"Come on," I said. "The sun will be chewing at us in another hour."

He stood frozen for a minute, and then he kicked his heels, stumbled a yard or two, and leapt onto the tailboard and moved in with the chicken and me. I couldn't abandon Lyle. Deadwood wasn't home for Nacogdoches. The sharps would steal his pants. The whores would eat the pockets off his shirt. The miners would shovel him into the canyon, and pick through him for pay dirt. An old husband was something. I got my education from him. What the hell!

I didn't have to cluck. The horse perked up his ears and pulled us out of Deadwood.